The Flight

M. R. Hall is a screenwriter, producer and former criminal barrister. Educated at Hereford Cathedral School and Worcester College, Oxford, he lives in Monmouthshire with his wife and two sons. Aside from writing, his main passion is the preservation and planting of woodland. In his spare moments, he is mostly to be found among trees.

THE FLIGHT is the fourth novel in M. R. Hall's CWA Gold Dagger shortlisted Coroner Jenny Cooper series.

m-r-hall.com
facebook.com/MRHallAuthor@MRHall_books

Also in M. R. Hall's Coroner Jenny Cooper series

M.R. HALL
The Flight

PAN BOOKS

First published 2012 by Mantle

This paperback edition published 2013 by Pan Books
an imprint of Pan Macmillan, a division of Macmillan Publishers Limited
Pan Macmillan, 20 New Wharf Road, London N1 9RR
Basingstoke and Oxford
Associated companies throughout the world
www.panmacmillan.com

ISBN 978-0-330-52661-6

Copyright © M. R. Hall 2012

3 5 7 9 8 6 4 2

A CIP catalogue record for this book is available from
the British Library.

Typeset by SetSystems Ltd, Saffon Walden, Essex
Printed and bound by CPI Group (UK) Ltd, Croydon, CR0 4YY

Visit www.panmacmillan.com to read more about all our books
and to buy them. You will also find features, author interviews and
news of any author events, and you can sign up for e-newsletters
so that you're always first to hear about our new releases.

In memory of Sergeant Ronald Rex Hall,
9th Battalion Parachute Regiment

And limping death lashed on by fate
Comes up to shorten half our date.
This made not Daedalus beware,
With borrowed wings to sail in air;
To hell Alcides forced his way,
Plunged through the lake, and snatched the prey.
Nay scarce the gods, or heavenly climes
Are safe from our audacious crimes:
We reach at Jove's imperial crown,
And pull the unwilling thunder down.

The third ode of the first book of Horace (23 BC)
(trans. John Dryden, 1685)

ONE

RANSOME AIRWAYS FLIGHT 189 to New York was one of 753 scheduled to depart from London's Heathrow that Sunday in early January. During peak times at the world's busiest international airport, one plane would take off and another land every minute. There was little room for error either human or mechanical, still less in the uncertain realm where the two connected.

At forty-six, Captain Dan Murray was one of the oldest pilots on the payroll. With a wife and three teenagers to support, he had chosen to sacrifice union representation and the perks he had enjoyed with his former company for the money in hand offered by Guy Ransome's buccaneering airline. His basic salary barely covered the weekly groceries bill, and stopovers were spent in the cheapest airport hotels, but each transatlantic return trip earned him a little over £2,500. In a shrinking industry you had to make your money while you could.

Departure was scheduled for nine a.m. Murray hauled himself out of bed at five, slowly came to life in the shower, and minutes later was behind the wheel of his eight-year-old Ford. The persistent headache that had been bothering him lately had thankfully failed to take hold, and for once he didn't have to spend his morning commute waiting for the painkillers to kick in.

It was an hour's drive to Heathrow, and even at this ungodly hour of the day the motorway was filling up with angry traffic. He pulled into the car park of the Ransome building on the outer fringes of the airport at a little after six-thirty, collected his flight case from his locker and took a shuttle bus to Terminal Four. The short journey was shared with a dozen drowsy cabin crew dressed in Ransome's trademark purple uniforms. Some would join him on the flight to New York; others were bound for Dubai, Abu Dhabi or Taipei. The younger hostesses discussed rumours of staff cuts on long-haul flights, but the older ones and Captain Murray kept their thoughts to themselves. Experience had taught them that Ransome Airways had little patience with gossips or trouble-makers.

First Officer Ed Stevens was already hard at work in the landside crew room when Murray joined him for breakfast. The twenty-eight-year-old had a newborn daughter and a wife who had been made redundant as soon as her pregnancy had started to show. He needed his job even more than his captain did and was keen to impress. After a few moments' chat, Murray opened his company laptop, hooked into the firm's intranet and listened while Stevens talked him through the flight plan.

The precise route they would follow from London to New York was contained in the electronic flight information pack, a series of files in an email issued in the early hours of the morning by Sky Route. The company's sophisticated software was designed to get aircraft to their destinations as cheaply as possible, taking account of the weather, and passenger and cargo payload. 10 per cent of flight costs were incurred in landing fees and over-flight charges, 90 per cent in aviation fuel. A strong headwind could add 30 per cent to the cost of a flight and turn it into a loss-maker for the company; finding the cheapest route on a given day was critical.

Sky Route had taken account of all the satellite-generated weather data and decided on a southerly course to avoid strong winds in the north Atlantic. They would fly due west from Heathrow, level off at 31,000 feet over the Severn estuary and make their way towards the southern tip of Ireland. Midway across the Irish Sea they would climb to their cruising altitude of 39,000 feet and follow an almost direct line across the ocean. An estimated flight time of eight hours would have them on the ground at New York's JFK at midday, Eastern Standard Time. Having talked his captain through the main points, Stevens drew his attention to several Notices to Airmen (NOTAMS) that warned of pockets of thunder cloud over the western British Isles and Irish Sea. It was unremarkable weather for the time of year and nothing to cause either pilot anxiety.

Captain Murray had always preferred flying the Atlantic to complex routes over a patchwork of countries. Beyond Irish airspace there would be no air traffic controllers to deal with until they skirted southern Canada. And once aloft the Airbus virtually flew itself; in fact, if correctly programmed, it would even land and come to a halt on the JFK runway without human intervention.

Satisfied with their proposed course, Murray ordered a second cup of coffee and set about checking the fuel-load calculations. Operating on the tightest of margins, Ransome Airways insisted its captains take on only the regulation minimum 3 per cent of total fuel load as a contingency, which amounted to approximately thirty extra minutes in the air. If a captain chose to take on more and didn't use it, he would be fined according to a sliding scale: every two litres of fuel taken on board required another litre just to keep it airborne. Satisfied that there were no weather systems reported over the Atlantic likely to require a significant deviation, Murray confirmed Sky Route's suggested order for 105 tonnes of kerosene and hit the send button, filing his flight plan with the company dispatcher.

It was ninety minutes before take-off.

Greg Patterson was having a bad weekend. His ten-year-old daughter, Amy, was in tears, people were staring, and nothing he said would console her. To make matters worse, he could feel his wife's disapproval across the three thousand miles of ocean that separated them. Taking the vice-president's post in London had seemed to him just the sort of fillip his tired marriage had needed, but Michelle had refused to leave Connecticut. A professor in applied mathematics at Hartford University, she had been offered a visiting lectureship at King's College, London, but when departure day loomed she claimed she couldn't bring herself to desert her elderly mother. Greg knew full well there was more to it than that, but for the sake of his daughter he had agreed to go alone, and to suffer a monthly intercontinental commute.

Michelle had brought Amy over for Christmas but had had to fly home four days early to look after her mother, who, with impeccable timing, had broken a hip during her absence. Greg had persuaded Michelle to let Amy stay on with the promise that he would fly to New York with her en route to a business meeting to Washington. He had seen very little of his daughter during the previous eight months and relished the prospect of a few days alone with her. All had been well until the previous Friday morning, when, in typically autocratic fashion, Greg's CEO cancelled his Washington trip, dictating that he had more pressing business to attend to in London. Greg had briefly toyed with the crazy idea of flying to New York with Amy on Saturday and back to London twenty-four hours later, but his plan was skewered when late on Friday evening the airline bumped them onto a Sunday flight, claiming that their Saturday departure had been unwittingly overbooked. Michelle had failed to be understanding. As far as she was concerned, Greg's intention to fly their daughter home as an unaccompanied minor was tantamount to child abuse.

Amy clung on to him and wept at the desk in the departure hall as he completed the forms entrusting her to the airline. The Ransome hostess tried her best to soothe the child, promising movies, video games and an endless supply of treats until she met her mother at the other end, but Amy wouldn't be mollified. Greg attempted and failed on three separate attempts to get her to put on the purple tabard that singled her out as a child travelling alone, and it was the hostess who finally insisted that he just go and leave them to it. With a lump in his throat he disappeared into the crush of travellers with his daughter's tearful pleas ringing in his ears.

One aspect of service on which Ransome didn't skimp was its VIP lounge. Cattle-class tickets barely covered costs; the airline's profit was made in business and first class. Attracting wealthy customers was the chief priority. One such was Jimmy Han – a name the young entrepreneur had adopted for the benefit of his Western business associates – who had clocked up more miles with Ransome Airways than any other customer. Once every two weeks he travelled from his company's manufacturing plant in Taipei to its offices in Frankfurt and London. This week, for good measure, he was adding a three-day hop across the Atlantic to his schedule. He had spent the previous night at the Savoy, but its luxurious spa had felt a little tired compared with the one he was currently enjoying in the newly overhauled Ransome lounge: lying face-down on a massage couch, he drifted into a doze as a beautiful young woman kneaded his back with scented oils.

The semi-educated boy from Shanghai had come a long way in twenty years. He had worked hard, been lucky and grown exceedingly rich. There was much he intended to give back in return for his success, but that was no reason not to enjoy his wealth. When an interviewer had once asked him if he ever tired of the high life, Han had replied that those who came from nothing appreciated luxury like no one else, for at the back of their minds was always the thought that it might all be suddenly snatched away.

The Airbus A380 was the world's largest commercial airliner. 73 yards long, 24 yards high and with a wingspan the length of a football pitch, it dwarfed the 747s that stood alongside it. Designed to carry 525 passengers in a normal three-class configuration, Ransome Airways bunched things up a little more tightly in economy to squeeze in closer to six hundred.

Pre-flight preparations were in full swing. Outside in the freezing drizzle a pumping truck transferred fuel from underground containers into the tanks in the aircraft's wings, while the ground engineers carried out their final inspections. Inside a team of cleaners was working against the clock as the eighteen cabin crew checked that the galleys had been correctly loaded and searched the passenger manifests for those with special requirements: the 'problems'. There were unusually few: three in wheelchairs and a smattering of fussy eaters. Amy Patterson was the only unaccompanied minor. The words 'Will need attention!' had been entered next to her name. The crew unanimously decided that she would be the responsibility of Kathy Flood, the newest and youngest of their number, whether Kathy liked it or not.

After twenty years flying US-made Boeings, Captain Murray had found retraining to fly the Airbus a challenge. But having conquered his initial scepticism at the aircraft's semi-robotic flight control systems, he was now a fully committed convert. It wasn't perfect – he would have preferred a conventional centre stick to the arcade-style electronic joystick positioned at his right side, and a nostalgic part of him would have liked at least a few mechanical analogue instruments for use in the last resort – but he accepted that he was flying an incomparably safe machine. Fly-by-wire technology meant that all the vital systems were controlled by a highly sophisticated network of computers and electronics. Rather than the rudder, spoilers and tail elevators being moved by cables and hydraulics operated manually from the cockpit, the pilot's controls transmitted only electronic signals to the various moving parts.

Instead of conventional instruments, the Airbus captain and first officer each sat before a console containing a number of LCD screens. Directly in front of each of them was an identical primary flight display, which showed the aircraft's attitude in the air in relation to an artificial horizon and its flight mode. Each also had a navigation display providing a constant visual of the aircraft's position, the weather up ahead and constant readings of ground speed and true airspeed. An onboard information terminal contained the electronic tech logs and manuals that in older aircraft were contained in thick and unwieldy paper files. In the middle of the centre console that ran between the pilots' seats were the engine/warning and system displays, and beneath them the four thrust levers. On either side of the levers was a multi-function display – the pilots' main interface with the aircraft's computers. Using a keyboard and tracker ball, each pilot could flip between pages relaying the status of various on-board systems or send and receive messages to and from air traffic control and the airline's home base.

The intention behind this bewildering array of technology was simple: insofar as it was possible, to remove pilot error. If a pilot made a mistake, the computers would detect and correct it. And the Airbus's computers would make constant minor automatic adjustments to the roll and pitch of the aircraft. Whether the pilot wished it or not, his commands were constantly being modified or overridden. By far the most controversial of the Airbus's fail-safe features was its refusal to allow the pilot any more than thirty degrees of pitch up, fifteen degrees down and sixty-seven degrees of bank. This was intended to prevent a potentially catastrophic stall by keeping the plane within the safe limits of speed, attitude and altitude, but left some pilots feeling that in an emergency they would have one hand tied behind their backs. The aircraft's designers took a dispassionate view based on many years' worth of hard evidence: in a crisis, a computer flies better than a human. A computer is rational. It has no desire to be a hero.

The chief ground engineer, Mick Dalton, arrived in the cockpit thirty minutes before take-off to brief Murray and Stevens on the few defects he had found. He advised them that an intermittent fault with an actuator operating one of the spoilers on the starboard wing had failed to recur, but warned them to keep an eye out for it and scheduled a precautionary repair to take place on the aircraft's return. There was the usual crop of niggles from inside the passenger cabin – several faulty video screens, a malfunctioning toilet pump – and a report from the previous flight crew of an anomalous autopilot action. While autopilot one had been engaged it had apparently skipped a pre-programmed level-off on ascent, climbing straight through to cruising altitude.

Dalton was dubious. He suspected that the first officer, a new recruit to the airline, had mis-programmed the system. Ed Stevens promised he wouldn't make the same mistake and double-checked the flight data. Despite his misgivings, Dalton recorded the reported error and certified the aircraft fit for flight.

Half an hour before take-off, the three wheelchair-bound passengers together with a sniffling Amy Patterson were brought along the gantry by ground staff and handed over to the cabin crew. Kathy Flood led the little girl to a seat near an exit door in the mid-section of the lower cabin where she could keep a close eye on her. She showed her where to find the kids' movies on the seat-back screen and how to press the call button any time she needed something. Before joining Ransome Airways Kathy had spent two years as an au pair to a wealthy Italian family with six spoilt children, and compared with them Amy Patterson was a delight. Kathy helped her to send a text message to her mother saying the plane was due to leave on time, and handed her some sweets to suck during take-off. After a few minutes of Kathy's reassuring attention, Amy's mood lifted and she finally smiled.

First-class passengers embarked ahead of the crowd and were ushered upstairs into a spacious cabin that resembled the interior of a Manhattan boutique hotel. Forty luxury pods, with fully reclining seats upholstered in cream leather, were arranged around a kidney-shaped champagne and sea-food bar. At the very front of the aircraft were six self-contained 'ultra suites' – glorified versions of the first-class pods – separated from the main cabin by sliding perspex doors.

Jimmy Han usually made do with the relative comfort of a regular pod, but it had been a hectic few days in which he had already travelled more than halfway across the globe. As soon as he slid the door of his suite shut and drew the blind he knew that he had made the right decision. Kicking off his shoes, he eased into the seat and adjusted it just so, stroking the controls until it moulded to the small of his back. Today was a rest day, a time for reflection. He closed his eyes and recalled a long-forgotten moment from his childhood: his father had kicked a stray dog that lay sunning itself in the street outside their drab apartment building. When he had asked why, his father had said, 'Because he looks more comfortable lying on the hard ground than I'll ever be.' Han smiled. Even now he wasn't as relaxed as that flea-bitten bag of bones; but he was worth more than 700 million dollars.

At eight-fifty the last of the sixteen cabin doors was secured and Captain Murray turned the simple ignition switch which commenced the automatic start-up of the four Rolls-Royce Trent engines. He watched the changing images on the engine screen as the aircraft's computers started each of them in turn and pressurized the hydraulic systems. Sophisticated sensors relayed a constant stream of information: the computers finessed the many interconnected electrical and mechanical processes in a way no human ever could. It was as if the vast machine had a life of its own.

The ground crew disconnected the push-back tractor and radioed the cockpit to set the brakes to 'on'. The aircraft's computers calculated where its centre of gravity lay based on the size and distribution of the payload, and decided on the correct angle at which to attack the air: too shallow and it would struggle to leave the ground, too steep and the centre of lift would slip behind the centre of gravity, risking a disastrous stall. The wing flaps and stabilizer (the horizontal section of the tail) adjusted themselves accordingly. On older planes the pilot would feel his way into the air, instinctively responding to the feedback on his centre stick and the pressure on his rudder pedals, but the Airbus pilot had no feedback, no tactile sense of the air pressing against the flying surfaces. He relied instead on the streams of information on his visual displays. Among the many acts of faith the aircraft demanded, those required on take-off were the most profound.

First Officer Stevens received the go-ahead from the tower and Captain Murray manoeuvred the Airbus towards the start of runway two. Inside the cabin passengers temporarily denied the comfort of electronic distractions buried themselves in newspapers or uttered silent prayers. In the cockpit the pilots' focus narrowed to the rigid procedure that lay ahead. The Boeing 777 directly in front of them sped off along the greasy tarmac, passed the point of no return and lumbered into the air, shearing a little to the left as the pilot compensated for a sudden gust of cross-wind. Thirty seconds passed; the tower confirmed cleared for take-off and Captain Murray pushed the thrust levers fully forward to the take-off-go-around setting.

The aircraft started to accelerate; the windshield streaked with rain. First Officer Stevens called out, 'Eighty knots.' Both pilots cross-checked their airspeed instruments; both were in agreement. Had they not been, take-off would have been aborted immediately. Upwards of eighty knots the pilot was obliged to ignore any minor faults and abort only to avoid imminent disaster. An automated voice called out, 'V1', indicating that the critical speed of 122 knots had been reached. Captain Murray removed his hand from the thrust lever, now committed to take-off. As they reached 141 knots, First Officer Stevens called out, 'Rotate,' and Captain Murray pulled gently on the joystick, easing the nose up through three degrees per second until at twelve-point-five degrees the massive craft began to lift and climb.

At a hundred feet Captain Murray called for 'Gear-up', then 'AP one'. Like most pilots, he would have preferred to fly the aircraft manually to 10,000 feet before switching to autopilot, but Heathrow being a noise-restricted airport, any deviation from the Standard Instrument Departure – such as a sudden throttle up – could infringe volume regulations and trigger a hefty automatic fine, a portion of which under Ransome's rules would have been docked from his salary.

The autopilot engaged. Only a few hundred feet from the ground the two human pilots became virtual spectators as the aircraft banked left and headed out on a westerly course, slowly ascending towards 10,000 feet. Their displays showed the constant subtle movements of the rudder, spoilers and stabilizer countering the effects of a blustery north wind. To have flown the aircraft as skilfully by hand would have been a physical impossibility.

At 1,500 feet Captain Murray pulled the thrust lever back to the 'climb' setting as they entered low-lying cloud and encountered minor pockets of turbulence. First Officer Stevens swapped formalities with air traffic control and obtained permission to pass through the first altitude constraint of 6,000 feet. At 4,000, the flaps retracted from take-off position and the engines responded to the reduced lift with an increase in power, accelerating to 250 knots. The cloud was thick and dense, making for a bumpier ride than many passengers would be finding comfortable, but the weather radar showed conditions clearing over the Welsh coast. The latest reports from the mid-Atlantic were of a clear, bright, turbulence-free day.

At 10,000 feet, both pilots called out, 'Flight level one

hundred': standard procedure designed to keep them working as a tight-knit team. Now high enough above the ground to be free of noise restrictions, the engines powered up to a more efficient climb speed of 327 knots. Captain Murray switched off the passenger seat-belt signs and enabled the in-flight entertainment system. First Officer Stevens checked in with air traffic control, who handed him over to Bristol. A brief exchange of messages secured permission to continue to an initial cruising altitude of 31,000 feet.

Both pilots began to relax; they were airborne. The hardest part of their day's work was already done.

As soon as the seat-belt signs were switched off, Kathy Flood came to check on Amy Patterson, and found the little girl so engrossed in her favourite video game that she barely noticed her. Relieved, Kathy went about her work. For the next seven hours she would be at full stretch tending to the sixty passengers in her section; there was simply not enough time to cope with a miserable child.

A polite tap at the door of Jimmy Han's suite signalled the arrival of a pretty stewardess who handed him the complimentary drinks menu. It was too early in the day for champagne, so he ordered freshly squeezed orange juice, giving her a smile which promised a handsome tip if she looked after him well. Reaching for the remote, he flicked to CNN, hoping for updates on the latest diplomatic spat between China and Taiwan. But the studio anchor was dwelling on another minor story and he impatiently scoured the ticker at the foot of the screen before a knot of tension stiffened his neck and reminded him that he was meant to be taking it easy. Business could wait. He switched across to the movie channels and picked out an old Clint Eastwood picture: *Dirty Harry*. It was one of his favourites. He had learned one of his most valuable lessons from American films: the good guys are ultimately more ruthless than the bad.

The altimeters ticked past 30,000 feet, prompting both pilots to call out, 'One to go,' affirming that their instruments were in sync and that they were nearing level-off. First Officer Stevens checked in with Bristol and learned that aircraft up ahead had reported a belt of thunder clouds, but that no deviation was necessary. At 31,000 feet the autothrust pulled back, downgrading to a softer mode which caused the engines to quieten to an almost inaudible whisper and settle to the optimum fuel-efficient cruise speed: a steady 479 knots.

'How's the baby?' Captain Murray asked his first officer. 'Getting any sleep?'

'Doing my best – on the sofa.' Stevens unbuckled his belt and rolled his stiff shoulders.

'Like that, is it?'

'I told her, I'll change all the dirty nappies you like, but getting up in the night, forget it. I've got a plane to fly.'

'Off the leash tonight, then? I hope she doesn't expect me to keep an eye on you.'

'In New York? You really think you'd keep up?'

'You'd be surprised.'

The interphone buzzed.

'Coffee time already?' First Officer Stevens glanced up at the entry screen and saw a stewardess standing beyond the outer of the two doors which separated the cabin from the cockpit. 'They could have sent the pretty one.'

'Who's that?' Captain Murray asked.

'You know – the little blonde one, Kathy, with the—' He held his hands out in front of his chest.

'Oh, yeah – *her.*'

Both men laughed.

'You're definitely on your own tonight,' Captain Murray said. 'Not my responsibility.'

Stevens tapped in the entry code which would let the stewardess through the outer door.

'Speed! Speed!' The automated warning voice called out from speakers mounted in the instrument consoles.

'What the hell is that?' Captain Murray said, more puzzled than alarmed. 'We're at 470 —'

'Speed! Speed!'

'Jesus —'

'Speed! Speed!'

There was a loud clatter and a scream of alarm from between the cockpit's two doors as the aircraft's nose pitched violently upwards and the stewardess was thrown off her feet.

'I'm sorry, say again, Skyhawk . . . Skyhawk, uh, are you still on?'

At his seat in the tower at Bristol airport Guy Fearnley saw Skyhawk 380 on his radar screen but heard only static through his headset.

'Skyhawk, are you there?'

The air traffic controller watched the numbers on his screen that indicated the aircraft's altitude was starting to fall; slowly at first, then faster and faster. He blinked twice to make sure he wasn't imagining it.

He wasn't.

The brief message from the Airbus had been too fractured to make out. He switched channels and tried again. 'Skyhawk this is Bristol eight-zero-nine —'

There was no reply.

TWO

THE WORN TYRES HAD LOST their grip on the bend. The
driver, who had been travelling at an estimated speed of
seventy miles an hour, had stamped on the brakes, causing
the already sliding wheels to lock. Skating across the wet
surface, the car had ploughed into an oak at the side of the
road, killing the single male occupant instantly. It was bad
luck: the tree was the only one for fifty yards in either
direction. That, at least, was the conclusion of the road
traffic accident investigation officer who had spent the small
hours of the morning measuring the skid marks on the
remote stretch of country lane. Another car travelling behind
appeared also to have skidded, probably to avoid the car
that had spun out of control, but there was no evidence to
suggest who the driver had been, and he or she had certainly
not reported the accident to the police. Ordinary people
could at times be shockingly callous. For the officer recon-
structing the scene it had been a routine technical exercise, a
matter of entering data in a computer that produced a neat
3D reproduction of the accident. But as a coroner who was
often far too diligent for her own good, Jenny Cooper had
been there to see the body and the wreckage, and to smell
the blood. The airbags had failed. The driver, a man in his
late thirties named Jon Whitestone, had bounced off the
windscreen, leaving no face for his wife to identify. Beyond

the fact that he was late coming home from work, no explanation could be found for the victim's excessive speed. It was a needless death.

Closing the lid of her laptop, Jenny wished she hadn't read the officer's report with her late-morning breakfast. The week had been fraught enough without work spoiling her Sunday, too. By the time she had finished dealing with the accident's aftermath it had been past midnight. It was nearly two when she'd made it back to her cottage deep in the Wye valley, and she had needed a pill to sleep. Now there were only a few precious hours of the weekend left in which to recoup. She would get some fresh air, make a start on the paperwork that had been mounting on her desk, and finally decide whether she would follow the advice of several well-meaning girlfriends and start searching for a date on one of the more upmarket singles sites. She had been putting it off for weeks: the very idea of meeting with a complete stranger filled her with dread. It also felt oddly like a betrayal. Whenever she allowed herself to think of Steve, her former lover, she ached for him. But it had been her choice. She had encouraged him to take the position at the architects' practice in Provence and to surrender to love if it came along. And it had, with almost indecent speed. Within months of arriving he had moved in with a beautiful dark-haired girl called Gabrielle, and was blissfully happy. He still sent the odd email, even a Christmas card which he had signed with a kiss, but his communications had become steadily less frequent as, without either of them saying so, they both acknowledged that it was time to move on.

Could she ever be as close to another man as she had once been to Steve? Could she imagine sharing her most intimate secrets? She carried these questions with her up the foot-worn boards of the narrow wooden staircase and came no closer to answers as she ran a deep bath.

She had plunged as much of her chilled flesh beneath the surface as the antique roll-top tub would allow when the telephone rang. Jenny closed her eyes and tried to ignore it. Whoever it was, she would call them back when she was ready. But they refused to give up. Ten, twelve, fifteen rings, still they persisted. It was no use. She forced herself out of the water, wrapped herself in a towel and hurried barefoot to answer it.

She picked up the phone in the living room, water pooling on the cold flagstones around her feet.

'Hello?'

'Mrs Cooper? You've heard the news —' It was Alison Trent, her officer.

'No.'

'Surely —'

'No. What is it?'

Alison paused. 'A plane crash . . . On the Severn.'

'Bad?'

'Nearly six hundred.'

It was Jenny's turn to fall silent. Six *hundred*. 'Not all dead?'

'We don't know. The good news is it's North Somerset's jurisdiction.'

Jenny felt a selfish sensation of relief. 'So we're not involved —?'

'I'm afraid we are, Mrs Cooper. South Gloucestershire police just called saying two bodies have been washed up at Aust. An adult male and a female child. I'm on my way. I thought you might want to come. Oh, and you'll probably want to bring your wellingtons.'

*

Jenny drove through the Wye valley as fast as she dared in the new Land Rover SUV with which she had reluctantly replaced her decrepit VW. Speeding through sleepy villages, she absorbed the constantly updating news of the disaster which had unfolded only a few miles to the south. A Ransome Airways Airbus A380, the world's largest and most technically advanced passenger airliner, had ditched in the middle of the Severn estuary two miles west of the new Severn crossing. The crash had happened some three and a half hours earlier around nine-thirty. Rescue boats were at the scene, but no survivors had yet been found. There was some flotsam on the surface and a number of bodies had been recovered, but the aircraft's fuselage had sunk beneath the water. The number of an emergency helpline was read out repeatedly. A shell-shocked air traffic controller from Bristol told a reporter that he had lost radio contact with the stricken plane without warning and had watched it plunge to earth on his screen. The descent had taken over six minutes, which already had a hastily assembled collection of experts speculating that by no means had it dropped like a stone. A physics professor explained that following a break-up an aeroplane travelling five and a half miles above the earth would take roughly two and a half minutes to fall to the ground. A descent lasting six minutes suggested that the pilot had retained some control and had struggled to remain in the air.

Search-and-rescue helicopters were sweeping the mile-wide stretch of water to her right as Jenny crossed the vast span of the Severn Bridge, their orange lights disappearing in and out of the curtains of grey mist that hung over the estuary. She took the first exit at the far end, and minutes later was pulling up at the edge of a mud and shingle beach between

Alison's Ford and a cluster of police vehicles. A young constable approached. Jenny wound down her window.

'Jenny Cooper. Severn Vale District Coroner.'

'They're expecting you, ma'am.'

He nodded towards two white tents that had already been erected over the corpses. Jenny climbed out and pulled on her boots, freezing drizzle pricking the back of her neck. The mud was thick and deep, sucking at her feet as she waded over.

Alison appeared from the nearer tent, swathed in a ski jacket and a plain woollen hat with flaps that hung down over her ears. 'The girl's in here,' she said with a studied absence of emotion. 'You can't tell me you haven't heard the news reports by now.'

'I've heard them,' Jenny said. 'But I can't say that it helped.'

She braced herself and followed her officer into a tent no more than ten feet square in which a young female forensics officer dressed in white overalls was taking photographs of the little girl. Daily exposure to death had largely inured Jenny to the sight of all but the most horrifically damaged adult corpses, but the sight of a dead child was something she had never grown used to. The girl lay face up on the mud just as the retreating tide would have left her. The first thing Jenny noticed was the fully inflated bright yellow lifejacket with the straps secured tightly around her slender waist. She wore blue jeans, pink canvas pumps and a pale blue T-shirt with what appeared to be a purple tabard over it. Her sandy-blonde hair was plaited in a single pigtail. On her forehead was a raised, dark, circular bruise.

'I think she might have been an unaccompanied minor,' Alison said. 'They make them wear those tops so the staff can spot them.'

Jenny forced herself to look closer and made out the edge of what appeared to be an airline logo. 'Has the medic been?'

Alison dug a folded piece of paper from her coat pocket and handed it to her. The form, hastily signed by a doctor twenty minutes earlier, confirmed that there was no sign of life and no realistic prospect of resuscitation.

'Her body temperature is less than ten degrees,' Alison said. 'She'd have been in the water well over an hour, probably more like two.'

Jenny noticed the small bloodstain on the left side of the girl's T-shirt that marked the spot where the doctor had taken her core temperature by liver puncture.

'Any idea who she is?'

'Not yet. I've left details with the incident room. I'll get a call as soon as they have an idea.'

Fighting her instinct to recoil, she studied the girl's plaster-white face, her smooth bare arms and her fingers curled up to form partial fists. Apart from the blow to the head there was no other sign of injury.

'I was expecting more damage,' Jenny said. 'And she obviously had time to put on a lifejacket.'

'Almost makes it worse, doesn't it?' Alison said. 'Knowing what's coming, I mean.'

Jenny recalled the experts' speculation on the radio. The stricken plane appeared not so much to have crashed, but to have crash-landed on the estuary. From what she had read of such disasters, bodies could emerge from the wreckage in all manner of conditions: some mangled beyond recognition, others more or less intact. It all depended what debris the body collided with. The brutal randomness of passengers' injuries added yet another layer of horror onto an event already too large for her fully to comprehend.

The forensics officer zipped her camera into a case. 'How soon till you take her to the D-Mort?' she asked. 'Only we could do with the tent.'

'D-Mort?'

'Disaster mortuary. They're setting one up on a field at Walton Bay – where the plane went down.'

'Who's "they"?' Jenny asked. 'North Somerset?'

'The Ministry of Justice is appointing someone more senior to take charge,' Alison interjected. 'They don't think us provincial hicks can be trusted.'

Jenny had been so shocked by the scale of the accident that she had barely turned her mind to the complicated logistics of managing it. There were standing protocols for handling a high-casualty event which involved setting up a disaster mortuary as close as practicable to the scene. There bodies would be identified, autopsied and stored until it was appropriate to release them to families. A handful of coroners had been specially trained to manage such situations, but despite the presence of an elderly nuclear power plant and several chemicals factories within her jurisdiction, Jenny had never been selected to be one of them, a minor snub that still rankled.

'Any bodies lying in my area will be taken to the Vale as usual,' Jenny said. 'They'll have enough to deal with at Walton.'

The officer gave an uncertain nod. 'How long are you going to be?'

'There's an ambulance on the way,' Alison said. 'You can spare your tent for ten minutes.'

'I'll be in the van,' the young woman said, letting it be known that she was being caused serious inconvenience. She picked up her two bags and marched out.

An odd, liquid sound issued from the girl's body. Jenny

looked down to see a small gush of water bubble up through her lips and trickle across her cheeks.

'Muscles contracting,' Alison said. 'Must have had water in her lungs.'

Some instinct prompted Jenny to lean down and touch the girl's face – just in case – but it was as cold as porcelain. 'If she inhaled water, she must have been breathing after the crash.'

Alison made no further comment and turned back to the entrance. 'You'd better have a look at the other one.'

The second tent lay some ten yards closer to the water's edge on a band of sticky black silt. Alison unzipped the flap and pulled it back to reveal the body of a bearded man lying with his right cheek on the ground, his arms spread out at his sides.

Jenny placed him in his upper thirties. He was sturdily built and looked nothing like an airline passenger. He was wearing dungaree-style over-trousers, calf-length orange rubber boots, and a red plaid shirt rolled up to the elbows with a white T-shirt underneath. His forearms were veined and muscular, those of a man accustomed to heavy manual work.

'He looks like a fisherman.'

'Not at this time of year,' Alison said. 'There's nothing in his pockets – we checked.'

She handed Jenny a second piece of paper similar to the first. The medic had recorded his core temperature as 13.5 degrees.

'He wasn't flying to New York dressed like that,' Jenny said. 'I think we might have our first casualty on the ground.'

She walked around the body on the duckboards the forensic officers had put down inside the tent and studied the man's face. Beneath the inch of reddish-brown growth on his left cheek she made out the outline of a disfiguring scar that his beard was probably intended to disguise: even in death there was a toughness in his features which said he would not have died without a hard struggle.

'I don't see any obvious injuries,' Jenny said.

'Nor did the medic,' Alison replied. 'He thinks it was hypothermia. It might not even be connected to the crash. He could have fallen in drunk anywhere between Weston and Gloucester. Until we identify him we won't know.'

Jenny knew that the water temperature would be less than ten degrees at this time of year. The man's body had yet to cool to that level. A drunk who had fallen into the river at some time during the night would have been at least as cold as the water by now.

She spotted a small silver medal on a chain around his neck. She stooped down for a closer look and saw that it was a St Christopher.

'The patron saint of travellers,' Alison said, with no hint of irony.

Jenny felt an involuntary and quite unexpected pang of emotion. She straightened, brisk and businesslike, trying to compensate for her irrational reaction. 'All right. Let's get them moved.'

Leaving Alison to organize the bodies' transfer to the mortuary, Jenny drove along the shore road until she reached a lay-by overlooking the water which was screened from passing traffic by a dense hedgerow. Shivering, she tried to reason through the feelings that had unexpectedly reared up on the beach. It had been many months since, in Dr Allen's consulting room, she had recovered the memories of the childhood accident – a word upon which he insisted – in which she had pushed her five-year-old cousin Katy down the stairs of her aunt's house to her death. For weeks afterwards the image of the little girl tumbling backwards through the air and landing neck first on the treads had been the constant backdrop to her every waking thought, and flashbacks would jerk her from her sleep. But, just as Dr Allen had promised, the haunting had slowly started to fade.

Gradually, she had been able to reason through the events of that afternoon nearly forty years ago and begin the slow process of forgiving herself. It wasn't her fault, the psychiatrist had insisted: they were merely two innocent children reacting to a painful situation not of their making. Her father and her aunt, Katy's mother, were the ones who had to bear responsibility. What had they expected in leaving their daughters to play on the other side of the door from their noisy, illicit love-making?

Responsibility. That was the word which triggered the tightness in her chest and the sensations of panic deep in her core. It carried an absoluteness from which there was no escape, as definite as death itself. And it was the hapless dead, the innocents, who caused her to feel it most acutely, those who bore no responsibility of their own. Those, she supposed, who reminded her of Katy. It would have been easy to have sent the bodies on the beach to the D-Mort and to have washed her hands of them, but the moment the suggestion had been made she had known it would be impossible. The little girl wouldn't let her. The past and the present were still too entangled; she had still to atone.

'Her name's Amy Patterson,' Alison said. 'American. Ten years old. I was right – she was travelling alone. Her father works in London, should be arriving any minute. Family liaison told him to meet us here.'

The buzzer sounded and Alison pushed open the door to the single-storey building that housed the Severn Vale District Hospital's mortuary. Despite the mortuary's pervading odour of disinfected decay, Jenny was glad to step out of the cold wind and into the airless warmth.

She followed Alison through the swing doors that opened onto a corridor lined with gurneys bearing corpses shrouded in envelopes of white PVC. A young mortuary technician Jenny hadn't met before exited the autopsy room wheeling the body of a man too large for the plastic to meet fully across his middle.

'Alison Trent, coroner's officer,' Alison said. 'And this is the coroner, Mrs Cooper. I had the body of a young girl sent over from Aust. Her father's about to arrive for an identification.'

'Dr Kerr's working on her now,' the young man said.

'He told me it wouldn't be until later,' Alison said with a note of alarm.

'He's meant to be over at the D-Mort, see. Everything here's got to wait.'

He gestured to the half-dozen or more corpses lined up against the opposite wall.

'I'll talk to him,' Jenny said, stepping forward. 'You wait outside. Hold Mr Patterson off until I phone you.'

Dr Kerr was leaning over the tiny female body on the table with his broad, muscular back to her. Although young for a pathologist heading a hospital department – still only in his mid-thirties – he worked with the calm assurance of a seasoned professional. The row of organs already laid out on the steel counter to his right told Jenny he was deep into the autopsy.

He glanced back over his shoulder at the sound of her approach. 'Mrs Cooper. I thought you might look in.'

'I thought you'd wait until later. Her father's arriving from London any moment.'

'Emergency procedures, I'm afraid. Wouldn't have been

able to touch her for a week if I hadn't dealt with her this afternoon. I'll try and get your man done too.' He carefully lifted the dead girl's stomach into a large kidney dish, which he carried to the counter.

Jenny's eyes flicked of their own accord into the opened, empty torso. White as ivory, the delicate, gracefully curving ribs were strangely beautiful.

'Can you hurry?' Jenny asked.

'That depends on whether you're expecting the bargain or the de luxe service.'

'I'd settle for a cause of death.'

'We've got that already. Hypothermia.'

He carefully squeezed the liquid contents of the stomach into the dish. Jenny smelt the acid, then felt it at the back of her throat.

'Are you sure?'

'I'm expecting to find some bleeds from that knock on the head, but I don't think it was fatal. There was some water in her lungs and there's some in her stomach, but not the amount you'd associate with a conventional drowning. If she was floating in a lifejacket in rough water she'd have slowly lost consciousness but continued to breathe with waves breaking over her.'

'That sounds like drowning to me.'

'It's the cold that would have stopped her reflexes. She'd have had twenty, twenty-five minutes at the most.'

'There's speculation the plane was breaking up in mid-air,' Jenny said. 'If that was the case, the cabin would have depressurized and dropped to the outside temperature.'

'About minus fifty degrees. You'd expect to see frostbite, maybe even signs of the eyeballs freezing. Really nasty stuff. It didn't happen.'

Jenny spotted Amy's wet clothes and lifejacket in a clear plastic bag stowed on the shelf of the gurney that would carry her body back to the refrigerator. 'From what I hear most of the bodies sank with the plane. It seems odd she emerged from the wreckage intact.'

'Stranger things have happened,' Dr Kerr said. 'I met a French pathologist who dealt with the Air France crash off Brazil a few years ago. The plane broke up in mid-air and fell five miles into the sea. Most of the bodies were in pieces, but some were virtually intact. Luck of the draw, I guess.'

'She was wearing a lifejacket. Why haven't I heard of any others recovered in lifejackets?'

'Nothing's going to make sense for a while yet, Mrs Cooper. We don't even know what happened to the plane.'

Jenny turned at the sound of Alison bursting through the door. 'He just called. He's five minutes away.'

'Buy him a coffee,' Jenny said. 'It won't be long.'

Jenny looked away as Dr Kerr went on to complete his removal of the major organs and tried to marshal what little knowledge she had of air accidents to imagine what might have happened. Wasn't it always said in the pre-flight safety announcement that in the event of ditching on water passengers should put on lifejackets? Surely six minutes was long enough for that to have happened? But how easy would it be to reach under your seat and pull a jacket over your head during the equivalent of a roller-coaster ride?

'As I thought,' Dr Kerr said a short while later.

Jenny watched him as he examined the partially exposed brain.

'Tiny bleeds near the point of impact, no major haemorrhage. There's no fracture to the skull. I doubt she'd have been rendered unconscious, at least not for long.'

'Any idea what she hit?'

'The screen on the back of the seat in front of her, probably. She got off very lightly, all things considered.'

'Not that lightly.'

He reached for a scalpel. 'You don't like this bit, remember?'

'No . . .' Jenny said. 'You will make sure she looks presentable?'

'Of course. Why don't you leave me to it?'

Greg Patterson's grim expression as Alison brought him along the corridor towards the refrigerator told Jenny that he understood the cause of the delay perfectly well. A tall, square-shouldered man recently turned forty, he looked as if he had been a sportsman in his youth. She noticed his shoes and expensive preppy clothes worn not for self-expression, but as a uniform of some kind. Corporate – that was the word; Patterson had sacrificed something of himself to be whatever he had become.

'Good afternoon, Mr Patterson. Jenny Cooper. Severn Vale District Coroner.' She offered a hand.

He shook it firmly, meeting her gaze with tired but grimly determined eyes. 'Greg Patterson.'

'All I need at this stage is a visual identification. If it's any reassurance, your daughter's body is virtually unscathed. Are you ready to proceed?'

He nodded, containing his emotion behind a tightly clenched jaw.

Jenny turned to the refrigerator cabinet. She opened the drawer numbered fourteen just far enough to expose the top half of Amy's body. She pulled back the flap of plastic to reveal the girl's face. Dr Kerr's technician had excelled himself: she looked peaceful; there was even colour in her cheeks.

Patterson glanced down briefly. 'That's her,' he said, determined not to falter.

Jenny covered the face and slid the drawer shut.

'Your officer said she was wearing a lifejacket,' Patterson said.

'Yes—' Jenny answered, unsure how much Alison had told him.

'How long was she alive in the water?'

'It's unlikely to have been more than half an hour, probably less.'

'Was she conscious?'

'It's impossible to say.'

'How soon was it till help arrived? Why wasn't she found?' His voice was clipped, his tone painfully dispassionate.

'I'm afraid I don't have that information, Mr Patterson.'

'What about the man who was found nearby? Who is he?'

'We don't know yet. Your daughter is the first to have been identified.'

Patterson stared at the closed refrigerator door, then down at the floor.

'There's talk of a bomb, an explosion.'

'There are a lot of questions to be answered, Mr Patterson,' Jenny said. 'I'm afraid it's going to take some time.'

He nodded, his thoughts held firmly within. Jenny wanted to ask him more, to fill in the details of why Amy had been flying alone, but the moment wasn't right. He had behaved with dignity and she didn't want to rob him of it. Instead she retrieved her card from her pocket and handed it to him.

'Feel free to contact me any time. I'll be in touch shortly.'

Patterson took out a soft calfskin wallet and carefully slotted the card inside. He paused and briefly closed his eyes as if letting a wave of emotion crash over him then wash away. 'Do you know if her mother has been told? . . . I didn't want to . . .' He swallowed. 'What I'm trying to say is that I would appreciate it very much if you were to make the call.'

Jenny and Alison traded a glance.

'Of course,' Jenny said.

He hastily pulled another card from his wallet and handed it to her. It read: *Professor Michelle R. Patterson, Department of Applied Mathematics, Hartford University, Hartford, Connecticut.*

'She'll want to come over,' Patterson said. 'The body will still be—?'

'It will have to remain here for several days at least,' Jenny said. 'As you can imagine, the investigation may take some time.'

He nodded. 'I understand.'

They looked at each other for a moment, both concluding that there was no more to be said, then Patterson turned abruptly and set off back along the corridor.

'He looked ever so guilty, don't you think?' Alison said, as soon as he had passed through the door at the far end. 'He's probably thinking he should have been there with her. I could never have let my daughter fly alone at that age.'

Jenny didn't answer. She was steeling herself to make a phone call.

THREE

IT WAS ALREADY FIVE O'CLOCK in the afternoon: almost the precise time at which Flight 189 had been due to land in New York. Jenny sat in her parked car outside the mortuary and dialled the cellphone number printed on Michelle Patterson's card. There was a long moment of silence, then the distinctive extended single ring of an American phone.

'Hello. Who is this?' The woman who answered sounded desperate and tearful.

'Mrs Patterson?'

'Who *is* this?'

Jenny could barely hear her over a noisy babble in the background. 'My name's Jenny Cooper. I'm the coroner for the Severn Vale District – near Bristol, in England.' Jenny paused as she was overwhelmed at Mrs Patterson's end by a flight announcement. She was taking the call in an airport. 'I've just been with your husband—' She sensed that she was no longer being listened to. 'Mrs Patterson?'

'Go on.' The mother's voice had become dull and flat: the tone indicative of shock.

'Your daughter was in the plane that crashed. Your husband asked me to telephone you . . . He has just identified her body. I'm so sorry.'

After a pause, Mrs Patterson said, 'Where is my husband?'

'On his way home, I assume.'

Another, longer pause followed. Amongst the clamour surrounding Mrs Patterson, Jenny heard the sound of women weeping and wondered what had driven them to gather at the airport nearly eight hours after they knew the plane had gone down.

'Did he . . .' Her voice cracked with emotion. 'Did he tell you what the hell he was thinking letting her travel alone?'

'No. He didn't discuss that.' Keen to bring the conversation to an end, Jenny said, 'I have your email address. I'll forward my details within the hour. Would you like me to attach a photograph?'

'Yes, please,' Mrs Patterson said, 'yes . . .' But her voice trailed away and she ended the call.

Jenny dropped the phone back into her pocket, fighting the numb sensation of grief which she invariably felt after breaking the news of a sudden and unexpected death. She felt irrationally responsible, as if there were something more she could have done. She reminded herself that it was always like this; that she had never evaded the sensation of the newly dead being close at hand, as if she were somehow involved in cutting the ties that bound them to their former lives. Dr Allen had told her that her reactions were tied up with her guilt over Katy; that the day she forgave herself her imagination would stop tormenting her. It still felt a long way off.

She switched on the car radio to catch up with the news. A studio presenter was talking to a journalist on the ground, who claimed that witnesses had reported hearing a loud explosion around ten a.m. Anti-terrorist officers were said to be working through the passenger lists, searching for anyone with known connections to terrorist organizations. There was speculation about a link to Somali Islamists known to have made threats against US and British interests. The latest expert to be called on claimed that British airport security had been allowed to slacken due to staff cuts.

Jenny started at the sound of a knock on the driver's window. She turned to see Alison's impatient features. She opened the door, letting in a blast of icy air.

'Dr Kerr wants you to come and see the man's body.'

'I'll be right there.'

'He's in a hurry. So am I, actually – they've just called and asked me to go over to the D-Mort to help with identifications.'

'They can get police in to do that. I need you to find out a little more about Mr and Mrs Patterson. She seems to think her husband shouldn't have let their daughter travel alone. I'd like to know what happened.'

'Don't you think the poor man deserves some time to let it sink in, Mrs Cooper?'

'The poor man didn't have the guts to tell his own wife.'

'All right. Whatever you say, Mrs Cooper.'

Jenny braced herself for another visit to the mortuary.

'Hypothermia,' Dr Kerr announced from the counter at which he was weighing the dead man's lungs on a pair of electronic scales. All the internal organs were lined up in a row, including the large intestine, which was spilling over the edge of a large steel bowl. The smell of faeces had now been added to the unpleasant mix. 'Colder than air temperature and not a drop of water in his lungs.' He gave her a look as if to say he was expecting her to draw an obvious conclusion.

'Are you saying he didn't die in the water?'

'Unlikely. He was a sailor. He was wearing the full kit: double-lined bib-trousers and Dubarry boots.'

'Should that mean something to me?'

'Made in Ireland. Top notch.'

'Sounds like inside knowledge?'

'A childhood spent sailing on Belfast Lough. My dad wanted to make a racer out of me, but I'm afraid I proved a disappointment.' He set the lungs aside and walked back towards the body. 'This guy was serious – calluses and rope burns across both hands.' He twisted the right hand towards her and pointed to the thick, rough patches of skin. 'You say he was found near the girl?'

'They were a few yards apart.'

'He's got scratches on his forearms that look like they could have come from fingernails. And a couple of marks either side of his neck.'

Jenny stepped round, fighting a growing sensation of nausea, and noticed a nick in the flesh at about collar height.

'I've taken scrapings from under the girl's nails. You never know—'

'You think he might have come to her rescue?'

'It's possible. You're sure he wasn't wearing a lifejacket?'

'He was found dressed in those clothes.' She nodded to the heap of clothing folded on the trolley at the foot of the table.

'I'm surprised. It's usually the old salts who take a chance – make it to sixty and they think they're immortal.'

Jenny said, 'Could he have floated without one dressed like that?'

'Oh yes,' Dr Kerr said. 'The air in his lungs would have kept him near the surface or thereabouts. It is slightly puzzling, though. If he didn't have a lifejacket I can only think he was holding onto something else.'

'The girl?'

Dr Kerr looked at her blankly for a moment as if distracted by a private thought, then said, 'Who found him?'

'As far as I know, both bodies were spotted from the air by a search-and-rescue helicopter.'

'Who arrived on the ground first?'

'The police, my officer, a medic, then me. Why do you ask?'

'I've a feeling you'll want to be sure of the chronology. Did any of these people check his clothing?'

'Alison said they'd checked his pockets. What is it?'

Dr Kerr said, 'Have a look at what he was wearing – under the shirt.'

Jenny stepped over the trolley and picked up the still-wet plaid shirt that was lying on top of the pile. Beneath it was a harness of some sort comprising two loops of padded nylon webbing connected by a single strap. Attached to one of the loops was a pocket about the size of a hand.

She was none the wiser.

'It's a Sidewinder shoulder holster,' Dr Kerr said. 'I just looked it up on the internet. It's designed to hold a serious handgun. He was wearing it over his T-shirt. It was empty. I didn't tell Alison – I thought you'd want to decide what to do with the information.'

Jenny paused to reorientate her thoughts. She had a dead sailor, possibly armed, recovered with no lifejacket and no water in his lungs, when all things considered he should have drowned.

'Was there anything else on him?' Jenny asked.

'No. That's it.'

She wondered what kind of man would be sailing a yacht in the Severn estuary while carrying a sidearm. 'I'll talk to the police. We won't know anything without an ID.'

'Check with them about the lifejacket. Maybe whoever found him took it off, then found the gun,' Dr Kerr suggested.

They exchanged a look, neither wanting to speculate more than was necessary, but both intrigued by the dark possibilities.

Jenny said, 'There's been a lot of talk on the radio about a possible terrorist attack – an explosion.'

'I've seen no evidence of that, not on the little girl, certainly not on this fellow.' He shrugged. 'Early days. Who knows what'll turn up?'

Jenny watched him stroll back to the counter and draw up a high stool on which he would sit to work at his dissection, his back to the autopsy table. In a moment she would leave him alone in a windowless mortuary surrounded by corpses, yet he couldn't have seemed more at ease. She envied his even calm. And as Jenny turned out of the room and walked swiftly towards the exit, she took care to stay on the opposite side of the corridor from the waiting bodies.

'They're desperate for help at the D-Mort now. There's really nothing more I can do here,' Alison announced, as Jenny arrived in the reception area of their humble ground-floor offices in Jamaica Street. The faded Georgian terrace close to the centre of Bristol was only saved from being shabby by the elegance of its proportions, but behind the facade, the small set of rooms they occupied was looking distinctly tired.

Jenny chose to ignore her challenging tone. 'How did you get on?'

Alison grabbed several pages from the computer printer and handed them over. 'The mother teaches maths. The father's something in computers as far as I can tell. Works for a company with offices round the world. Oh, and there's a passenger list for the plane if you're interested – took all day, but the airline just released it.'

Jenny glanced at the biographies Alison had gleaned from various websites. From her photograph, Michelle Patterson appeared as earnest as her husband, perhaps even more so.

Jenny said, 'Would you mind emailing Mrs Patterson a photograph of the body? She asked for one.' She reached into her pocket and handed Alison the card Greg Patterson had given her.

Alison leaned over her computer, producing a sound like machine-gun fire as she attacked the keys. It was obvious that something was troubling her, but now was not the moment for Jenny to address it.

'So Dr Kerr thinks our second body was a sailor,' Alison said.

'Yes. You don't happen to remember who was there on the beach when you first arrived?'

'Just a constable and two forensics. Why?'

'Did anyone search him?'

'I checked his pockets, that's all,' Alison answered, stepping away from the desk to pull on her coat.

'Who was the first on the scene?'

'The constable.'

'You're sure?'

'I spoke to him. He went to both the bodies, saw they were dead and called in assistance. Is there a problem?'

Jenny hesitated, but could think of no good reason not to tell her. 'He was wearing a shoulder holster, but there was no gun in it. And it seems strange he wasn't wearing a lifejacket.'

'A gun? What would he have a gun for?'

Jenny shrugged.

'I'll talk to DCI Molyneux if you like. He's heading up the incident room they're setting up over at the D-Mort.'

Jenny said, 'Why don't I do that? You let me know the word on the ground.'

Alison gave her a look. She didn't need to say that she disapproved of Jenny's continued suspicion of the police, among whom she counted many friends and former colleagues. And Jenny didn't have to say that her caution was based purely on experience. She'd yet to meet a serving detective who'd give an honest answer when a dishonest one would leave more room for manoeuvre.

'I'll see you in the morning then, Mrs Cooper,' Alison said, and swept out of the office. Her footsteps sounded heavily along the corridor that led to the front door.

Resisting the distraction of trying to fathom the reason for Alison's latest mood shift, Jenny went through the heavy oak door to her own office and found DCI Molyneux's number on her computer. He answered his phone against the sound of heavy machinery. The incident room was being assembled next to the mortuary from bolted-together Porta-kabins, he said. It was like a full-scale bloody building site in the middle of the Somme. Jenny told him about the sailor with the holster.

'As if we didn't have enough crap to deal with,' Molyneux said wearily.

'I take it you've no clue who he is.'

'I've got two hundred bodies on the floor of a tent, Mrs Cooper, four hundred more washing about in the river and God knows how many hysterical relatives standing around in the pouring rain. You'll have to wait your turn.' He rang off, yelling orders to workmen as he did so.

Grateful for the fact that the plane hadn't come down five miles to the east, Jenny gave up any hope of identifying the man before morning and turned her attention to Amy Patterson's parents. Alison's description of Mrs Patterson was somewhat short of the mark. According to her online résumé, she was a graduate of Stanford and had gained a PhD in applied mathematics at Yale before taking up a teaching post. She specialized in aerodynamics and had acted as a consultant to industry. Her husband had also studied applied mathematics at Stanford, but from there had gone on to the Massachusetts Institute of Technology, where he had spent several years on the staff of the mathematics department. He left academia in his late twenties to join a company called Cobalt Inc. From the little information Alison had gathered, she deduced that its principal business was the development of specialist computer software.

Jenny found Cobalt's website and quickly reached the limits of her understanding. The company described itself as a provider of 'turnkey software systems incorporating bespoke algorithmic solutions'. A search for the meaning of 'algorithm' taught her only that it was a term that described a mathematical formula designed to carry out a specific task. Computer software, she learned through another, more detailed search, depended on algorithms: they were the logical mechanisms, or formulae, through which tasks were ordered and results achieved. If you wanted to assemble and process any significant amount of data, you needed algorithms to apply certain rules to it in order to generate the desired outcomes. Greg Patterson, she concluded, was most probably an expert in mathematical codes, but codes for what, she had no idea.

She turned to the passenger and crew list. It ran to several pages, listing names in alphabetical order. There was no clue as to which section of the aircraft each passenger had been sitting in. The names sounded mostly British or American and a few oriental. None was familiar except that of Lily Tate, a fashion model whom Jenny had already heard mentioned several times on the radio: she had been en route for New York, where she was due to shoot a commercial. Jenny had never seen the inside of the first-class section but she wondered if that had made it all the more lonely for Lily Tate and the others sitting near her on the way down. First-class passengers wouldn't have reached out to hold each other's hands, would they? No, she couldn't imagine that.

It was getting late and a long week lay ahead. Jenny dropped the documents into her briefcase and stood up from the desk, her eye catching the photograph of her son, Ross, on the mantelpiece above the Victorian fireplace. He was nearly nineteen and over six feet tall, but whenever she thought of him the first picture that entered her mind was of a small boy with bright blue eyes and a gap-toothed grin, and it made her want to cry. She remembered the smell of his skin, and the way he would run to hug her. And now he was at university in London and even more distant since he had learned about Katy.

The desk telephone rang, scything through the silence and jarring her brittle nerves. Jenny instinctively glanced at the caller display, expecting to see Alison's name, but it was an unfamiliar number.

'Jenny Cooper.'

'Glad to have found you, Mrs Cooper. Sir Oliver Prentice, Director General, Ministry of Justice. Among my many responsibilities, I oversee public inquiries and the legal end of major disasters. I don't believe we've had the pleasure.'

'No—'

'You're on my list to entertain, but I'm afraid it's not in alphabetical order.'

Jenny felt she was expected to banter a little before getting to whatever the serious business was, but he had caught her off guard. Her reply inadvertently came out sounding sarcastic: 'Is this a special invitation?'

'Rather the opposite, I'm afraid. You might have heard – I've asked Sir James Kendall in to act as coroner for this crash.'

'I had heard it wasn't going to be handled locally.' She recognized Kendall's name as that of a recently retired High Court judge. He had made the headlines the previous year for dealing robustly with a terrorist conspiracy to deliver suicide bombers into the trading rooms of several City banks disguised as maintenance men. The evidence had been flimsy

– discussions between young men that might have been nothing more than bravado, but which earned them each eighteen years' imprisonment.

'You'll like him. He's a good man – fearless.'

Jenny sensed the word was added for her benefit. 'I'm sure.'

'I hear two bodies turned up on your patch. There's no point duplicating effort, so I suggest you pop them over to the D-Mort right away, keep everything under one roof.'

'Only one of those bodies came from the aircraft,' Jenny said. 'The other is an adult male dressed in full sailing kit. His death might even be unconnected.'

'Do you know who he is?'

'Not yet, no.'

Prentice paused to consider the situation. Jenny knew what he was about to offer as well as she knew he would have her file, with its history of irritatingly successful insubordination, open on the desk in front of him. The law entitled him to appoint whomsoever he wished as coroner for any particular case, but there was still protocol to be considered and, of course, the fear that she might create an embarrassing fuss.

'Well, if you're sure he's not from the plane there seems little point making Sir James's life any more complicated than it need be. You'll take the girl's body over this evening, all her clothing and possessions, hand over the file? He's already on site, he'll be expecting you.'

Jenny didn't recall telling Prentice that the body was that of a girl. 'If you insist,' she said.

'It would be most helpful, Mrs Cooper. I hope it doesn't prove too late a night for you.'

He rang off, leaving her with the distinct and uneasy feeling that the ground was moving beneath her feet.

*

Jenny was turning off the lights in reception and about to head out when the phone rang again. She answered it at Alison's desk.

'Hello, Jenny Cooper speaking.'

She was met with silence, then a catch of breath as if the caller were about to speak, only to lose courage. There was a click, followed by the burr of the dial tone. Jenny attempted to retrieve the number but the synthesized voice at the exchange reported that it had been withheld. An instinct told her to wait, that whoever it was would try again, but five silent minutes passed and no call came. Perhaps it had been a wrong number after all?

She should remember to ignore her instincts, she told herself as she bolted the office door. Acting on them had sent her down many blind alleys, and Dr Allen was always most insistent that the hallmark of sanity was rationality. From now on, she promised herself, she would act strictly according to the evidence before her.

FOUR

JENNY FIRST SPOTTED THE HALOGEN GLOW of the D-Mort
from over a mile away along the flat, coastal road that ran
alongside the estuary. Arrays of arc lights suspended from
cherry pickers a hundred feet up in the air illuminated a large
field in which several cranes were at work. As she came closer,
she saw that they were assembling a number of portable
cabins into a small office block, which stood alongside several
vast marquees connected by covered walkways. Still more
canvas structures were being erected around them.

A roadblock had been positioned several hundred yards
before the entrance to the field. Jenny pulled up at the
checkpoint, which was protected on either side by concrete
barriers of the kind used to shield government buildings
from terrorist attack. It was a female police constable who
leaned down to inspect her identification, but to either side
of the barrier stood young regular soldiers carrying rifles.
Jenny stated her business and informed the constable that an
undertaker's van would be arriving shortly. She received
instructions to turn into the field and park in the green zone
reserved for staff.

Jenny drove slowly between two rows of plastic bollards
which led to the field entrance, noticing several more armed
soldiers standing watch in the darkness on either side. Turning through the open gateway, she rattled across a cattle grid

and followed notices to the green zone, passing along a temporary road that appeared to have been constructed from plastic matting. Parking her Land Rover amidst a large assembly of police and military vehicles, she glanced over at the blue zone and deduced that it was where the relatives of the dead were being taken. Several young female soldiers and police officers were directing them to a marquee, in which, no doubt, they would be greeted by a host of whispering counsellors and chaplains.

Following a colour-coded walkway to the staff reception tent, Jenny's suspicion was confirmed that this was precisely the sort of disaster for which Home Office contingency planners had been preparing for more than a decade. She remembered from a training course she had been obliged to attend the previous summer that the government had sufficient resources to erect six such D-Morts at any one time. All the necessary equipment was stored in warehouses at strategic locations around the country ready to deal with multiple terrorist attacks or fatal epidemics. Somewhere on site there would be a handful of officials who had been planning this day for years.

Her phone rang as she approached the entrance of the tent. She glanced at the screen with the unrealistic hope that it might be Ross. It was a London number.

'Mrs Cooper, its Greg Patterson. I just picked up your message.' He sounded fraught.

'I did try you several times, and your wife—'

'I know. Look . . .' He paused, as if gathering strength. 'I don't want you to move my daughter's body. Neither does my wife.'

'I'm afraid I haven't been given any choice. The Director General of the Ministry of Justice has instructed me—'

'Her body does not belong to anyone except her parents,' Patterson said, 'and we do not give permission.'

'Mr Patterson, until a certificate is signed releasing her for burial I'm afraid that's not the legal position.'

He made no reply.

'I can make representations on your behalf, though,' Jenny said. 'Is there any particular reason—?'

After a pause, Patterson said, 'Her mother doesn't want her body in with all the others. She doesn't feel it's appropriate.'

'Is this a religious objection of some sort?'

He fell silent for an even longer moment.

'I can't speak for my wife, but there's something I need to know . . . it won't happen if she's lumped in with six hundred others.'

'What's that, Mr Patterson?'

'She . . . Amy, called me while the plane was going down . . . she said the plane was falling, I could hear people screaming around her, I could hardly hear her voice . . . I said, "Put your lifejacket on, put it on, now." I thought they'd be out over the Irish Sea, it was all I could think of . . . I haven't told her mother any of this, it would be too distressing. But I need to know if I might have saved her, if she'd only been found more quickly . . .'

Jenny gave him a moment. 'Mr Patterson, there's no reason to presume your daughter's death won't be fully investigated along with all the others.'

'Mrs Cooper, this is an Airbus 380, the world's biggest and most advanced passenger airliner. The companies who operate these planes are committed for the next thirty years. These aircraft are the arteries of world trade. Measured against that, my daughter's death will count for nothing.'

Jenny said, 'Even if I believed that were true, it's not an argument that would hold any sway, I'm afraid. I'm sorry, Mr Patterson. If you wish to pursue this issue further, you'll have to take it up with the Ministry of Justice. In the meantime, your daughter's body is being transferred to the disaster mortuary at Walton Bay.'

Patterson said, 'There was no explosion, Mrs Cooper. Amy didn't say anything about a loud bang.'

They listened to each other in silence. It was Patterson who ended the call.

He had been talking for his wife. It was always the mother – the one who had given and sacrificed most in raising the child – who insisted on clinging to the body. Men, in Jenny's experience, put distance between themselves and the shell of their dead offspring almost immediately. Mrs Patterson wanted her daughter's uniqueness preserved for as long as possible, and her separation from the others who had died stood as a symbol that she remained special.

Jenny stepped into the reception tent. Nothing could demand greater sanity than the investigation that now confronted her. A young man in naval uniform greeted her from behind a trestle table serving as a desk and issued her with a temporary staff badge to be worn around her neck 'in all places and at all times whilst on site'. He directed her along one of two covered walkways that led from the tent to a single Portakabin that stood at ninety degrees to the stack being erected behind it.

Walking the thirty yards from the reception area to the coroner's office, Jenny looked out over the main area of the site and saw that three marquees were already standing and that one more was going up. One would be reserved for relatives, one would serve as a canteen and rest area for staff, one would act as a holding bay and identification suite for bodies, and the fourth would house the autopsy tables and a forensic laboratory. The modular offices would be divided between the police, the Coroners' Service, the search and rescue coordinators and air accident investigators.

Over the rumble of the cranes and the chug of the diesel generators, she was sure she heard DCI Molyneux shouting at someone to getting his bloody phone lines sorted out.

She knocked at the door of the coroner's office and stepped into an oasis of calm. Sir James Kendall, a courteous silver-haired man dressed in sober pinstripes, stood up from behind a desk to greet her. As a retired judge he would have to have been over seventy, though he retained the physique and moved with the suppleness of a far younger man.

'Jenny Cooper, Severn Vale District Coroner.'

'Ah yes. Good of you to come.' He shook her hand and gestured her to a chair opposite his. 'This is Inspector Colin Harris, my officer.'

A fleshy-faced man, whom Jenny assumed was a specially appointed detective seconded from the Met, nodded to her from behind the screen of his laptop.

'You've brought the body over, have you?' Sir James asked, lowering himself into his chair.

'The undertakers are on their way. Her clothing is with her, and the lifejacket she was wearing. But I ought to warn you, the parents aren't happy with her being moved.'

'Oh? Why's that?' He seemed to take it almost as a personal slight.

'I think they might see their daughter as a special case. She was wearing a lifejacket. The results of the post-mortem suggest she survived for some time after the crash.'

'We may have many such cases, Mrs Cooper, it's simply too early to say.' He knitted lean, liver-spotted fingers in front of his chest. 'But you'll appreciate that the Director General would like to keep this all under one roof. We don't want things any messier than they have to be.'

'No.' Jenny took the few formal documents relating to Amy's body from her briefcase and handed them across the desk. 'Finding constable's report, my officer's statement and notice of identification. And with any luck a written post-mortem report to follow first thing tomorrow.'

Sir James pulled on a pair of reading glasses and inspected the documents thoroughly.

Jenny said, 'I expect you know there was a second body on the beach. A male. A sailor, we think.'

'Yes.' He looked at her over the tops of his spectacles. 'The navy divers have found the wreckage of a yacht. I received the message a few moments before you arrived.'

'Struck by wreckage from the plane,' Harris added without looking up from his work.

'Do you know anything else? Were there others on board?'

'That's all the information we have, Mrs Cooper,' Sir James said, carefully securing Amy Patterson's documents with a paper clip.

'Do you have any idea what brought the plane down?'

'There are plenty of theories, but none of them worth a breath until we locate the flight data recorders.'

'Doesn't this aircraft transmit flight data back to base all the time it's in the air? That's what I heard on the radio.'

'There appears to have been an interruption in communications, no doubt connected to the cause of the accident.' He gave her a patient smile which told her he now had more important things to occupy his time.

Jenny stood up from her chair. 'You'll let me know about the yacht, won't you?'

'Directly, Mrs Cooper. And please, do feel at liberty to have a look around while you're here. I must admit, I've never seen anything quite like it. I hope not to again.'

'Quite,' Jenny said, finding herself mimicking Kendall's courtly language. There were questions she would like to have asked and issues she would like to have raised – the dead man's holster for one, and Amy Patterson's phone call for another – but something stopped her. The judge was trying to *manage* her, and that instinctively made her want to manage him back. 'We'll discuss the yacht tomorrow. I'll probably want to bring what's left of it over to Avonmouth. I've got a friendly salvage firm who'll organize that if it's a problem for you.'

Sir James Kendall exchanged a glance with Harris. 'All in good time, Mrs Cooper.'

Jenny stepped out of the office into a cold blast of wind that was whipping sheets of rain noisily against the canvas overhead. She turned left along the walkway which led to the largest marquee on site. A police constable at the nearest entrance marked 'Staff Only' checked her ID badge and nodded her through. She entered to find a long corridor stretching the length of the tent, from which branched several sectioned-off areas. She stopped at the entrance to the first and saw rescue workers bringing in body bags on stretchers from outside. The atmosphere was one of sombre efficiency and strange associations. The marquee was not unlike those in which grand wedding parties took place. It smelt of wet grass and damp canvas and the sound of the generators summoned images of a fairground. Jenny watched as bags were laid out on the floor and dealt with by a small team of mortuary technicians dressed in green surgical scrubs and latex gloves. The bodies were searched for identifying documentation and a note of anything found was made by one of several police officers, who moved up and down the line carrying clipboards. Even from forty feet away, Jenny could tell that some were so damaged as to be unrecognizable. Each was given a numbered tag, and a photograph was taken before it was zipped up and carried through to the next section. There was no easy or sanitized way of identifying the remains of so many dead. Those bodies that had had documents in their clothing were laid out on the floor of the identification area in alphabetical order; the rest were placed at the end of the line under a sign which read simply, 'Identity Unknown'. Jenny looked on as Alison and three other coroners' officers from surrounding districts escorted clusters of relatives to carry out their grim task. Most were silent, or sobbed quietly, overwhelmed by the incomprehensible scale of the disaster.

'She hasn't got a next of kin, not within twelve thousand miles.'

Jenny turned at the sound of the raised voice and saw a man of about her age remonstrating with the constable guarding the entrance.

'Please, sir—'

'I thought you wanted the bodies identified. Isn't that what you want?'

Alison left the couple she was dealing with to a colleague and hurried over.

'What seems to be the problem?'

'I'm being told I can't identify my friend because I'm not a relative or partner.'

'What is your relationship to the deceased?'

'Her name was Casey. Nuala Casey. We used to be together. Her brother's her only family and he lives in Auckland, New Zealand.'

Alison inadvertently caught Jenny's eye and seemed to sense her disapproval at the intrusion of the petty rule. She consulted her list. 'All right, sir, you can come through.'

Jenny turned to go, but she found herself compelled to look back. Alison led the man to near the start of the line. He moved purposefully, not flinching or averting his eyes from the other bodies which were in the process of being identified. His voice was that of a professional, but the deep lines in his face and his wiry frame didn't belong to someone who spent their days cooped up in an office.

Alison stopped by one of the body bags and stooped to unzip it. Jenny caught a glimpse of blonde hair and a badly bruised and swollen face.

The man stared hard, then nodded. 'That's her. Do you have any of her effects?'

'Those can only be released to next of kin with permission of the coroner, I'm afraid, sir. Perhaps her brother could contact him?'

'Of course.' The man signed his name on Alison's clipboard then walked quickly to the exit, forcing Jenny to step aside.

Alison gestured to her to wait while she zipped up the bag, then came to meet her by the doorway. 'I heard about the little girl. They took her straight out to one of the storage trailers.' She pointed towards a flap in the marquee's outer wall. 'There are ten of them parked out there. They can fit fifty in each. They've been stored in a warehouse near Taunton, apparently, just waiting for something like this to happen.' She seemed impressed. 'We've recovered more than two hundred already. The divers are going to be working through the night. Can you imagine it?'

Jenny said, 'What's the latest word on the cause?'

'You name it – bombs, surface-to-air missile, hijacked by terrorists then shot down by our own fighters, it all depends who you talk to.'

'Such as?'

Alison quickly scanned the area, checking they weren't being listened to. 'The farmer who owns this field told the police he heard an explosion. He claims he drove down to the estuary, couldn't see a thing through the mist, but heard engine noise out there, like helicopters or something.'

'When was this?'

'Ten or fifteen minutes after it went down.'

'You haven't heard anything about a yacht? Kendall said the divers have found one.'

'I'd heard that; nothing about any more bodies though. What did Molyneux say about our sailor and his gun?'

Before Jenny could answer, another group of relatives arrived at the entrance: an elderly man supported by two younger women whom Jenny assumed to be his daughters. 'I think you might be needed,' she said, and left Alison to her work.

The brief glimpses Jenny had caught of the recovered bodies had all revealed faces that had suffered impacts of varying ferocity. They reminded her of road accident victims whose heads had whipped forward and struck the dash or airbag. These were precisely the kinds of injuries she would have expected to see following a violent crash landing, and their frequency made Amy Patterson's unbattered condition even more puzzling.

The heaviness in Jenny's limbs told her it was time to go home and get the sleep she would need to cope with the days ahead, but she knew that even a sleeping pill wouldn't stop the questions from churning in her mind throughout the night. She couldn't leave without finding out more.

The autopsy room was at the far end of the corridor and accessed through a solid doorway with an electronic mechanism that could only be operated by the swipe card held by the constable guarding it. Jenny was let through to find a fully equipped mortuary that was barely distinguishable from those in the most modern hospitals. There were six tables, six modular units containing surgical instruments, dissection bench and sink, and along the far wall a row of a dozen refrigerators each with three shelves stacked one on top of the other. Pathologists were hard at work at each station. She recognized two of them as locums who were regulars at the Vale. Dr Kerr was working at the far table. He lifted a hand in greeting and gestured her over.

Jenny carefully crossed the linoleum floor made slippery by the splashes from the shower hoses used to sluice down the bodies when a post-mortem was complete. She found him starting work on a male in his twenties. The face was badly bruised from a frontal impact and the slim, muscled torso had been virtually severed above the pelvis at the level of the lap belt.

'Morbid curiosity, Mrs Cooper?' Dr Kerr said.

'That and being ordered to give up the little girl to Kendall. I'm not to be trusted, apparently.'

He smiled across the body at her. His eyes were tired and bloodshot. 'No comment.'

Jenny said, 'What's your theory?'

'We know the hull split in three as they're designed to on impact. All the bodies we've seen so far have been recovered from the front section. It's stuck nose-down in the silt under fifty feet of water. A lot of them were severed by their lap belts; some shot right out of their seats and crushed their skulls on the overhead lockers. Seats ripped clear of their moorings – that's what we're hearing.'

'Any more in lifejackets?'

He shook his head.

Jenny said, 'Any evidence of an explosion?'

'No. That's one theory that's losing traction all the time. If there'd been a sudden depressurization at altitude you'd expect to find air embolisms – froth in the heart ventricles from blood gases suddenly expanding – but we've not found any. No hypoxia either – the blood's fully oxygenated.'

'Meaning the plane hit the water intact?'

'It's looking increasingly likely. Tail-end first probably, with enough force to snap the hull in two places – could have been weakened already, of course. However it happened, the front end flipped forward and sank down to the bottom nose first. The rear and mid-sections are lying on their sides, but the tide is too strong for the divers to get inside until later.'

Jenny said, 'All the bodies I've seen are in a real mess. Any idea why Amy Patterson's isn't?'

'She was probably sitting along the line of fracture, most likely at the join between the rear and mid-section. If the hull was sufficiently weakened it would have snapped as the tail hit the water. Once that happened, there might not even have been a seat in front for her to hit.' He lowered his voice, 'We've had a couple from first class. You know the model everyone's so excited about – Lily someone? – in pieces, literally. Identified from her jewellery.'

Jenny said, 'Where are you getting all this information?'

'It gets passed up the line. The rescue crews bringing the bodies ashore are talking to the guys who bring them back here, who are passing what they've heard on to our technicians. Kendall gave us all a big speech about how we weren't to speculate, let alone talk to the press, but you can guess how well that's working.'

Jenny said, 'Do you think they'll let me go down to the beach?'

Dr Kerr shrugged. 'They can only shoot you.'

Kevin and Dave were off-duty ambulance men who had been diverted from their usual beat in central Bristol to spend the night ferrying the dead from the makeshift pontoon at the water's edge up to the D-Mort. A damn sight easier than dealing with fighting-mad drunks in the city centre was Kevin's assessment of their night's work. Jenny rode with them three abreast in a vehicle that looked like a golf buggy with caterpillar tracks instead of wheels. Behind them, they towed a trailer large enough to hold four body bags. They bumped over a rutted mud road that had been bulldozed out of the field and which snaked between the dunes down to the shore. At the head of the beach they were waved down by two soldiers, who ordered Jenny to stay back while the others collected their load of bodies from the pontoon. Rescue workers and ambulance crew only were allowed down to the water's edge, but on whose orders they were unable or unwilling to say.

Jenny stood on the muddy shale huddled in the outsize waterproof coat Dave had loaned her and took in a scene of intense activity. A large vessel she recognized as a Severn dredger was moored about three hundred yards out. A bank of spotlights on its deck lit up the water to its port side, facing the shore. Within the illuminated area – the size of several sports fields – were three smaller vessels from which teams of divers were operating. Their powerful searchlights moved like apparitions beneath the silty water. She counted more than half a dozen inflatable dinghies ferrying bodies and equipment to and from a floating pontoon. Some were manned by civilian crew, others by the Royal Navy. The pontoon itself was accessed by ramps and was anchored to the shore by cables attached to two large military trucks. With a tidal range of three vertical yards, the water was constantly moving up and down the muddy beach, and the pontoon had to be moved with it.

Jenny wasn't sure what she had been expecting to see – some trace of the wreckage perhaps, some small clue as to how it happened, what it had looked like when an airliner carrying six hundred souls fell to earth and shattered. But there was no visible detritus on the water or lying on the mud.

Nothing.

It struck her then that what she was witnessing, and what

she had already seen at the D-Mort, was a logistical operation that surpassed anything she could ever have imagined
the civil authorities being capable of. In twelve short hours
they had raised a small tented city in a Somerset field,
assembled an armada of boats and brought together police,
coastguard and military in seamless configuration. If Jenny
needed any reminding, it confirmed to her that no event
could have been dealt with any more seriously.

'Excuse me, madam. Stand aside, please.' The young
infantryman motioned her away from the makeshift road as
several sets of headlights appeared through the dunes.

Three black Range Rovers rounded the corner in single
file and gunned straight down on to the beach.

'Who's that?' Jenny asked, not expecting a reply.

'Guy Ransome,' the soldier said. 'But you didn't hear it
from me.'

She watched the cars pull up at the shore. A driver climbed
out of the middle vehicle and opened the rear door for the
tall, good-looking entrepreneur, not yet fifty, who had made
his first fortune in electronics before staking it all on an
airline. It seemed to her that it was a lonely figure who
walked out along the pontoon, pausing to watch the body
bags being unloaded from a dinghy. How did the mind of a
rich man work, she wondered? Was he counting the cost to
his business or to his own soul?

'You wouldn't swap places with him now, would you?'
the soldier remarked.

Jenny didn't answer.

FIVE

EDWARD MARSHAM, A PRINCIPAL INSPECTOR with the
Air Accident Investigation Branch, spoke with the reassuring
calm of a former test pilot. He was telling the interviewer
that although it was too early to say what had brought down
Flight 189, the theory with the most weight was that the
aircraft had been struck by an unusually powerful bolt of
lightning at high altitude. This would have shorted out
critical circuits in the aircraft's avionics, causing the captain
to lose control.

Wasn't the aircraft supposed to have many layers of back-
ups and fail-safes? the interviewer asked.

No number of back-up systems could prevent a freak
accident, Marsham said regretfully. The one crumb of comfort was that such lightning strikes were incredibly rare. In
the entire history of commercial aviation only a handful of
passenger craft had been lost in such a way.

Should aircraft be flying near thunderstorms when they
could be avoided? the interviewer pressed.

According to the Met Office weather data, there was only
a small storm in the area at the time, Marsham said. What
they could be looking at was an even rarer occurrence: the
plane itself causing a bolt of lightning to be discharged from
the surrounding clouds; in effect, acting as a conductor for
positively and negatively charged areas of cloud. The inci-

dence of lightning, and just what caused the build-up of electrical charge in the atmosphere, was still a phenomenon science was unable fully to explain.

What evidence beyond the weather data was there for a lightning strike? the interviewer enquired.

Divers had photographed a pronounced scorch mark on the forward starboard section of the hull, Marsham said. It was close to the avionics bay, which was situated forward of the hold beneath the cockpit. A bolt of lightning could be many thousands of volts and up to 30,000 degrees centigrade – the temperature at which sand and silica fuse to form glass.

The reception on the car radio broke up and vanished temporarily as Jenny entered the forested gorge between St Arvans and Chepstow. She caught only fragments of the remainder of Marsham's interview, but what she did notice was that he was allowed to go largely unchallenged.

Her phone rang as she was driving the straight mile alongside Chepstow racecourse. Alison's sleep-laden voice came over the speakers, talking to her from all four corners of the car.

'They've delivered your yacht, Mrs Cooper.'

'*Delivered* it?'

'It's on the quayside at Avonmouth. DCI Molyneux just called to let me know. They had a dredger bring it up on the early tide.'

'Why's he being so helpful all of a sudden?'

'They wanted it away from the main site,' he said. 'They're clearing the rear section of the hull this morning and raising both sections to the surface this afternoon. It's going to be a hell of a job getting it all ashore and transporting the pieces by road to the AAIB hangar at Farnborough.'

'No word from the incident room on our John Doe?' Jenny asked.

'Do give me a chance, Mrs Cooper. My head barely touched the pillow.'

'Let me know what they say, oh, and see if you can get me a number for that farmer who saw the lights.'

'What for?'

'I want to buy some sheep – what do you think?'

'Fine. But don't expect me before ten,' Alison said curtly and hung up.

The security guard at the entrance to Avonmouth docks greeted Jenny like an old friend and directed her to the quay. Late the previous summer the bodies of twelve emaciated Somali stowaways had turned up in the bilge tanks of a cargo ship registered in Karachi. The find had caused her many trips to visit the ship's captain and crew, who had refused to come ashore for fear of arrest. She had reluctantly certified the deaths as having occurred accidentally, but she had had her doubts. Talking to men in the docks canteen, she had heard lurid second-hand tales of foreign crews tossing stowaways overboard in the middle of the ocean.

Wearing the obligatory yellow hard hat she had been issued with at the gate, she walked out along the quay towards what was barely recognizable as the wreckage of a yacht. She could see a section of mast and the pointed end of the stern, but the rest was a broken heap of wood and canvas. A man dressed in the ubiquitous fluorescent yellow coat was standing nearby, taking photographs with a camera mounted on a tripod.

'Good morning. Jenny Cooper, Severn Vale District Coroner.'

The man looked up from his work. 'Dick Corton, Marine Accident Investigation Branch.' He squeezed her hand in a powerful grip. 'Not much of this left.' His voice was gentle and his accent pronounced. He wasn't local – Norfolk, Jenny guessed. She placed him in his early sixties, though it was hard to say. His face was a lattice of veins broken by the weather; his eyes were narrowed to slits as if permanently fixed on a far horizon.

'I'd forgotten you'd be involved as well,' Jenny said.

'Not a lot to trouble us, to be honest,' Corton replied. 'You can see it's been ripped in half. I'd say part of the plane's wing caught it as it ditched on the water. Bad luck – only vessel out there as far as I can tell.'

Jenny could see that half the hull was virtually intact. The wheel was still bolted to the deck, but the stairs that would have led down to the cabin below were absent. The galley area was still recognizable: there was half a table, some cupboards, a stove, but beyond that there was little remaining that resembled a boat.

'It looks as if there's a lot of it missing,' Jenny said.

'Smashed to pieces,' Corton said. 'Some of it would have been washed out on the tide. I'd put money on one of the engines having struck it. Look at where the hull's fractured and you can see burn marks.'

Jenny stepped closer and examined the jagged edge of the broken hull. Even with her untrained eye, it looked as if the wood had been scorched, and the layer of foam between the inner and outer skin of the hull appeared in places to have melted to the consistency of burnt treacle.

'Would the aircraft's engines have been that hot? We're not even sure if they were still working.'

'I wondered about that. One for the AAIB, I'd say,' Corton said, returning to his camera. 'I'm just boats.'

Jenny looked up and down the wreckage for any identifying marks, but there were none that she could see. 'Do you have any idea where it came from?'

'I can tell you exactly.' Corton dug into his pocket for a notebook. 'She's called the *Irish Mist*, 43-foot ketch registered in Dublin. Built in '85 and owned by a Mr Peter Hylands. I got hold of him first thing and he tells me he's just sold it through Hennessy's yacht brokers in Dublin Bay to a fellow called Chapman in Jersey. The sale went through last week and Hennessy's took possession. They didn't answer their phone. I left them a message.'

'How does that work – with the broker, I mean?' Jenny asked.

'Often they'll employ a man to deliver the vessel to the buyer – for a fee, of course. Sometimes two men, depending on the size of the boat.'

'What about this one?'

'One man could do it,' Corton said, moving his tripod around for a side-on shot of the wreck. 'What I couldn't say, though, is what they'd be doing this far up the Bristol Channel en route from Dublin to Jersey. The weather was nothing ugly, even around Land's End. He was forty miles out of his way – unless he had business in Bristol. I called the coast-guard, but he hadn't put any messages out on the radio.'

Jenny thought of the dead man's holster and asked herself why she had no intention of telling Corton and why she hadn't yet mentioned it to the police. She had no answer, except that experience had taught her to share information only with those in whom she had complete trust. She couldn't yet get the measure of Corton, and she could sense he felt the same about her.

'Where would you keep the lifejackets on a boat like this?' Jenny asked.

'There'd be a locker either side of the cockpit. Nothing to see now, though – that part's all gone.'

Jenny stepped over a section of broken mast to take in another angle. She wanted to imagine the accident from the perspective of the dead man, presuming he was at the wheel as the plane came towards him. With what remained of the vessel lying on its side, the handrail that ran around the stern was at shoulder height. She peered over it at the section of deck on which he would have been standing and saw that individual planks had been ripped out. Several remained in place, though they were largely splintered and broken.

'What's happened here?' Jenny said. This damage doesn't look like it was caused by the accident. It looks fresh.'

Corton finished taking his picture and wandered over, carefully studying the shattered boards.

'You're right. That's been done since it's been out of the water. Someone's chopped open the deck to check the void beneath.'

'Why?'

'Just to be sure, I expect,' Corton said. 'I wouldn't read anything into it.' He strolled back to his equipment and started to dismantle it. 'I take it you've got a body, or you wouldn't be here.'

'Yes. A male, dressed in sailing gear. No identity as yet.'

Corton nodded and quietly continued with his task.

'The pathologist said he looked like a regular sailor – Dubarry boots, apparently – but no lifejacket. Does that strike you as odd?'

'A solo sailor would normally wear one, certainly.' Folding the tripod into its case, Corton went on, 'Will you be wanting to hold onto the wreck or shall I arrange for it to be disposed of? I've no more use for it.'

'I won't get rid of it just yet,' Jenny said. 'You never know what might be needed.'

She watched him for a moment, wondering if he knew any more than he was letting on. It occurred to her that he had offered less than he might have done.

The farmer's name was John Roberts and he wasn't answering his phone. Jenny left a message but was impatient to talk to him. As far as she or Alison had been able to ascertain, he was the closest thing to an eyewitness that existed. The farmhouse was half a mile from the D-Mort, several hundred yards outside the cordoned-off area, yet close enough to it to hear the constant throb of the generators.

She approached the farm down a rutted track and turned into a yard in which two rusting tractors stood idle. The business had clearly seen better days.

It was Mrs Roberts who answered the door to her, a younger woman than Jenny had expected, with a worn-down face and a grizzling infant on her hip.

'He's not here,' she said, when Jenny explained the reason for her visit.

'Will he be back soon?'

'No idea.' She shrugged one shoulder, her guarded expression saying she hoped Jenny would hurry up and go.

'Do you mind if I ask where he is? Does he have a phone?'

'He's over there.' She nodded towards the D-Mort. 'They wanted him to give a statement or something.'

'My inquiry relates to a boat the plane seems to have struck when it crashed.'

The woman shook her head. 'He never said nothing about a boat.' She took a step back and went to close the door. 'Sorry.'

'You must have heard it too. Is that your kitchen window looking out over the estuary?'

'I didn't see nothing, just heard the bang, that's all.'

'What kind of bang?'

'How many kinds are there? Like a bomb going off, I suppose. There was nothing to see out there – just mist.'

'No flames?'

Mrs Roberts shook her head and switched the child to her other hip.

'Didn't you hear the plane flying in low? It must have come very close.'

'No.'

From where she was standing, Jenny could see between the gaps in the farm buildings all the way over the fields to the crash site. She could even hear the buzz of the dinghy engines and the low rumble of the dredger's crane.

'How loud was this explosion?'

'Not very.'

'But loud enough for your husband to go and investigate.'

'He was more curious than anything, especially when he heard the helicopters.'

'Oh? When was that?'

'Right after.'

'Can you be any more precise? It would be very helpful.'

Mrs Roberts said no, she couldn't. The baby had been crying and she hadn't been paying much attention.

'But you're sure there were helicopters?' Jenny persisted.

She shrugged. 'That's what he said.'

There were protocols to be followed, procedures set down in the Coroner's Rules which required her to make written requests for production of computer records, all of which in due course she would do, but in Jenny's experience there was never any substitute for an unannounced visit. A worried-looking junior official was sent out to meet her at the staff entrance to Bristol International Airport with orders to schedule a formal appointment, but Jenny insisted there were time-critical questions she needed answered immediately. Buckling under her veiled threat that failure to cooperate might amount to an obstruction of justice, the official signed her in at the gate and instructed her to follow her car to the air traffic control tower.

They were met inside the entrance to the new building by a man who introduced himself as Martin Chambers, the assistant director of the facility. Dismissing the young woman, he led Jenny directly to a first-floor meeting room that could have belonged to any modern office block in the country.

Chambers did a poor job of covering his irritation at her arrival. 'I've already made arrangements for the transfer of our data to the coroner's office. I discussed it all with Inspector Harris last night. Disks are going over later today.'

Jenny tried to explain the difference between her inquiry and Sir James Kendall's, but Chambers saw only an attempt to make him duplicate his efforts when he was struggling with staff absence and the trauma of the country's largest ever aviation disaster having happened in his airspace.

'I am sympathetic, Mr Chambers, but I will need my own copies of those disks.'

'Fine. We'll send them to you.'

'Will they include voice recordings of conversations between the ground and the pilots?'

'There were virtually none. They had only just sought clearance when they lost contact.' His tone was clipped and brittle.

'Do you recall the nature of their last communication?'

'It was something perfectly routine about the weather. There was no Mayday, no indication of anything amiss, just a loss of contact. My controller tried all possible channels but there was nothing. He just had to watch the plane fall out of the sky.'

'When you say "fall" —?'

'You'll find a graph. It won't be as accurate as the one that'll be produced from the flight data recorder, but it shows the rates and angles of descent.'

Jenny said, 'You make it sound like a *series* of incidents.'

'The pilots clearly didn't give up without a fight.' He glanced away, the picture in his mind evidently not one he was eager to put into words.

'I've had information that helicopters were at the crash site within minutes of the accident. Will your data cover that period?'

'Our radar isn't effective at very low levels. If they were below 500 feet they're unlikely to show up.'

'But surely you would have known if they were there?'

'Everything below 2,000 feet is uncontrolled airspace. Coastguard, police, air ambulance – they'll all check in with us. As far as I recall, it was at least thirty minutes before air sea rescue arrived. They're from the Royal Navy and have to fly up from Cornwall.'

'Is there any chance I can talk to the controller who was on duty at the time?'

'His name's Guy Fearnley. I let him have the day off,' Chambers said. 'I think that's reasonable, don't you?'

The interview was over in less than ten minutes and Chambers had stuck rigidly to the company line. He refused to speculate about causes of the crash or about the movement of low-flying aircraft in its aftermath. Air traffic control was a commercial business, and there could be no admissions.

Leaving the control tower, Jenny found herself drawn towards the high fence that separated the car park from the apron on which the smaller aircraft that used the airport operated. There were small cargo planes painted in the livery of courier companies, a handful of sleek private jets and a number of single-engine light aircraft of the kind she often saw flying over the Wye valley on summer afternoons. There was something about planes that both excited and terrified her. She needed a Valium before making even the shortest holiday flight; for every moment she was alive to the slightest change in the pitch of the engines and her stomach would lurch at the mildest encounter with turbulence. The very thought of travelling through the air at 500 miles per hour in an aluminium tube only ten inches thick had always seemed absurd to her, yet at the same time strangely exhilarating. But it seemed only right and just that the audacious freedom offered by an aeroplane came with an element of risk.

'Are you with the police?'

She turned abruptly to see a man with a vaguely familiar face standing watching her. He was wearing a waist-length flight jacket with a company logo on the breast: Sky Drivers. She tried to place him. Had he been one of those she had held up at the perimeter gate as she argued her way in?

'No, I'm not with the police,' Jenny said.

The man studied her face and seemed to accept her answer. 'Sorry to have troubled you.' He turned away and started towards the building to their left, which looked like a freight depot.

The voice. She remembered now – he was at the D-Mort, the man who had insisted on identifying a woman who had been his girlfriend.

'Excuse me,' Jenny called after him. 'I'm a coroner. Is there anything I can do?'

He stopped and looked back.

'Not the coroner dealing with the crash. Mine is the next jurisdiction along – Severn Vale.' His searching expression made her feel obliged to explain further. 'I'm dealing with a fatality that may be connected – a boat was hit.'

He swept her with mistrustful eyes. Then Jenny detected a flicker of recognition.

'I was at the disaster mortuary last night,' she said, 'in the identification suite.'

'I know. That's why I thought . . .' He shook his head. 'It doesn't matter.'

As he turned to go, Jenny said, 'Are you a pilot?'

'Yes . . .' He sounded wary.

She didn't like to bother a man who was grieving, but something in his demeanour told her it would be all right. There was a toughness about him, a detached quality she had noticed the night before. 'Maybe you can help me answer a question—'

He didn't look too sure.

'It's just that some helicopters arrived at the crash scene very soon after. I don't see any helicopters here – do you know where else they might have come from?'

'Within what area?'

'A witness said they headed off to the east.'

'Do you have a description?'

'Not yet.'

'I should try Beachley – the army base. That'd be the closest.' He half-turned, then hesitated, as if he were reluctant to carry the conversation any further than he had to. 'I hear they think the plane was brought down by lightning. Is that the official line?'

'As far as I know.'

'As good a story as any, I suppose.'

'Do you know a better one?'

He met her gaze. She felt something in his attitude towards her slowly shifting.

'I really don't know very much about planes,' Jenny said. 'Would you have a moment to talk?'

He took her to the unglamorous canteen used by pilots and other airside staff and told her his name was Michael Sherman. There was a gossipy, cliquey feel to the place, pilots sitting with pilots and ground crew keeping to their own. Sherman seemed to pass unacknowledged by any of them as he led her between the crowded tables to one by the window that was free. Not a man to waste time on small talk, Jenny observed.

He sipped his coffee in silence, waiting for her to make the running.

'What kind of plane do you fly?' Jenny asked finally.

'A Cessna 208, sometimes a 182. Private charter. Most of my business is flying jockeys between racecourses – the firm's got a contract with some of the big owners. Helicopters are more convenient, but never as safe.'

He made himself sound like a glorified taxi driver. It didn't fit with Jenny's feeling about him: the history in his features, the way he spoke – as if he was used to operating under pressure.

'You had a friend on 189?'

He nodded. 'Nuala. It's an Irish name. We were together for a while. She was a pilot, too – worked for Ransome as a matter of fact. Flew the Airbus short-haul. They still don't like female captains crossing the big oceans. Some sort of superstition, I guess.'

'She was what – a co-pilot?'

'No. A passenger, as far as I can tell. They get cheap tickets . . .' He turned to gaze out of the window as a big airliner came in to land, its tyres sending out puffs of smoke as they touched the runway. 'I expect she was just taking advantage of the perks, getting a few days away.'

Jenny sensed there was more. Now she was sitting close to him she could almost feel the shifting layers beneath the surface. There was some anger he was hiding, and a big unanswered question.

'You thought I was a detective. What did you think I wanted?'

He turned his gaze back from the window, a little startled.

Jenny noticed his deep blue eyes. They seemed to tell her they had seen a lot.

She watched him silently ask himself a question: should I trust her?

'Anything you tell me is entirely confidential, Mr Sherman.'

He gave a trace of a nod and stared down into his coffee. 'Nuala and I parted about a year ago, not on the best of terms. We didn't speak for months; not at all, in fact . . . But she tried to call me three times in the last few days. She left messages on my phone – it's a personal one, I don't tend to switch it on very often. My name was still written in the back of her passport – the person to contact. That's how they got hold of me.'

'What did she say in these messages?'

'She wanted me to call her, that's all—'

Jenny said, 'There's something more, isn't there?'

Sherman didn't answer.

'Or you wouldn't have the thought the police would be interested in her messages.'

'It's probably nothing, it's . . .' He shook his head. 'Accidents are like that, they start making you ask stupid questions—'

'I might be a better judge of that than you right now. Look, this conversation is strictly between the two of us, Mr Sherman – there's no reason not to say what's on your mind.'

'You're very persuasive, aren't you? '

'Sorry. I'm curious, that's all.'

'You'd have liked Nuala – she didn't take no for an answer either. Most pilots just deal with what's in front of them at the present moment – anything else is a distraction – but she was never content with that. She had studied engineering, did a degree and two years' research before she

71

ran out of money and got a job, but she never lost that instinct.' His eyes quickly scanned the room, then returned to Jenny. 'Nuala's big concern was safety. Times are tight, airlines are shrinking and cutting corners and everyone's too frightened for their jobs to speak out . . . She ran a forum on the internet – anonymously, of course – which pilots would visit to swap stories or offer each other advice. Keeping her involvement secret was very important to her. She made me swear I'd never mention it to anyone, not in the business or outside it.'

'And you thought the messages she left you might have been connected with this forum?'

'The first thing I did when I heard, even before I knew she was on board, was try to log in, but it had been taken down. I can see the airlines' lawyers might have wanted to stop the rumour mill turning, but that quickly?'

'Had you visited it recently?'

'About a week ago.'

'Maybe her messages were about that? Perhaps she was having some sort of trouble with the forum and thought she'd better check you'd not said anything.'

'I guess it's possible,' Sherman said, 'but she knew she could trust me.'

'Is there anyone else she might have spoken to?'

'I called her brother in New Zealand. He didn't know anything. Didn't even know she was going to New York. She's got a friend or two in London. I haven't tried them yet, I'm not sure they'll want to hear from me.'

'That sort of break-up, was it?'

Sherman said, 'She went in with her eyes open . . .' He let out a sigh that expressed an emotion somewhere between anger and regret. 'You don't fly Tornados for eighteen years and come out as Mr Home Improvements. Nuala knew that.'

'You were in the RAF?'

He nodded. 'I got out, but like I told her, it would never get out of me.'

Jenny was intrigued, but he was already getting up from the table. 'I've got some jockeys to fetch. Nice meeting you.'

'I'd like to talk to you again, Mr Sherman—'

He pointed to the logo on his jacket. 'You know where to find me.'

SIX

THE CALL FROM THE NURSING HOME came as she was
turning out of the airport. It was the disapproving matron,
Mrs Stewart, informing her that her father had suffered
another minor stroke, his third in as many weeks. He was
comfortable, she said, and the doctor hadn't seen any need
to take him to hospital. The unspoken subtext was that
Jenny should hurry up and visit if she wanted to see him
alive again.

It was becoming awkward. Despite his rapidly failing
health, Jenny hadn't visited in over a month. She was his
only daughter, his only close family. Mrs Stewart knew
Jenny's history, of course. All the staff did; it would have
been impossible not to. It had been plastered across the local
newspapers the previous summer. Worse still, the reports
told only a fraction of the truth. None had mentioned that
her father had been having sex with his own brother's wife
when it happened; there was no mention of the fact that
he had sworn his five-year-old daughter to silence on pain
of death. He was always referred to as 'a respected local
businessman' and that was how his nurses thought of him.
It was Jenny they shrank from in the corridors and whispered about the moment she had passed by.

'How ill is he?' Jenny asked, frightened to hear the
answer.

74

'He's weak, Mrs Cooper. He can take a little fluid, but that's all.'

'Does the doctor think he'll improve?'

'You know how it is. If you want my honest opinion, I'm not sure he will.'

Jenny said, 'Thank you. I'll be over shortly.'

'I think that would be best,' Mrs Stewart said, adding, 'you never know how much in his condition he might understand.'

If a dirty secret had a smell, Jenny thought, it would be the smell of the first-floor corridor at the end of which her father lay. It was a hopeless smell, one of living decay and of futile attempts to disguise it.

The door to his room was ajar, but she knocked anyway and was met with the inevitable silence. Her nerves dampened by the beta blocker she had taken during the drive over, she stepped inside to find the room neater than she had ever seen it. The nurses did that, she had noticed: treated decline with increasing orderliness until eventually the unwanted item in the bed was tidied away too.

'Hello, Dad. It's Jenny.'

He lay still, staring at the ceiling, as if all that remained of his life force was concentrated into the effort of breathing.

'I heard you'd not been well.'

She drew up a chair and positioned it close, but just beyond his reach. It was as though entering his presence propelled her back into the mind of her childhood self – full of fears and dark imaginings.

You will only be free when you have forgiven him, Jenny. She could hear Dr Allen's words repeating in her mind like a mantra. Logically, she understood it all; she was suffering under a burden her father alone had placed on her; her buried associations with death had even affected her choice of career, but sitting close enough to touch, hearing the breath rattle in his dying lungs, she felt no understanding, only anger. And she hated herself for it. She could summon pity for every undeserving drunk scooped dead off the streets, but not an ounce for her own father. She wished he were dead, gone, finished, extinct, and even as she had the thought, she felt the black space open beneath her.

'I'll take you with me, Smiler,' he seemed to say from behind his old man's mask. 'There'll be no getting away from me.'

As she left his room, hurrying along the corridor to avoid the prying eyes of the nurses, she knew that he had her still, as surely as if he were gripping her with those powerful hands that had so often stung the back of her legs. And he wanted to bring her tumbling down with him.

'No,' Jenny snapped. 'You'll put me through to him now.'

'I'm sorry,' the adjutant protested, 'but—'

'I said I'll speak to him now.'

Cowed by her ferocious insistence, the junior officer placed her on hold. She waited moodily, fully aware that it was her father she was angry with, not a man merely trying to do his job, and tried her best to calm down.

'Mrs Cooper? Brigadier Russell. What can I do for you?' He spoke in the sharp, impatient way of a military man annoyed at being diverted from more important business.

'I'm investigating a death connected with the plane crash yesterday – a yachtsman. I've had a report that there were helicopters on the scene only minutes later and that they headed off in your direction. I wondered if they were yours.'

The Brigadier took a moment to reply. When he answered her, he had radically adjusted his tone to one of polite enquiry. 'And where did this report originate?'

'From a member of the public who happened to be nearby,' Jenny said, being deliberately vague.

'I'm quite sure we had no helicopters operating at that time. I provided some air support later in the afternoon as back-up to search and rescue, but that's all.'

Jenny pressed on. 'If the witness is correct they would have passed your base at approximately ten-fifteen yesterday morning. Might anyone have seen them?'

'There are always lots of civil aircraft in the area, Mrs Cooper. I'm sure you appreciate we don't keep a log of everything that passes by.'

Jenny was in no mood to be lied to. 'An army base across the estuary from a nuclear reactor? You must maintain some regular surveillance.'

'If only we had the resources you imagine, Mrs Cooper. I can assure you, we don't.'

As Brigadier Russell put down the phone, it occurred to her that somewhere deep in the bowels of government, the same people who had so rapidly erected the D-Mort must also have formulated plans for dealing with the flow of information in the wake of a major accident. They would need to be seen to be in control, and that meant damping down speculation. All her phone call would have achieved was the ringing of another alarm bell somewhere in White-hall and the addition of her name to a list of trouble-makers.

Avoiding the mounting pile of routine death reports collecting on the side of her desk, Jenny flicked to the latest online news reports and found a page accumulating photographs of the lost passengers. Top billing was given to Lily Tate, the model, but next to her in the A-list was a name Jenny had never heard before: Jimmy Han. His biography said he was forty-three years old and the CEO of Han Industries, a computer-chip manufacturer worth several billions of dollars. He had fled China for Taiwan aged twenty, where, despite a lack of university education, he had single-handedly built up his global computer manufacturing business from scratch. Much to the annoyance of the Chinese government, he had been an outspoken critic of their attempts to stifle access to information, especially through the internet. Wherever Han went he seemed to court suspicion and controversy. During a recent address at Cambridge University, a fight had broken out between pro- and anti-government Chinese students; while in India he had been photographed meeting the Dalai Lama. His death was described as a major loss to the cause of Chinese democracy. There were several other wealthy businessmen on board, though none as colourful, rich or young as Han.

'I've identified the yachtsman.'

Jenny looked up to see Alison entering. Her expression was grim.

'Gerry Brogan, thirty-eight. He's been working for Hennessy's for a year. Before that he did the best part of five years for sailing illegals into Ireland who he'd picked up in France. He's also got form for violent assault, possession of cocaine with intent to supply and the Garda suspect him of having sailed guns out of the country to Scotland for the IRA during decommissioning. What you might call a real professional.' She slapped a print-out on the desk headed Irish Criminal Records Bureau.

Jenny looked down the list of convictions, which stretched back to one of shoplifting handed down by the Waterford Juvenile Court. 'Have you spoken to his employers?' she asked.

'Just now. They knew nothing about his past except that he'd been skippering some tycoon's yacht in the Caribbean for the last six years. They say he could sail all right, and single-handed, too. He'd set out to deliver the *Irish Mist* to

Jersey, but had phoned them early that morning to say he had a problem with the rudder and was putting in to Swansea for repairs. That's the last they heard. They've no idea why he came all the way up the Bristol Channel.'

'Is he married, single . . . ?'

'There's a girlfriend. I've got a number but she's not replied yet.'

Jenny recalled the freshly broken boards on the yacht's deck. 'I presume our police had been in touch before you were?'

'No. I had to break the news.'

Jenny nodded, deciding to keep her questions about Brogan and what had happened to his yacht to herself.

'We know why he was wearing a holster now, don't we?' Alison said. 'The man was a villain.' *And he got what he deserved*, she might have added.

'We'll see,' Jenny replied.

'Oh, and he definitely had a lifejacket. Top of the range, apparently – illuminated on contact with water, and stayed lit up for twenty-four hours. I'm surprised no one's found it.' Changing the subject, Alison pointed to a box on the floor as she turned to leave. 'The police left that for you this morning. It's the effects from that man's car on Saturday night. He was a photographer, apparently. I spoke to his wife but she didn't seem that interested. Still in shock, I expect.'

In the drama of the plane crash Jenny had almost forgotten about Saturday night's road accident. 'I'll deal with it,' she said.

Alison glanced pointedly at the pile of papers sitting just as she had left them on the corner of Jenny's desk four hours before. 'I'll believe it when I see it, Mrs Cooper.'

Now that she knew what the box contained, Jenny couldn't have left it untouched if she had wanted to. There was always something troubling about objects retrieved from the scene of a traumatic death, as if they had absorbed something of the event into themselves and might pass the contagion on. She lifted the cardboard flaps with a sense of dread, half-expecting to find the contents were stained and crusted with the dead man's blood. But what she found inside was a sturdy canvas holdall zipped shut. She opened it to discover that it contained a camera and two large albums bearing the name of his business – Whitestone Studios – which were filled with prints. The first album contained samples of work that she assumed made up the bulk of his business: wedding pictures, a smiling young woman at her graduation ceremony, team photographs taken at a rugby tournament and informal shots captured at a black-tie dinner of the kind that made their way into the back of trade magazines. The second folder felt more like an artist's portfolio and consisted largely of artfully composed landscapes and studies of shifting skies. As she turned through the pages, Jenny saw the photographer's themes emerge more clearly: the clouds, the sun, a fiery harvest moon; the mood on earth set by what appeared in the sky. Some macabre instinct made her reach for the camera and switch it on to search for the very last photographs the dead man had taken. The images that greeted her were far removed again from those in the folders. She scrolled through a series of beautiful portraits of a slender, dark-haired woman whom Jenny placed in her early forties. She wore an enigmatic half-smile, though her dark brown eyes were sad. The photographs were taken inside with a lens that blurred the background into obscurity. There were several of her head and bare shoulders, and a single picture of her leaning against a plain white wall, naked.

A memory stirred of opening the wallet that the technician at the mortuary had retrieved from the dead man's blood-drenched coat. There had been photographs inside: two children and a woman she had assumed to be his wife. Her face had been pretty, but ordinary. And it definitely hadn't belonged to the woman in the photograph.

Jenny heard determined high-heeled footsteps outside her office window which came to a stop at the front door. The buzzer sounded. She hurriedly replaced the camera and closed the box.

'It's Mrs Patterson,' Alison called through from reception.

'Who?'

'The dead girl's mother. She wants to see you.'

Already? She must have caught an overnight flight and travelled straight to Bristol. How could she have forced herself onto a plane so quickly?

She got her answer as soon as Alison brought Michelle Patterson through the door. Jenny could tell before she had spoken that here was a woman who had turned grief into anger and a furious desire for retribution.

Jenny gave a sympathetic smile and offered her hand, but Mrs Patterson ignored it, or was too preoccupied to notice, and launched straight in with her demand. 'Where is she? I want to see my daughter's body.'

Alison took her cue to leave.

Jenny proceeded gently. 'Your husband may have explained to you – your daughter's body has been taken to the main disaster mortuary. Her case has been handed to Sir James Kendall. He's the coroner for those who died in the crash.'

'I don't understand. Yesterday you called me and said her case fell within your jurisdiction. As far as I can ascertain it's all to do with where a body is lying when it's found.'

'Usually, but in this case the Ministry of Justice inter-vened.'

'Why? Why would they do that?'

Jenny motioned her to a chair.

'Administrative reasons. They don't want the confusion of parallel investigations taking place.'

'Is that lawful?'

'Yes, it is.'

Mrs Patterson met Jenny's eyes. She had the keen, searching expression of an academic.

'Has my husband told you the precise reason why Amy wasn't on the plane she was meant to be flying on?'

'When my officer last spoke to him, he said something about the airline changing the reservation.'

'Really? He's hardly said a word to me. I knew I shouldn't have trusted him.' Her voice quavered slightly. 'She had never flown on her own before.'

'I'm sure there was nothing he could have done.'

'He could have done what he'd promised in the first place and flown with her. At least she wouldn't have died alone.' She pulled a handkerchief from her pocket and pressed it briefly to her eyes, as if attempting to force the tears back inside.

Jenny waited, attempting to gauge how much she should tell her.

Mrs Patterson answered the question for her. 'How did she die? Did she suffer? I need to know.'

Jenny said, 'I don't think your daughter did die alone. Initial post-mortem examination shows that in all likelihood she died of hypothermia – she probably survived the crash with non-life threatening injuries and was alive for some time in the water.' She hesitated. 'A man was found on the beach close to her, a yachtsman whose boat was struck by the plane. He appears to have died the same way. There's a chance he was with her, but we don't know for certain.'

The mother's face became immediately animated. 'Who was this man?'

'His name was Gerry Brogan. He was delivering a yacht from Dublin to Jersey. We haven't been able to get hold of his girlfriend yet.'

'May I have her number?'

'I'm really not sure whether—'

'Are you a mother, Mrs Cooper?'

'Yes.'

'Then you'll need to understand why I need to know who was with my daughter during the final moments of her life.'

Jenny felt her stomach turn over and a lump form at the base of her throat. 'I have be honest with you, Mrs Patterson – you may not like what you find out.'

'What do you mean?'

Telling herself that she was only doing her duty, Jenny pulled Brogan's record from among her papers and handed it across the desk. She looked away as Mrs Patterson read it through.

'I've no reason to think that he behaved any differently from how any other human being would in that situation,' Jenny said.

Mrs Patterson stared, unfocused, into space. Finally, she said, 'Part of my work outside academia has been acting as a consultant to the aerospace industry – mostly in the field of aerodynamic modelling. In fact I did some of the early work on Boeing's competitor to this aircraft – calculating the optimal surface area of the wings to carry such weight. I've a lot of faith in planes, you might be surprised to hear – scientists, on the whole, try to get things right. But politicians on the other hand . . .' She left her thought half-spoken. Shifting to a more combative mood, she sat to attention in her chair, her hands folded on her lap. 'Would you consider that my daughter's case was taken from you partly for political reasons, Mrs Cooper?'

'I very much doubt it,' Jenny said, anxious that it wouldn't be constructive to encourage that line of thinking, given Mrs Patterson's current state of mind.

Mrs Patterson seemed to sense that she wasn't being entirely truthful. 'And what would you say to taking it back?'

'I really can't see how that could happen,' Jenny answered tactfully.

'My question is whether you would be *prepared* to take it back?'

'I could hardly refuse, but it would take court action – a judicial review. The decision to take your daughter's case away from me would have to be proved perverse or unlawful. Neither of those things is very likely.'

'You meet grieving mothers all the time, Mrs Cooper – you must know what they're capable of.'

Jenny paused. 'I understand how you feel, Mrs Patterson, but a lot more will emerge in the next few hours. Why don't we speak again in the morning?'

'I'm at the Marriott on College Green,' Mrs Patterson said. 'And you should know this from the outset – I won't be leaving this country without my daughter, or without the truth.'

Alison was scathing in her judgement, which she passed barely a moment after their visitor had left the office. 'I know the poor woman's lost a daughter, but you can tell the type – you could lay down your life for her and it wouldn't be enough. I should steer well clear, Mrs Cooper.'

Jenny had learned to tolerate Alison's eavesdropping, but lately her officer had abandoned all pretence and begun to treat Jenny's private meetings as her own. The day was fast approaching when Jenny would have to have a stern word, but she hadn't the energy for a confrontation right now. She was scheduled to meet Dr Allen after work and needed all her reserves of emotional strength.

Instead, she carried the photographer's box through from her office and placed it on Alison's desk. 'It's just a camera and some photographs he'd taken recently. There's no reason they shouldn't go back to his wife, except—' She hesitated. 'There are some pictures on the camera . . .'

Alison's interest was piqued. She dived into the box and brought it out, working the controls like an expert. 'They're rather good.' She clicked through several frames, studying the woman critically. 'You know, I think I might know her. I'm sure I've seen her face somewhere . . .'

'His office is just down the road. The chances are she's local, too.'

Alison arrived at the shot of the woman standing naked. 'Oh . . .'

'What do you think we should do?' Jenny asked.

Alison considered the dilemma. 'I think his widow could do without seeing these, don't you?' She started to delete them.

'No, don't—' Jenny said. 'We should try to find whoever she is in the pictures. She might want them.'

Alison peered closely at the woman's face. 'Yes, I think I may have seen her in the street with a little child. I pass a nursery school driving to work, perhaps it was there.' She placed the camera back in the box. 'I've no idea, but I'll certainly look out for her.'

'I'd be grateful,' Jenny said.

Alison set the box on the floor, then gave Jenny a look that seemed to read her thoughts.

'Are you all right, Mrs Cooper? You look a bit pale.'

'I'm fine,' Jenny lied. 'A little tired, that's all.'

SEVEN

SHE HAD FAR MORE IMPORTANT things to think about than herself. The briefcase sitting at the side of her chair contained the air traffic control data plotting the last moments of a doomed airliner; somewhere in Dublin a young woman who had just learned that her lover was dead was waiting for her call. But here she was – yet again – sitting opposite the eternally patient and punctilious Dr Allen, who persisted in the belief that he could make her feel whole. Over the course of three years, the consulting room where they met in the compact, modern Chepstow hospital had become as familiar as her own home.

'Do you love your father, Jenny?'

'No.'

Dr Allen smiled. 'I don't recall you ever having answered a question so emphatically. It makes me suspicious.'

'I was with him this morning,' she said, deliberately softening her tone for the psychiatrist's benefit. 'He's had a stroke, several in fact. He won't live long. I have examined my feelings and I felt nothing towards him except fear. He can barely breathe, but merely being in the same building makes me feel panicked.'

'He was the monster in your nightmares, wasn't he?' He flicked back in his notebook through many pages of meticulously handwritten notes. 'The persistent dream – the crack opening in the wall of the room you slept in as a young child, the malevolent, unseen presence beyond—' He glanced up at her. 'When you're in your father's physical presence you experience the same sensation as you did in that dream.'

'It's similar, certainly.'

'But it is him? The monster?'

Jenny felt her eyes suddenly well with tears, but she hadn't been *feeling* anything.

'You seem irritated by your reaction.'

'We've discussed this before.'

'It's not weakness, Jenny. Far from it. You were weak when you had no mechanism for dealing with your feelings, when they simply overwhelmed you and caused you to break down. Now at least you're expressing them.'

She concentrated on drying her eyes and swallowing the lump in her throat.

'Tell me, have you been feeling emotional at unexpected or inappropriate moments?' he asked.

Jenny recalled her reaction to the two bodies on the beach. There had been other moments, too. She had wept after a perfectly mundane phone call from her son, and again after she spotted her ex-husband in a supermarket car park with his young partner and their new baby. She nodded.

'And tell me, were these occasions when you would expect a person able to experience feelings normally to have a genuine, spontaneous emotional reaction, albeit a less dramatic one?'

'Yes,' Jenny said, disconcerted by the fact that he seemed to be several steps ahead of her.

'Good.' He made a neat and precise note in his book. 'Alarming as it may be for you, that tells me that we're making very good progress indeed.' He set down his pen and knitted his fingers. Although he was no more than thirty-five, Dr Allen had already assumed the aura of a sage. 'Recapturing the memory opened a channel to your subconscious – the buried vault you've talked about. It may be a narrow channel, but trust me, the force of the tide behind it will make a wider and a wider one. Your challenge is no longer accessing feelings, it's allowing yourself to experience them.'

'Even when it's inappropriate?'

'Especially then. Although I wouldn't ask you to break down in public.'

'Just my style.'

He smiled, then studied her face. She felt self-conscious under his gaze and glanced away.

'If you don't mind my saying, Jenny, when you arrived today, I sensed something was weighing heavily on your mind – other than your work, of course.'

'What do you mean?' she asked, feeling suddenly defensive.

'We talked about the plane crash. It's clearly as distressing to you as to everyone else, but your mind was elsewhere.'

'How would you know that?'

'Why don't we concentrate on the question?'

She felt a surge of anger pass through her body. 'You presume to know my thoughts, but I've a right to know where that comes from. You asked me to express my feelings, I'm expressing them.'

'Of course,' he conceded. 'You mustn't worry about this, and it's only a rough guide, but I noted the line of your sight. If someone is looking down and to the right they tend to be accessing feelings, up to the left, a visual memory, and so on. You were very much in the realm of your own feelings before I even mentioned the crash, and you stayed there.'

'Is that mainstream science?'

'Now you are straying from the point. Tell me. Please.'

He was right. Her mind had filled with images of her

father even as she drove through the dark evening across the Severn Bridge. By the time she sat in the chair they were so vivid he might have been standing in the same room.

'I was thinking about my father.'

'What about him?'

'Images, pictures . . . memories—'

'From what period of your life?'

'Long ago. As a child, I suppose – when things were still clear and sharp. Somehow your senses seem to become blunted as you get older.'

'The central image, Jenny. What is it?' He suddenly raised his finger – a deliberate, momentary distraction. 'Tell me.'

'He's young, in a suit and tie. A summer suit, a rose in his buttonhole – it's at a wedding, I think. Yes, his youngest brother was getting married. A pretty girl—'

'Your father's expression?'

'Smiling.'

'His demeanour?'

'Happy. My mother's with him.'

'Jenny?'

She startled, as if coming suddenly awake.

'Would it surprise you to hear that you were smiling too?'

She looked at him blankly, aware of two competing voices in her head in heated but incoherent conflict.

'You'll have to take my word for it. But it tells me you have a big opportunity now.'

'And what's that?'

'To make your peace with your father. It's important to do it before he's gone.'

'I don't think I can.'

'What are you frightened of exactly?'

She tried to put her complex feelings into words. 'It's almost a superstition . . . You'll think I'm stupid—'

Dr Allen shook his head.

'I know he's going, but when I think about it I'm frightened . . . that he'll take me with him.'

'You feel your destinies are entwined. That's because he has always intruded on you. Your feelings have never been your own. And failure to express yourself is a form of living death, is it not?'

'I suppose so,' Jenny said. And for the first time since the feeling of imminent doom took the breath from her in a crowded courtroom nearly five years before, she allowed herself truly to believe that the beast that had stalked her was him, her father.

Dr Allen thought carefully before continuing. 'I can say this to you now because you're well enough to bear the responsibility. To live is a choice made consciously or unconsciously. It takes effort and will. Similarly, people may choose not to live, consciously or unconsciously – for example, people who skydive for a hobby, don't, in my opinion, die altogether by accident.'

'What about people who die in plane crashes?' Jenny said, challenging his dubious theory.

'There is a school of thought that says there is no such thing as an accident, but that's a little too simplistic for my tastes. I'm just advising you to be very aware of your choices, that's all.'

'Are you telling me I've got a death wish, doctor?'

'No . . .' He sounded less than convinced. 'But to pursue your analogy of the aeroplane, it takes constant propulsion to stay in the air. The moment the engines stop, it falls.'

'I get it – living is a conscious choice, but you think I spend all my time thinking about death, so I'm more attracted to that than life. You never did approve of me being a coroner.'

'It's a very necessary profession,' he said. 'Just be careful not to give everything you've got to the dead.'

Michael Sherman had answered his phone in the cockpit of a Cessna he was flying back from Newmarket to Bristol. Jenny had offered to drive over to the airport to meet him, but he said he would prefer to come to her—his boss had already warned him not to speak to any officials without his approval and it wouldn't be wise to be seen together. Since the accident a collective paranoia seemed to have gripped the airlines, he explained, even his small outfit.

He suggested they meet at the St Pierre. A few miles west of Chepstow on the Welsh side of the estuary, it was a fourteenth-century manor house that had been converted into a hotel and country club. Jenny approached along a winding drive and arrived in front of an imposing castellated building. She parked amongst the rows of Mercedes and BMWs and made her way to the entrance.

She spotted him sitting at a corner table in the wood-panelled lounge bar, quietly sipping beer from a tall glass. He looked over to her and waved. As she picked her way between the club sofas she noticed that he looked different. He'd shaved and put on a fresh white shirt.

'One of your favourite haunts?' Jenny said, sitting in a chair at an angle to his.

'It's where the jockeys and owners stay,' he said. 'They know me here. I get to use the gym and shoot a round of golf if I've got nothing better to do. Can I get you a drink, Mrs Cooper?'

'Red wine,' she said, flouting Dr Allen's long-standing ban. If he wanted her to act on her feelings, she would. 'And, please, call me Jenny.'

'Michael.'

He called over a waitress, who took the order. He displayed little outward sign that he had just lost someone he had been close to, but she could nonetheless sense it in him: a pervading sadness beneath the surface that felt heavy with regret.

'Are you sure you're all right with this?' Jenny asked.

'Fine,' Michael said. 'It's not like I haven't known people die in planes.'

'In the RAF?'

'There were a few. Not as many as you'd think.'

Jenny had never met a fighter pilot. She was curious to know more. 'You must have seen a lot of active service.'

'Kosovo, Afghanistan, Iraq, Afghanistan again.' He fired off the answer as if he was used to giving it, and quickly changed the subject. 'What have they given you?'

Jenny pulled her laptop from her briefcase and loaded the disk that Chambers had had couriered to her office. They moved a little closer together so they could both see the screen.

'It's just the raw air traffic control data,' Michael said. He clicked open a file. 'See – it's a playback.' They were looking at a video file, showing the air traffic controller's screen exactly as he would have seen it. It was dotted with moving aircraft symbols. 'There she is, RA189.' He pointed to a triangular symbol approaching from the right-hand side of the screen. 'The initials and the number identify the flight – RA189 – the two numbers underneath are airspeed and altitude – 470/20,000.'

Voices crackled over the image:

'*Skyhawk 1–8-9, identified, climb flight level three one zero, unrestricted.*'

'*Climb to flight level three one zero, Skyhawk 1–8-9.*'

'That's Bristol giving them clearance to climb to a cruising height of 31,000 feet, and the first officer confirming,'

Michael said. 'All looks pretty routine so far. Normally the route would take them north-west over Wales, but you can see they're all being sent out over the Severn estuary.'

'Any reason?'

'Could have been military aircraft manoeuvres in the Welsh valleys. That's where we used to do a lot of our low-level practice.'

'*Bristol, Skyhawk 1–8–9 – do you have any reports of turbulence on our routing?*'

'*Skyhawk 1–8–9, light turbulence reported at your level and your route for the next fifty miles. Nothing to worry about.*'

'*Thank you.*'

'They sound quite chatty,' Jenny said. 'I thought it would be full of "rogers" and "wilcos".'

'It's like anything – you get a feel. If reception's bad you revert to formality to make sure the other party knows where your message begins and ends. But this is all run of the mill. The first officer just has to check in with Bristol to let them know he's there, and then he'll be talking to Shanwick over in Ireland, getting clearance to head out across the Atlantic.'

'He seems worried about turbulence,' Jenny said.

'It's just a standard precaution to check there have been no reports of heavy turbulence from flights up ahead. He'd mostly be thinking about whether it was safe to switch off the seat-belt signs. A lot of passengers need to pay a visit after take-off. OK – we're coming up to level-off now, 30,000 –'

Jenny watched the altitude figures tick up to 30,500, then 31,000 feet. The time read 09:52.

'Wow,' Michael said. 'Look there – the airspeed's falling away, 450, 430 . . . 400, but he's climbing steeply. And nothing on the radio.'

They moved in closer to the laptop, straining to hear any trace of a message.

The air traffic controller spoke when the airspeed had ticked down to 350. *'Skyhawk 1–8–9, I see your airspeed is three-fifty. Confirm all OK.'*

There was no reply.

'Skyhawk, this is Bristol eight-zero-nine. Please confirm airspeed. I'm reading three-ten.'

Jenny and Michael continued to watch in silence as the airspeed figures tumbled rapidly through the two hundreds and the controller made repeated unsuccessful attempts to gain a response. There was a momentary sound through a cloud of static, not clear enough even to be certain that it was a human voice.

'I don't see how that happened,' Michael said. 'It looks as if he stalled . . . but how?'

The controller was panicking now. *'I'm sorry, say again, Skyhawk . . . Skyhawk, uh, are you still on? Skyhawk, are you there?'*

'What happens then?' Jenny asked. 'I mean, technically.'

Michael ignored her question, transfixed by what he was seeing on the screen. 'There. Look at that.' He sat back in his seat as the altitude figures started to tumble, slowly at first, then faster. 'He did stall. If you slow down too much you lose lift at the wing tips first. The pilot, more likely the autopilot, compensates by dipping the nose. But if it dips too far, and if for some reason you've got less than full control, on a big aircraft you're in danger of getting into a dive you can't pull out from. On a small plane, you'd jam on the rudder, hope to flip over on your side and win it back that way. But with something the size of the 380, once it's falling the forces involved are phenomenal. It's designed for steady, stable flight–' He paused, watching a shift in the rate of fall. 'My God – he almost does it. He's almost levelling out at 15,000 . . . Thought so—' The altitude figures resumed their rapid tumble. 'My guess is he managed to bring the nose up, but probably too far. It may only be a matter of a few degrees, but if the centre of lift shifts ahead of the centre of gravity, the nose is forced up even higher.' He demonstrated with his hand, tilting his palm upwards to forty-five degrees. 'You need more thrust to push you out of it, but now the engines are below the centre of gravity and even if you had the power, it would just force the nose even higher.' His fingers were vertical. 'Then you start to slip backwards. This is bad.'

They watched the pattern repeat itself – a level-out at 8,000 feet, then another rapid dive until the aircraft symbol simply vanished from the screen.

Michael stared at the screen for a moment longer, then clicked to another file. It was a graph produced by air traffic control software which plotted the flight's descent from 31,000 feet to the ground over a period of five minutes and forty-two seconds. It resembled a series of three mountains of diminishing height. 'He was fighting it all the way down.'

Jenny took a sip of her wine, a rich, oaky Rioja, and felt glad to be alive. 'Could a lightning strike have caused that?'

'Like I said, it's virtually never happened. And this is the most advanced aircraft in the world.' He shook his head. 'Losing the radio, losing speed – it looks like everything went at once, but the pilot still had some control, otherwise he wouldn't have come so close to winning it back. If there was a bomb, you could understand it, but if there wasn't . . . There isn't just one fail-safe system on that plane, there are four or five, and probably more.'

'Give me a theory,' Jenny said. 'What will the Air Accident Investigation Branch be looking for?'

'The on-board flight data and cockpit voice recordings will tell them a lot, but looking at this trajectory I'm guessing that they'll be searching for something that could have caused almost complete electrical failure leading to engine shutdown. Either that, or pilot error that's off the scale of negligence. I suppose he could have throttled right back at level-off and disengaged the autopilot somehow, but I don't see how – there would have been audible warnings.'

'And that wouldn't explain loss of radio.'

'If you're dealing with that sort of emergency you may not have time to radio. It's all hands on deck.'

Jenny said, 'I'm told it landed tail first on the water, but the hull split in two places.'

'That wouldn't surprise me,' Michael said. 'The stress that pulling out of several stalls must have placed on the airframe could easily have been enough by itself to have broken the aircraft apart. It would certainly have been severely weakened by the time it came down. And hulls are designed to split cleanly in three – the idea is that survivors can escape without having to negotiate jagged metal.' He suddenly looked tired, as if the reality of the accident had finally hit home. 'I'll expect you'll find Nuala was sitting at the back. She always insisted that was the safest place.'

Jenny said, 'We've only found one body with a lifejacket. A little girl travelling alone. She called her father on the way down and he told her to put it on. That's all he could think to do . . . I'm guessing the captain didn't have time to make an announcement.'

'Or his PA wasn't working.'

'But Nuala was a pilot. Wouldn't she have thought to wear one?'

Michael took a mouthful of beer and gazed down at the table. 'If she thought it would do any good . . .'

She waited for him to explain.

He reached into his pocket and drew out his phone. He looked at it for moment, then hit some buttons. He showed the screen to Jenny. It was the call log. The date was yesterday's. *Nuala* appeared three times in a row. She had tried to call him three times in the space of two minutes.

'She was trying to reach me as they were going down,' Michael said, his voice close to a whisper. He switched away from the missed calls log to his message folder.

'Then she sent me this, at nine fifty-seven. The ground was coming up fast by then. Can you imagine texting?' He handed the phone to Jenny. The message said simply, *Tyax x*.

'What does it mean?' Jenny asked.

'It's the name of a little place in British Columbia – our one and only holiday together. We hired a float plane in Vancouver and flew up there ourselves, stopped off on a crystal-clear lake in the middle of nowhere. Just us and the grizzly bears . . . And I think it's what she called herself on Airbuzz – that was the name of her forum.'

'Which do you think she was referring to?'

Michael put the phone back in his pocket. 'Probably both.' He gave her a look which she couldn't interpret. He seemed lost, as if he was relying on her for answers.

Jenny said, 'Are you going to share this with the coroner?'

'Do you think I should?'

'Why wouldn't you?'

'Because, despite everything, it was me she was trying to talk to.' Michael drained his glass. 'We were meant to be getting married at one time, but it turned out not to be in my nature. We'd hardly spoken in nine months.'

'You think she had some information she wanted you to know?'

'She wasn't trying to rekindle the romance.'

'Why are you telling me this, Michael?'

His gaze lingered on her for a moment. 'I'm a pilot, I rely on a sixth sense.'

EIGHT

AFTERWARDS SHE THOUGHT SHE MIGHT only have been imagining Michael's pass. The conversation had quickly moved on and wrapped up along businesslike lines. What had shocked her most was her reaction to the prospect. She had felt hot and anxious. Had it not been for the beta blocker she felt sure she would have suffered a panic attack right there in the hotel bar, her first in months. It was curious, but also disturbing. Throughout her dark years, sex and desire had always been an antidote to her anxiety. When Steve had touched her, she was instantly transported into the moment. Nothing else mattered. But Michael's unexpected look had produced the opposite effect. The brief flash of excitement, like an electric pulse through her body, had been followed by a sense of dread that seemed to rise like a dark tide inside her. And it was made all the more confusing by the fact that she hadn't for a moment thought of him that way.

During her morning commute through the frosted forest and across the estuary, she tried to isolate the feeling that had haunted her the previous night and that refused to be banished by the startling January sun. It was not one but several sensations, she concluded. Grief, shame, and a guilty feeling that she realized she hadn't experienced since she was a teenager. Giving in to it, as Dr Allen would have told her to, she felt her cheeks start to burn and the taint of disapproval – her father's. She remembered the day, sitting at the kitchen table opposite him, during the painful time after her mother had left home. She was fifteen years old, and still very innocent. He had quizzed her about the party she was longing to go to and made her list the names of all the boys who would be there. He had made her feel as if she was betraying him.

Things were getting mixed up. It was as if the walls of her inner compartments had been broken down and her emotions were slopping from one to the other; the past and present were equally potent. She was middle-aged, a young woman, a child, all at once. The realization brought a measure of relief. It was just as Dr Allen had predicted. She was experiencing again, and the pain would pass if she would only let herself *feel* it. That was fine in theory, but it left her frightened of making an irrational judgement. Could she trust herself in this state of mind?

She had no option.

It had been Michael's parting suggestion to check the traffic cameras on the Severn Bridge for any sign of helicopters. Jenny called the bridge authorities as soon as she arrived in the office, but was referred to the Welsh Assembly government, who passed her around five different officials until someone finally informed her that all original footage had already been handed to Sir James Kendall. Jenny tried her contacts in the Chepstow police to see if they might work an angle she hadn't thought of, but got the same answer: the data had been seized within hours of the plane going down. The order had come directly from Whitehall even before Sir James Kendall had been formally appointed.

Perhaps it was just slick contingency planning that had prompted the authorities to move so quickly, but Jenny doubted it. As she and Michael had been leaving the hotel, he had talked about an incident in Afghanistan in which a colleague had bombed the wrong target and killed seventy innocent civilians at prayer in a makeshift mosque. If they'd run the war as well as they'd organized the cover-up it would all have been over in a couple of years, he said. A small army of men and women from anonymous departments emerged from nowhere to make sure every potential channel of information was blocked. Jenny was beginning to see parallels with her own investigation.

Pushing the creeping sensation of paranoia from her mind, she opened the email that had just arrived from Dr Kerr. It was the results of DNA analysis carried out on the scrapings taken from beneath Amy Patterson's fingernails. It confirmed the presence of Brogan's skin cells.

The phone rang in the outer office as she was reading his accompanying note: *Evidence suggests Amy Patterson was not only alive in the water, but fully conscious. Abrasions to Brogan's forearms indicate the application of considerable force, presumably in panic.*

Alison forwarded the call to her desk, 'It's a Mr Galbraith. He says he's the Pattersons' lawyer.'

'Mrs Cooper?' The voice belonged to a man in his thirties, who was both pushy and ambitious.

'Speaking.'

'Nick Galbraith, Caldwell Rose. I represent Greg and Michelle Patterson.'

She recognized the name of Bristol's most upmarket firm of solicitors from an inquest she had conducted into the death of a wealthy young woman at a private clinic. The firm had represented the clinic, and her impression of them had been of charming old-school manners masking a determined streak of ruthlessness.

'How can I can help you?'

'I presume you've seen the result of the DNA test.'

'Yes,' Jenny answered, asking herself how the information had managed to reach him first. She checked the email again and noticed she had merely been copied in as a courtesy. Sir James Kendall was the first named recipient.

'This evidence seems to suggest that Amy didn't die in the crash,' Galbraith said.

'That's correct. Though we already suspect that was—'

'Mrs Patterson would like to meet you,' Galbraith interjected. 'In fact, we both would.'

'What do you wish to discuss?'

'Best not to on the phone, don't you think? Can you make her hotel, two o'clock?'

Jenny made him wait while she checked her diary. 'If you're absolutely sure it's necessary.'

'Thank you, Mrs Cooper. Goodbye.' He gave her no time to change her mind.

'I spoke to his girlfriend.' Jenny looked up to see Alison bustling in with the pile of mail Jenny had deliberately ignored when she arrived.

'Oh?' Jenny said, preoccupied. 'Whose?'

'Gerry Brogan's. Her name's Maria. They'd only known each other a year, but she was devastated, poor girl. No one had told her. She'd been trying to call him all yesterday evening.'

'Did she have any idea what he was doing this far up the Bristol Channel?'

'She didn't even know he had a criminal record. I don't think she believed me when I said he'd been to prison. He told her he'd spent the last twenty years sailing yachts.'

'What else did she say?'

'Only that he was living on a boat until he moved in with her. He sounds like a bit of a drifter, if you'll pardon the pun.' She looked at Jenny with maternal concern. 'You seem a bit tired, Mrs Cooper. You should try getting some more exercise, you'd feel much better for it. I know I do.'

'I can see,' Jenny said, feeling an irrational stab of jealousy. Alison had been regularly visiting a gym and, as she often told anyone who would care to listen, had lost twenty pounds. It had taken years off her.

'I know it's not easy – being alone.'

'You seem to be managing.'

'Just about—'

Jenny waited, sensing that Alison needed to unburden herself.

'It's Terry, my husband.' She made an attempt at a shrug. 'His girlfriend walked out on him last month and he's been on the phone saying he wants to get back together. Spain's suddenly not so wonderful now it's just him in a rented flat.'

'Would you have him?'

'No,' she said with less than certainty. 'He's got no right to me any more. He's had my best years, now I want some for myself.' She was trying hard to convince herself. 'I'm sorry. I shouldn't be troubling you with this—' She turned to go.

Jenny said, 'Alison – there was a call here on Sunday night, after you'd left. I answered, but whoever it was didn't speak. Do you think it might have been Terry?'

'He calls my mobile . . .' She hesitated, as if hiding something. 'I know who it might have been, though. It won't happen again.'

Jenny nodded, knowing not to probe any further. 'And the photographer's camera—'

'I'll deal with it,' Alison said, and hurried out on heels that threatened to snap her ankles.

Tired? No one had ever called her that before. But when she inadvertently caught her reflection she saw a face that had been attractive once, which was still slender, but which life had worn and grooved. A history had emerged in her features; there were threads of silver in her hair; she was a woman who could never again be called a girl.

It was less than a half-mile walk to the Marriott on College Green, which stood only a few yards from Bristol Cathedral in the ancient heart of the city. The narrow side streets that led off in several directions with their scruffy old pubs and faded Georgian buildings were a gateway into the city's seafaring past. This had been England's first port in the days of tall-masted ships that rode the trade winds across the Atlantic. The thoroughfares and marketplaces would have been filled with American and African voices. Even more so than London, Bristol had been the crossroads of the world.

Galbraith strode out of the downstairs lounge to meet her in the lobby and squeezed her hand in a large fist. 'Good of you to come, Mrs Cooper.'

He was just as she had pictured him: tall, dark-haired and broad-shouldered. She remembered that the senior partner of his firm, a man named Duncan Rose, liked to tell anyone who'd listen that he had twice played rugby for England. He had recruited in his own image.

'I've booked us a meeting room upstairs,' he said, leading the way towards the elevator. 'I thought it might be best.'

Michelle Patterson had set up office in a small meeting room on the second floor. She had a notebook computer, a printer and two phones – one for research, one for fielding calls from the families of other passengers, she explained as Jenny took a seat. This was clearly her way of coping, and if outward appearances were anything to go by it was working. Dressed in a formal business suit and with her hair neatly arranged, she could have been about to address an academic conference.

'I apologize for my husband's absence,' Mrs Patterson

said. 'We both find it easier to cope alone, at least for the moment.'

'I understand,' Jenny said, although she didn't. Not at all.

'My clients would like their daughter's inquest dealt with swiftly,' Galbraith explained, pouring them each a glass from an expensive-looking bottle of mineral water, 'and I've advised them that the best way to achieve this is to have the case returned to your jurisdiction. This latest evidence seems to prove beyond doubt that their daughter's death was subsequent to the crash, in which case I don't see any reason why she shouldn't be dealt with separately.'

'I doubt the Ministry of Justice would agree,' Jenny said.

'Their decision was taken in ignorance of the full facts,' Galbraith said. 'A vital part of the coroner's function is to provide swift and conclusive findings for grieving families. I can't see why they would stand in the way of that.' He smiled. 'We would need your full support and cooperation, of course.'

'My husband and I really would be most grateful,' Mrs Patterson added expectantly.

Jenny noticed a look pass between them. She suspected that there was an aspect of their request that they had yet to share with her.

Jenny said, 'If you're worried about the release of your daughter's body, I'm sure that can happen imminently, perhaps even in the next few days.'

'It's a concern, of course—' Mrs Patterson said, but left her sentence incomplete. She glanced again at Galbraith.

'What's your feeling about the correct procedure, Mrs Cooper?' he asked. 'Do you agree with us that it would be unfair to ask grieving parents to wait possibly a year or more for Sir James Kendall to make a finding when you could deal with matters much more rapidly?'

His speech felt to Jenny like a clumsy attempt to disguise

his true intentions. Having spent several minutes in the room, she was beginning to form a clearer picture.

Caldwell Rose probably charged out at over £200 an hour. They were eager for business, and in her grief, Mrs Patterson was prepared to give it to them.

'Let's be frank, Mrs Patterson,' Jenny said. 'You want to know why an aeroplane fell out of the sky. Even if I were to get your daughter's case back, it would be on condition that I left that particular question to the disaster inquest. I would be strictly confined to determining her immediate cause of death, which we already know.'

'That's true up to a point,' Galbraith began, 'but—'

Mrs Patterson cut across him. 'I've read reports of your previous investigations, Mrs Cooper, and my lawyers have confirmed their accuracy. You've made quite a reputation out of asking the questions from which others have shied away.'

'I'm afraid the system is conspiring to keep people like me in their place, Mrs Patterson. Recent changes in the law mean that I'm no longer quite the free agent I once was.'

'Which makes it all the more important to keep up the fight, surely?'

Jenny could tell from Galbraith's expression that his client had already strayed well beyond their agreed script. He gave an apologetic smile. 'I think what Mrs Patterson is trying to say—'

'I understand perfectly,' Jenny countered, 'but what neither of you has told me is the reason you think Sir James Kendall won't deliver what all the relatives of the deceased would expect.'

Galbraith looked at her with the troubled expression of a lawyer suffering a conflict between his own feelings and his professional ethics. But if he was asking her to help trick a court into believing her inquest would be one thing when they all intended it to be another, she felt he had an obligation to get his hands dirty too.

She looked him in the eye and waited.

'As I think my client may already have told you, she has some experience of the aerospace industry,' Galbraith said. 'It's a global business upon which all major countries depend, yet there are only a handful of major aircraft manufacturers. You wouldn't have to be a conspiracy theorist to imagine that a government would work extremely hard to protect those interests.'

'A coroner is an independent judicial officer. I don't conduct inquiries according to any agenda.'

'Which is precisely what we fear Sir James Kendall might be tempted to do. You might be interested to see this.' Galbraith motioned to Mrs Patterson, who handed a two-sheet document across the table.

It was a report written on Civil Aviation Authority stationery and headed: *Ramp-Check on Ransome Airways Airbus A319*. The text below was marked *CONFIDENTIAL*.

The body of the text was couched in technical language which Jenny barely managed to follow, but she caught the gist: the previous July, a CAA inspector had, for a reason unspecified in the document, carried out an unannounced inspection of a Ransome Airways plane at Heathrow airport. He had checked the aircraft's defect log and found evidence that the plane had flown with a significant fault that should have been repaired before it took to the air. The summary paragraphs read:

Approximately forty minutes into the flight from Heathrow to Prague an ELEC GEN 1 FAULT message appeared on the Electronic Centralized Aircraft Monitor (ECAM) and a FAULT caption illuminated on the overhead panel. The crew checked the Electrical System page on the ECAM and confirmed that the No. 1 generator had tripped off-line. Attempts to reset the generator proved unsuccessful, and in accordance with prescribed procedure the No. 1 generator was selected OFF. The Auxiliary Power Unit (APU) was started and its electrical generator supplied the left AC bus. Twenty minutes later an ELEC GEN 2 FAULT message appeared on the ECAM. The crew again checked the Electrical System page on the ECAM and confirmed that the No. 2 generator had tripped off-line. Attempts to reset were similarly unsuccessful, and No. 2 generator was selected OFF. The APU was therefore engaged to supply the right main AC bus. The flight continued to Prague without further incident. Once on the ground, an airline engineer successfully restarted both No. 1 and No. 2 generators and recorded a finding of NO FAULT FOUND in the defect log. He certified the aircraft fit for take-off.

These faults demanded thorough and detailed investigation, but the flight log shows that the aircraft returned to Heathrow ninety minutes after landing. The airline maintains that the decision to accept the engineer's certification was the pilot's alone, but Captain xxxxx denies this, claiming that instructions to return the aircraft to Heathrow as scheduled came directly from the airline. There was no reported repeat of the faults during thirty-two subsequent flights by the aircraft and no detailed investigation of the faults has been conducted by the airline.

Recommendation: refer to prosecuting authorities

'I've emailed it to a number of pilots, who were all appalled,' Mrs Patterson said. 'The general consensus seems to be that the airline was fortunate not to have all its planes grounded immediately. A major electrical failure could be catastrophic, all the more so on a fly-by-wire plane. We can find no record of a prosecution.'

'How did you come by this?' Jenny asked.

'Interesting you should ask,' Galbraith said. 'One of Mrs Patterson's colleagues found it posted on the internet on Sunday afternoon. An hour later it had gone, along with the whole site.'

'What was this site?' Jenny asked.

'It was called Airbuzz,' Mrs Patterson replied. 'Apparently it was a forum for insider talk in the airline business. According to my colleague, this was just one of a number of similar hair-raising reports from around the world.'

Jenny looked at the blacked-out spaces covering the captain's name and wondered if it was Nuala Casey's. Even if it was, it might just be a collision of coincidences: for all she knew such risk taking might be commonplace in the airline business, but her gut told her it was more than that. And despite its chemical straitjacket, her heart was beating hard against the inside of her ribs.

'It's not exactly a smoking gun,' Galbraith said, 'but it does say something about Ransome's attitude to safety.'

'Right,' Mrs Patterson added. 'It's not worth losing money over.'

'Would you agree, Mrs Cooper?' Galbraith said.

Jenny could see trouble ahead, a lot of trouble, but she could also see the little girl lying on the beach, swept to her on the tide along with Brogan.

'Yes,' Jenny answered.

'Then you would be as anxious as we are to see that every avenue is explored in determining the cause of the crash.'

'That goes without saying, but we have to be realistic,' Jenny said. 'If you're correct about the intentions behind the official inquest, then I can't see any court returning jurisdiction over your daughter's death to me.'

'That may or may not be necessary,' Galbraith said. 'We may not need that. In fact, it might be best if we didn't go down that avenue. I imagine the last thing you want is to attract more controversy.'

Jenny was confused. 'What do you mean?'

'The thing is, Mrs Cooper,' he said, gesturing with his palms like a skilful politician, 'most, if not all, of the questions we would like to be addressed could fall within the scope of your inquest into Mr Brogan's death. If you were to allow us full representation as interested parties, then it might serve all our objectives.'

It was a perfect lawyer's play. Caldwell Rose would get to collect their fees without running the risk of having to convince a sceptical High Court judge that their clients alone amongst six hundred grieving families deserved special treatment. All they needed to seal the deal was for Mrs Patterson to hear Jenny promise to give her what she wanted.

Jenny would have been justified in getting up from the table and leaving the room without another word. She was being manipulated and so was Mrs Patterson. Some disasters were simply too big, their ramifications too far-reaching to allow the whole truth to emerge and Galbraith and his employers knew it as well as she did.

But it was already too late. She had been touched by a mother's grief and pushed beyond the point at which she could forgive herself for walking away, and secretly she was more than a little curious to know what else Mrs Patterson and her lawyers would unearth that otherwise might remain suppressed.

'I have no objection to you being represented at my inquest into Mr Brogan's death,' Jenny said. 'You are a legitimately interested party. But I must warn you now, there may be no answers and, if there are, they may not be the ones you want to hear.'

'I'll take my chances, Mrs Cooper,' Mrs Patterson said. 'It's not as if I have anything more left to lose.'

NINE

OPENING HER INQUEST ONLY a week after Flight 189 came down had seemed the best way to catch evidence before it was buried, but Jenny had seriously underestimated the obstacles that would be placed in her path. The first warning shots had come in off-the-record phone calls from Simon Moreton, a Director in the Ministry of Justice, and her superior insofar as a coroner could be said to have one.

Despite all that she had got away with in the past, he warned her, she wouldn't be repeating the experience. A wise coroner, he suggested, would recognize that this was one of the rare occasions that required all public officials to pull in the same direction. It was civil service code for 'back off now or expect consequences'. When she reminded him that the law required a coroner fearlessly and independently to inquire after the truth, she was met with silence.

When Moreton's pleading failed, his superior, the politely imperious Sir Oliver Prentice, requested her to postpone 'to allow the media to calm down'. She responded with a request of her own: where in the Coroner's Rules did it require her to time her inquiry according to the level of press hysteria? Then there were no more phone calls, merely a two-line email informing her that counsel had been instructed to keep a watching brief at her inquest on behalf of Sir James Kendall's inquiry. Determined to make life difficult for her, Sir James

Kendall declined to release traffic camera footage from the Severn Bridge, curtly informing her that she had no right to evidence already lawfully in his possession. Nor would he hand over statements taken from rescue workers or the farmer, Roberts, who, as far as she was aware, remained the closest anyone had to an eye-witness. Meanwhile, Kendall's carefully managed inquiry ground on slowly and in silence. The only news that had emerged from his office was that the autopsies were complete and that the process of reassembling the wreckage of the aircraft was under way at the AAIB's hangars at Farnborough in Hampshire.

When the Courts Service claimed there was no courtroom available within a fifty-mile radius, Jenny's patience snapped. As a calculated act of revenge, she chose the remotest and most inaccessible venue within her jurisdiction in which to conduct her proceedings. If they wanted to keep tabs on her, she was going to make sure they suffered for it.

The village of Sharpness, situated twenty-five miles northeast of the centre of Bristol, was once a flourishing deepwater port crammed with cargo ships. Later eclipsed by the container port at Avonmouth, it had declined to a sleepy dormitory midway between the cities of Bristol and Gloucester. The tired-looking docks saw one or two ships each week, but the atmosphere was of a settlement that had been left marooned by time.

The village hall was a single-storey brick building that could have been built in any of the post-war decades. Jenny followed Alison into the echoing interior, feeling a perverse delight at bringing such momentous events to a place that still bore the stubs of Christmas streamers. The rooms were cold and a faint smell of damp hung in the air. With no sign of the helper they had been promised, Jenny and Alison took off their coats and set out the chairs and tables themselves. It was a long way from the air-conditioned comfort of the modern court buildings many coroners enjoyed, yet there was something profoundly pleasing in such basic surroundings; the truth was so much harder to disguise when there was no ceremony or ornament for it to hide behind.

Jenny hunkered down in the small committee room at the back of the building where, boosted by several cups of coffee, she attempted to focus on the task ahead. There was no avoiding the fact that her inquiry was limited to determining Gerry Brogan's immediate cause of death; she wasn't expected nor was she legally permitted to stray into the territory that had been marked out for Sir James Kendall. If she crossed the line, she faced the prospect of a higher court summarily halting proceedings and handing them over to another, more compliant colleague. In the few years she had been in her post, the law had gradually shifted to exert unprecedented levels of political control over the office of coroner, which for eight hundred years had managed to remain almost entirely free from outside interference. It was a fact that infuriated her, and she was determined to do all in her power to roll back the tide.

Alison's familiar knock sounded on the door at precisely ten minutes to ten. As she stepped inside, Jenny heard a hubbub of voices from the hall along the short corridor.

'We've got more than enough lawyers, Mrs Cooper, but I don't think Mr Ransome's going to be showing his face, and there's a message from DCI Molyneux asking to be excused attendance unless it's absolutely necessary.'

'It is. Tell him to be here after lunch or I'll issue a summons. Is Brogan's girlfriend here?'

'Just arrived. I feel sorry for her, poor girl. She'd just walked through the door when Mrs Patterson cornered her and started asking about terrorists. I had to ask her to leave her alone.' She handed Jenny the witness list. 'Corton's here, and Mr Hennessy from Dublin.'

'Good. Who told you about Ransome? His lawyer?'

'Mr Hartley. You must remember him from the Danny Wills case a couple of years back?'

Jenny's heart sank. Giles Hartley was the Queen's Counsel who had represented the private company that owned a prison in which the fourteen-year-old boy had been murdered by a member of staff. When the truth had begun to surface, Hartley had personally seen to it that the facility's director fled to safety in the USA, where she still lived, a fugitive from justice as far as Jenny was concerned.

'I think he'll be making an application for Mr Ransome to be excused from appearing,' Alison said.

'He can try.' Jenny ran her eye over the list, deciding in what order to take the witnesses. She decided on the least contentious first, if only to keep the Pattersons' lawyers from revealing their hand too soon. 'All right. Give me a moment, I'll be right with you.'

Alison gave her a concerned look. 'You won't let Mrs Patterson bully you, Mrs Cooper? There's no reason this shouldn't be open and shut.'

'No,' Jenny said. But even as the word passed her lips, she felt her diaphragm tighten and her heart begin to pick up speed. As Alison left, closing the door behind her, she was gripped by the same claustrophobic sensation she felt buckling into the seat of an aeroplane ready for take-off. Only today she was at the controls.

'All rise.' Alison's voice brought the room to silence.

Jenny entered from the back of the hall and passed along the aisle between half a dozen rows of chairs containing witnesses and journalists. Occupying the seats at the front was a small army of lawyers. As she reached her desk and turned to face them, she felt severely outnumbered and more than a little intimidated.

As the assembled company resumed their seats, Giles Hartley QC remained standing. A tall man with an imposing aristocratic demeanour, he spoke in a precise, genteel manner designed to make any opposition appear pitiably unreasonable. 'Ma'am, I represent Ransome Airways. My learned colleague Miss Rachel Hemmings represents Mr and Mrs Patterson, Mr Leonard Crowthorne appears for the Commissioner of the Somerset Constabulary and Mr Rufus Bannerman QC is representing the interests of Sir James Kendall's inquiry.'

Jenny looked along the line of barristers in the front row. Rachel Hemmings possessed the only face that couldn't be called intimidating. An attractive, though tough-looking woman in her late thirties, Jenny had heard she was earning a fearsome reputation in the family courts. Crowthorne was a big bully of a man, who had become Bristol CID's favourite prosecutor, and Bannerman was his opposite, a thin, bookish type with the expression of one permanently pained by others' failure to see things as clearly as he did. Hartley and Bannerman, the senior men, each had pretty female juniors at their sides, and all the barristers had at least one instructing solicitor sitting in the row behind.

Nick Galbraith sat slightly apart from his colleagues in the second row alongside Mr and Mrs Patterson. He looked content, safe in the expectation of a large cheque for his firm whatever the outcome of the hearing. The Pattersons, by contrast, appeared uncomfortable in each other's presence, their body language that of two very separate and self-contained individuals.

'Before we begin, ma'am, I would like to address the issue of your request for Mr Ransome's attendance,' Hartley said.

'There is no issue,' Jenny said. 'I expect to hear from him.'

She saw Mrs Patterson nod in approval.

'I need hardly remind you, ma'am, that your terms of

reference do not extend to any investigation into the cause of the downing of Flight 189. That being the case, I cannot see any reason why Mr Ransome's testimony, such as it might be, would be of any assistance to you.'

'Mr Hartley –' Jenny strained to remain patient – 'Mr Brogan was sailing a yacht which appears to have been sunk when an aeroplane owned by your client ploughed into it. Unless you are arguing that a man who fires a gun has no responsibility for the bullet once it has left the barrel, Mr Ransome is not only a relevant witness, but my inquiry could not possibly proceed without him.'

'Ma'am, as far as I can ascertain from the few documents you have chosen to disclose, Mr Brogan was alive for some time after my client's aeroplane came down—'

'Your client will attend, Mr Hartley.'

'Ma'am, I'm afraid that—'

'I'll spell it out, shall I?' She lifted her eyes to the journalists seated behind the lawyers. 'If Mr Ransome fails to answer his summons voluntarily, he will find himself doing so involuntarily.' She turned her gaze to Crowthorne. 'The same goes for Detective Chief Inspector Molyneux.'

Hartley exchanged a glance with Bannerman. 'Your comments have been duly noted, ma'am.' He smiled thinly and lowered himself into his chair.

Jenny addressed the lawyers collectively: 'Is there anything else?'

She watched Bannerman, Sir James Kendall's representative, touch his index fingers thoughtfully to his lips, then decide to bide his time.

'Very well.' She turned to Alison. 'We'll have the jury, please, Usher.'

Jenny drew in a breath and offered a silent prayer for strength. She would need all she could muster.

Alison left the hall and returned from the large meeting

room with the nine citizens who had been summoned to form the coroner's jury. There were six mostly middle-aged women, one man nearing seventy and two much younger men, one black and well dressed, the other white, shaven-headed and tattooed. She seated them in two rows at the side of the room and took each one through the ordeal of reading the juror's oath aloud to the packed and impatient hall. Some were visibly nervous, others merely confused by their call to immediate public duty in an obscure corner of the countryside.

'Let me make one thing clear,' Jenny said to them at the start of her opening remarks. 'This is neither a criminal nor a civil court. No one is on trial. You are not being asked to determine guilt or innocence, or even liability. You have one task, which is to determine the cause of death of a thirty-eight-year-old man named Gerry Fergus Brogan.

'A little over a week ago, Mr Brogan was sailing a yacht named the *Irish Mist* on the Severn estuary, approximately twenty miles to the south-west of here. At around one o'clock in the afternoon his body was found washed up on the beach on the English side of the old Severn Bridge. Not far from his corpse lay the body of a ten-year-old American girl named Amy Patterson. She was wearing a lifejacket and had been a passenger in an airliner that had come down in the estuary a little over three hours earlier. The following day, the wreckage of the yacht Mr Brogan had been sailing was found close to the sunken remains of the aircraft. It appears the plane struck it as it crash-landed. Having heard all the relevant evidence, I will ask you to determine Mr Brogan's cause of death. The most common verdicts are accident, misadventure, suicide, unlawful killing or an open verdict – meaning that the cause of death remains unknown.

'Please try to remember that we are not concerned with deciding between competing cases. Our task is purely and simply to unearth the truth, or as much of it as we can.' The lawyers traded subtle glances, amused at Jenny's hopeful idealism. Ignoring them, she held the jury firmly in her gaze. 'It is a duty unique to the coroner's court and I expect you to perform it to the best of your ability.'

Maria Canavan was the first to come forward to the chair positioned in the no-man's-land between Jenny and the lawyers that would serve as the witness box. She was slightly built, with long red hair that fell across her freckled face. Her voice barely carried as she stumbled through the words of the oath.

Jenny spoke to her gently, leading her by the hand through the preliminaries. She was twenty-six years old and worked as a part-time secretary for Hennessy's, a yacht brokerage which operated from offices at Dublin Harbour. She had another job as a waitress in a seafood restaurant on the quay, which was where she had met Gerry Brogan almost exactly a year ago. He told her he had been crewing on yachts in the Caribbean since the late nineties and had come back to Ireland intending to set up in business on his own. He had talked about starting an ocean-going sailing school, but was looking for work while he was studying for his instructor's licence. It was she who had introduced him to Mr Hennessy and got him work delivering yachts to customers around Europe.

'When did this friendship turn into a relationship?' Jenny asked.

'It was after he started working at Hennessy's.' She spoke in little more than a whisper. 'We just sort of got friendly, you know.'

'Did you live together?'

'That was later, last November time. He'd been staying on his boat down at Bray. It was tough in the winter, so I said he should move in to my place. I've a little flat in Rathmines.'

'And did you know much about his personal history at this time?'

'Only what I've just told you. And I knew he grew up in Blackrock up near the border there.'

'He didn't tell you he had a number of criminal convictions?'

Maria Canavan shook her head.

Jenny motioned to Alison, who handed her a copy of Brogan's criminal record and distributed several more among the jury and lawyers.

'His first recorded offence was one of theft from a shop in Waterford, County Kilkenny. He was fourteen years old. There's another for violent assault when he was twenty-two, also in Waterford, for which he was sentenced to twenty months in prison. Aged thirty-one he was convicted in Dublin for the possession of 800 grams of cocaine with intent to supply. He went to prison for three years.'

Maria Canavan stared blankly at the piece of paper in her hand.

Jenny moved on. 'I've spoken to an officer in the Garda, an Inspector Padraig Murphy. He tells me that Mr Brogan was suspected of helping to sail IRA guns across to Scotland during the late 1990s. He wasn't charged with any offence, but it seems his name was one of those mentioned by intelligence sources.'

'I don't know anything about that,' Maria said. 'But I do know his references from Antigua were all good. He'd worked on the same yacht for six years. An American owned it, a banker. Gerry skippered it for him during the summer and took care of charters over the winter. It was a legitimate business.'

'Did his employer say why he left?'

'Gerry had told him the same thing as he told me – he wanted to make a life in his home country.'

Where his connections were. Where there was money to be made from his old friends, Jenny thought to herself, but there seemed little point pushing the witness into territory she knew nothing about. Gerry Brogan had a murky history; he was a man whom the Garda had marked down as involved in the criminal rather than the political activities of the IRA. There were hundreds like him across Ireland, Murphy had said during their ten-minute telephone conversation; and a lot of them had made hay during the early years of the peace process, around the turn of the century, when former paramilitaries were given an easy ride by the police on politicians' orders. It was more than likely that Brogan had skipped off to the West Indies only when he felt he could ride his luck no more.

'Did he ever mention his family?' Jenny asked.

'Not much. Only that his parents had both died when he was younger.'

Jenny addressed the jury. 'I have received information from the Irish authorities that Mr Brogan was taken into the care of the social services when he was nine years old and spent a number of years in a children's home in Waterford. His mother's name is recorded as Mrs Annie Brogan, but thus far attempts to locate her have proved unsuccessful.' She looked back at Maria Canavan. 'Did he talk to you about his early years?'

'He told me he came from Blackrock in County Louth.' She seemed puzzled. 'Maybe he had friends there? He knew the town, right enough. We made a trip there once.'

It was one of the ports closest to the Northern Irish border. Inspector Murphy had been reluctant to discuss details, but Jenny suspected Brogan had operated from there before he left the country. A little research had taught her there was a long tradition of smuggling illicit arms and goods in and out of Ireland through its many isolated harbours. In the 1970s and '80s, weapons supplied to Irish Republicans by Libya had been brought in that way.

Jenny turned to more practical matters. 'Did you have any personal involvement in arranging the delivery of the *Irish Mist*?'

'I dealt with some of the emails, that's all. The buyer was a businessman from Jersey. He sent a surveyor over before Christmas and I gave him all the paperwork. Gerry said he'd be gone three days. He'd sail down there and catch the plane back via London.'

'And he sailed alone?'

'He always did, unless it was a big boat, you know.' Her voice wavered. 'He was a fine sailor, right enough. He always got the boat there perfect – in all weathers.'

Jenny attempted to probe further into what Maria Canavan knew of Brogan's past, but learned nothing new. It seemed he had preferred to say little, rather than construct a tissue of lies as a fantasist might have done. He had been a quiet, hard-working man, the young woman said, studying for his instructor's licence in the evenings. They had even started talking about their future together. Brogan had had a yearning to build his own house further down the coast.

'Miss Canavan – did Mr Brogan contact you after he had set sail in the *Irish Mist*?'

'No. I heard he called the office – about the rudder – but I wasn't there at the time.'

'And you didn't attempt to contact him?'

She shook her head. 'He wasn't the sort of man you'd think to bother that way. A free spirit. Yes, that's what he was.' She smiled, pushing her hair away from tear-stained cheeks. 'You know, it doesn't bother me that he did those things. He never said an unkind word to me. Never.'

Jenny paused, then nodded to Alison, who from beneath her desk produced an evidence bag containing the holster Brogan had been wearing. As far as she was aware, only she, Dr Kerr and Alison knew of its existence till now.

Alison handed the bag to the witness. The lawyers waited expectantly for an explanation.

Jenny said, 'You're looking at a Sidewinder shoulder holster. It's designed to carry a handgun – in the case of this model, a 9mm Ruger pistol – and to be concealed beneath clothing. Mr Brogan was wearing it under his shirt when he died.'

Maria Canavan began to shake her head.

'I saw it on his body, Miss Canavan, as did the pathologist—'

It was Crowthorne who hauled himself upright to object. 'Ma'am, it's quite extraordinary that such a piece of evidence should not have been disclosed along with the post-mortem report. The Coroner's Rules clearly state—'

'That I have discretion. Which I exercised,' Jenny snapped. 'Sometimes there's a value in surprise. As a criminal lawyer, you should understand that.'

'Was there a gun? Have any ballistics tests been carried out? It's almost impossible to conceive of evidence that it would be more inappropriate to withhold.'

'I have no evidence of a gun, Mr Crowthorne, and tests on Mr Brogan's hands show no signs that he had discharged a weapon, but he had been in the water for some hours. That's all there is to know.'

Crowthorne's face reddened with outrage. 'Were the police told?'

'The police have shown little interest in communicating

with me, and I have returned the favour,' Jenny said. 'Can we please continue?'

Crowthorne thumped into his chair and turned to the pair of police solicitors behind him who were already in a tight huddle and reaching for their phones. Jenny switched her attention back to the witness. 'Did you ever see this holster, Miss Canavan?'

'No.'

'A gun?'

'Never.'

'Do you have any idea why Mr Brogan would have been carrying one?'

Maria Canavan stared back blankly, the shock in her face as real as Jenny had ever seen in a witness. 'No.'

'Thank you, Miss Canavan. Wait there.'

Hartley and Crowthorne were locked in whispered conversation with their teams and declined Jenny's invitation to cross-examine. Bannerman, who had still to utter a word, merely shook his head and wrote careful notes in his legal pad. Rachel Hemmings, representing Mr and Mrs Patterson, was the only lawyer to rise to her feet.

Jenny could tell at once that she had learned her trade in the family courts. An interested smile instinctively appeared as she turned to Maria Canavan. She addressed her in a relaxed, conversational style.

'Tell me, Miss Canavan, was Mr Brogan a trustworthy man?'

'Yes. Yes, he was.'

'But he didn't tell you the truth about himself.'

'Maybe he was afraid I'd judge him.' A note of defiance entered her voice. 'I wouldn't have.'

Hemmings nodded, as if she approved of the answer. 'You say you met in the restaurant where you were working—?'

'That's right.'

'Was it he who approached you?'

She hesitated. 'It might have been.'

'Well, was it or wasn't it?'

'I think he might have said hello to me first.'

'And can you remember – did he seem to know that you worked for Hennessy's?'

'No. I don't think so.'

'You don't sound altogether sure.'

'I don't remember.'

Hemmings paused. Maria Canavan was rattled and she wanted the jury to witness the fact.

'I appreciate this has all come as something of a shock, but thinking back, do you think that it's possible Mr Brogan used you as a way of getting an introduction to Hennessy's?'

The young woman hesitated again.

'Let's try and put the pieces together, shall we?' Hemmings said. 'Mr Brogan committed various crimes in his teens and twenties and served several years in prison. Thereafter the police suspect him of having been involved with smuggling Republican weapons out of the country. He left Ireland for the Caribbean, where he remained for a number of years before returning to get a job delivering yachts. When he died, he was more than a hundred miles off course and in all probability armed with a gun.' She looked up from her notes to the witness. 'Do you have any idea what he was doing so far up the Bristol Channel?'

Maria Canavan shook her head miserably. 'No.'

Eamon Hennessy was equally puzzled. The fifty-year-old owner of a family business that had been passed on through four generations, he was the closest thing the Irish maritime world had to aristocracy. His secretary, Miss Canavan, had made the introduction, he recalled, but he had been thorough in pursuing Brogan's references. Brogan's former employer was a man named Jonathan Budowski, a director of a well-known Wall Street firm of stockbrokers. From the inside pocket of his tweed jacket, Hennessy produced a copy of the emailed reference Budowski had provided, dated 12 September the previous year. It confirmed that Brogan had skippered his yacht for nearly six and half years without incident. He described him as entirely trustworthy and an accomplished seaman. As Hennessy spoke, Jenny saw that Mrs Patterson was noting down his every word.

During his brief period of employment, Hennessy said, Brogan had carried out fifteen deliveries and collections, all single-handed, and all without incident. He couldn't have performed better. On the morning the *Irish Mist* went down, he had left a message on the office phone to say that he had a problem with a jamming rudder and that he planned to put in to Swansea for repairs. But by the time he had made the call, he must already have been at least thirty-five miles past the port of Swansea and most of the way to Bristol. Asked why Brogan wasn't wearing a lifejacket, Hennessy answered that he should have been. He had been issued with a Baltic offshore model designed both to inflate and illuminate on contact with water.

'Did you have any knowledge of Mr Brogan's criminal past?' Rachel Hemmings demanded, when Jenny had finished with the witness.

'I did not.'

'Do you know why he might have been carrying a gun?'

'No.'

'Have you ever been approached by criminals or terrorists seeking to use your vessels for their activities?'

'Never.'

'Do you have any political affiliations yourself, Mr Hennessy?'

'I do not. I am a Protestant, my wife is a Catholic. My employees come from both traditions.'

Rachel Hemmings persisted with a series of questions designed to encourage Hennessy to admit to some degree of suspicion about Brogan, but according to his employer Brogan had distinguished himself only by being exceptionally competent at his job.

With each failed attempt to secure a revelation, Mrs Patterson grew more frustrated. She tugged impatiently at Nick Galbraith's sleeve and issued whispered instructions which he dutifully wrote down and passed to Rachel Hemmings. When, reluctantly acting on one of these notes, Hemmings put it to Hennessy that his yacht business was being used as a front for terrorists, Jenny stepped in to draw a halt.

'There are limits, Miss Hemmings, and you've reached them. You've no evidence for any of these assertions, have you?'

'No, ma'am,' Hemmings replied, relieved to have an excuse to resist repeating her client's outlandish allegations.

'Then we'll end it there. Thank you, Mr Hennessy.'

Mrs Patterson glared at him as he stepped away from the witness chair.

Jenny made a note on her legal pad that Hennessy had struck her as a rare commodity: a man with nothing to hide.

Jenny gave Dr Kerr the dubious privilege of being next in the witness chair. It was not a duty he relished. The fearlessness with which he tackled his work in the mortuary abandoned him when confronted with a row of critical lawyers. Reading nervously from the report he had drafted following his post-mortem, he told the jury that Brogan would have succumbed to hypothermia within twenty minutes of entering the chilled waters of the Severn estuary. His body had been washed up on the beach at Aust, a few yards to the east of the Severn Bridge, close to that of ten-year-old Amy Patterson, a victim of the plane crash. The absence of water in his lungs suggested that he had kept his head above water throughout his ordeal, and might in fact have died after reaching dry land. With his body temperature already severely reduced, he could have remained conscious until getting clear of the water, only to die within minutes. The presence of scratches on his arms and neck suggested that he might have had contact with Amy in the water. Beyond that, it was impossible to say what had happened to him between entering the water and his eventual death. Had he been wearing a lifejacket, it was possible that he might have been rescued while still alive, or even have swum to the shore, but without one the mere effort of staying afloat would have quickly drained his energy.

It was an unspoken rule of practice that a coroner would occasionally ask questions with the purpose of painting the deceased in a positive light, especially where there was any hint of suspicion or blame. Jenny asked if it was possible that Brogan might have died attempting to rescue Amy Patterson. Dr Kerr agreed that it certainly couldn't be ruled out.

Doggedly representing the interests of Ransome Airways, Giles Hartley QC followed on with several questions, seeking to place the blame for Brogan's death squarely on the sailor himself for failing to wear a lifejacket.

'You're surely not seeking to deny that your client's aircraft hit Mr Brogan's yacht?' Jenny interjected.

'It was struck by lightning, ma'am – an unforeseeable act of God,' he asserted. 'Mr Brogan's negligence was entirely his own.'

'Thank you, Mr Hartley. You have made your point.' She

looked over the heads of the lawyers to the dead man's girlfriend. 'I do apologize for counsel's insensitivity, Miss Canavan.'

'For the avoidance of doubt, ma'am,' Hartley said in his most courtly voice, 'I make no apology.' He gave a nod of mock deference and sat down.

Rachel Hemmings was interested in only one thing: the whereabouts of Brogan's gun.

'Could the weapon have been removed before you took custody of the body, Dr Kerr?' she asked.

Jenny willed him to stop and think before answering. He didn't.

'It's possible.'

'The police constable who was first on the scene gave a statement,' Jenny interrupted. 'You have seen it. No weapon was found.'

Undeterred, Hemmings pressed on. 'There were many opportunities for the body to be searched, weren't there? It didn't arrive at your mortuary until nearly three o'clock in the afternoon.'

'I don't consider it very likely,' Dr Kerr said, quickly backtracking.

'Did you test the hands for evidence of explosive discharge?'

'I did. None was found, but given the time spent in the water it's impossible to say whether the results are definitive.'

'So Mr Brogan *may* have fired a gun?'

'He may or may not. I can't say.'

Mrs Patterson had produced her notebook computer and was typing furiously. She brought something up on the screen which she showed to Galbraith, who in turn passed it forward to Rachel Hemmings.

'Ma'am, my client has found what she believes to be a picture of a lifejacket matching that which was issued to Mr

Brogan. Can Mr Hennessy please be asked to confirm its accuracy?'

'Certainly.'

The computer was passed back to Hennessy, who confirmed that the picture was indeed a Baltic offshore lifejacket of the kind issued to Brogan. A superior model, it was secured tightly to the body with the aid of a crotch strap and was designed to keep the wearer's head clear of the water.

Hemmings said, 'Dr Kerr, please describe the layers of clothing Mr Brogan was wearing.'

'He had on a T-shirt and underpants, bib-style waterproof trousers, a thick plaid shirt and boots.'

'You missed something out. Where was the holster?'

'Over his T-shirt.'

'So to fetch out a gun he would have had to reach through his shirt and down through the bib of his trousers?'

'Correct.'

'Wearing a properly secured lifejacket, that would have been virtually impossible, wouldn't it?'

'Yes, I suppose it would.'

Mrs Patterson came as close to a smile as her grief would allow. Her husband crossed his hands across his stomach and lowered his eyes to the floor. Whatever theory his wife was formulating, he showed no sign of sharing her enthusiasm for it.

Dick Corton, the investigator from the Marine Accident Investigation Branch, was as inscrutable while giving evidence as he had been on the quayside at Avonmouth, offering not a word more than was strictly required of him. He told the court that the *Irish Mist* had been struck on the port side of the hull, which, given that the plane had been approaching from the west, indicated that the yacht had been heading upstream towards Bristol at the time. The impact had smashed the port section of the deck and the timber below, fatally holing the hull. It would have sunk in seconds. Weather reports indicated that visibility was as low as three hundred yards. If, as had been suggested, the aircraft was travelling in the region of 180 knots, that would have given the skipper all of three seconds between seeing the plane and the collision. There was no time to take evasive action. The wreck of the yacht was found in fifty feet of water some three hundred yards upstream from the remains of the aircraft.

Jenny next went through the half-dozen photographs Corton had produced, showing what was left of the *Irish Mist* on the quayside. 'Picture number four, Mr Corton – please tell us what that shows.'

'It's the damaged section of hull near the bow of the boat – the front, if you prefer – just about where the aircraft, assuming that's what it was, struck.'

'I think we can safely assume it was the aircraft,' Jenny said. 'What I'd like you to comment on is what appears to be evidence of scorching – the insulating foam between the inner and outer hull appears burnt.'

'I would agree with that.'

'Caused by what, in your opinion?'

'The aircraft's four engines are sited beneath the wings, so I'm prepared to speculate that it was one of those which made impact.'

'What sort of temperatures are required to scorch insulating foam and timber?'

'The ignition point of timber is around 250 degrees centigrade.'

'You would agree, then, that whatever hit it was very hot.'

'That would be a safe assumption.'

Jenny glanced across at Rufus Bannerman QC, counsel

for Sir James Kendall, and saw him poised, ready to intervene should her questions start to intrude on the condition of the aircraft. Tempted as she was, she resisted, and moved on.

'In your inspection of the vessel, Mr Corton, did you examine the rudder mechanism?'

'I did.'

'And did you find anything to be wrong with it?'

'No, ma'am. The rudder was undamaged and the steering couplings were in good order.'

Mrs Patterson was busy whispering to her lawyers again. Her husband looked weary and embarrassed.

'Picture number six, Mr Corton – what does that show?'

'It's a section of the deck by the stern, ma'am. The deck boards have been ripped out, I assume by the naval team that salvaged the vessel.'

'And why might they have done that?'

'It would be perfectly routine to check the voids,' Corton said.

'For what, precisely?'

'Anything. It was the only vessel in the area. You would want to examine it closely.'

Jenny turned to the jury and explained as neutrally as she could that while Sir James Kendall, the coroner charged with investigating the deaths in the aircraft, had reserved all members of the salvage crew as witnesses to his inquiry, he had written to confirm that nothing of relevance to her inquest had been found in or around the wreck of the yacht.

Experienced as she was in dealing with the demands of an irrational client, Rachel Hemmings nonetheless coloured with embarrassment as she commenced her cross-examination.

'Mr Corton, you are an experienced mariner yourself, aren't you?'

'I am.'

'You spent twenty-five years in the merchant navy and latterly skippered cargo vessels.'

'That's correct.'

'Tell us, if you can, why so few yachts are to be seen in the upper reaches of the Bristol Channel – the area to which we also refer as the Severn estuary.'

'It has one of the highest tidal ranges in the world – as much as fifty feet in places.'

'Meaning that it's an exceptionally treacherous stretch of water?'

'For the inexperienced, most certainly.'

'The area of water in which the *Irish Mist* went down is only navigable at high tide – is that correct?'

'You would have to sail in on the rising tide, if that's what you mean.'

'Thank you for correcting me, Mr Corton. But my point is that Mr Brogan would have to have been navigating according to a carefully prepared plan.'

'Either that or he was fortunate with his timing.'

She paused briefly to take a sip of water. Behind her, Mrs Patterson was waiting, her eyes fixed on Corton.

'Let's assume it wasn't luck – there was nothing wrong with his rudder, after all. High tide occurs roughly once every twelve hours – is that correct?'

'More or less.'

'And it was some sixty minutes before high tide when the accident happened.'

'Fifty-seven.'

'Mr Brogan knew he was going to be in that spot at the time, didn't he?'

'I have no idea.'

'Doesn't it strike you as more than mere coincidence that a man with his history was the only person at the scene of an aircraft disaster?'

Corton frowned. 'I couldn't possibly speculate.'

Jenny cut in just as Rufus Bannerman QC was squaring himself to object. 'Miss Hemmings, please restrict your questions to the physical evidence.'

She continued regardless. 'Contrary to every rule of good seamanship, Mr Brogan was wearing no lifejacket. That can only be because he intended to fire a gun.'

'Don't answer, Mr Corton,' Jenny said. 'Miss Hemmings, I have warned you—'

'Mr Corton,' Hemmings persisted, 'have you been told to tell only partial truth to this inquest?'

'No, ma'am, I have not.'

'You're lying, aren't you, Mr Corton? What was in that boat? What aren't you telling us?'

'Miss Hemmings, that's enough. You may stand down, Mr Corton.'

Corton gratefully stepped away from the chair.

Hemmings was in full flow. 'Ma'am, you expressly stated that this inquest exists to uncover the truth. I am doing no more or less than that requires.'

'That does not include making unfounded allegations.'

'I am entitled to ask the witness if he is withholding information.'

'And you got your answer. Please sit down.'

'With respect, ma'am, I did not get an answer. You discharged him before he could reply.'

Jenny was pulled up short. Hemmings was right. In her haste, no, her *fear* of trespassing across the boundaries she had been set, she had denied Mrs Patterson her chance to have her questions put. It was a new and disconcerting experience: she was usually the one sniffing out unlikely conspiracies. She needed time out to reconsider, and decide how far she could let Hemmings go before the Ministry of Justice pulled the lever and let her swing.

'We'll adjourn there until two o'clock,' Jenny said, and stood up from her desk.

Mrs Patterson's voice cut through the sound of scraping chairs as she turned on her lawyers. 'What was wrong with the question? The man had a gun. He was a known terrorist . . .'

Greg Patterson tried to calm her, but her voice rose in indignation. 'Why can't we ask about that? What's she hiding, Greg?'

Jenny walked quickly to the office and closed the door, Mrs Patterson's words ringing in her ears like an accusation. It was at moments like this that she envied her tough-skinned colleagues who remained immune to the emotions of grieving familes; she felt Mrs Patterson's grief like a physical force.

'Mr Bannerman would like to see you,' Alison announced, as she appeared a short while later with coffee. 'I think he's got a message from the Ministry.'

Jenny would normally have refused to see counsel in private during an inquest, but on this occasion she decided to make an exception. It wasn't cowardice, she told herself, it was merely the sensible thing to do. Just as Dr Allen had instructed, she was no longer acting on whims and hunches, but reasoning her way to answers. It was as if Mrs Patterson had held a mirror up to her: the sight of a formerly rational woman collapsing so spectacularly under the weight of emotion was no more or less than had happened to her. But while Michelle Patterson had only just begun her descent into madness, Jenny was on the last leg of the journey home and had no intention of retracing her steps.

'How can I help you, Mr Bannerman?' Jenny asked, as he sat in the plastic chair opposite hers.

'It's not so much a case of helping me, perhaps, as helping

yourself, Mrs Cooper.' Bannerman spoke with a kindly smile that must have disarmed many opponents in a long and successful career at the Bar. Up close, he looked even softer and more benign than he had across the hall. 'You will be aware that the Ministry of Justice is understandably most anxious that your inquest doesn't intrude on Sir James's territory, so to speak. It's no reflection on your abilities, of course; the concern is merely that were you inadvertently to make any premature findings of fact, it would play havoc with the eventual inquest into the plane crash. You can imagine what fun we lawyers would have if his findings threatened to contradict yours. He could find himself snagged up in judicial reviews for years. That surely wouldn't be in anybody's interests, least of all those of the families of the dead.'

'What do you suggest?' Jenny said, trying hard to reveal nothing in her expression.

'As you might expect, I have briefed both Sir Oliver Prentice at the Ministry and Sir James Kendall on this morning's proceedings, and Sir Oliver is very much of the view that you have already called sufficient evidence to return a verdict. On the narrow issue of what caused Mr Brogan's death, I can't imagine there is any more to be said.' Bannerman took a measured sip of coffee. 'And as regards Mr Ransome, I have to inform you that he will not be attending, and that Mr Hartley and his team are poised to go to the High Court should you attempt to force the issue.'

Up until recently Jenny would have told Bannerman exactly what she thought of a man such as him, who was prepared to sacrifice the principles of his profession to suppress the process of justice and to hell with the consequences. But something had changed; her newly manifesting survival instinct told her to hold fire.

'Won't his absence merely add to the speculation, Mr Bannerman? Isn't that what you're seeking to dampen?'

'How shall I put this, Mrs Cooper?' He pushed his small, round spectacles up his short beak of a nose. 'It has come to my notice – I have to admit through conversations I have overheard, rather than been party to – that Mrs Patterson is under the impression that she has struck some sort of bargain with you. "She promised us we'd get to ask about the plane," to quote her directly. "She told us there would be no cover-up on her watch."' He smiled at her over the rim of his cup. 'I can't for a moment imagine that that is true, but she does rather seem to have got hold of the idea that you assumed the mantle of her personal champion.'

Jenny didn't permit the uncomfortable irony of the moment to show on her face. She realized now that she had truly done Mrs Patterson a disservice in promising her an inquiry she knew in all but the most irrational parts of her would not be permitted to happen. She had allowed herself to be swayed by a mother's grief and by her own selfish need to atone for ancient sins. Far from being noble, she had been weak.

'Sudden tragedy can unbalance the sanest of people,' Jenny said.

Bannerman nodded, assuming that they had reached an understanding. 'I can tell Sir Oliver that proceedings will be concluded swiftly?'

Jenny thought she had made up her mind, but felt a sudden and powerful tug in the opposite direction; as if the dead were imploring her. She resisted it.

'I intend a verdict to be delivered this afternoon.'

Bannerman smiled. 'A very wise decision, Mrs Cooper.'

Jenny had written her lines on her legal pad and carefully prepared her response to Rachel Hemmings's protests and the inevitable outburst from Mrs Patterson. Her justification would be firmly rooted in the law: her decision to limit the evidence framed as being in the overall interests of justice. By the time she had mentally rehearsed her speech several times over, she was almost convinced by it.

She remained calm even as she heard the lawyers reassembling and Mrs Patterson issuing instructions to Rachel Hemmings to stiffen her spine and remember she was being paid to get answers. Jenny felt strangely powerful, as if in one short lunch hour she had finally become absorbed into the great legal machine against which she had so often imagined herself to be opposed.

Alison's unmistakable tap-tap-tap sounded on the door. 'We're ready for you, Mrs Cooper.'

As Jenny made to leave, she felt the silent buzz of her phone in her pocket. She reached for it by reflex. The name on her screen was that of Owen Williams, the Chepstow detective with a hatred for the English. They hadn't spoken in months.

Jenny called through the door. 'Won't be a moment.' She answered his call. 'Sergeant Williams?'

'Inspector Williams now, if you please. Even I still don't believe it.' He sounded more sing-song Welsh than ever, his voice rising and falling between baritone and soprano. 'You're conducting the inquest into the death of that sailor, aren't you?'

'Yes,' she said, straining to hide her impatience. 'Right now, in fact.'

'Oh,' he said. 'Only I think we've found his lifejacket. I thought you might want to pop down and claim it.'

TEN

Hartley and Bannerman had looked appalled when Jenny announced that the hearing would be adjourned while further evidence was obtained. They had demanded full particulars of precisely what had been discovered, Rachel Hemmings adding her voice to the clamour, but Jenny had told them only that a lifejacket had been discovered, not by whom or where. All parties insisted they be granted the right to have their experts inspect it simultaneously. Jenny refused, asserting her right to have evidence tested first and as she saw fit.

Leaving the building, she saw Greg Patterson and Nick Galbraith steering Mrs Patterson away from predatory news cameras. No wonder Bannerman was nervous: a forceful woman with a fearsome intellect – there could be no one harder to contain.

Jenny headed north across the Severn Bridge into Wales with her conscience clear. She had come close to being compromised, but had found the courage to resist at the last minute. Her search was still on.

She followed Williams along the corridor of the quaint, stone-built police station in the main street of the little market town of Chepstow, and into a locked evidence room. The few rows of aluminium shelving were decidedly bare. Business was slack at the moment, he was pleased to report.

And as far as Williams was concerned, trouble usually came in the form of foreign – invariably English – interlopers who had dared to venture onto the wrong side of the border.

He handed Jenny the orange lifejacket in the clear plastic evidence sack in which it had been stowed. It was deflated and smeared with mud.

'It was one of the boys from the sailing club who found it. It was washed up on the shore opposite the castle. Must have come right up the mouth of the Wye on the tide. You can see it's been tampered with.'

Jenny peered through the plastic. One lifejacket looked much the same to her as any other.

'Look here—' He took the bag from her. 'You see this?' He pointed to one of the two inflatable pouches at the front of the jacket. 'It's been punctured. It's a clean cut, about two inches long. Looks like it was done with a knife.'

'Is that how it was found?'

'Hasn't been touched. I took a statement from the fellow myself. And here.' He fumbled through the plastic for one of the nylon webbing straps. 'This is the bit that's meant to go down your back and between your legs. Clips together at the front. It's been cut up there, by the shoulder.'

'I can see,' Jenny said. 'It was like that when he found it too?'

Williams nodded gravely, enjoying a rare moment of drama in his steady line of work 'It was, Mrs Cooper. The man only brought it in because it didn't look right to him. I'll expect you'll want someone to have a look at it.'

'Yes—' Her mind was already racing with possibilities.

As Williams handed her the bag she saw that the words 'Hennessy's, Dublin Bay', and beneath them the company phone number, were written in faded black marker pen on the rear side of the jacket. There was no doubting it was Brogan's.

'Can I take a copy of the finder's statement?'

'Certainly,' Williams said, sensing that he might have become involved in something portentous. 'Is there anything else I can do to help, Mrs Cooper?'

Jenny pulled herself back from her distracted thoughts. 'There is one thing. There's a witness on the Somerset side of the estuary who heard a helicopter flying back in this direction from the scene of the air crash very soon after it happened. I tried to get hold of the CCTV footage from the bridge, but I was beaten to it by Kendall and he's keeping it to himself.'

'I know. Some of my boys were drafted in to the D-Mort, said he was a right uppity English bastard.'

Jenny gave a patient smile. 'You do know I'm half-English, Inspector.'

'We've all got a touch of the mongrels, Mrs Cooper, but always remember – the beautiful bits are Welsh.'

Jenny took a circuitous route back to the office, stopping off at the depot of a courier company, where she arranged for the immediate dispatch of the lifejacket to a private foren-sic laboratory in Oxford. Her phone didn't stop ringing for the entire hour, and like one of the people she used to smile at pityingly in traffic jams, she conversed with her callers as animatedly as if they were sitting in the seat next to her. There were calls from the lawyers anxious for information she wouldn't give, and another from an official in the Ministry of Justice demanding to know when her inquest would be concluded. As soon as possible, she replied, refus-ing to be pinned down.

Simon Moreton joined the procession and informed her that he had postponed an important meeting with the Justice Minister, no less, to find out what the devil she was playing at.

'It's hardly sinister, Simon. New evidence has turned up.'

'What evidence?'

'A lifejacket.'

'And?'

'I don't know yet. It'll take the lab a few days to run some tests.'

'What kind of tests?'

'Why don't you trust me for once?'

'I've tried that before, Jenny. It's not done either of us any favours.'

'Would you believe me if I told you I intend to do this strictly by the book?'

'Jenny, it's not betraying any official secrets to tell you that this disaster is being treated as an issue of national security. The PM has already chaired three meetings of a specially convened disaster management committee. There are military and intelligence people crawling all over this. You don't honestly believe you can improve on their efforts?'

'If they were behaving properly they'd pass their evidence on to me.'

'Always the constitutionalist when it suits you.'

'You don't have to deal with grieving mothers.'

Moreton let out a weary sigh. 'I can't shield you any more, Jenny. I won't say it again – the world's safest airliner falling from British skies is out of your league. *Dangerously* out of your league.'

'Noted. Haven't you got a minister to suck up to?'

'Goodbye, Jenny. You're on your own now.'

'Goodbye, Simon.' She hit the overhead button that ended the call.

She was fumbling for her phone, intending to switch it off in order to gain a few moments' peace, when it rang again. It was Michael Sherman.

'Michael?'

'Hi. Look, sorry to bother you—'

'What can I do for you?'

'Can we meet for a few minutes? I'd rather not talk on the phone.'

'Any particular reason?'

He chose not to answer. 'I'm not far from your office.'

'I'll be there in ten minutes.'

'How about the Mexican place on the corner? I could do with a drink.'

There were student bars on Whiteladies Road, and those that were strictly for the after-work crowd. Montezuma's was squarely in the former category. Jenny had never been tempted to step inside, and now knew why. The floor was tacky with spilt beer and everything, including the paper napkins, smelt of last night's tacos. But Michael appeared neither to notice nor to mind. As he sat down in the corner booth, his mind seemed to be elsewhere. Sliding into the bench seat opposite, Jenny noticed that his eyes were heavy with tiredness.

She waved her hand in front of his face. 'Is this a social visit, only I'm rather busy?'

'Sorry—' He shook his head as if to wake himself. 'Long weekend. Race meetings from Plymouth to Carlisle. Some of the jockeys seem to spend more time in a plane than they do on a horse.'

'There was something you didn't want to say on the phone—'

His eyes instinctively swept the largely empty room. It was a habit she guessed he had picked up in the Air Force – always alert to who might be listening. 'I spoke with Nuala's brother last night. Called him up in Auckland. He's feeling bad that he hasn't come over, but he's a young guy, twenty-five – he's trying to get the money together for the fare.'

She waited while he gathered himself to continue.

'He said she called him a couple of weeks ago – on a Wednesday. They usually skyped every couple of weeks on a Sunday, so it took him by surprise. Anyway, she said she was going to New York at the weekend – Saturday, he thinks she said – and might not be able to make their usual time. He asked was it another one of her free flights she got through the airline. She said, no, it was "sort of a work thing". He thought she was hinting she might have been going for a job out there – she'd often talked about leaving Ransome – but she didn't really want to discuss it.' Michael glanced out through the window at the passers-by, his thoughts turning inwards once again. 'She could be like that. If there was something she didn't want to talk about, there was no way you'd prise her open.'

'That all sounds perfectly plausible.'

Michael nodded distractedly.

'Was there anything else?'

'I called one of her old friends – I used to know her when Nuala and I were together. Her name's Sandra, calls herself Sandy. Sandy Belling. She's chief stewardess on the London–Dubai route. She said Nuala had stepped up from short-haul to the Middle East destinations two months ago and was loving it. She'd been due to fly to Dubai the Thursday before she set off for New York, but had called in sick on the Wednesday. She was going to be out of action for a week is what Sandy heard.'

'She called in sick then booked herself onto a Ransome flight? That doesn't make a lot of sense.'

'Sick for a pilot can mean just a little under the weather. I wouldn't draw too many conclusions.'

Jenny was dubious. 'What is it, Michael? There's something you're not telling me.'

'The text she sent me – *Tyax*. I keep picturing her in that plane. Have you any idea what that must have been like? You'd have people screaming, stuff flying through the air. Once she realized they were in a deep stall she'd have known exactly what was coming next. It's the nightmare descent people like her train for on the simulator and pray never happens . . .' He took a long pull on his beer.

'There are huge resources being thrown into finding out what brought that plane down,' Jenny said. 'The military, the security services – I've heard it from the horse's mouth.'

'I've been in the military. Believe me, the truth doesn't come into it.' She saw the deep anger in his eyes. 'When someone fouled up, bombs went astray, innocent civilians got killed, our officers weren't interested in the truth, only in working out the lie.'

'My inquiry doesn't extend to the causes of the plane crash, Michael. I'm not being allowed to go there.'

'You're not curious?'

'Of course I am.'

'According to Sandy, Nuala's entire life was on her smartphone. Her contacts, diary, all her computer passwords and pins. She was never without it. I asked for access to her effects at the D-Mort, but was told the coroner had to give permission. Apparently he's not releasing anything, not for anyone.'

'Did she have a computer?'

'Maybe it was with her, maybe it was at her flat. I'm guessing she had her house keys with her. She used to keep them in her pocket. She never carried a handbag.'

'Someone else might have a key.'

'Not that I know of. I'm not sure she would have trusted anyone.'

'What are you trying to find? Why not let the inquiry run its course?'

He tapped both sets of fingers on the edge of the table, as

if seeking reassurance from its solidity. Jenny could see that his thoughts were taking him to a place where he felt disconnected from whatever version of reality it was he normally inhabited. 'I don't believe in conspiracies, Jenny – not even the British Army can organize them properly. But I have seen cover-ups. In my experience there's never been a military plane crash that's been reported straight. There's invariably a spin on it. The technology's never allowed to fail, somehow or another it's always pilot error.'

'You said it was the text message that was troubling you – that word. If it had the kind of significance I think you're implying, then it must have been related to something she already knew; something before the plane went down. Be straight with me – is that what you're thinking?'

He gave an uncomfortable shrug. 'She knew lots of things. She made it her business to.'

'Such as?'

'It was all on Airbuzz. Ill-maintained planes taking to the air, planes with faulty parts. Ground staff told not to record faults in the tech log. Pilot errors, computer errors, air traffic control errors. Pilots forced to fly dog-tired or unfit. Most of this stuff's down to natural human error and the pressures of business, but a 380 . . .' He shook his head. 'This is a machine that is meant to fly itself. It's the pinnacle of a hundred years of innovation, millions of man hours, billions of dollars of R and D. It should not have dropped out of the sky like that.

'And I've been thinking about the air traffic control data you showed me. That's not a lightning strike. The plane was levelling off at 31,000 feet – that's above most of the weather. But think about it. Bam! Lightning strikes the hull. Even if it's the most powerful bolt there's ever been, the worst it can do is short out some of the electrics. There are back-up computers, back-up generators, and if the worst comes to the worst, a propeller flips out beneath the aircraft which we call a ram air turbine. The air makes it spin. It generates enough electrical power for the pilot to operate the basic controls – rudder, stabilizer, some of the ailerons, throttles – and to maintain his primary flight display. You'd expect to see a controlled descent, not a stall.'

Jenny said, 'Let's say the AAIB are right and there was a giant lightning strike, couldn't it have so disrupted the electrical systems that nothing worked correctly? There are no mechanical controls between the pilot and flying surfaces, are there?'

'I'm not a physicist, I don't know what massive electrical fields can do, but everything I do know about planes tells me that lightning would have to have blown a hole in the fuselage and damaged the avionics to bring it down. But there are five avionics bays in a 380 – I still can't see it. A missile literally blowing them apart maybe, or a bomb . . .'

Jenny pictured the diagram of the 380 she had retrieved from the internet. The avionics bays were right beneath the cockpit, accessed from above through a trapdoor, and from outside the aircraft via a door beneath the nose cone.

'The avionics bays are pressurized,' Jenny said. 'If the hull was breached anywhere close to them, surely the passenger cabin would have depressurized, too?'

'Of course,' Michael said.

'That didn't happen. As far as I know, none of the bodies show any signs of depressurization. And the little girl who phoned her father as the plane was going down said nothing about a bang.'

'That's my point. If it wasn't lightning, and if it wasn't a bomb, then the only explanation is a catastrophic technical failure. That aircraft's computers monitor every aspect of flight; the pilots are being constantly reminded and warned. If they were in danger of stalling, an electronic voice would have called out a warning to them, and if they didn't respond the plane's computers would have adjusted the speed and attitude.'

'And if anyone would have known about a weakness in that aircraft—'

Michael met her gaze. 'It would have been Nuala. You've got it.'

Alarm bells sounded in her head. It was human nature to want a neat explanation for disturbing and unexpected events, and to search for causes and connections where none existed. But there was also a time to acknowledge that the circumstantial evidence had mounted to an extent that couldn't be ignored. And it wasn't so much Nuala's text that troubled her – it might have been nothing more than a message of affection – but Brogan's lifejacket. The severed straps, the seemingly deliberate puncture. The niggling suspicion that something that Sir James Kendall already knew was being hidden from her.

Jenny said, 'I don't hold out any hope of getting access to Nuala's personal effects, and I'm not even sure it would help to attempt it. I've no legitimate grounds to make a request and, even if I did, it's a sure-fire way of getting it looked at by Kendall's people first.'

'So, that's it? You're not even going to try?'

Jenny said, 'I have to be careful. Let me think about it overnight.'

'Up to you.' He finished his beer. 'I can always go it alone.'

Jenny made it back to Jamaica Street just in time to catch Professor Colin Dacre before he left his office on the pretty outskirts of north Oxford. Forenox was the most expensive of the laboratories she employed to conduct forensic investigations, but their links with the university made them one of the best in the country. When he wasn't busy with his day job, the former chemistry don was lecturing postgraduate students and overseeing numerous research programmes. He was renowned as one of the world's leading experts in the rapidly evolving field of the portable detection of explosives. Thanks to Dacre and his team, soldiers on active service would shortly be receiving a hand-held device able to sniff out buried landmines from up to twenty yards away. The equipment would also be employed at airports: any passenger, item of luggage or cargo that had been in contact with explosives could be detected immediately.

She told him about the lifejacket that would be arriving by courier within the hour, and that she needed to know as much about its history as his team could tell her.

Dacre's curiosity was aroused by the challenge. He replied that the chances of learning anything about the provenance of the implement that cut the straps were slim, but that if Brogan had indeed fired a gun in the proximity of the jacket they were likely to find some telltale molecules embedded in its fabric.

Then the awkward question: could he make it his top priority?

'How soon do you need it?' Dacre asked.

'Yesterday?'

'I won't be able to conduct the tests personally, but I've a team of eager young technicians who are always grateful for the overtime. Would you like them to burn the midnight oil?'

'I'd appreciate it. Thank you.'

Setting down the phone, Jenny glanced at her email inbox and saw at least half a dozen messages from Mrs Patterson, each pointing out what she had convinced herself were anomalies in the evidence. There was also one from her solicitor apologizing for the missive he assumed she would have sent in defiance of his express instructions. His client was over-wrought and underslept, he explained, and he promised to do his best to rein her in. Jenny sent all the messages to the recycle bin and switched the machine off. She needed some uninterrupted time to plot her way forward.

Instead the phone rang, making her start. She grabbed the receiver.

'Jenny Cooper.'

'Oh,' a man's voice said, in mild surprise. 'I was trying to get hold of Mrs Trent.'

'Hold on.'

Jenny called through the door to Alison and heard her step out from the kitchenette, where she was tidying up, their meagre office budget not stretching to a cleaner.

'Who shall I say is calling?'

'Paul,' he answered hesitantly.

Alison came to the doorway.

'It's Paul for you.'

Alison reddened, staring panic-stricken at the receiver. 'I'll take it at my desk.' She hurriedly pulled the door closed behind her.

Jenny detected the signs of another minor romantic drama and tried not to eavesdrop. But the snatches of Alison's stage whisper that carried through to her were too enticing to ignore. Paul, it seemed, was an unwelcome admirer, or at least one who seemed to be placing her in a dilemma. Jenny heard her say, 'I don't know . . . I just don't know if I should—'

It was a childish stab of envy that prompted her to remind Alison on the way out that she had yet to deal with the dead photographer's camera, which, along with his other pos-sessions, was still sitting in a box at the side of her desk.

'I'm sorry, Mrs Cooper. I've hardly had a moment.'

Jenny looked at her dubiously.

'I'll see to it, I promise,' she snapped.

Jenny felt a twinge of shame as she left the office, realizing at once what had provoked her fit of pique. She resolved to take hold of herself. If she was lonely, she must do something about it, just not now.

'Is this Mrs Cooper, the coroner?' The voice was that of a young and very precise man.

'It is.' Barely awake, Jenny struggled to focus on the small digital clock that sat on the windowsill by her desk. It was two forty-five a.m.

'My name is Ravi Achari. I'm calling from Forenox. Professor Dacre informed me that you wished to receive information on the lifejacket as soon as it became available.'

'Oh . . . yes. Please.' She struggled to sound alert.

'Regarding the strap and the puncture wound, we can confirm they were caused by the same sharp object – we have detected minute traces of steel swarf on each of the severed surfaces. It had two cutting edges, suggesting a bayonet-type knife. Some preliminary research suggests there are various military-style knives of this nature, all commercially available, with self-sharpening sheaths. We suggest this may be the most fruitful line of inquiry.'

'Interesting. I'm grateful.'

'There is more, Mrs Cooper.' She heard him tap on a keyboard. 'Microscopic examination of the front surface of the jacket revealed evidence of flash burns to the left-hand front face of the jacket, suggesting brief exposure to intense heat.'

'That makes sense. He came close to an aircraft engine.'

'Ah.' He hesitated. 'That may be the case,' he said guardedly, 'but we have tested some of the affected area using terahertz spectroscopy and found minute traces of PBX embedded in the same surface of the fabric. This is currently being confirmed by two separate chromatography techniques. We suggest this is post-blast residue, or, if you prefer, unreacted material. Not all of the explosive is fully combusted, you understand. Judging by the very limited damage, we suggest the jacket was some distance from the blast.'

'Hold on. PBX – ?'

'Plastic bonded explosive,' Achari said, as if it were common knowledge. 'Though, interestingly, the traces we have detected don't appear to contain the chemical marker indicating its provenance as required by the Montreal Treaty.'

Jenny's tiredness vanished. She felt the blood pulsing through her veins. 'The lifejacket has been in the presence of an explosion?'

'Undoubtedly, Mrs Cooper.'

ELEVEN

JENNY COULDN'T SLEEP. For three restless hours her mind buzzed with possibilities, each more outlandish than the last. At six a.m. a now weary-sounding Achari telephoned a second time. The two further tests had confirmed the presence of unmarked PBX on the lifejacket and detailed thermal testing of the fabric indicated that the wearer had been at least fifty yards from the centre of the explosion. Jenny quizzed him hard about where the explosion had taken place. In the air? On the water? Underwater? Definitely not underwater was all he could confirm.

By six-thirty she was at her desk in the study drinking strong coffee and struggling with the weight of responsibility the new evidence had heaped on her shoulders. Strictly speaking, the ethical course would have been to release it to all the interested parties immediately, including to Sir James Kendall. If she were to do that, she felt sure that the Secretary of State for Justice would invoke his powers under the Coroners and Justice Act to suspend her inquest immediately, citing issues of national security. It would be a neat and certain way of washing her hands of the case, but each time she contemplated the prospect, her conscience pulled her back from the brink.

She tried to predict how events would unfold at the reconvened inquest were she to produce a surprise witness from Forenox. If she wasn't silenced immediately, she could guarantee that there would be a huge effort to uncouple the evidence of an explosion from the scene of the air crash. And therein lay a problem: as things stood, there was nothing in the forensic evidence to link the two. She made a note to ask Dr Kerr to forward swabs from Brogan's body to the Forenox team. If there was explosive residue on his skin, there could be no argument.

She dreaded Mrs Patterson's reaction. She would inevitably seize on evidence of an explosion as irrefutable proof of terrorism and demand that Jenny carry out inquiries that no amount of explanation would convince her were beyond Jenny's remit. And then there was the media firestorm that would undoubtedly follow. The moment she released this evidence she would find herself the centre of global news and responsible for even greater numbers of passengers staying away from beleaguered airlines. The potential consequences were limitless.

Whichever way she looked at it, she was faced with a straight choice: to share her evidence such as it was with the official crash inquiry, or to reinforce it further by digging deeper into what, if anything, Nuala Casey knew.

She prayed that it wasn't just her ego making the decision as she lifted the telephone.

'Michael? It's Jenny.'

'Hi,' came his non-committal reply. In the background, she heard the sound of a small plane sputtering into life, its engine rising to a dragonfly hum.

'I've thought about what you said, and there is no way I can get Nuala's property from the D-Mort.'

'Uh-huh.' He sounded unsurprised and unimpressed.

'But what if I were to come with you to her flat? It's stretching the boundaries of my inquiry rather, but I'm sure I could persuade a friendly locksmith to let us in.'

He was silent for a moment. She sensed his wariness. 'Why the sudden change of heart?'

'I'll tell you when we meet. How soon can you do it?'

'I'm giving flying lessons over at the Cotswold airport this morning. I finish around one.'

'I'll meet you there.'

Telling Alison only that she would be out of the office for the rest of the day on a research trip, Jenny switched off her phone and drove the forty miles across Gloucestershire to Kemble. The winter countryside had a stark, stripped-down beauty that she had learned to appreciate since moving out of the city. Frost clung to the clefts of hillsides untouched by the sun. In the centres of bare fields ancient oaks that in summer were perfect domes of green revealed their bent and twisted limbs.

The Cotswold airport was in fact little more than an airstrip: a handful of buildings and a scattering of light aircraft and helicopters parked on the grass. Jenny stayed in the warmth of her car, watching the tiny planes coming and going and wondering what impulse it was that possessed people to take to the sky in such fragile machines.

A few minutes before one o'clock, a tiny Cessna made an erratic descent towards the airstrip, wings tilting left and right. The nose jerked suddenly upwards as it came in to land. It hit the ground heavily, bounced once, then twice, before skewing slightly as it drew to a halt. It turned at the end of the runway and taxied over the grass towards the car park. Michael climbed out of the cockpit together with a young man who was laughing self-consciously at his efforts and hoping his instructor would share the joke. But Michael had already spotted Jenny. He hastily scratched a note in the student's logbook and made his way over to her.

She wound down her window. 'I hope that wasn't you at the controls.'

'It's only his third lesson – you should have seen the first.'

'You must be insane. I couldn't even set foot in one of those things.'

Michael smiled. 'What are you scared of?'

'What do you think?'

'You don't fancy going up for ten minutes?'

'No thanks.'

'Come on – you'll love it. It's a perfect day. I'll cure your fear for good, I promise you.'

'I doubt that very much.'

'Just once round the field, that's all.' He opened the car door, refusing to take no for an answer.

The two-seater Cessna Skycatcher was cramped and claustrophobic. Jenny's heart was already pounding as Michael fastened her belt and fixed on her headset and was fit to explode by the time he had taxied to the start of the runway. As hard as she tried to relax and disappear into inner space, each sound and sudden movement wrenched her back to unwelcome reality.

'Just a light headwind this morning – nothing too bumpy. All set?'

Jenny nodded, feeling anything but. Even as they were accelerating along the runway she would have gladly thrown open the door and taken her chances.

'Here we go—'

Michael eased back the stick and aimed the nose towards the sky. The little aircraft clawed its way upwards. Jenny gripped the sides of her seat as they juddered through pockets of warm air, the plane's flimsy-looking wings shaking alarmingly.

'Look over there.'

Michael pointed left towards far-off hills, monumentally beautiful in the sharp sunlight, but Jenny couldn't enjoy the view. She took a slow, deep breath and tried to relax her clenched muscles, telling herself that it was good that she was facing her fears.

The plane banked sharply leftwards, the wing tilting to what felt like ninety degrees to the ground.

'It's perfectly safe,' Michael said. 'These things can glide. You don't even need the engine to land safely.'

'Can we not try that?'

He smiled, his eyes brighter and more alert than she had seen them before. It was as if since leaving the ground he had come alive.

'A thousand feet. Doesn't feel like it, does it?'

'Are we going down soon?' Jenny said. 'I thought it was going to be just once around the field.'

'We've got twenty minutes of fuel. My students have paid for it—'

'Please?'

The plane took a sudden dip, the engine revving as it momentarily lost purchase. The whole fabric of the craft seemed to strain as they levelled off with a violent thud.

'Just a touch of turbulence.' He pointed to the west. 'Look, you can see Bristol.'

Jenny nodded, losing her battle against her phobia.

'Are you going to tell me what happened to change your mind?' Michael said.

'Can we please go back now?'

'I'm confused. I'm having to put a lot of trust in you.'

'What do you mean?'

'One minute you don't want to get involved, the next you want to break into Nuala's flat. I was taught to be wary of people who change their minds. They're not usually who you want in a crisis.'

'I've got some new evidence, that's all. *Please* can we go back now?'

'How about sharing it with me?'

He was staring straight ahead. The nose of the aircraft was pointing upwards; Jenny's eyes ran over the dials and saw the altimeter climbing. Her anxiety crossed the threshold into panic.

'Why are we still going up?'

'I thought you might want to know how a stall works – it's a routine training drill. Ease back on the throttle, lower the nose a touch—'

'Are you trying to scare me, Michael?'

The whine of the engine trailed off to an idling tick-tick. The airspeed wound back towards zero. For a moment they seemed to hover on the edge of a precipice. Jenny felt her fingers bite into the fabric of the seat. She was too terrified to make a sound.

The sensation was like falling backwards off a cliff. One moment they were looking straight up at the sky, the next they were sliding towards earth. Jenny heard herself scream as they tumbled through one full somersault, then another. Now she was staring straight down at the ground, which was spinning clockwise in front of the windshield. Michael was pounding the foot pedals and pulling hard left on the stick. Just as it seemed the ground would rush up to meet them, the spinning abruptly ended and they were swooping in a tight arc that left her stomach somewhere far behind them. The engine growled back into life and slowly they levelled off at what felt like little more than treetop height.

'Sorry about that,' Michael said calmly. 'I usually pull out a little more sharply.' He turned back for the airfield.

Jenny sat in silence, struggling to catch her breath. Her throat was raw from screaming. Michael looked pale and rattled: she could tell he had managed to frighten himself as much as her.

Neither spoke until they had touched down and taxied to a halt.

Jenny yanked at her seat belt. 'I thought you might apologize.'

'I already did.'

'Really? I should report you. You obviously can't be trusted.'

Michael said, 'That lasted twenty-five seconds. Try doing that twelve times over and sending a text while you're at it.'

'Did you think I hadn't got that point?'

She searched for the door handle.

'All right, I shouldn't have done it. I didn't plan to . . . It was just an impulse – to make you understand.'

'How do you get out of this thing?'

'Listen, Jenny—'

She spun round in her seat and slapped him hard across the face. 'You bastard!'

Stunned, Michael pressed a hand to his stinging face. 'I'm sorry.'

'What's *wrong* with you?'

He threw open the cockpit door and jumped out. 'Long story.'

She would gladly have hit him again. He had been sitting in the passenger seat staring out of the window for close to an hour. No more apologies, no explanation. Not a word.

Then it started, out of nowhere.

He'd killed his first civilians as a young pilot in Bosnia in September '95. He was part of NATO's Operation Deliberate Force, flying Tornados out of Aviano in Italy. His job was to take out a bridge the Serbian army was using to transport supplies up to its encampments in the hills surrounding Sarajevo. He hit the bridge first time, only it happened to be covered with refugees travelling in the opposite direction: thirty-five men, women and children. Their shattered remains were filmed by an Italian film crew and all the airmen got to watch the results of their handiwork on the evening news.

During the fortnight of raids he notched up several more civilian kills; how many he never found out. Their officers told them it was justifiable collateral damage; a few lives lost to save many more. It was a doctrine that was carried into the Afghan and Iraq campaigns. They attacked few purely military targets: the groups of militia they hunted were mostly holed up in civilian villages and compounds. You learned to be accurate, he said, the video replay proving that you'd slotted the missile straight into the ring of sandbags where the gunmen were sheltering, but often you'd see the figures scattering in the background: women, children, goats, all running for their lives.

It was strange how different men reacted to killing. Some appeared genuinely to thrive on it, each death seeming to build them up further, while others buckled and lost themselves in drink or drugs. While he was still in uniform, Michael believed he had managed to get away without permanent damage. He hardly drank and always slept at night. He counted himself one of the few lucky ones. Then one day, nearly three months after becoming a civilian, he was standing on a tube platform on the London Underground when he saw a young woman dressed head to foot in a light blue niqab just like the ones Afghan women wore, and an image rushed back to him. He had been called in to clear out a wadi along which a group of Taliban fighters had fled, having ambushed a British foot patrol. He swooped in low and saw about a dozen of them: men with rifles and RPGs running down the dried-up riverbed, the banks too steep for them to scramble up to the safety of the surrounding undergrowth. He mowed them down so easily he almost felt cheated. Having turned about for a second pass to mop up any he had missed, he saw another figure darting out from behind a rock. His finger had hit the trigger before his brain had registered who he was killing. It was a woman with her hands up. And they remained above her head even as the bullets ripped her in half and sent her severed torso flying high into the air. And from that moment on she had never left him, not for a single hour. He even had a name for her: Nikoo. It meant good and beautiful in the Afghan language.

One of the reasons it hadn't worked out between him and Nuala, Michael said, was that each time they made love, all he could see was Nikoo flying into pieces. And now Nuala had died too, it felt like divine retribution.

Jenny said, 'Have you had any help?'

'A psychiatrist? I'd lose my pilot's licence.'

'Should you be flying if you're suffering flashbacks?'

'It doesn't usually happen when I'm flying.'

She glanced over at him, 'It did today, didn't it?'

Michael shrugged.

'Let me guess when else it's happened,' Jenny said. 'The trip to Tyax – you and Nuala in the little float plane.'

He looked at her in astonishment.

'It doesn't take a lot of working out. You killed a woman from a plane. You feel guilty. And now you fly male jockeys for a living. I bet you find reasons not to teach female students, too.'

'Nuala didn't know about it. I handed her the controls . . . I told her I was feeling ill.'

'You didn't tell your lover, but you tell me.'

'It's different . . . I don't know . . .' He searched for a reason. 'It must be that you're older or something.'

'Thank you.'

'You know what I mean. You don't expect a young woman to understand things like that. They're full of energy and hope, you don't want to bring them down.'

'Keep going, you're really building me up.'

'Forget it. You wanted to know my story.'

'I did not.'

'In the plane – you said: "What's wrong with you?"'

'Rhetorically.'

'No.'

'Oh – you know what I'm thinking, do you?'

'I didn't say that . . . But I think I might know what you're feeling.'

'Uh-huh?'

'The same as me . . . Interested.' He glanced at her, then turned his gaze out of the window.

Jenny said, 'I think I preferred it when you weren't talking.'

A silence fell between them.

Michael was the first to break it. 'You haven't told me about your new evidence. It's something big, isn't it?'

It was Jenny's turn to look surprised.

Michael smiled. 'I thought so. I read on the internet about the guy with the gun, but I don't think he's got anything to do with it. Just another drug runner is my guess. You've got to be a genius or an idiot to get a serious amount through the airports nowadays. Out in the Caribbean for six years – he would have had all the connections he needed.'

'Maybe.'

'So if it's not him, what is it?'

'It's confidential.'

'I told you my secrets.'

Jenny sighed. 'Promise me it goes no further.'

'Swear to die.'

She had a feeling that this was going to lead somewhere she could choose to avoid. But it was too late; she had already gone in too deep with Michael to back away now. 'The sailor's lifejacket was found washed up in the mouth of the Wye. The straps had been cut, the inflatable chamber had been punctured, and it had been roughly fifty yards away from an explosion of unmarked PBX – there was explosive residue on the fabric.'

Michael withdrew into himself as he seemed to turn the information over and over in his mind. His silence stretched on for several moments.

'Aren't you going to tell me what you're thinking?' Jenny asked.

'Is there the same residue on his body?'

'I'll have test results tomorrow.'

'What about the girl?'

'I no longer have access to her.'

He gave a dismissive grunt.

'What does that mean?'

'It means whatever we think we know now it's bound to be wrong.'

At least it was something they could agree on.

Nuala's flat was on the second floor of a converted Victorian house in a side street off the Uxbridge Road; as close to town as a pilot's wage would allow, and a thirty-minute drive to the airport. She could have lived in a leafy village in Berkshire on the other side of Heathrow, Michael said, but she preferred the restless energy of the city, the streets full of Asian and Afro-Caribbeans, all the ethnic shops and food stores. He struggled to share her enthusiasm for London.

Having spent many hard years in godforsaken places, he could think of nowhere he would rather be than the quiet of the English countryside.

The locksmith company sent an eager and talkative boy of eighteen called Mohammed, who barely glanced at Jenny's ID before going to work as keenly as a thief. His jobs were mostly for bailiffs, he said. They'd get a warrant, wait for the debtor to leave home, then sneak in and seize the goods while he, or just as often she, was out. That way you avoided trouble. If the debtor was holed up indoors there were crafty ways of prising him out. He knew a bailiff who would phone saying he was from Western Union and had some money waiting for collection at the local franchise. To make it fun, he'd sometimes pretend it was a prize from an online lottery. One time, he told a man he'd won ten million euros. Mohammed claimed to have found the victim of the prank dead from a heart attack, the phone still clenched in his hand.

Michael and Jenny waited patiently, the job turning out to be trickier than Mohammed had anticipated. There was no one at home in the downstairs flat, meaning first they had to negotiate the front door. There was a deadbolt and a separate spring-latch mortise, both of which had to be picked. Nuala's front door on the upstairs landing was a bigger challenge: a multi-point system that required two keys to be turned simultaneously. Jenny learned more about locksmithing in twenty minutes than she had ever wanted to.

When at last the door swung open and Mohammed had taken his £200 in cash, Jenny asked Michael if he would like to go in first, perhaps to spend a few moments alone.

The prospect seemed to alarm him. 'I'd rather not, if you don't mind,' he said.

Jenny stepped inside and he followed.

It was just as he remembered it, Michael said, apart from the new set of blinds at the windows. It had a modern, pared-down feel, more like a hotel suite than a place someone called home. Apart from the small bedroom and bathroom, the flat was open-plan: a simple, white and chrome kitchen diner opening onto the main living space. There was a pair of simple Japanese-style sofas arranged around a low glass table, a flat-panel TV and a handful of novels stacked on a slender steel rack that snaked up the wall.

'She liked to live simply,' Michael said. 'She used to say this place was the one thing in her life over which she had complete control.'

'I'm still surprised,' Jenny said. 'I suppose you would expect a woman to have more stuff. There are no photographs, no pictures on the walls.'

'She didn't feel the need. She claimed not to have a sentimental bone in her body.'

Jenny drifted towards the desk and filing cabinet at the far end of the room. 'Did you believe her?'

'I never really questioned it . . . I remember one time she said that she had always known she would never have children.'

'Like a premonition?'

'No. Not like that.' He joined her at the desk. 'I think she meant that she would always be too caught up with her work. All her energy went into worrying about people flying in planes.'

Jenny nodded, but privately she thought it sounded like the kind of thing a young woman who was frightened of remaining alone might say. She speculated that Nuala would have bet a lot on Michael, seeing him as a man to share her future with. Having him leave her as she turned thirty would have been a heavy blow.

'I see a scanner and printer but no computer,' Jenny said.

Michael checked under the desk. 'It's not here – this is where she always sat down to work. She always had a laptop.'

He pulled open the single drawer beneath the desk and found several bunches of keys and airside passes for various airports in continental Europe and the Middle East, along with a photocopy of her pilot's licence and her most recent medical certificate.

He sifted through the keys. 'Spare house keys, car keys, and company locker.'

'We'd better take them,' Jenny said.

Michael slipped them into his pocket. 'She'll have left her car at Heathrow – there's a staff car park at the Ransome building. That's where her locker is. I think she might have kept her company laptop in it.'

'She had two computers?'

'The company machine is just for flight planning and official notices and emails. Not for personal use.'

'We'll call by on the way home,' Jenny said. She scanned the few shelves above the desk: a handful of technical manuals, and an old university textbook on mechanical engineering. 'Not many books.'

'She read as much as she could online,' Michael said. 'She had a thing about not wasting paper. Guilt at wrecking the climate with passenger jets, I expect.'

Jenny drew open the upper drawer of the stylish wooden filing cabinet. It contained all of Nuala's personal papers: domestic bills, wage slips, bank and credit card statements. Glancing through them, there was nothing out of the ordinary. Nuala was paid between four and five thousand pounds each month and spent less. There was close to forty thousand sitting in a deposit account.

Michael pulled open the bottom drawer.

Jenny knelt beside him and saw that the contents were

divided up into six hefty suspension files marked MECHAN-ICAL, ELECTRICAL, SOFTWARE, NAVIGATION/ATC, EMPLOYMENT and MISCELLANEOUS.

'It's all her Airbuzz stuff,' Michael said.

'Printed out on paper,' Jenny remarked.

'Didn't want to lose it, I guess.'

He pulled out the MECHANICAL file and laid it on the floor. They sifted through pages of reports filed by air accident investigation authorities around the world that Nuala had downloaded from the internet. All the cases she had collected related to mechanical faults on commercial airliners. From malfunctioning landing gear to burst hydrau-lics, to toxic engine fumes penetrating the cabin, to an incident in which an entire wing severed from a small passenger prop with the loss of all lives. The doomed plane's wing had suffered metal fatigue and been repaired in so many places that one afternoon it simply sheared off at 5,000 feet.

'These all look like official investigations,' Jenny said, 'not anecdotal reports.'

'I know,' Michael said, reaching for the SOFTWARE file. 'I doubt she would have printed anything out that would have linked her directly to the Airbuzz forum. She wasn't stupid.'

They worked through each of the files in turn and found the same thing: Nuala had collected a library of official reports into accidents and major mechanical faults that had occurred during the last five years. The documents were in precise chronological order, the most recent nearest the front.

'Why was she doing this?' Jenny asked.

'All pilots care about this stuff, but she was a little obsessed.'

'Did she work entirely alone? There must have been other pilots who were frequent visitors to the forum.'

'I don't think you're understanding quite how sensitive these incidents are—' He stopped mid-sentence, his attention caught by a document he had just pulled out of the MISCEL-LANEOUS file. 'Wow . . .'

'What is it?'

'Something that proves my point.'

He handed her the single sheet of paper. It was headed *Side Letter* and was dated 18 November the previous year. It read:

> *As a further fundamental condition of employment, the pilot hereby promises and undertakes to seek the advice and guidance of the airline's legal department prior to notifying the Civil Aviation Authority in the UK, or the equivalent relevant authority in any foreign country, of any incident that might be deemed a 'serious incident' or 'accident' or other reportable event. Notwithstanding any legal requirement to report any such incident, the pilot hereby accepts that failure to act in accordance with the guidance of the airline's legal department in relation to any such incident may result in termination of employment.*
>
> *Further, the pilot hereby accepts that any disclosure to any third party of any or the whole of this side letter shall constitute a fundamental breach of the contract of employment and shall result in summary dismissal.*

The printed names and signatures of the parties beneath the text had been blacked out prior to copying.

'The commander of an aircraft has a legal duty to report an accident or any serious incident that could have resulted in an accident,' Michael said. 'What amounts to a serious incident is something of a grey area. There's not a passenger plane in the sky that hasn't got a handful of faults logged at any one time. It all comes down to how jumpy the pilot is as to how he responds.'

'I'm no expert in employment law,' Jenny said, 'but surely you can't threaten to sack a pilot for doing his legal duty.'

'You can try,' Michael said. 'What's an airline got to lose? It's a buyer's market. Qualified pilots are ten a penny.'

Jenny studied the letter closely for any further clue as to its origin. There was none. The only hints lay in the fact that the text was blotchy, suggesting it had been scanned and emailed before being printed out. The absence of a web address at the top of the page indicated that it hadn't been printed from the internet but rather sent directly to Nuala.

'It's the kind of thing she was dealing with all the time,' Michael said. 'It's just odd that she printed it.'

'Maybe it was hers?' Jenny said. Then the thought struck her: there was not a shred of unwanted paper on or around the desk, not a spent envelope or a discarded note. 'You don't think she might have left it here on purpose?'

'What do you mean?'

'Well, look at this place. It's immaculate. Even for a tidy person this is spotless. Every document in date sequence, all her personal papers perfectly ordered . . .' She stopped herself.

'Tell me what you're thinking,' Michael demanded.

'It feels unnatural . . . It's the kind of thing I've seen with suicides.'

'She was in a plane crash.'

'But what was she doing on that plane?'

Michael shrugged. If he had a suspicion, he wasn't committing to it.

Jenny said, 'Let's load this stuff into my car. I want to talk to your friend Sandy.'

TWELVE

SANDY BELLING LIVED ALONE with her seven-month-old child in a semi-detached house in one of the anonymous suburban streets in Heston, on the far western fringes of London. It was an area distinguished only by the thunder of the aircraft engines which passed over every forty-five seconds, sixteen hours a day, and was home to many of the thousands of low-paid aircrew, ground staff and myriad airport workers who flooded into Heathrow each morning.

She had just returned from three back-to-back round trips to Abu Dhabi and hadn't seen her baby for four days. In common with many other female cabin crew, she had to rely on her mother to do the child-minding while she was away working and it was evidently causing tensions. She told Michael she was thinking of switching to a job on the check-in desk. The pay was less, but the hours regular. Jenny noticed that the baby had dark olive skin with tightly curled thick, black hair. Sandy was pale with mousy hair and freckles, and the kind of friendly, open face you expected to see when nervously stepping through the door of an aircraft.

They sat at the kitchen table while Sandy spooned something orange from a jar into her son's mouth, trying to remind him who was mother. It felt almost indecent to talk about her dead friend when she was so clearly under strain, but Michael had promised Jenny she was tough enough to take it.

Jenny got her to talk a little about how she and Nuala had become acquainted, and learned that they had met at a staff party nearly three years ago. Nuala had recently joined Ransome Airways and Sandy, already an old hand at twenty-six, had let her in on some of the company secrets. There was a lot of gossip between pilots and cabin crew, mostly about who had slept with whom, but also office politics. Personality traits became exaggerated in the enclosed space of an aircraft cabin; small niggles very soon became big issues and the best captains liked to be kept abreast of tensions. Sandy and Nuala had continued to work on the same routes and had become a regular team, priding themselves on running a happy plane.

'Did she ever talk to you about technical issues to do with aircraft?' Jenny asked.

'No, only things that affected the cabin – electrical faults, all that—'

'But you knew she was interested in air accidents?'

'She mentioned it.' Sandy wiped the baby's mouth with a paper towel. 'That's not really the kind of thing I like to think about.'

'It wasn't always shop talk with Nuala. When we were together these two were always partying,' Michael said, in a failed attempt to lift the mood.

Sandy shot him a look which told of a painful history. Jenny could imagine the long hours she would have spent consoling her friend after Michael left her.

'Did she ever discuss her employment?' Jenny asked.

Sandy looked puzzled. 'No.'

'She didn't complain about working conditions?'

'Only as much as anyone else. At least we had jobs. Lots of my friends in other airlines have been made redundant.

It's just as bad for pilots – if you're over fifty, you can forget it.'

'Tell me how she had been lately.'

'Busy. She'd been flying to Dubai several times a week. A new route takes some getting used to – you have to adjust your body clock as well as everything else. She came over for a meal a couple of weeks before Christmas and she seemed tired and bit stressed. Not herself.'

'Did she say why?'

'No . . .'

Sandy unbuckled the baby from his high chair and lifted him into the playpen. Jenny exchanged a look with Michael, both of them having the same thought – that Sandy was hiding something.

'But you had a suspicion?'

Sandy dangled some toys in front of her child, but he was more interested in beating the mat with his fists.

Jenny persisted. 'What do you think was the matter?'

Sandy glanced again at Michael. 'As far as I know, she hadn't been seeing anyone for . . . well, since Michael and her. I asked her how she'd been getting on with the first officer she'd been flying with to Dubai. He's a guy called David Cambourne – he's not the most popular. She said "fine", but in a way which said she didn't want to talk about it.' She aimed her remark at Michael: 'You know how she could do that.'

'So there was a problem between them?' Jenny said.

Sandy was reluctant to answer.

'Anything at all you can remember would help.'

'How? What's her personal life got to do with a plane crash? I knew the pilot and the co-pilot of that plane, and half the cabin crew. All of them had problems – they were human beings.'

Jenny backed off, only now fully appreciating just how

much grief Sandy and her colleagues must have been dealing with in the ten days since the crash. 'I'm sorry.'

'There was gossip, that's all,' Sandy said. 'One of the girls thought she'd seen him coming out of her hotel room in Dubai. It could only have been a rumour, but that's enough. Pilots aren't allowed to be in relationships together, and they're certainly not allowed to break the law in a foreign country. If that had got back to management they'd both have been sacked.'

'That sounds very serious. Didn't you ask her about it?'

Sandy shook her head.

Jenny made a guess. 'Because if you knew, technically you'd be obliged to tell someone.'

Sandy said, 'I'm a single mother. I need my job. Nuala knew that.'

'Did they continue to fly together?'

'Yes. I was on one of their flights just after Christmas.'

'And the rumours?'

'For all I know they could have been malicious. Let's face it, male pilots don't want women taking their jobs. A woman can always be looked after by a man – that's how people think, especially when things are tight like they are now.'

Michael said, 'Sandy knew Nuala better than me, but I don't think she would have risked her job that way. Let's just say she had powers of self-control not possessed by most.'

Sandy looked at him in a manner that was more pitying than accusing.

'Did she tell you she was going to New York?' Jenny asked.

'No. I already told Michael – all I heard was that she had phoned in sick.'

'You didn't call her?'

Sandy sucked in her cheeks and turned back to the baby. She looked as if she might cry.

Softening her tone, Jenny said, 'You were worried it might have had something to do with the rumours?'

Sandy gave a hint of a shrug.

'You shouldn't feel guilty,' Jenny said. 'It's not your fault the airline's being run this way.'

'I was meant to be her best friend . . .' She wiped her eyes with the back of her hand.

Michael said, 'This guy Cambourne, what's he like? Could Ransome have been trying to get rid of two problems at once?'

'He's a bit distant, that's all. Fond of himself.'

'One to stick strictly to the rules?'

'You'd think so.'

'Any incidents on any of his flights that you know of? Anything that could have led to an accident? October, November time, perhaps?'

Sandy cast her mind back. 'I heard about a flight to Zagreb that overshot by fifteen minutes. By the time they'd turned round they had only just enough fuel to land. That was about November. He might have been first officer.'

'What was this, a canteen rumour?'

'I overheard some of the young girls talking on the staff shuttle. No one with any sense gossips in the canteen.'

Michael glanced at Jenny, both of them having the same thought: the side letter could have been imposed on Cambourne's contract.

'Did you ever hear any more about it?' he asked.

Sandy said no, it was just the once.

The baby started to grizzle. Sandy lifted him out of the playpen and pressed him to her shoulder. She looked exhausted, her four days in the air catching up with her.

'I think we should go,' Michael whispered to Jenny. He eased his chair away from the table and turned to Sandy. 'I don't suppose you've got a number for Cambourne?'

'I think so. But you didn't get it from me.' She handed Jenny the baby. 'Would you mind?'

'No—'

Jenny took the grumbling child in her arms while Sandy crossed the room to pick up her phone to search her contacts. It had been years since Jenny had held a baby. She had forgotten how delicate they felt; they were fragile like nothing else.

'Here,' Sandy said, and showed the number to Michael. He punched it into his phone.

Sensing Jenny's awkwardness, the infant started to cry. Sandy hurried over and took him back, her gentle strokes and reassuring whispers instantly soothing him into a torpor. It was a gift Jenny had never possessed.

Jenny said, 'I can see you're a natural.'

'Thanks.' Sandy seemed touched.

'If anything else occurs to you, you'll let me know? It'll be strictly confidential, of course.'

'Sure.'

Jenny turned to leave. As she followed Michael to the front door, a huge jet rumbled overhead. The house shook.

'That'll cost someone a fine,' Michael said. He turned to say goodbye and saw that Sandy was weeping.

'I'm sorry.'

'No. You had to . . .' She rocked to and fro, seeking comfort in the embrace of her child. 'A man phoned last week. I'm not in the book, but he got hold of the number and phoned here. He said he was part of the official investigation into the air crash. He knew I was a friend of Nuala's. He wanted to know whether she had her computer with her on the flight. I told him I didn't know . . . He didn't want to believe me.'

'Did he give his name?' Jenny asked.

'Sanders. He sounded very severe, like an army officer or something.'

'Did he say anything else?'

She nodded. 'He said he would be back in touch, and next time I had better have an answer . . . Do you know who he is? He frightened me.'

'No,' Jenny said. 'But if I find out, I'll be sure to let you know.'

Cambourne didn't answer his phone, but several minutes after Jenny had left a message saying she would like to speak to him about a flight to Zagreb that had overshot, he called her back.

'Who is this?' he demanded.

'My name's Jenny Cooper. Coroner for the Severn Vale District. I'm very interested in why Nuala Casey was on a flight to New York.'

'I've no idea.'

Michael urged her on from the passenger seat.

Jenny pushed her luck. 'I know enough about your relationship with Miss Casey to think that's not very likely, Mr Cambourne.'

He fell silent.

'You're not in any kind of trouble. All I want is to talk to you off the record for a few minutes. I'm fifteen minutes from Heathrow, where are you?'

'I'm flying out of Terminal Five later this evening. I'll be there in just over an hour.'

'Perfect. I'll give you a call.'

*

She left Michael in the car park outside the Ransome building, searching for Nuala's Fiat, while she went inside. The
airline's cut-price ethic extended to the tired decor in their
reception area. She approached a grimy desk and spoke to
the sour-faced employee seated behind it. A man determined
to make full use of his sliver of power, he studied Jenny's
identification with officious attention to detail before lifting
the receiver to call through to the office.

Interrupting him, Jenny said, 'I have a key to Captain
Casey's locker. All I need is for you to show me where it is.'

Wilfully ignoring her, he continued with his call, telling
the person at the other end that there was a coroner in
reception asking for access to a pilot's locker.'

'A *deceased* pilot,' Jenny emphasized.

'I see. Of course.' He put down the phone. 'I'm sorry,
madam. There's no one available to meet you right now.
Perhaps you would like to make an appointment.' He turned
the page in the desk diary and reached for a pencil.

'Who was that you just spoke to?'

'I beg your pardon?'

'I'd like to speak to whoever that was.'

He looked dumbly at the phone as if it might answer for
him. 'I can't do that, I'm afraid.'

'Because?'

'It's nine o'clock in the evening, madam. You have to
make an appointment for tomorrow.'

Jenny leaned over the desk and read the name on his
security tag. 'Listen, Mr Preston, I'm conducting an inquest
into a death caused by one of your employer's planes. You
can either come to give an account of yourself in my
courtroom later this week – and I will gladly have you
arrested if that's what it takes – or you can let me through
that security barrier and tell me where I can find what I'm
looking for.'

She suddenly became aware that several cabin crew who had been on their way out had stopped to watch the show. Preston glanced between her and his audience, then turned his gaze back to the diary.

'Someone show this lady where the staff lockers are,' he muttered.

Jenny turned to the young woman nearest to her. With an anxious glance to her colleagues, she swiped her pass over the electronic reader on the turnstile. 'Through the glass doors, turn right. End of the corridor – pilots' rec room.'

'Thank you.'

The stewardess hurried away.

Jenny walked along the corridor, passing empty offices, and nudged open the door to the pilots' recreation room. It too was empty. It reminded her of some of the shabbier areas set aside for lawyers in outlying court buildings: a few desks, some waiting-room furniture and three walls lined with wooden lockers. To her right was a door marked WOMEN. She stepped through it to find a similar room to the first, only in miniature. There were eight lockers, and a large wall mirror with a make-up shelf beneath. She tried the key in each of the locks. It turned in the last of the row. She opened the door to find it as she had suspected – empty.

'The car's not there. I asked one of the lads in cabin crew and he thinks it might have been towed,' Michael said.

'Where to?'

'There's a pound where all the abandoned cars from the long-term car park end up.'

'Why would anyone work for this company?' Jenny said.

'Lousy conditions but more money in the hand. It's the choice you make.'

Jenny climbed back into the Land Rover and dialled Cambourne's number. It rang three times.

'Mrs Cooper?'

'Yes.'

'What do you wish to discuss?'

'I'd like to find out what, if anything, Nuala knew about the plane that came down.'

'I'm afraid I can't help you with that. And nor would I be able to discuss it with you even if I did. I've taken some advice. You're not the official coroner. Ransome employees aren't permitted to speak to you.'

'Your company's legal department may not be the most reliable source of advice, Mr Cambourne.'

'I have a wife and child, Mrs Cooper. Captain Casey never jeopardized a colleague's position, nor would she wish that to happen now. That's all I have to say. What car do you drive?'

'I beg your pardon?'

'Don't make me repeat myself.'

Jenny was confused. 'A green Land Rover Freelander.' She glanced through the window wondering if he was nearby. 'Why?'

'Wait two minutes.'

'I beg your pardon?'

Cambourne rang off. Jenny tried his number again and got an automated voice telling her that his number was unavailable. He had switched his phone off.

'Did he say *wait two minutes*?'

'That's what I heard,' Michael said. 'He didn't sound like the kind of man Nuala would have slept with. She couldn't stand public school types. She wouldn't have been with someone married, either, for God's sake.'

'It's a little late to be jealous, don't you think?'

'Why would I be jealous?'

'You were thinking of going back to her, weren't you?'

'You're full of it.'

'Tell me you hadn't been thinking about getting help to deal with the flashbacks. Every time you woke up with a hangover and a plane to fly you knew you were shaving the odds finer.' Jenny looked at him. 'You don't strike me as a man ready to give up on life. You want to be happy.'

'You really should have been a fairground mystic. Are you sure you haven't got a crystal ball in the glove box?'

'I know what it's like.' Jenny said. 'I have flashbacks too.'

She had taken him by surprise. He looked at her dubiously. 'Flashbacks to what?'

Jenny's phone rattled in the cupholder between their seats. She picked it up to find a text message: *Short Stay 1, level 3, end of row.*

She showed it to Michael. 'It's not Cambourne's number.'

'Try calling it back.'

She pressed the green button and got a message from a synthesized voice: *you have dialled an incorrect number.*

'Anonymous text,' Michael said. 'Easy enough to do. It'll be him.'

Jenny silently scolded herself as she drove across the airport towards Terminal One, at a loss to explain why she had felt compelled to give so much of herself away. Why, of all men, was she about to share her secret with this one? He was troubled, damaged, irresponsible, lost – all the things she had promised herself she would avoid – yet she'd felt something from the moment she first saw him. It wasn't a physical attraction, nor was it a compulsion. It was just as he had described it himself – an interest. A sense that somewhere beneath all the layers that separated them, there was an affinity.

She glanced sideways and inadvertently caught his eye. Not for the first time that day she could tell they were sharing the same thought: where was this going to lead?

They passed through the barrier into Short Stay 1 and slowly spiralled upwards towards level 3, Jenny still nervous handling the Land Rover in a tight space.

'Why would he want to meet us here?' she said. 'There are more cameras in this car park than inside the terminal.'

'He'll have a reason,' Michael said.

She crested the top of the ramp onto level 3 and turned right.

'What does he mean, end of the row? Which row? There are lots of them.'

They were nearing the end of the building and about to make a right turn, when a silver estate car shot out from a space directly in front of them and took off at speed. Jenny stamped on the brakes.

'What are you doing? Get after him,' Michael said.

Jenny found first gear and stepped on the accelerator.

'Stop!' He slammed his hand his hand on the dash.

'Jesus—'

She hit the brakes again, slewing to a halt halfway around the turn.

Michael threw open the door and jumped out.

'What are you doing?' Jenny called after him.

The driver of the car behind angrily sounded his horn.

'OK, OK!'

She tried to ease forward and stalled. He honked again.

Michael shouted at him to calm down before he had a heart attack, and jumped back into the passenger seat as he leaned on the horn again: one long, continuous blast. Jenny hardly noticed it. Michael had a briefcase on his lap.

'Nuala's flight case. It was left in the space,' he said, unfastening it. He looked inside. 'Company laptop.'

'Cambourne had it.'

Michael shook his head. 'The guy behind the wheel was older, bald with glasses.'

'I didn't get a look at him.'

'You're not a pilot.' He glanced over his shoulder. 'Will that guy ever shut up? You'd better drive on.'

Flustered, Jenny crunched the gears.

Michael placed his hand on top of hers. 'Why don't I drive?'

He took a route through the back roads towards Windsor and stopped at a thatched pub tucked away down a lane away from the main road. They ordered sandwiches and retreated to a table in the corner of the quiet saloon bar to unpack Nuala's case. Besides the company laptop, there was a hand-held GPS device, some flight charts of Europe and the Middle East, a spare white shirt, basic wash kit and underwear.

'She travelled light,' Jenny said. 'No moisturizer, not even a lipstick or mascara.'

'It was a point of pride. Anything a man could do she could do better.'

Jenny picked up the GPS. 'What's this for?'

'No idea. But she did like gadgets. Maybe she got a pilot's discount somewhere.'

'What does it do?'

Michael took it from her and switched it on. 'It looks like a global position system. It tells you exactly where you are, and if you program in some coordinates, it'll point you in the right direction – see?' He showed her the screen displaying their current location. 'Just like a car sat-nav only a bit fancier.'

He put it aside and lifted the lid of the laptop. After a few moments booting up, it asked for a password. He typed in *Tyax* and up came the desktop.

'She certainly enjoyed that trip,' Jenny said, then felt ashamed.

Michael didn't respond.

There were the usual icons for email and word processor, but there was no general internet access, only a button to click linking the user to the Ransome intranet.

The few documents Nuala had stored on the hard drive were from her recent Sky Route flight plans.

'Looks like she kept this one clean. Strictly a work tool,' Michael said.

'Try the email,' Jenny urged.

He opened the email program, which also housed her company calendar. Jenny took over, scrolling through the last six months. The diary entries were in a standard form that looked as if they had been entered by the company and lodged automatically on the machine. Nuala had kept up a steady routine of three or four short-haul turnarounds through late summer and early autumn, and then in late October had shifted to a pattern of twice-weekly runs to either Dubai or Abu Dhabi.

She had flown to Dubai on Christmas Eve and flown back on Christmas Day itself. December 26th and 27th were marked *LEAVE*.

'Not much of a holiday,' Jenny commented.

A further flight to Dubai scheduled for the 28th had been marked *CANCELLED*. There was no entry for the 29th, and from the 30th it was business as usual for the following week.

'Look – five days' leave,' Jenny said.

The dates Saturday 8 January to Wednesday 12th had been marked *UNAVAILABLE*, but above them, two round trips to Abu Dhabi scheduled for Sunday 9th and Wednesday 12th had been struck out and marked *CANCELLED*.

'It'll be in the emails,' Michael said impatiently.

Jenny opened the inbox and followed the trail between Nuala and flight-crew scheduling. There was no hint that she was taking leave until Wednesday 5 January. In a short note, Nuala had written, '*Re: temporary leave of absence. I shall be available to resume normal duties as from Thursday 13 January.*' A reply sent at 14.08 later the same afternoon, read: '*You are scheduled to fly to Dubai RA340 at 13.30 on Thursday 13 January. Please confirm availability.*' To which Nuala replied, '*Availability confirmed.*'

On Thursday 6th she had received an email from the Ransome Airways bookings desk confirming her staff-discounted flight to New York on RA189 departing at 9 a.m. on Saturday 8 January, with an onward connection on American Airlines to Washington DC. Her return flights were scheduled for the afternoon and evening of Wednesday 12th.

'What was she doing there?' Jenny said.

Michael shrugged.

There was only one more email in the inbox. It was dated Friday 7th and was sent at 18.35. Headed, '*Urgent change to your itinerary*', it read:

We regret to inform you that due to an error in our reservations system, you were unfortunately booked onto a flight that was already full. Ransome Airways apologizes for any inconvenience this may cause, and unless we hear from you to the contrary we will transfer your reservation to flight RA189 departing Heathrow Terminal 4 at 9 a.m. on Sunday 9 January. Your return flights remain unaffected and your staff discounts still apply.

You need not reply to this email.

Jenny said, 'Amy Patterson was booked onto the Saturday flight, too.'

'It happens,' Michael said. 'There's no excuse, but it does.'

'*Temporary leave of absence* – that doesn't sound like the woman you've described.'

'No.'

'Sandy said she was off-colour, so why then would she have been flying to Washington? That's no way to recover.'

Michael sat back in his chair and stared up at the huge oak beam that ran the length of the room, his pensive expression telling Jenny that he was battling with contradictory thoughts.

'She wouldn't have called in sick and then booked staff-discounted tickets,' Jenny said. 'The airline must have approved her leave. But it wasn't holiday, it was *leave of absence*. It's almost as if there was some sort of official reason.'

'Yes,' Michael said, keeping his warring thoughts to himself.

'Could she have been going on a training course?' Jenny asked.

'Unlikely. We've got all the simulators you could need here.'

Jenny closed down the laptop. 'It could all have been perfectly innocent, of course. A few days away. Crossing the Atlantic would be nothing to a professional pilot.'

Distracted by a private thought, Michael said, 'Do you mind if we make one more stop on the way home?'

'It's late, Michael—'

'Captain Dan Murray's widow. I've met her a couple of times with Nuala. Nice lady.' He took out his phone. 'We'll call it a social visit.'

It was eleven p.m. when they drew up on the driveway of the house outside the village of Wokefield, further west into the Berkshire countryside. Diane Murray came to the door as they were walking up the brick path. She was a handsome woman in her late forties, but her face had a hollow, washed-out appearance, the shock of her loss still printed in her dazed expression. Recognizing Michael, she greeted him by his first name.

She had heard about Nuala, and offered her sympathies. There was something ritualistic in their exchange, as if among airmen and their loved ones such encounters were conducted according to an unwritten code. The possibility of sudden death, it seemed to Jenny, was accepted as part of the deal.

Diane led them through to the homely, farmhouse-style kitchen where they sat at the family table surrounded by reminders of her late husband. His farmer's jacket still hung on the peg at the back door; several pairs of his boots were lined up on the rack. She apologized for the mess; the kids hadn't yet returned to school since the crash. It had been hard to stay on top of things.

Michael was about to pass Jenny off as a friend when she stepped in to pre-empt him. She tried to explain that she was a coroner, but not part of the official investigation into the causes of the crash. Mrs Murray said she had lost count of the number of people who had visited during the previous week. There had been detectives, air accident investigators, agents from the security services, air traffic control executives, airline managers and even Guy Ransome himself.

'Everyone's very sympathetic,' she said, 'but I know they're all desperate for me to say that there was something wrong that made him take his eye off the ball. Human error would be the perfect explanation, wouldn't it? It's the one outcome that wouldn't mean anyone else taking responsibility.'

'It's always the same,' Michael said. 'If in doubt, blame the man at the controls.'

Jenny said, 'If it helps, we've seen the air traffic control data. The aircraft slowed down for a reason that's not apparent at the moment. Michael doesn't think it looks like pilot error.'

'They showed it to me, too,' Diane said. 'Then asked me if he had been depressed.' She shook her head in disbelief. 'He loved flying. It was his life. God knows, he wasn't doing it to get rich.'

'He was fit and well the day of the crash?' Michael asked.

'I think so. He'd been having a few headaches, but that's because he had been working so hard. He wasn't sure he'd have many years left in the business, so it was a question of earning while he could . . .' She paused, determined not to let herself give way to emotion. 'He only took on this flight the day before. The pilot who was scheduled to captain it got the flu.'

Michael said, 'Nuala was bumped from the Saturday flight. Just bad luck, I guess.'

Jenny's felt her toes curl, but Diane seemed to find his directness reassuring and managed a ghost of a smile.

'How long had he been on the 380?' Michael asked.

'About eight months. Half a dozen Ransome pilots trained. Dan scored the highest of all of them.'

'He'd flown Boeings most of his career, hadn't he?'

'It was his choice to retrain. The Airbus took some getting used to, but he said that once you had learned to trust the computers it was far more relaxing.'

'No problems he'd told you about?'

'He only ever mentioned one. It was back in the summer, on one of his early flights – I think he said it was a problem with the thrust levers coming in to land. He thought it was some sort of computer glitch, but he booked in for some extra sim time to make sure.'

'Did he tell you any more?'

'Why? Was there something wrong with the plane?'

'No idea, but it would be good to have all the information.'

Diane pushed her hands anxiously through her shoulder-length blonde hair as she tried to summon up the details. 'It was something about how automatic thrust was meant to disengage when you pushed the levers forward a click, but for some reason it didn't. The engines were still putting out power when they were meant to be idling. He had to switch to manual and throttle back. It meant they stopped too close to the end of the runway.'

Michael said, 'I've heard of pilots forgetting to disengage autothrust, but not the switch failing to work. That's a serious incident. Did he report it?'

'To the airline, I think. He must have done.'

'What about to the Civil Aviation Authority or AAIB?'

'I'm not sure . . . I don't remember him saying anything about that.'

Jenny and Michael exchanged a glance.

'Any other scrapes he told you about?' he asked Diane.

'No. As far as I know it was a one-off.' A note of alarm entered her voice. 'You don't think it was the same fault?'

'I doubt it very much – it probably wasn't even the same aircraft.'

Jenny said, 'Mrs Murray, you wouldn't happen to have a copy of your husband's employment contract? We've learned that some airlines may be trying to stop their pilots reporting incidents as the law requires them to.'

'I can look in his desk . . .' She turned uncertainly to Michael. 'You do think there was a fault, don't you?'

'I'm keeping an open mind,' Michael said, 'but that sounds a lot more likely than an experienced pilot having made a stupid mistake.'

He went with her along the passage to the alcove under the stairs where her husband had dealt with all his paperwork. Jenny heard them talking quietly as they went through the drawers of his desk. Michael was good with her, calm and reassuring, and able to confront her loss head on. Jenny cast her eyes around the kitchen and spotted mementos of Dan Murray's career as an airman: a photograph of him as a young pilot posing on the steps of an airliner; another of him at the controls in mid-flight; a row of miniature planes lined up on the dresser.

Michael returned to the kitchen alone, closing the door quietly behind him. 'She's a bit upset. I told her she should go to bed – we'll let ourselves out.' He handed her a document – Dan Murray's contract with Ransome. 'He signed it five years ago, but have a look at the last page.'

Attached to the back with a paperclip was a side letter identical in form to the one which they had found at Nuala's flat. Dan Murray had signed and dated it on 8 July the previous year.

'We just checked his diary,' Michael said. 'His first flight as captain of a 380 was on 28 May. If the incident with the thrust lever was a month later, it looks as if the company gagged him straight away.'

Jenny said, 'He can't have reported it, or the aircraft would have been grounded.'

Michael nodded. 'Like a shot.'

THIRTEEN

IT HAD BEEN A VERY LATE NIGHT. Stopping off at Michael's for the coffee Jenny had needed to sustain her for the rest of the drive home had turned into several hours spent poring over the files they had retrieved from Nuala's flat. She had been worried that there would be awkwardness between them after all that Michael had confessed to her earlier in the day, but their visit to Captain Murray's widow had seemed to switch him into a different mode. He was a military pilot again: detached and purposeful, and determined to unearth any clue about what had gone wrong with Flight 189. Jenny hadn't made it into her own bed in Melin Bach until nearly four a.m.

Their close examination of Nuala's papers revealed that over the course of the previous six months she had printed out a vast number of documents relating to crashes and near-misses. Many makes of aircraft featured, but it was the Airbus in which she seemed to have the greatest interest. It might simply have been explained by professional curiosity – after all, it was the plane she flew – but both Jenny and Michael had sensed that she was searching for something in particular.

The incidents and accidents she had researched in detail fell into two broad categories: runway overruns and anomalous behaviour of aircraft systems while in the air. Michael had been of the opinion that the overrun incidents all seemed to have an explanation based in human error. A 320 that overran a runway in Portugal with no loss of life seemed simply to have landed too far along the runway. Another 320 that overran in Honduras the same year, killing the captain and a passenger, also seemed to have come to grief as a result of the pilot misjudging his final approach. Three years earlier a 340 landing at Toronto's Pearson International Airport had skidded off the end of the runway and come to rest in a ravine. Miraculously there was no loss of life. Again, the plane seemed simply to have set down too late, probably due to poor visibility during a violent rainstorm.

More disturbing were the incidents without an immediate human explanation. Qantas Flight 72, a 330-300 flying from Perth to Singapore, made a pair of uncommanded pitch-down manoeuvres at 37,000 feet. So violent were they that passengers were flung around the cabin, many sustaining serious injuries. The subsequent investigation found that computer errors had given false stall and overspeed warnings, which in turn had caused flight control computers to command a sudden nose-down movement resulting in a dramatic plunge of 650 feet lasting twenty seconds. Fortunately, the pilots regained control and made an emergency landing at a nearby airport. A little over two months later, another Qantas Airbus travelling the same route, but in the reverse direction, suffered a spontaneous disengagement of the autopilot and the crew received a warning of a malfunction in the Air Data Inertial Reference System – the same system that had malfunctioned on Flight 72. The crew switched off the suspect instruments and returned to Perth to make a safe landing.

The incident which had engaged Nuala most deeply was the catastrophic loss six months afterwards of Air France

Flight 447. A 330-200 en route from Rio de Janeiro to Paris plunged into the Atlantic with the loss of all 216 passengers and 12 crew. The precise cause of the crash remained a subject of ongoing discussion, but a trail of evidence pointed to problems in the system responsible for determining the airspeed. Messages automatically transmitted by the aircraft's computers in the minutes before the disaster suggested that one of the three airspeed indicators having been found faulty and switched off, the remaining two continued to give contradictory readings.

Investigators' attention focused on the pitot tubes, the small hollow pipes positioned beneath the aircraft's nose which measure airflow and thereby airspeed. If the tubes had frozen and become blocked with ice crystals, it was suggested, no accurate airspeed readings would have been possible. The flight data recorder, retrieved two years later from the deep ocean floor, revealed that the two co-pilots at the controls (the captain was on a rest break) appeared disorientated by the automated stall warning generated as a result of the false speed readings. It was an unexpected event at high altitude and they instinctively responded by pulling up the nose. The aircraft climbed rapidly out of the flight envelope, lost lift, and entered a disastrous stall – precisely the thing they were trying to avoid – from which they failed to recover.

Shortly after the crash Airbus operators were advised to update all pitot tubes to a modern heated version designed to prevent icing. On a copy of the US Federal Aviation Authority's directive ordering the change, Nuala had written a note in her own hand: the two initials MD. Michael had no idea what they meant, except that it might have related to one of her many contacts on the Airbuzz forum; perhaps another pilot who had encountered similar problems.

Jenny switched on the radio as she crossed the bridge into England to catch the eight-thirty news. Flight 189 was once again the lead story. The BBC's aviation correspondent excitedly reported that the AAIB had taken the unusual step of releasing a transcript of a portion of the cockpit voice recording. It had already been shown to the relatives of the dead and would be made available to the media later in the day. At the same time, a newspaper journalist had apparently got hold of the story that Flight 189's ACARS transmissions had mysteriously stopped a little over three minutes before the aircraft started to fall from the sky. The source of the rumour was reported to be a French engineer close to the investigation. A pair of aviation experts drafted in to comment read this as a highly significant fact, but disagreed violently as to the reason why. As well as allowing communication between the aircraft and the airline, the ACARS system relayed essential flight data back to the airline's computers. One of the experts saw the absence of this data as suspiciously convenient for Ransome Airways; the other saw it as further evidence to bolster the theory that there had been a sudden and disastrous failure of the aircraft's electrical systems.

Jenny recalled all that she had read about the Air France flight. What little information that had survived the disaster had come from ACARS messages reporting fault codes in the aircraft's system. Against her better judgement, she felt herself siding with the expert who sniffed important information being buried.

Armed with excuses and platitudes, Jenny pushed through the office door ready for the inevitable hail of complaints from Alison at having been left abandoned for an entire day, but the face that looked up from behind the reception desk was unexpectedly cheerful.

'You've got visitors, Mrs Cooper,' Alison said. 'I hope you don't mind – I told them to go through.'

Jenny waited for further explanation, but Alison merely smiled and returned to her typing.

Jenny nudged open her office door to find Mrs Patterson and Nick Galbraith waiting for her.

Galbraith was quick to his feet and instantly apologetic. 'Sorry to intrude, Mrs Cooper—'

Mrs Patterson was far from contrite. 'We thought you'd disappeared.'

'No—' Jenny began.

Mrs Patterson interrupted her. 'Well, that's certainly the impression you've given, and not just to me.'

Jenny addressed herself to the lawyer. 'Mr Galbraith, you're aware that this meeting isn't strictly appropriate: the inquest is still being heard.'

'Well, that's news to us,' Mrs Patterson interjected. 'Thank you. Now are we going to hear about this lifejacket, or is that secret information, too?'

Galbraith hid his embarrassment well. 'The purpose of our visit is merely to bring some further evidence to your attention, Mrs Cooper.' He fixed Mrs Patterson with a firm gaze. 'Not, I emphasize, to discuss the substance or conduct of your inquiry.'

'I suppose that falls within acceptable bounds.'

She hung her coat on the back of the door and walked around to her side of the desk, trying to banish the unkind thoughts she was having about her uninvited visitors: after all, Mrs Patterson was only doing exactly what she would in her situation.

'Right, what have you got?' Jenny asked.

'All the relatives were emailed a copy of the CVR, or a small part of it, at least,' Mrs Patterson said. She handed a document across the desk.

'I heard about this on the news,' Jenny said. 'I'm surprised a copy hadn't already leaked out.'

'All the relatives signed a confidentiality agreement,' Galbraith explained. 'They receive information before the media in exchange for a strict undertaking not to release it.'

'You're happy for me to read this?' Jenny asked.

'Please do,' Mrs Patterson answered.

Jenny studied the surprisingly short transcript of the cockpit voice recording which began as the pilots finished their preparations for take-off.

KEY

CAM	Cockpit area microphone voice or sound source
PIL	Pilot
FO	First Officer
*****	Expletive
INT	Interphone voice or sound source
TWR	Radio transmission from the Heathrow Controller
DEP	Heathrow Departure
BRI	Radio transmission from the Bristol Controller

08.58.06	TWR:	Skyhawk one eight nine cleared for take-off
08.59.02	CAM:	TOGA (take-off go-around)
08.59.04	PIL:	TOGA set
08.59.25	CAM:	(sound similar to increase in engine speed)
08.59.45	FO:	Eighty knots
08.59.47	PIL:	Check
09.00.01	CAM:	V one
09.00.03	FO:	Rotate
09.00.18	FO:	Positive rate
09.00.20	PIL:	Gear up
09.00.23	FO:	Gear up
09.00.40	PIL:	Engage AP one (autopilot)

THE FLIGHT

09.00.55	DEP:	Skyhawk one eight nine, Heathrow Departure, good morning
09.01.00	FO:	Good morning Skyhawk one eight nine super passing one thousand five hundred feet on Detling two Golf departure
09.01.10	DEP:	Skyhawk one eight nine Heathrow Departure radar contact, maintain one thousand five hundred
09.01.13	CAM:	(sound similar to decrease in engine speed)
09.01.18	DEP:	Maintain fifteen hundred Skyhawk one eight nine
09.01.22	FO:	One thousand five hundred
09.01.35	DEP:	Skyhawk one eight nine continue climb through six thousand
09.01.39	CAM:	(sound similar to increase in engine noise)
09.01.45	PIL:	A little bit cloudy today
09.02.47	FO:	Radar's showing clear over the Irish Sea
09.02.55	PIL:	Flaps one please
09.02.57	FO:	Flaps one
09.03.02	PIL:	Flaps up please after take-off checklist
09.03.05	FO:	Flaps up
09.04.08	FO:	After take-off checklist complete
09.06.01	PIL:	Weather?
09.06.05	FO:	Dense cloud over Bristol through to Welsh coast
09.06.07	PIL:	No problem
09.06.09	FO:	Do you want to keep cabin seat belts on?
09.06.12	PIL:	See how we go
09.10.12	FO/PIL:	Light level one hundred

09.10.15	CAM:	(sound similar in increase in engine noise)
09.11.13	PIL:	OK, nice and smooth. Disengage passenger seat-belt signs
09.11.15	FO:	Sure?
09.11.17	PIL:	Sure
09.15.12	BRI:	Skyhawk one eight nine this is Bristol, good morning
09.15.14	PIL:	Good day. Skyhawk one eight nine super passing flight level one four five climbing level two hundred
09.15.16	BRI:	Skyhawk one eight nine identified, climb level three one zero, unrestricted
09.15.18	PIL:	Climb level three one zero unrestricted. Thank you, Bristol
09.16.05	CAM:	(sound similar to objects moving in the cockpit)
09.16.07	FO:	Bumpy. Seat belts?
09.16.18	PIL:	We're OK
09.16.20	FO:	(hesitant) OK
09.18.10	FO/PIL:	One to go
09.19.05	FO:	Bristol, this is Skyhawk one eight nine. Any weather to report over the Channel?
09.19.08	BRI:	Cactus two one zero ten minutes ahead of you reports light turbulence to mid Channel. Storm clouds moving in from the north. Nothing major
09.19.19	FO:	Thank you
09.19.30	CAM:	(sound similar to decrease in engine noise)
09.19.32	PIL:	Cruise
09.19.34	FO:	Decimal eight
09.19.47	PIL:	How's the baby? Getting any sleep?
09.19.49	FO:	Doing my best, on the sofa

09.19.53	PIL:	Like that, is it?
09.19.56	FO:	I told her, I'll change all the dirty nappies you like, but getting up in the night, forget it. I've got a plane to fly
09.20.04	PIL:	Off the leash tonight, then? I hope she doesn't expect me to keep an eye on you
09.20.10	FO:	In New York? You really think you'd keep up?
09.20.14	PIL:	You'd be surprised
09.20.22	CAM:	(sound of interphone buzzer)
09.20.22	FO:	Coffee time already? They could have sent the pretty one
09.20.27	PIL:	Who's that?
09.20.27	CAM:	(sound of seat belt unbuckling, footsteps across the cockpit)
09.20.29	FO:	You know – the little blonde one, Kathy, with the . . .
09.20.31	PIL:	Oh, yeah – her
09.20.31	CAM:	(sound of laughter from PIL and FO)
09.20.35	PIL:	You are definitely on your own tonight. Not my responsibility
09.20.41	CAM:	(synthesized voice) Speed. Speed
09.20.42	PIL:	What the hell is that?
09.20.43	CAM:	(sound of footsteps then belt buckle being fastened)
09.20.43	PIL:	We're at four-seventy
09.20.44	CAM:	(synthesized voice) Speed. Speed
09.20.46	PIL:	Jesus
09.20.47	FO:	No ECAM actions listed
09.20.49	CAM:	(synthesized voice) Speed. Speed
09.20.50	PIL:	What does it mean?
09.20.51	FO:	Nose down. Nose down
09.20.53	PIL:	What—

09.20.55	CAM:	(sound of objects clattering)
		(synthesized voice) Stall. Stall
09.20.58	PIL:	It can't . . .
09.21.01	FO:	Disengage AP (autopilot)
09.21.03	CAM:	(sound similar to a grunt)
09.21.06	FO:	There's no, there's no—
09.21.08	PIL:	(shouts) Alternate law
09.21.09	FO:	No ECAM actions
09.21.12	PIL:	Direct law
09.21.13	CAM:	(sound similar to a grunt)
09.21.15	FO:	No ECAM. No ******* ECAM . . . Radio's
		dead. We're flying blind
09.21.17	CAM:	(sound of objects including heavy object
		clattering)
09.21.19	FO:	Dan. Dan
09.21.20	CAM:	(sound of objects clattering. Sound
		similar to grunt)
09.22.23	FO:	Dan

(no further conversation or discernible words)

| 09.26.57 | | Recording ends |

When Jenny looked up, Mrs Patterson said, 'It manages to be both rather clinical and rather banal, don't you think?'

'It certainly looks as if they were taken by surprise. Has there been any analysis of this that you know of?'

'I'm sure it'll come,' Galbraith said. 'It's clear the speed warning came out of the blue. They seem to have slowed to stall speed without realizing. I'm told that simply shouldn't happen.'

'I noticed that they had a bump – about three minutes before. Here we are – nine sixteen and five seconds: *sound similar to objects moving in the cockpit*. The first officer seems to react in surprise and ask if they should engage the seat-belt signs. According to what I heard on the radio, that's when the ACARS stopped transmitting flight data. I suppose it could have been a jolt of turbulence.'

'That wouldn't disable all the aircraft's electrical systems,' Mrs Patterson said. 'And you'll notice there's no mention of lightning. Surely they would have seen it?'

'I imagine that depends,' Jenny said. 'From what I've read, lightning can strike an aircraft from any angle.'

'I'm sure something happened at the moment you suggest, Mrs Cooper.' Gailbraith frowned. 'But I think we can safely exclude the possibility of a lightning strike. They weren't flying through a storm; there was turbulence, yes, but nothing untoward.'

Jenny said, 'I'm glad to have read this, Mrs Patterson, but I'm really not in a position to comment. This is a matter for aeronautical engineers.'

'I have to say I agree with Mrs Cooper,' Galbraith said.

His client wasn't ready to defer. 'The problem is not even the greatest so-called experts in civil aviation may know the real answer, even if they were permitted to give it.'

Galbraith shot Jenny another apologetic look. Whatever was coming, he was telling her, was not to be taken seriously.

'You won't necessarily know about this, Mrs Cooper,' she began, 'but private defence companies around the world have developed weapons more than capable of destroying an aircraft's avionics. One such device is mounted on a surface-to-air missile. It detonates close to an aircraft, releasing a blast of microwave radiation that could quite literally fry the plane's circuitry. You've just read the transcript – all their instruments failed. They lost their ECAM display – they had no idea what had malfunctioned or why. You saw what the first officer said: "We're flying blind".'

Jenny tried to respond patiently. 'I understand that the need for an explanation is overwhelming, honestly I do, but perhaps we all ought to accept that this will take some time to unravel.'

'The longer the truth remains untold, the deeper it gets buried,' Mrs Patterson replied. 'Let me share a few facts with you. One: any terrorist group with sufficient funds can obtain such a weapon. Two: Brogan could have launched such a weapon from his yacht. Three: Brogan had a history with Irish Republican terrorists – your evidence. Four: terrorists have a history of subcontracting their atrocities to other terrorists. Brogan could have been working for the Real IRA or for al-Qaeda, it's all business. Five: the British government has a long and ignoble history of covering up the reasons for air crashes. We still don't know for certain who planted the Lockerbie bomb in '88, for goodness' sake. And lastly, not just my daughter, but lots of passengers were moved onto that flight at the last minute, and many were moved off. I've been in constant communication with other relatives. No one believes it's a coincidence – modern computerized booking systems simply don't do that.' She sat back in her seat with a look of grim triumph.

'I understand your suspicions, but the other day you sought to convince me that Ransome Airways had a history of inadequate maintenance and that that was the reason for the crash.'

'They do. But I've discovered so much more since then.'

Jenny glanced at Galbraith. 'And there is still far more to know, I've no doubt. But as I have explained to you, for reasons outside my control, my inquiry only extends to the cause of Mr Brogan's death.'

Mrs Patterson fell silent for a moment, as if weighing whether any more words would be wasted, and then with quiet certainty said, 'It wasn't just any flight. There were passengers on board someone wanted eliminated. If you are unwilling or unable to inquire further, then I will.' She stood up from her chair. 'Good day, Mrs Cooper.' She addressed Galbraith: 'I'll see you at the Marriott,' and marched from the room.

'I do apologize—' Galbraith began.

'Apologies accepted, but please don't bring her here again.'

'Not the easiest, is she?' Alison said, passing Jenny the messages she had managed to dodge the day before. 'I don't think she quite understands the process. Apparently the coroner's officer at the D-Mort simply refers to her as "that effing woman".' She pointed to a document she had flagged. 'Dr Kerr had some test results for you. I told him you were incommunicado. And Mr Moreton and Sir Oliver Prentice's office called as well, and all the lawyers at the inquest. In fact, I'm not sure that there's anyone who wasn't desperate to talk to you yesterday.'

Jenny should have apologized, but Alison's sarcasm was too much to swallow. 'I noticed the photographer's things are still sitting in that box next to your desk. Perhaps you might deal with them today.'

'I'm afraid I didn't have a moment to leave my desk, Mrs Cooper, the phone didn't stop ringing. Oh, and of course there's a slew of new death reports to deal with. I'll bring those through now, shall I, or will you be away "researching" again?'

Jenny fought to contain the barbed insults she would have gladly hurled in her officer's direction.

Emboldened by her silence, Alison continued, 'I don't like to point out the obvious, but this wouldn't happen if you didn't let people take such advantage of you, Mrs Cooper. Anyone can tell that woman's paranoid. You shouldn't be dancing to her tune.'

'I am not dancing to anybody's tune,' Jenny snapped.

'If you'll pardon me for saying so, you could have fooled me.' Alison turned to go.

'While we are on the subject of inappropriate behaviour, do you think we can try to keep our personal relationships out of the office. I think we may have crossed the line a little recently.'

'I'm sorry, Mrs Cooper?'

'I don't mind you talking to boyfriends, just try to keep it within sensible limits.'

Alison looked at her incredulously.

'I've had one call – from a man I've hardly spoken to in twenty years.'

'That's not quite true—' Jenny halted mid-sentence. Alison's eyes had flooded with tears. It was a reaction that startled them both.

She turned and fled through the door to her desk.

Jenny waited a moment, then followed. 'I'm sorry—'

'It's all right, Mrs Cooper.' Alison swabbed her eyes with a handkerchief, but the tears were refusing to stop.

His name was Paul, Alison explained, when her sobbing had subsided sufficiently for her to talk. Along with her husband, Terry, he had been one of the young officers she had worked with when she first joined the police force. Not long after they met she and Paul had had a brief but very passionate affair. It might have led to other things, except that he was newly married to a woman with whom he wasn't truly in love. Not long after, Alison fell into a relationship with Terry, and six months later they were married. He had definitely been second choice, she admitted, a situation made even more uncomfortable by the fact that he and Paul had remained friends. But time and parenthood gradually healed the wounds. Paul transferred to the Met and eventually lost touch. Alison never forgot him, but his memory dimmed and life moved on.

She had heard nothing from him in fifteen years, until quite unexpectedly she received an email, then a phone call – the one that Jenny had picked up. Already divorced for five years, he had learned about Alison and Terry's split through a mutual friend. He wanted to see her again, but so did her husband. After nearly three decades of marriage, she had found herself right back where she started.

'What does he want from you?' Jenny asked.

'To pick up where we left off,' Alison said. 'I could feel it the moment he started talking – all the old feelings came flooding back.'

'So—?'

'Terry . . . He'd never get over it. He still doesn't know what happened between us.'

'He left you for some woman in Spain. I think he's forfeited the right to feel jealous, don't you?'

'That's not how feelings work though, is it? I knew it wasn't serious between them. This is completely different . . . I'm not sure he could take it.'

Jenny said, 'Would you say your marriage was happy? Were you in love with Terry?'

'I was always very fond of him.'

'Is that enough?'

Alison buried her face in her hands.

Jenny said, 'Sometimes it's easier to avoid your one chance of happiness than to seize it. Believe me, I should know.'

Alison's confusion seemed to add to Jenny's own. Nothing seemed simple or straightforward. She was in a world of false perspectives and crooked angles. Dr Kerr's lab results confirmed that Brogan had been exposed to a brief burst of intense heat. There was evidence of singeing to his hair and beard on the left side of his face and head, and microscopic examination of exposed areas of skin showed evidence of flash burns, also exclusively on the left side. It gave some credence to Mrs Patterson's wild theories about him launching missiles from his yacht, but a phone call to Forenox swiftly established that the rocket propellant used in missiles was of an entirely different composition to plastic explosive.

Confronted by the bewildering array of disjointed and implausible evidence mounting on her desk, Jenny had to admit that she was dealing with a conspiracy theorist's dream, and the weaker part of her wanted to be seduced. She reminded herself that nearly all such theories were merely an emotional avoidance mechanism. Anything was easier to believe than that your innocent loved one had been singled out for destruction by an arbitrary and unforgiving universe.

And it wasn't just Mrs Patterson who had been infected with improbable ideas. It seemed increasingly likely to Jenny that, having felt unloved and betrayed by men, Nuala Casey had transferred her sense of injustice to the impersonal forces upon which she relied to keep the planes she flew in the sky. Her meticulous files stood as a testament to a mounting paranoia that bordered on an obsession.

Surrounded by madness, Jenny craved a dose of cold, hard reality. It came just as she was about to call Sir Oliver Prentice to reassure him that her inquiry would be concluded by the end of the week.

The call was from Michael. He was at Bristol airport. 'I just saw the CVR transcript. One of the pilots here managed to download a copy.'

'I've read it.'

'You know those things are worse than useless.'

Jenny let out a silent sigh. Not him, too.

'You can't tell a thing without knowing what the pilots were seeing on their instruments. You've got to re-create the precise conditions. Are you interested?'

'In what, exactly?'

'I just spoke to a man called Glen Francis. Nuala was his first officer when she started on the Airbus. These days he works for a training company based outside Gatwick. They've got an A380 simulator. He's prepared to re-create the flight for me. I thought you might want to come along.'

'Michael, I'm up to my eyes.'

'This evening. He can see us at eight. I can fly you down.'

'In the dark? No thanks. I think I'll drive.'

FOURTEEN

IT WAS OFFICIAL. Jenny had a gun to her head. Sir Oliver Prentice had made it plain that unless she recommenced her inquest by the end of the week, steps would be taken to abort it. The accumulating lists of grievances filed by the various lawyers were in danger of leading to the unavoidable conclusion that she was proving herself unfit. What he had really been fishing for by issuing such blatant threats was an explanation of the evidence which had caused her to suspend proceedings, but Jenny had blustered, claiming the delay was purely due to the forensic lab examining the lifejacket. He had remained unpersuaded. The inquest was too important to be mishandled he told her; either proceedings were to resume first thing on Friday morning or she would be relieved of her responsibilities.

It left thirty-six hours for her to keep looking. But for what? Like the pilots of Flight 189 she was flying blind.

It was some time past eight o'clock when she found Michael waiting outside the entrance to the industrial unit set among the cargo depots and cheap hotels in the netherworld between Gatwick airport and the Sussex countryside. He looked fresh, relaxed and more than a little smug after his solo night-flight from Bristol.

'How was the traffic?' he asked.

'Safely on the ground,' Jenny said.

'You haven't missed anything – Glen's been setting up. He managed to extract a copy of 189's flight plan from Sky Route. Pilots like to re-enact the events leading up to real-life disasters when they check in for their six-monthlies. Apparently you can't call yourself an Airbus pilot these days unless you've successfully landed on the Hudson.'

The reference, which a week previously Jenny would not have understood, was to United Airlines Flight 1549. The Airbus 320-214 lost all engine power shortly after take-off from New York La Guardia when it struck a flock of migrating geese. The pilot, fifty-seven-year-old Chesley 'Sully' Sullenberger, managed to glide the stricken plane to a safe landing on the Hudson River. Many experts thought that this miraculous feat – the only occasion on which a fully laden passenger jet had ever successfully ditched on water – was in no small part due to the contribution made by the Airbus's flight computers, which, powered by the aircraft's back-up generator, continued to augment the pilot's input all the way down. No lives were lost. In fact, there were barely any injuries. In aviation circles and far beyond, Sullenberger had become a legend.

Glen Francis came to meet them in the deserted reception area. A tall, imposing man in late middle age, he had the calm, unflappable demeanour one expected in a commercial pilot.

'Pleased to meet you, Mrs Cooper. Michael tells me you're particularly interested in how 189 landed.'

She saw the two men exchange a glance and played along. 'Yes. My inquest concerns a man whose yacht appears to have been struck by one of its engines.'

'I'm not sure how much I can help you, but I can't see that it'll do any harm.' He swiped his security tag across a reader and led them inside. 'Now I've got the route programmed in, every 380 pilot who comes through here will have to fly it. That's how we learn best – by our mistakes.'

They passed through a short corridor that opened into a vast, barn-like space lit by dim fluorescent light. Two simulators were mounted fifteen feet above the ground on telescopic hydraulic legs. From the outside they closely resembled the rides erected in museums and town squares at holiday times.

Glen led the way up the metal staircase to the gantry via which the simulators were accessed. He explained that for a commercial airline or a pilot paying his own way one hour of simulator time would cost over six hundred pounds. Each was loaded with genuine A380 avionics and handled exactly like the real aircraft. Both were certified by the Civil Aviation Authority to Level D, meaning they were so realistic that they could be used for zero-flight-time training. In theory, a pilot already qualified to fly other aircraft could embark on his first commercial flight in an A380 having learned only in this facility – although it wasn't something Glen would personally recommend.

Jenny and Michael followed Glen through the doors of the larger of the two sims into an exact replica of the 380's cockpit. Here the resemblance to a fairground ride ended. Every detail was exactly reproduced, Glen explained, even down to cup holders.

'Who's coming to sit up front with me?' he asked.

'That had better be you,' Michael said, and motioned Jenny forward.

She buckled into the right hand of the two pilots' seats. Glen sat to her left; Michael clipped into the observation seat behind them.

'A quick tour,' Glen said. 'Overhead are the control switches for engines, cabin pressure, electrical and fuel systems. In front of us we have identical sets of controls and three identical screens. Moving from the outside towards the centre, the first is the onboard information terminal. We use it to access a vast technical operating manual if you like, and also to communicate with the airline. Right in front of us is the primary flight display with the artificial horizon, airspeed, altitude and flight mode, and closest to the centre the navigation display. Bang in the middle is the engine or warning display – it tells us what's going on with all four engines at any given moment. That leaves the three screens between us on the lower console. The centre one we share: it's the system display. Using the buttons down here beneath the thrust levers, we can access the electronic centralized aircraft monitoring system and call up a schematic of any of the aircraft's systems to see how they're functioning. Either side, we each have our own multi-function display. These are our interfaces with all the aircraft's on-board computers. We each interact with them using our own keypad and tracker-ball mouse.

'If it looks complicated, that's because it is. We're not just flying the craft, we're monitoring every system and making adjustments where necessary. Right in the middle of the central console we have the four thrust levers. Each controls one of the engines. The red button on the outside disengages autothrust and hands us back manual control. You'll see they have four settings or detents. Fully forward is take-off go-around, giving you maximum thrust; one click behind is flexible maximum continuous thrust, a setting used in take-off; behind that is "climb", which is also the switch for autothrust. Autothrust is the mode in which you'll spend 90 per cent of the flight, the computers taking care of everything. And right at the bottom is zero, for minimum idle. It may be a little hard to get your head around, but the basic point is that even when you're taking off and landing one of these things it's the computers, not you, determining the level of thrust.'

'There's no manual control?' Jenny asked.

'Only if you disengage autothrust, and then only within certain parameters – the computers shouldn't let you stall by going too fast or too slowly. They know exactly how much power is needed to maintain a constant speed, and they're extremely good at it.' He pointed into the footwell. 'Down here you've got the rudder pedals, and to my left and your right we each have a joystick. This is how we control our attitude in the air, except that on this aircraft we have six computers monitoring every flying surface and making adjustments as we go. In normal flight this stick only allows us a safe degree of movement – I couldn't pitch the nose too far up or too far down even if I wanted to. The whole point of Airbus technology is that pilots are fallible. The computers don't miss things or take risks.' He smiled, realizing that Jenny was barely keeping up. 'I'd told my boss we'd be out of here by nine. We'd better get going.'

Glen flicked some switches and the windshield, which until now had been a blank screen, flickered into life. They were looking out at the Heathrow runway.

'I took the liberty of taxiing this far,' Glen said. 'No point simulating the take-off queue.' He pointed to his multi-function display. 'You'll see the waypoints already programmed in all the way to New York. These radio beacons take us up to the Bristol Channel.'

Jenny looked at the list of odd-sounding names – VAPID, NORRY, INLAK.

'All right, we're cleared for take-off.'

Glen pushed the thrust levers forward to the take-off-go-around detent and Jenny heard the sound of roaring engines as they started to pick up speed along the runway. The sensation was uncanny: the cockpit vibrated just as a real one would; the simulator mimicked every bump in the tarmac. Jenny instinctively shrank back into her seat.

'Relax,' Michael said, touching her shoulder. 'It's only pretend.'

Glen eased back on the joystick and they were airborne. 'Here we go . . . and gear up. That's the first officer's job.' He pointed to the lever next to Jenny's seat. She pulled it towards her and heard the familiar whine of the landing-gear servos followed by a thump as virtual doors closed over them.

The aircraft rolled gently to the left and Jenny found herself looking through the side window at the M4 motorway heading west. There even appeared to be traffic moving along the carriageway. But within moments wisps of cloud streaked past the windshield and they were bumping through mild turbulence.

'We can mimic the weather conditions, but not replicate them exactly of course,' Glen said. 'All right, we're at 1,500 feet. I'm shifting the thrust levers back into climb mode with the autothrust engaged. Now I'm engaging autopilot one. It's going to take us all the way up to 31,000, then it'll level off until we're over the Irish Sea, when we'd climb up to a cruise altitude of 39,000. In theory, this will take us all the way to our destination without me touching the controls.'

'We're sure Dan Murray engaged the autopilot?'

'I can't conceive of any reason why he wouldn't have.'

'How did you rate him?'

'Very highly. Some pilots fit together with the Airbus naturally, others want to be the Red Baron and no amount of training will shake them out of it it. Dan Murray was one of the easiest students I've taught; Ed Stevens, too.'

'And Nuala Casey?'

'She was good. A little too much imagination for my taste, but that's a personal opinion.'

'What do you mean by imagination?'

'A pilot should think ahead, but only within reason. It's

possible to spend so much time thinking about what might happen that you miss what's going on in front of you. That was my only concern. But she wasn't the one flying 189, was she?'

'No.'

There was not much to see apart from one dense bank of cloud after another rushing up to meet them. There was neither ground beneath them, nor sky above. The only indication that they were flying level were the artificial horizons on the two primary flight displays. Even to Jenny's untrained eye, they looked vulnerable compared with the analogue instruments and dials in Michael's little Cessna.

'What happens if these instruments go down?' Jenny asked.

'The idea is they don't,' Glen said. 'With multiple computers and generators there's no reason for them to fail short of a bomb going off.'

'Are you sure you'd know about it, if it did?'

'The avionics bays sit right beneath these seats,' Glen said. 'All that separates us from them is a floor a few inches thick. If the hull was breached, I don't think we'd last very long, not at 31,000 feet.'

Jenny put Mrs Patterson's crazy speculation out of her mind. She wanted to hear the rational explanation.

The climb from 1,500 to 14,000 and through on up towards 30,000 feet was, apart from the odd jolt of turbulence, largely uneventful. Glen explained that the aircraft was more than capable of coping with all but the most extreme of thunderstorms. For the most part, lightning was discharged harmlessly along the hull. The only real threat was from the intense heat in the fraction of a second that it struck, but this wasn't sustained enough to melt the composite hull. The avionics themselves were fully insulated and tested to withstand electro-magnetic discharges way in excess of anything a lightning strike would generate.

'You seem to have convinced yourself lightning wasn't the reason,' Michael said.

'We don't know everything about lightning,' Glen replied. 'But we do know how to protect aircraft from it, and we also know that the conditions that morning were nothing like the tropical storms these things are built to withstand. If you want my honest opinion, I think it was more likely to have been zapped by a UFO.

'One to go,' he went on. 'That means we've 1,000 feet to level off.'

Jenny heard the engines slowly wind down as they neared the top of their climb. They were still encountering angry-looking clouds.

'Don't we get above the weather at this height?' Jenny asked.

'Perhaps if we were to climb another 5,000 feet,' Glen said. 'But you can get cloud and storms at 40,000. OK, look at your primary flight display.' He pointed to his own. 'We're at 31,000 feet, autopilot one is engaged, the thrust levers are in the climb detent and altitude cruise mode. Look across to your navigation screen and you'll see true airspeed is 479 knots, exactly as Stevens called it on the cockpit voice recording. I've no reason to doubt this isn't what they were seeing. But fifty seconds later they had a speed warning, and Stevens called out *nose down*, meaning they needed to lower the nose to avoid a stall. I don't know exactly how Murray responded, but the next thing we know there was a stall warning and we hear Stevens being thrown around the cockpit.'

Jenny found it more than a little unnerving to hear Glen talk so dispassionately about men he had known and trained, but sitting behind the controls, even though she had only the sketchiest understanding of them, she sensed the pilot's awesome responsibility, and appreciated how the mind would narrow its focus to the few significant instruments upon which so many lives depended.

Michael said, 'Either the airspeed indication or the speed warning was wrong. It can't have been both.'

'I agree,' Glen said. 'We've seen anomalies on the Airbus and we have protocols to deal with them, but if I'm honest a false speed alert isn't something I've come across. Normally I would say the pilot's first instinct would be to trust his instruments. If he's keeping level, not losing height and his airspeed indicator is telling him he's at 479 knots, there's no reason to push the nose down – it's simply a case of three lots of data versus one.'

Jenny sensed a 'but' coming.

'But since the Air France and Qantas incidents, I've noticed a tendency among some pilots to doubt what their instruments are telling them, especially in a stressful situation. And once the mind has disengaged from the protocols you're into the realm of emotional, irrational reactions. Instead of a man working *with* a machine, you're suddenly dealing with a man fighting one.' Glen started flicking switches.

'What we can definitely ascertain from the speed warning is that there was some sort of computer failure. From the cockpit voice recording we can tell that the aircraft switched from normal law to alternate law to direct law, giving the pilot mostly manual control of the flying surfaces. That could be caused by a generator problem or even a temporary computer fault. The proper reaction would have been to check the ECAM actions and to keep the plane straight and level while the first officer worked through them on the multi-function display. If all three primary flight computers fail, it's a case of managing the transition to the secondary ones.

'But let's imagine Dan Murray panicked. Let's say he wasn't content to work through the protocols and skipped to the assumption that this was an Air France type incident, that something was wrong with his airspeed indicator, and that the aircraft's computers were about to carry out a pitch-down of their own accord in order to avoid a stall. According to the CVR transcript he was in alternate, then direct law, so he more or less had full manual control of the aircraft. To a certain extent he could do things with it that the Airbus systems won't normally allow. Not trusting his instruments, he pulls up the nose even though his first officer was sticking closer to the protocols and suggesting nose down . . .'

Jenny and Michael were thrown back in their seats as the nose pitched violently upwards, the engines rising to a deafening roar.

'He thinks he's taken control,' Glen called out above the noise, 'except he could easily have flown straight out of the flight envelope. He's pulled up so hard the centre of lift has shifted below the centre of gravity, meaning the more thrust we put on, the more the laws of physics rock him back into a vertical position until we're virtually at ninety degrees to the ground—'

They were looking vertically upwards.

'Look at the airspeed – it's slowing right down to nothing. Ed Stevens has been thrown off his feet and knocked out cold, so it's just down to Dan Murray. He can't carry out complicated manoeuvres and reset the computers at the same time. It's simply not possible.'

Jenny could barely force open her eyes, let alone contemplate trying to operate the computer on her console.

'Here we go—'

Jenny experienced a brief sensation of weightlessness as the aircraft clawed emptily at the air before gravity started to suck it back towards earth. Artificial as it was, the sensation was every bit as dreadful as it had been in the Cessna. Her stomach rushed up towards her throat. Closing her eyes only made the nausea worse.

Glen wrestled with the joystick and pumped on the rudder pedals. 'In direct law I haven't got the plane's systems to help me; all that computing power is useless. It's just me trying to wrest control of the world's largest commercial airliner. Perfect for level flight, but an absolute pig in a stall . . .'

They jolted violently to the left as the aircraft tumbled over onto its right side. Glen fought simultaneously with the thrust levers and joystick, and seemed for a moment to regain control, only for the nose to dip violently and once again they were pinned to the back of their seats, scything vertically downwards through the clouds.

Glen pulled the joystick back as far as it would go, but the nose refused to lift.

'Dan did better fighting gravity than I did,' Glen said. 'We're not pulling out of this.'

Jenny watched the figures on the altimeter hurtle downwards . . . 15,000, 10,000, 5,000, 2,000.

'It's no good!' Glen said.

Jenny instinctively brought her hands over her face, bracing for impact, but as the altimeter slid past 1,000 and she caught a glimpse of the River Severn between the clouds, the lights went up, the screens clicked off, and the simulator slowly reorientated itself to the horizontal.

There was a moment of silence as all three of them seemed to turn their minds simultaneously to those who had experienced it for real.

'I'm afraid I didn't manage to pull off your landing,' Glen said. 'I'll hazard a guess and say that he must have had some power in the engines to get anything like level – I hear it landed belly down.'

'That's what the passenger injuries suggest.'

'We could try again. We've time.'

'It's all right,' Jenny said, unbuckling her seat belt. 'I think I've seen enough.'

Michael said, 'So your best guess is that Murray responded incorrectly to a computer or an electrical error?'

Glen said, 'On the voice recording you've got Stevens reacting to what sounds like a jolt of turbulence three minutes before the level-off. It could be that was a lightning strike. It's even possible that tripped something in the electrical system and caused a fault that triggered the speed warning. That, in my opinion, was the real bit of bad luck. A false speed warning would have brought all the Air France and Qantas incidents flooding back. But the fact is the 380 has state-of-the-art pitot tubes. Post-Air France, the Airbus has probably got the most reliable airspeed indicators in the world.'

'A mismatch between man and machine,' Jenny said. 'A machine copes with crisis through brutal logic; the human mind reverts to intuition.'

'I couldn't have put it better,' Glen said.

'Which is what you meant by Nuala having too much imagination. She wasn't robotic enough to work hand in glove with the computers.'

Glen glanced at Michael. 'If the pilot of a modern passenger plane isn't prepared to trust his equipment absolutely, he's no business strapping into the cockpit. I'm not saying Dan Murray would definitely have landed that craft if he'd stuck to the protocols, but he would have stood a much better chance. And so would all the people in the back. The Airbus doesn't just prevent crises, it knows how to deal with them – and in my long experience, better than most pilots do.'

'You seem disappointed,' Jenny said, as she and Michael walked out of the building into the cold, damp night.

He shrugged. 'Maybe I'm biased – one pilot not wanting to believe another would screw up like that.'

'What about Glen – are you sure he doesn't have an agenda?'

Michael shook his head. 'You won't find a straighter guy in the business.'

Jenny was still struggling to fit what she had just experienced together with all the many questions in her mind which still remained unanswered. 'Say it was pilot error, we still don't know what Nuala was doing on the flight, or why Brogan had traces of plastic explosive on his lifejacket.'

'It really doesn't matter, does it? They're all dead.' He turned away and started off across the car park towards the roadway.

'Michael?'

He kept on walking.

'Michael, please—' She was confused. She hadn't expected him to react emotionally.

As she started after him, her phone rang. It was a caller she couldn't ignore – Simon Moreton.

'Hello, Simon.'

'Ah, Jenny – good news all round, I hear?'

'Really?'

'You're being sensible and Sir James Kendall is addressing the world's press at the D-Mort in the morning. I was thinking of making the trip down. I'm so grand these days, they'll even give me a car.'

'There are nicer places for a day out.'

'Why don't we go together? Spot of lunch afterwards? It's about time we caught up.'

Moreton always couched his invitations as if they were pleasant social engagements, but Jenny had learned that was just the way the game was played. The only reason he left London was to stamp his authority on the rebellious provinces, and if he could manage some gentle flirting at the same time, so much the better.

'Why not?' Jenny said.

'Excellent. I'll pick you up from your office at ten.'

As she put away her phone, Jenny scanned the darkness for Michael, but he had disappeared through the gates and away down the road. She jumped into her Land Rover and drove in the direction she thought he had gone. There was no sign of him on the deserted pavements. He seemed determined not to be found.

As she turned round and began the long journey home, she pictured him flying through the night back to Bristol, alone with his ghosts. And for a fleeting moment she wished she were with him.

FIFTEEN

SIMON MORETON WAS ON SPARKLING FORM. Revelling in his elevation to the rank of Director at the Ministry of Justice, he now referred to himself as a 'mandarin'. Jenny was supposed to be impressed, but she had never been one to admire a man for his status. Her ex-husband was an eminent heart surgeon, but in her experience the higher up the greasy pole he climbed, the more self-important and objectionable he had become. Her former lover, Steve, had been a failed architectural student scratching a living from the land when they had first met, and his complete disinterest in all the things by which most men marked their achievements had been one of the qualities that attracted her most.

As Moreton whisked her through the north Somerset countryside in the back seat of a sleek government Jaguar, she was expected to play the willing consort, and she dutifully obliged.

Whatever he had come to say, he was leaving it until later. For the time being it was all gossip from the corridors of power intended to make him seem important and to seduce Jenny into feeling part of the in-crowd. The latest excitement centred on a senior High Court judge (no names, only subtle hints at his identity) who, it turned out, had been entertaining a young man at his official lodgings at the public expense. It was sufficient grounds to demand his resignation, only he had intimated to the Lord Chief Justice that were he to be pushed out he would make sure that the dirty linen of an unspecified number of his colleagues would also be washed in public. Everyone in the Ministry was on tenterhooks, waiting to see who would blink first.

'That's the problem with today's world,' Moreton mused, 'no sense of honour.'

'I hope you're not trying to make me go quietly, Simon,' Jenny joked.

'Good gracious, no – I'm your number one fan. Think how complacent I'd become without you to keep me on my toes.'

The government car swept unhindered through the roadblock outside the D-Mort and deposited them at the entrance to a covered walkway leading directly to the marquee, which the previous week had served as the reception centre for the relatives of the dead. Once inside, they were greeted by a young lance corporal from the Welsh Guards who directed them to the seats in front of the dais from where Sir James would be making his announcement. In the large open space behind the few rows of chairs, the world's press and broadcast media were jockeying for position. Photographers and news cameramen perched on stepladders, TV and radio reporters rehearsed their intros in a dozen different languages, and the old-fashioned newspaper men gathered in huddles trading rumours.

'I can't say I've ever been to one of these before,' Moreton said excitedly.

'What about the families?' Jenny asked. 'Are they allowed to attend?'

'As far as I know this is strictly for the media and the likes of us. It's not in anyone's interests to have a lot of grieving relatives exploited for the cameras.'

'Or asking awkward questions.'

'Jenny, Jenny, you really are a cynic.' He found their reserved seats at the centre of the front row. 'Best in the house – you can't say I don't look after you. All I ask in return is that you give me a brief tour of the campus afterwards. Heaven forbid we'll ever need to build another, but you never know.'

'My pleasure,' Jenny said drily.

As the final minutes to midday ticked by, she was struck by a mounting sense of unreality. The anticipation among the waiting crowd was like that of an expectant theatre audience. The tragedy of the previous week had given way to the drama of the unfolding story. The relentless twenty-four-hour news schedule demanded another segment of the narrative, and Sir James Kendall and his colleagues knew that if they didn't provide one someone else would. If they were to stay in charge of events, they had to lead the media.

Sir James mounted the platform with a man whom he introduced as Edward Marsham of the Air Accident Investigation Branch. Jenny had heard Marsham on the radio and had pictured a more imposing figure than the man who hovered at Kendall's side. The primary purpose of the news conference was, Kendall explained, for Marsham to outline initial findings into the cause of the accident. Then Kendall would give a brief update on the status of the bodies held in the D-Mort.

Uncomfortable in the glare of the spotlight, Marsham's forehead gleamed with perspiration as he stepped up to the microphone. Relying heavily on his notes, he introduced an animated re-creation of the last minutes of the flight. Displayed on a pair of large, flat-panel screens mounted either side of the dais, it showed the ill-fated 380 climbing upwards towards the level-off height of 31,000 feet.

'Initial weather data from the Met Office suggested that

there were no storms active in the flight's path,' Marsham explained. 'However, data has now been gathered which establishes beyond doubt that between fifteen and eighteen minutes into the journey, the aircraft passed through a dense bank of cumulonimbus, responsible, we believe, for the turbulence which caused First Officer Stevens to remark at 09.16.07 on the cockpit voice recording that it was "bumpy". He also appears to query whether passenger seat belts might be appropriate, but Captain Murray seems to disregard the suggestion. We also know that several seconds after this, at approximately 09.16.24, the aircraft stopped transmitting flight data via ACARS.

'It's a well-documented fact that the action of an aircraft passing through clouds containing positively charged ions can actually provoke a discharge of lightning. It is highly probable that this is what occurred here. The American FAA estimate that each commercial airliner is on average struck by lightning once a year. Aircraft hulls are so designed that the lightning is simply conducted along the outside and back into the air. The electrical systems on the A380 are further shielded with surge and grounding protectors. In nearly all cases lightning has no discernible effect on the aircraft or its systems, except perhaps for a small flickering of lights or instruments lasting less than a second. Indeed, in comprehensive tests carried out by NASA in the early 1980s, aircraft were deliberately flown into storms on 1,400 separate missions. They were struck by lightning a total of 700 times with no ill effect.

'That said, while most lightning carries a negative charge to the ground, the rarer form of positive lightning – which, as its name suggests, carries a positive charge to the ground – is characteristically up to ten times more powerful than its negative counterpart. Positive lightning can travel distances of up to ten miles, and may be triggered by man-made objects in the atmosphere such as rockets or aircraft. While there has only been one aircraft lost to positive lightning in the last forty years, it is conceivable that a bolt of a billion volts or so may have caused a temporary disturbance in some of the aircraft's electrical systems, including flight computers. While it's too early to say exactly what effect that might have had, we are increasingly certain that this was the inciting cause for the sequence of events that followed.'

The image on the screen showed a lightning bolt striking the aircraft on the lower side of the nose beneath the cockpit. Marsham tapped some keys on the computer and switched the image on the screens to a still taken of the aircraft's nose on the quayside at Avonmouth.

'Look carefully on the underside of the nose directly beneath the cockpit windows. You will see a distinct black discoloration, a streak, if you will, angled upwards from right to left. We believe this was caused by the heat of the lightning.'

He clicked to another image, which showed a closer view of what resembled a scorch mark on the white hull.

'There is the point of impact, on the hull directly outside the avionics bay. It caused no physical damage to the structure of the aircraft, but may – and I stress *may* – have caused an electrical failure of some sort. What we now know from the cockpit voice recording is that a speed warning was issued at 09.20.41 at a time when data from air traffic control suggests that the aircraft was travelling at a cruising speed of 479 knots. The speed warning was repeated several seconds later.' He paused, and for the first time in his presentation looked up from his notes. 'The speed warnings were clearly anomalous.'

The marquee was momentarily lit up by a barrage of camera flashes capturing the moment of admission. The reporters had their story: the world's largest airliner humbled by the forces of nature.

The image on the screen flicked back to the animation of the aircraft in flight. In a deadpan voice, Marsham explained the final movements of the aircraft through the air as it pitched upwards, then began its erratic, see-sawing descent. The journalists fell silent as professional objectivity was temporarily replaced by raw, human horror at what nearly six hundred passengers on board must have endured throughout those six tortuous minutes.

The precise sequence of stalls was a matter of educated guesswork based on the air traffic control data, Marsham emphasized, but what was known from the condition of the wreckage was that the aircraft struck the water belly first, snapping cleanly in two places due to the force of impact combined with the stresses it had endured in the air. The animation on the screen showed the final break-up: the hull hit the water tail-first and broke into three pieces; the fore section tipped forwards and torpedoed down to the seabed, where it lodged in the silt; the mid- and tail sections flooded with water in a matter of seconds and sank.

'Again, this remains a matter of speculation, but we are of the opinion that, given perhaps only a few hundred feet more, the aircraft might have slowed sufficiently to have avoided break-up on impact. We are of the view that Captain Murray had succeeded in gaining at least partial control. At this early stage it remains impossible to say what precise effect pilot actions had on the final outcome of the flight, but we are as certain as we can be that neither Captain Murray nor First Officer Stevens was responsible for initiating the fatal chain of events.'

Jenny wondered why Marsham hadn't seized on the conclusion that Glen Francis had reached in the simulator – that

Murray had reacted out of fear and contrary to correct protocols, in effect causing the sequence of stalls – but then realized that his preliminary findings had left the door open just enough to allow that possibility through at a later date. The lightning theory was convincing enough for now. The news media would be kept amused for the next few days trawling universities for experts on freak weather to fill their schedules. The blame could yet be switched to Murray if circumstances demanded.

Sir James Kendall stepped forward to chair the brief question-and-answer session that followed. For the most part, the press made only predictable enquiries. Could Marsham be certain a bomb hadn't been detonated inside the plane? Had the possibility of hijack been ruled out? Could he discount the rumour that an RAF jet had been scrambled to shoot the aircraft out of the sky when communications with the ground failed? All of these Marsham dealt with easily. It was only when discussing Captain Murray that he displayed signs of anxiety.

'Is it true that Captain Murray was called in as a last-minute replacement for the pilot scheduled to fly the plane?' a journalist from the Spanish newspaper *El País* enquired.

'Yes, I understand Captain Murray took the place of Captain Finlay, who was unable to fly through illness,' Marsham said, 'but there are often changes to flight crew late in the day, especially in the wintertime, when pilots come down with colds and flu like the rest of us.'

The journalist persisted. 'Is it true that Murray hadn't taken leave for over seven months?'

'I must confess I haven't examined his flying records in detail.'

Sir James Kendall pointed to a young female reporter from CNN. If he had hoped she would prove more sympathetic, he was to be disappointed.

'Why didn't Captain Murray switch on the seat-belt signs when First Officer Stevens suggested it? It leaves the impression that he wasn't overly concerned with the safety of his passengers.'

'Captains make these judgements every day,' Marsham stalled. 'I'm sure he would have done nothing to jeopardize the safety of those on board.'

The young woman shot back. 'You had a captain who was clearly overworked, and an under-slept first officer who was planning a wild night out in New York. Is this responsible behaviour for men with hundreds of lives in their hands?'

'We will of course be checking that flight crew were abiding by all the appropriate regulations.' Marsham's voice held steady, although it was clear from the sweat now trickling from his temples that he had been caught off his guard.

'This is all about money, isn't it?' the reporter countered. 'When you have two tired men flying six hundred passengers you know too many corners are being cut. Does Ransome Airways skimp on its maintenance engineers too?'

Sir James Kendall eased Marsham aside. 'The purpose of this news conference is to share with you what we already know, not to speculate on things about which we have incomplete knowledge. The practices of the airline involved will of course be examined closely. We've time for one final question. The man in the brown jacket—'

A reporter with a pronounced Chinese accent spoke up, announcing that he was from Taiwan Television news. 'Can you please tell us, are you investigating the theory that this aircraft was targeted because it was carrying several important and noteworthy passengers?'

Sir James Kendall looked uncomfortable. 'The evidence all points to this aircraft having been brought down by a freak natural event, and every transatlantic flight invariably carries important and noteworthy people.'

'So you have closed your mind to this possibility?'

'My task as coroner is to deal with the evidence as it presents itself, not to indulge in theorizing. Thank you, everybody.'

Kendall gathered his papers and, ignoring the clamour to answer further questions, ushered Marsham from the platform.

'There's always one, isn't there?' Moreton said. 'Why can't people be content to believe that there's such a thing as an accident?'

'Perhaps if they trusted the messenger they would.'

'Kendall's as straight as they come,' Moreton protested.

'I'm sure he is.' Jenny changed the subject. 'Well, if you're still feeling strong enough, I'll give you a tour of the sights, shall I?'

'Excellent.' He glanced beyond her to one of the dignitaries sitting further along the front row. 'I'll catch up with you outside in just a moment. It's the Permanent Secretary from the Department for Transport – I ought to say hello.'

'No problem.'

Leaving Moreton to grease the wheels of government, Jenny seized the chance to disappear into the crowd of departing journalists and catch up with the Taiwanese reporter whose question had prompted Kendall to bring proceedings to a halt. Dodging between news crews busy sending live pictures out across the world, she collared him just inside the entrance to the marquee.

'Excuse me,' she said, tapping his shoulder.

He turned, a little startled by her unannounced approach. 'Yes?'

Her eyes dipped to the press pass all journalists were

obliged to wear around their necks and she saw that his name was Wen Chen.

'Jenny Cooper, Severn District Coroner.' She fished into her jacket pocket and brought out a business card. 'I'm inquiring into the death of the man who was sailing a yacht—'

'I know about your investigation, Mrs Cooper.'

'Oh –'

'I've spoken to Mrs Patterson, or rather she has spoken to me.'

'I see.' She glanced back through the crowd and saw that Moreton was deep in conversation with his colleague. 'Would you have a moment, Mr Chen?'

His eyes flitted left and right and he motioned towards the exit.

They stepped out of the marquee and sheltered from the steady drizzle under the canvas awning.

'What can I do for you, Mrs Cooper?' Chen asked cagily.

'I was interested in your question. I know about Jimmy Han, but you seemed to imply there were other passengers on board with significant enemies.'

'Yes—'

'I'd be interested to know who you think they are.'

Chen looked at her with an expression she couldn't fathom. 'Talk to Mrs Patterson.'

'With all due respect to Mrs Patterson, I'm not sure—'

'She has all the information.' Chen waited for a group of fellow reporters to pass out of earshot. His voice dropped to a whisper. 'I've got kids, responsibilities – you understand?'

Jenny struggled to reconcile the timid man in front of her with the aggressive journalist she had witnessed only a few moments before. 'Has something happened since you asked those questions, Mr Chen?'

'Speak to Mrs Patterson.' He handed back her business card. 'Good luck.' He turned and walked hurriedly away.

The strange shift in Chen's demeanour continued to play on Jenny's mind as she led Moreton on a tour of the D-Mort. She kept up a steady flow of chatter even as they were touring the mortuary and examining the banks of refrigerators which would continue to hold the bodies of the victims in a state of limbo for months to come, but her thoughts were preoccupied with what had caused the journalist to clam up.

In the company of Simon Moreton it was possible to believe that everyone in authority was as fair and benevolent as he appeared to be. She wanted to believe Marsham and Kendall's version of events – nothing was more appealing than a neat, logical explanation leaving no one to blame – but the inner voice she had tried so hard to silence was crying out to her that she couldn't.

'Are you all right, Jenny – too much for you?'

'Sorry, I was miles away.'

'I could tell. It doesn't say much for my conversation.'

They were walking back along the covered walkway from the mortuary, passing a stack of portable offices signed Evidence and Effects.

'I was thinking about the little girl on board – Amy Patterson.'

'What about her?'

'The fact that she so nearly survived . . . Did you know she called her father on the way down? He told her to put on a lifejacket. According to the pathologists, she was the only one in the whole craft to have been wearing one.'

Moreton paled. 'Oh? Did she say anything that might be of use to us?'

'Us?'

'To the inquiry, I mean,' he added hurriedly.

'There was no explosion, no bang.'

'Well, we know it wasn't a bomb.' He seemed relieved.

'You'd think a billion-volt bolt of lightning would be every bit as loud as a bomb, though, wouldn't you?'

'I've no idea,' Moreton said.

'No,' Jenny lied. 'Nor do I.'

Lunch was aboard the Glassboat restaurant in Bristol docks. Moreton was a weekend sailor and had a fondness for dining on boats, he explained. On a wet Thursday afternoon in January customers were thin on the ground; they had nearly one half of the restaurant to themselves and an unobstructed view through picture windows. Lights twinkled in the trees along the quayside and reflected off the water, giving the dark afternoon a cosy, almost magical feel.

Jenny surrendered to Moreton's cajoling and joined him in a glass of wildly expensive Rioja Gran Reserva. She couldn't deny that he had exquisite taste in wine and after a few mouthfuls amusing and indiscreet conversation to match it. She counted him saying, 'I really shouldn't tell you this . . .' at least half a dozen times, but each time he did.

He waited until their plates were cleared and coffee ordered before reluctantly switching to the subject that he had travelled from London to discuss.

'I can assure my superiors that you're reconvening tomorrow, can I?'

'That's the plan,' Jenny said, now beginning to wish she hadn't weakened into accepting a refill.

'And would it be too much to expect a speedy and uncontroversial conclusion?'

Jenny smiled. 'I'm afraid I can't second-guess my jury, Simon. We'll just have to wait and see.'

He toyed with the stem of his glass, giving her an enigmatic look that she felt she was meant to understand.

'You might as well get it over with. You didn't prise yourself out of Whitehall just for lunch.'

'Lunch with you is always worth travelling for, Jenny, but I must confess there is one issue I feel obliged to raise. I suppose you could call it a matter of national security.'

'Go on.'

'It's come to my attention that a lifejacket was recovered believed to have belonged to Mr Brogan.'

'Yes—?'

'And that the lab testing it detected traces of plastic explosive.'

Jenny nearly choked on her wine. 'Who told you that?'

'Let's just say there are certain understandings between the security services and forensic laboratories such as Forenox.'

'They handed over my evidence? They had no right—'

'They had no choice, Jenny. It was requested from them. I'm sorry, but some things are just too important—'

'To be left in the hands of a provincial coroner?'

'No—'

'Don't treat me like a fool, Simon. I should go to the press with this.'

'There'd be a D-Notice.'

'Then I'd go to the American papers, and the internet. You couldn't gag me if you wanted to.'

'Please don't overreact. It's simply a question of acting in the national interest. You said it yourself – it wasn't a bomb that brought 189 down. Brogan, however, appears to have had historic links to Irish paramilitaries. We know that bizarre coincidences happen, but we also know what the press do with them. The last thing we want is another Lockerbie, with conspiracy theorists polluting the public consciousness for the next thirty years.'

'What precisely are you asking me to do?'

'We know what brought down the plane and we know

that Brogan died of hypothermia. It doesn't take a genius to suppose that he might have detonated whatever illicit cargo he had on board to prevent detection, but your job isn't to rake over all that. It's a police matter. All the law asks of you is to determine the immediate cause of death.'

'You want me to suppress the evidence of the explosives.'

'It would be rather helpful.'

'And if I were to refuse?'

'We'll just have to manage the situation the best we can, but I can assure you, once that particular genie's out of the bottle, forces will be unleashed that none of us will be able to control. And, fairly or unfairly, it will be you who gets the blame.'

Jenny considered his words for a long moment. The fairy lights along the quayside shone like stars in a childhood dream. No, nothing seemed to fit together as it should. 'Could *you* be rather helpful and pour me the last of the wine,' she said.

Moreton looked at her uncertainly. 'Of course.'

He filled her glass beyond halfway with the last of the plum-red Rioja.

'Your very good health, Jenny.'

'And yours.' She picked it up in a trembling hand and threw the contents into his astonished face.

SIXTEEN

JENNY WALKED OUT OF THE RESTAURANT, leaving Moreton staring disbelievingly after her. To hell with him. Let
him do his worst. To think that he could ever have believed
that she would assist him in a sordid cover-up. She would
gladly have tipped the coffee over his lap too. He was a
worm; a worm crawling through the bodies of the dead.

She marched past the waiting Jaguar, ignoring the driver,
and walked the half-mile through the drizzle back to the
office, her elegant shoes squeezing her feet until they were
raw. But all she could feel was anger. Outrage. How *dare*
he.

She slammed through the front door at Jamaica Street and
resolved to get her inquest firmly back on track. She would
hear all the evidence, no matter how inconvenient or bizarre.

'Tell me everything's set up for tomorrow morning,' Jenny
barked, as she arrived in the office.

'Yes, Mrs Cooper,' Alison replied warily. 'Has something
happened?'

'Only Simon Moreton trying to pervert the course of
justice.' Jenny was in no mood to offer lengthy explanations.
'Is that box still there? We're meant to be running a public
service.'

'I'm dealing with it this afternoon, Mrs Cooper, I promise

you. I think I know who the woman in the photographs is now.'

Jenny sighed and made for her room.

'Actually, I've spent the last hour dealing with Mrs Patterson and her lawyers. They haven't left me alone,' Alison called after her.

'What do they want now?'

'What don't they want? They've got evidence they want to submit ahead of the inquest, inquiries they want you to pursue, and they want to know what was said at the press conference – the "secret bits" that didn't make the news.'

'What sort of evidence?' Jenny said.

'They won't discuss it over the phone. She's got it into her head that all her calls are being listened to. I think the poor woman's lost her grip, I really do.'

'I'll speak to Galbraith.'

'Oh, and the detective from Chepstow left a message asking for you to call when you got back.'

'He's probably been warned off as well.'

'I beg your pardon?'

'Nothing. Please deal with that bag, Alison. I don't know why, but it's really starting to bother me.'

She yanked open the heavy oak door to her room and banged it shut behind her.

The untended heap of papers on her desk would have to wait for the weekend. She had what was left of the afternoon to finalize her preparations for tomorrow. There were witnesses to contact and several formal statements still to be taken, not least from Ravi Achari and his team at Forenox.

She called Achari first, but reached a lab technician who couldn't locate him and promised her call would be returned shortly. It was the same story with DI Williams, except that the dopey-sounding sergeant said he was on a rest break. Down at the betting shop on the corner, Jenny guessed, or more likely watching the racing in the snug bar of the George with a beer in his hand. Nick Galbraith, however, answered his phone smartly.

'Mrs Cooper. Thank goodness.'

'My officer mentioned something about new evidence.'

'Yes. I don't suppose you'd be able to pop down to Mrs Patterson's hotel?'

'If you insist on meeting, I'd rather it was my office. I'm very busy this afternoon.'

'Of course, but . . .' He hesitated, as if embarrassed by what he was about to say. 'The thing is she's become rather suspicious.'

'You mean paranoid?'

'That would be an unkind way of putting it, but yes. She's had the hotel meeting room swept, you see. She considers it the only safe place.'

'And you expect me to play along with this?'

'I'm not the sort to believe in ghosts if you get my drift, but I have to admit, were this an inquiry into the supernatural, I would reluctantly be on my way to becoming a believer.'

'I'll be there in fifteen minutes. She can have half an hour more, but I'd prefer it if you did the talking.'

'I'll do my best.'

The mini function room on the second floor of the College Green Marriott had been converted into a full-scale office. There were phones, a photocopier, desk-top computer, printer and two carousels stacked with carefully labelled box files. A young woman sat at the head of the table next to Mrs Patterson, who introduced her as Alix, her PA, who would be keeping a shorthand note of the meeting.

Jenny fixed Galbraith with a look that demanded an on-the-record explanation for why she had been summoned to this less than conventional meeting.

'Thank you for accepting our request to receive additional evidence which may be of assistance to your inquest, Mrs Cooper,' he said formally, choosing each word with care. 'Mrs Patterson and I are most grateful that you agreed to meet here in the College Green Marriott in a conference room which Mrs Patterson is satisfied is free of covert surveillance devices.'

'I emphasize that I am here only to receive your evidence,' Jenny said, 'not to discuss the inquest into Mr Brogan's death.'

'Understood,' Galbraith said. He turned to Mrs Patterson, who wasn't enjoying her forced silence. 'Do remind me if I miss something out, Mrs Patterson. I would be grateful if you would direct any remarks to Mrs Cooper through me.'

She gave him a terse nod.

Galbraith reached for a small pile of loose papers and pushed them across to Jenny.

'I'm handing you a batch of email correspondence between my client and various members of the deceaseds' families. As you may know, the relatives have been corresponding with each other on a dedicated internet forum in which Mrs Patterson has taken a leading role. One issue of particular interest is the fact that more than twenty passengers on Flight 189 had initially been booked onto the flight that left twenty-fours earlier, on Saturday morning. They were each contacted by the airline and told their reservations were being transferred to Sunday's flight due to over-booking. Mrs Patterson's husband and daughter had both been booked onto the Saturday flight. His employers requested that he stay in London to attend to urgent business and he was forced to send Amy as an unaccompanied minor on the Sunday flight.'

Jenny flicked through the pile of emails in front of her as she listened and saw a number of identical messages sent from Ransome Airways' reservations department apologizing to passengers and offering them alternative seats on Flight 189.

'We accept this occasionally happens,' Galbraith continued, 'but a little research has revealed that it's far rarer these days than you might assume. Ransome Airways operates a system using dedicated software hosted on its own servers. In theory, tickets should not be sold for flights that are already full. What's more, a request for comments from frequent fliers on Ransome Airways elicited numerous responses from passengers who say they have never previously known their reservation to be transferred. Mrs Patterson has sought clarification from the airline, but so far they have refused to comment.'

Jenny said, 'This is all very interesting information, Mr Galbraith. I've no doubt it merits proper inquiry, but I don't see its relevance to my inquest into Mr Brogan's death.'

'If you'll hear me out, Mrs Cooper, you may conclude otherwise.'

Jenny glanced at her watch. The precious minutes before the end of office hours were ticking away fast.

'Mrs Patterson has also succeeded in contacting a number of people who were on board the Saturday flight. They were able to confirm that the plane wasn't in fact full, but contained a number of empty seats. Again, we have sought an explanation from the airline, but with no success.' He pushed another small stack of papers towards her. 'More significant perhaps are the identities of some of those whose reservations were moved onto Flight 189.'

Jenny held up her hand to bring proceedings to a halt and gestured to Alix to put down her pencil. 'Could I please ask you a question off the record, Mrs Patterson?'

'You can try,' she answered guardedly.

Alix's pencil hovered in mid-air as she looked from one woman to the other.

'All right,' Mrs Patterson said. She turned to Alix. 'Don't write anything down until I tell you.' She looked back at Jenny. 'Go ahead.'

'At the news conference this morning I spoke briefly to a journalist named Wen Chen. He was from Taiwan Television. He asked a question about "notable" passengers on the flight. It went pretty much unanswered. I caught up with him afterwards and he said that the two of you had been in contact.'

'He's been very helpful, quite possibly invaluable.'

'He seemed reluctant to talk to me.'

Mrs Patterson nodded, ruminating on a private thought. 'I'm surprised he was brave enough to ask questions at all. With six hundred lives taken, another wouldn't cost much.'

Jenny saw Galbraith's eyes moving apprehensively between them.

'Shall I continue?' he said. 'And it might be better for all concerned if we were on the record from now on.'

'Agreed,' Jenny said. 'Tell me what you've heard.'

Alix resumed her note-taking.

'Mrs Patterson's research amongst the relatives disclosed that among those whose seats were moved from Saturday to Sunday were two New York detectives – Lieutenants Arnold Berners and Leonard Halpern. Their wives say they were on a trip to the UK to liaise with anti-terrorist officers. Their inquiries related to suspected Islamist militants based in London. They were travelling under their own identities and their passports stated their occupation as police officers. A twenty-five-year-old passenger named Dr Ali Mathar, an academic from the School of Oriental and African Studies, was booked onto the Sunday flight all along, but a US sky marshal named Curtis Stevens was booked on at the last minute – his wife says she only got a call on Saturday evening from him with Sunday's ETA. This could be a pure coincidence, but Dr Mathar has published papers sympathetic to various anti-Western clerics. He's certainly someone whom the US law enforcement authorities would be expected to look at very closely.'

'I don't mean to interrupt,' Jenny said, 'but as far as I know, a lot of flights have marshals on board, and I don't believe there is any evidence of there having been a disturbance on the plane—'

'We appreciate that, Mrs Cooper,' Galbraith answered. 'The presence of those people on one aircraft can indeed be explained as coincidental, but we have to cover all possibilities. What's far more interesting is the presence of Mr Alan Towers.'

Galbraith handed her a brief biography which looked as if it had been downloaded from a company website.

'Aged fifty-five, Mr Towers is the founder and managing director of a Surrey-based defence contractor, Winchester Systems Ltd. He was booked onto the Saturday flight with an onward connection to Washington, but was bounced off it on the Friday. That's most unusual in first class.'

An alarm bell rang in Jenny's head. Nuala Casey had been going on to Washington.

'What was he doing in Washington?' Jenny asked.

'His wife can't tell us. He travelled all the time and she didn't keep track. His company is refusing to answer our inquiries. What we do know is that Winchester Systems are involved in the development of high-tech weaponry. Needless to say, their website is a little cagy, but all their staff seem to have backgrounds in either computing, aerospace or satellite technology. We appreciate that's not particularly remarkable, but there is an interesting coincidence. In business class was a twenty-eight-year-old physicist named Dr Ian Duffy. His seat had not been reallocated, but he did have an onward ticket to Washington on the same flight as Towers. Duffy was a leader in his field. His lab at Cambridge University is sponsored by a consortium of British defence contractors including Winchester Systems. We're trying to get a fix on his research, but so far we've established that he was involved with computers that work using pulses of light instead of electrical connections – this is really futuristic stuff, the sort of technology that if you were to have it first could make the interception of your data close to impossible.'

'Were they travelling together?'

'Not that Mrs Towers knew. Duffy was single and his parents are an ordinary middle-aged couple who are quite frankly baffled to have produced a leading physicist. They haven't a clue what he was doing. Their best guess is that he was attending a conference of some sort.'

'I have to add something here,' Mrs Patterson interjected. 'The company my husband works for leads the world in encryption software. Information is power. If you can keep it secret, it's even more potent. He and my daughter were moved onto the Sunday flight.'

Jenny felt herself begin to disengage. Another conspiracy theory was on the way.

'And if he and Duffy and Towers had all been killed, that would have been three men whose careers revolve around cyber security.'

'And where does Chen come into this?' Jenny asked.

'He was the one who told us about Dr Duffy. He had been looking for passengers with links to Jimmy Han. Apparently Han and Duffy sat on the same panel of experts at a symposium in Frankfurt last year.'

Jenny said, 'I'm grateful for what you have told me, but I

do feel that it's evidence that will be far more relevant to Sir James Kendall's inquest than to mine.'

'He won't listen to any of this,' Mrs Patterson said. 'You were at his news conference, you've heard the party line. As far as he's concerned it was lightning. Why would he trouble himself to dig any deeper than he has to?'

Jenny felt the urge to explain what to Mrs Patterson as a mathematician should have been blindingly obvious: that the class of people who regularly travelled the globe was a vanishingly small sliver of the population, and that among any group of five hundred of them there would be all manner of coincidental links and associations that could be moulded to fit any number of sinister theories. But that would have been callous. She reminded herself that Mrs Patterson was coping with the only tools she possessed. Other relatives would be numbing themselves with drugs or making pilgrimages to places they had once visited with their loved ones; she had set up an office and given herself an almighty problem to solve. What good would it do to tell her that the pain would slowly pass, and that what at this moment seemed like unanswerable logic would eventually resemble nothing more than wishful thinking? That was a journey she would have to take alone.

Jenny turned to Galbraith. 'I suggest you assemble what you have into a formal dossier. I'll happily accept it in evidence, but you appreciate my hands are partially tied.'

As Jenny left the room, Mrs Patterson called after her, 'The truth hurts, Mrs Cooper – why else would people lie?'

As the elevator doors closed shut behind her, Jenny felt the cold, familiar press of anxiety on her chest. The descent to the lobby felt like an eternity. She bore down against the feeling of rising dread, but quietly and stealthily it had already taken root and was tightening its grip. Her heart began to beat faster. Bursting out of the doors into the lobby, her head swam as she turned to the exit, her legs threatening to buckle beneath her. Changing course, she made her way unsteadily across the corridor and dropped into the closest armchair in the lounge. She forced herself to breathe slowly and deeply as the spasms of panic peaked, then slowly tailed off, leaving her feeling powerless and spent.

She longed to reach for a chemical crutch, but she had taken more than her permitted dose of beta blockers, and the tranquillizers which had so magically lifted her out of pain were no longer an option. According to Dr Allen, she was strong enough to cope with these episodes now that she could trace them back to their root. She would feel acute anxiety only when her rawest nerves were touched, he had assured her; when events tapped into the guilt that had lived with her from childhood. As the breath slowly returned to her lungs, she realized that it was Mrs Patterson's parting shot that had cut through her defences. She had managed to hold her nerve all throughout the long morning with Simon Moreton, his threats only strengthening her determination, but a few simple words from a grieving mother had felled her.

By accusing her of colluding in a lie, Mrs Patterson had unwittingly hit her where she was most vulnerable. It was the lying about her cousin Katy's death, even more than her hand in it, which had caused the poison to accumulate over three and half decades. Intimidated by her father, her enforced silence had hollowed her out until the fragile walls had collapsed in on themselves. It was as clear to her now as it was daunting: she couldn't look the other way. And if she did there would be only one outcome: her painstaking efforts to crawl back up to the light would end with a plunge back into the abyss.

It felt as if she had been dealt an impossible hand. So many dead, so many lives broken, and so many reasons why it wasn't her business to find the answers. Not for the first time in her short career as coroner, she felt unequal to the task that confronted her. She hauled herself to her feet and made her way to the exit, the papers Galbraith had given her weighing as heavily in her hands as lead. What should she do?

The beginnings of an answer came far sooner than she had expected. She was making her way gingerly down one side of the hotel's ornate double-sided front steps when she felt the vibration of her phone in her jacket pocket.

'Mrs Cooper?' a familiar Welsh voice said. 'Inspector Williams. Those helicopters you were asking about—'

SEVENTEEN

THE WITNESS'S NAME WAS LAWRENCE COLE, and for as long as anyone could remember his home had been a caravan outside the village of Portskewett, three miles to the west of Chepstow, and a short walk from the tidal beaches of the Severn at the end of the Black Rock Road. Jenny noted this little irony: Brogan had claimed to come from the town of Blackrock in County Louth on the Irish border. A notorious, but good-natured poacher and thief, Cole fed himself and supplemented a meagre income as a casual farm labourer by illegally netting salmon and shooting the odd goose on the mudflats.

Williams's background for the man they were about to meet didn't inspire Jenny with confidence. And as they trudged the fifty yards of muddy track from the lane in the icy darkness, she wondered if she would have been better off spending the last working hour of the day at her desk.

They rounded a sharp corner and entered an untidy wire compound encircling the ramshackle caravan through a makeshift wooden gate. Two dead rabbits and a duck hung from a hook on a tall wooden post. A ragged collie strained at the end of chain barking excitedly.

'Quiet down, boy,' a voice yelled from inside.

The flimsy door creaked on its hinges and Cole came stiffly down the cinderblock steps to greet them. A short, squat man with sharp green eyes that smiled impishly at Williams, he was probably in his fifties, though a hard outdoor life had added extra years to his weather-worn face. He squeezed Jenny's hand in a callused palm and ushered them both inside.

A pall of tobacco smoke and the fumes from an elderly paraffin stove competed to thicken the air inside to an unbreathable fog. They sat on the tatty bench seats arranged around a table while Cole lit the gas under a kettle. Jenny shot Williams a glance, urging him to move things along before they were embarrassed into accepting a cup of tea in one of the filthy mugs heaped on the drainer.

'We can't stop, Lawrence,' Williams said. 'Mrs Cooper's in a hurry. Why don't you tell us what you saw?'

'Like I told that boy of yours – it was a couple of helicopters.'

'When?' Jenny asked.

Cole lit a hand-rolled cigarette from the stove and eased his legs under the table.

'Can't have been more than ten minutes after the plane came down. I was packing up my tackle – I'd been out fishing, see.' He smiled at Williams. 'Hook and line, mind. All legal.'

'I don't doubt it,' Williams said, humouring him.

Jenny said, 'You saw the plane?'

'I did. Came screaming over, light flashing on the wings – never seen nothing like it. Heard it hit the water too, I did. Just like a crack of thunder.' He spoke with an accent that only existed in this pocket of South Wales: the lyrical Welsh rise and fall meeting the rich piratical vowels of the Forest of Dean. A genuine character, Jenny thought, but how would a jury perceive him?

'Did you see it hit the water?'

He shook his large head. 'Too far away. It was that misty

out you couldn't see a hundred yards, look. I felt it, though.'
He slapped a hand on his chest. 'Went right through me, it
did. I knew it was bad.'

'Tell me about the helicopters.'

'I was walking back up the lane there when I heard them
coming over. There were two of them, low on the water,
like. One of them had a searchlight – yellow, it was.'

'Did you notice any markings?'

'No. They just looked black from where I was standing –
shadowy, like.'

'You're sure it was only ten minutes?'

'Might even have been less. I was in a hurry to get back
here and switch on the wireless to hear about that plane.'

'You didn't see them come back?'

'Can't say I did.'

His sighting was interesting, but hardly concrete proof.
And if the powerful smell of whisky on his breath was any
indication, his idea of time might have been less than accurate.

'You told the constable you'd try to draw them for us,'
Williams said.

'So I did.' He cast a vague eye over his jumbled belongings.

'Here,' Williams said, fetching out his notebook and a
pen, 'have a go with this.'

Squinting though the smoke curling up from the cigarette
clamped between his lips, Cole began to draw with surprisingly delicate strokes. His forehead creased with concentration, he sketched the outlines of two aircraft that not only
had rotors, but also appeared to have short wings jutting
out from their sides.

It was Williams who pointed it out. 'What's that, Lawrence? Looks like wings.'

'That's what they had. I can still see them, clear as
anything.' He tapped his temple with a thick finger.

Williams glanced at Jenny. 'That's not what the search and rescue look like. They're in Sea Kings – no wings on those.'

Jenny said, 'Let's get this clear. You heard the sound of the airliner hitting the water, and some ten minutes or so later you saw these two helicopters flying downstream about a hundred feet up.'

'That's it.'

'Did you hear anything else?'

Cole frowned. 'I might have heard a bit of a bang a few minutes later, but it could as easily have been someone letting off a shotgun. It's hard to say.'

'When was the bang?'

He screwed up his face as he struggled to remember. 'Just as I was coming up from the lane, I think. I can't be sure.'

Jenny tried to imagine him being cross-examined by Giles Hartley and his colleagues and had to conclude that he wouldn't stand up well. If his evidence were to be believed it would have to be corroborated. That meant more legwork and more delay. And with each hour that passed, her inquiry hung by an ever thinner thread.

'What do you mean, *postponed*?' Alison said, her angry voice distorting over the speakers inside Jenny's car as she drove back along the narrow lanes to Chepstow. 'I've just spent the last two hours making sure everyone's ready to reassemble tomorrow morning.'

'Something's come up – more new evidence.'

'You know what's going to happen, Mrs Cooper?'

'It's a risk I'll have to take. We'll start again on Monday, I promise.'

'And I'm meant to sit here all evening soaking up the abuse? Do you have any idea how angry these people are going to be?'

'I'm sorry. It can't be helped.'

There was a moody silence on the line.

'Alison, look—'

'Don't worry, Mrs Cooper, I don't mind cancelling my plans for tonight. Just don't expect me to run any more errands for you. I'd better make a start.' She rang off.

Alison's outburst was intended to make Jenny feel guilty and she had succeeded. Jenny toyed with the idea of driving back to the office and taking over the task of telling angry lawyers and witnesses to reschedule once again, but decided there were more pressing matters demanding her attention. She could clear the air with Alison once the inquiry was over.

She scrolled through her contacts and found Michael's number. Another call that would carry an unwelcome load. It rang several times before he answered.

'Michael, it's Jenny.'

'I know,' he said warily.

'I was wondering if you could help me.'

'With what? Everyone who matters has already made up their mind.'

'I like to think I matter, and I'm still very much in the dark. A witness saw a pair of helicopters heading east only minutes after the plane went down. He's drawn a sketch for me. I need to know where they came from.'

It was late in the evening by the time Michael arrived, tired and subdued after a day criss-crossing the country between racecourses. A colleague had called in sick and the boss had insisted he take up the slack, keeping his extra journeys 'off the log'. It was criminal, but when there were twice as many pilots as jobs, he hadn't much choice.

Jenny sat him in front of the fire and poured him some wine, treating herself to a glass of orange juice.

'You're making me drink alone?'

'I'm meant to avoid it.'

'Oh? Why's that?'

'Too long a story to tell you now. I've made some pasta – do you want to eat first or can I show you the picture?'

'Let's see it.'

She retrieved Cole's sketch from between the leaves of a legal pad and handed it to him.

'Wow.' He seemed puzzled. 'He's sure this is what he saw?'

'I've no reason to think he's making it up. Why – what are they?'

'They look like Apaches. Helicopter gunships. These things sticking out of the side are called stub-wing pylons – they're mounts for missile launchers. The RAF don't have any, but I think the Army and Navy have a few. The Yanks have got hundreds of them, but none in the UK as far as I know. What colour were they?'

'He couldn't see. It was misty.'

'I've overflown Beachley lots of times. I've seen Pumas and Chinooks, but never any Apaches. But I can't think of anywhere else they could have come from that wouldn't have taken at least twenty minutes.'

'The brigadier at Beachley insists they were nothing to do with him.'

'Maybe he's right.' Michael rubbed his tired eyes. 'Oh, God.' The words slipped out in little more than a whisper.

'What?'

'I don't know what the current protocols are, but—' He paused to take a steadying mouthful of wine. 'There are standing orders about the shooting down of civilian airliners if radio contact is lost.'

'The aircraft wasn't shot out of the sky, Michael. I've seen photographs – there's a scorch mark on the underside nose, that's all.'

'That's a photograph. Have you seen the actual hull?'

'No. It's in the AAIB's hangar down at Farnborough.'

'I wouldn't believe anything until I've seen it with my own eyes.'

Jenny said, 'Have you changed your mind? When we came out of the simulator you seemed convinced the initial stall was at least partially Captain Murray's fault.'

'I don't know what to think.' He swallowed the rest of the glass. 'I trust Glen Francis, but then I've seen misinformation enough times to know that even something as big as this could be stage-managed.'

'The witness thinks he heard a bang or an explosion several minutes after the helicopters passed. Brogan's lifejacket bore traces of explosive residue and it had been punctured by a double-sided knife – the lab said it could have been a military one.' Despite the warmth of the fire, Jenny felt herself shudder as if from the cold. 'I hadn't allowed myself to put it all together like this before, but it's almost as if whoever was in those helicopters cut Brogan out of his lifejacket and cast him adrift . . . Who would do that? Why?'

'There'll be a reason,' Michael said. 'Just don't expect to find it.' He reached for the bottle and refilled his glass.

Jenny thought of what Mrs Patterson had told her about the businessmen and law-enforcers on board the aircraft, and remembered Chen's panicky reaction outside the press conference. It was almost unthinkable that anyone would sacrifice hundreds of innocent lives to make sure of killing one or two men, but the truth was that unthinkable things happened all the time. Then there was Nuala's involvement. There was still no satisfactory explanation for her presence on the aircraft, still less for the fact that, in common with several of the passengers Mrs Patterson had isolated, she was booked onto a connecting flight to Washington. She wrestled with conflicting feelings over whether to share with Michael all that she had heard. But as badly as she wanted to, she had to remind herself of her duty to remain clear and objective. She couldn't allow her opinions to be coloured by anyone's grief, not even his.

'You're right,' Jenny said, 'I won't be sure of anything until I see the plane for myself.'

'Do you think they'll let you?'

'It was directly responsible for Brogan's death. I don't see how I can be stopped.'

'Would I be able to come?'

'I don't think that would work.'

He seemed to accept her unspoken reasons, and they lapsed into silence as they stared into the fire.

After a while, Michael said, 'I ought to tell you – I looked you up online. I saw the newspaper stories about what happened when you were a kid.'

'I thought you might,' Jenny said, surprised that she didn't feel more shocked.

'It must be tough. At least I can keep what happened to me during the war to myself.'

'Take it from me – keeping secrets doesn't work.'

Michael nodded, his eyes fixed on the flames. 'I always thought it would be me who'd die in a plane, not Nuala.'

Jenny said, 'Is that what you wanted?'

'You sound like a psychiatrist.'

'I visit one – there, another secret. He tells me living is a conscious choice; it's something you've got to keep finding a reason to do.'

'What are your reasons?'

'My work . . . and my son, I guess.'

'You never mentioned you have a son. How old is he?'

'Eighteen. He's at university. At least, I assume he is – he never calls.'

'He's finding his feet. We all have to do that.'

'How about you?' Jenny asked.

'Pass.'

'You should find something, Michael.'

He gave her a sideways glance. 'I have to be in the air early tomorrow. I should go.'

He got up from the sofa and fetched his jacket that he'd thrown over a chair.

Jenny looked at the half-empty bottle on the rug. 'Are you sure you'll be safe?'

'Safer than I would be if I stayed here.' He smiled, leaving her unsure if he was joking or deadly serious.

As he headed for the door, he paused, as if hesitating over a decision, then reached into his inside pocket. He drew out a brown envelope folded lengthways. 'They sent me a copy of Nuala's post-mortem report.' He placed it on the table. 'We think we're at the controls, but I guess ultimately we're all just passengers along for the ride.'

He let himself out, closing the door quietly behind him.

The single-page report was written in Dr Kerr's brief, inimitable style. Two short paragraphs outlining the fatal injuries – severe trauma to the head resulting in massive haemorrhage, and deep lacerations and trauma to the abdomen caused by the force of the lap belt on impact – and a third under the brief headline *OTHER FINDINGS*. It read: *Recently healed scarring to the lower abdomen caused by surgical sterilization. Both fallopian tubes stapled. Evidence of early stage lymphoma confirmed by biopsy. No evidence of diagnosis on medical records.* Attached to his report was a photocopy of a set of lab results confirming *morphologic cell type in a nodular pattern consistent with malignant non-Hodgkin's lymphoma.*

Jenny heard Michael's car pulling away down the lane. It

was too late to call him back to try to persuade him that none of this made any difference, but had he stayed she doubted if she would have convinced him. This must have looked to him like the final proof that his leaving Nuala had closed the door to hope. If she couldn't have him, she was going to have no one, and certainly no one's child. The early-stage cancer was most likely fully treatable in an otherwise healthy young woman, but that's not how Michael would have read it. He would have seen Nuala dying on the inside, and it all being his fault.

Safer than I would be if I stayed here. His words lingered with her as she folded the report back into its envelope and carried it through to her study to stow in her briefcase. Michael was both drawn to and frightened by her; she had seen it in his eyes. She hated to feel the pull of another troubled, damaged man when all she longed for was to be free of complication, but she sensed it was too late. The winter wind had blown him to her as surely as the tide had delivered Brogan and the little girl.

EIGHTEEN

FRIDAY BEGAN BADLY. No sooner had Jenny made it through the freezing rain into the office than Alison announced that Simon Moreton had demanded she call him immediately. She retreated to her room expecting the worst, and wasn't disappointed.

'I've two things to tell you,' Moreton said in the brisk, dispassionate tone he reserved solely for relaying bad news. 'Firstly, your conduct of the Brogan inquest will be treated as a formal demonstration of your competence to continue in the office of coroner. I have been personally requested to report on your handling of the case to the Director General, and I needn't tell you that any goodwill that has previously existed between us was conclusively exhausted by your actions yesterday afternoon.'

'Do you have any idea how pompous you sound?'

'I haven't finished, Mrs Cooper. Do hear me out.'

Jenny sighed. Now it was *Mrs Cooper*.

'Secondly, all matters connected with the downed aircraft remain strictly outside your purview. Sir James Kendall's inquiry will deal with the issue fully and with the benefit of all appropriate expertise. You will kindly inform the Patterson family that any hope they have of manipulating your inquiry to extend its scope is entirely misplaced. Do you understand me?'

'I'm entitled to inspect the wreckage, Simon. To deny me that would be as absurd as preventing me from viewing a murder weapon.'

'Not even Sir James Kendall's experts are being granted access until the Anti-Terrorist Branch formally announce that there is no line of criminal investigation they wish to pursue. That will take some weeks at least. There is no question of you gaining access in the meantime.'

'Then I'll have no option but to postpone until I can inspect it.'

'Do you wish to hand me your resignation now?'

Jenny thought of several smart remarks at once, but resisted all of them. 'No, Simon, I don't. Have a nice day.'

She dropped the phone back in its cradle and jabbed an angry finger at the on switch of her computer. As it whirred and groaned into action she tried to imagine what life would be like if she were to call Moreton's bluff and resign. For the first time in her tenure as coroner she had to admit that she was tempted. There was a far easier existence waiting for her if she wanted it.

Alison appeared in the doorway. 'Mr Patterson called while you were on the phone. He said he's nearby and wondered if he could talk to you.'

'Did he say what about.'

'No, but reading between the lines –' Alison lowered her voice – 'I think he might have had a set-to with his wife.'

More private meetings with relatives only risked compromising herself further, but having met with Mrs Patterson several times it hardly seemed fair to refuse.

'All right. Tell him I'll see him, but please stress I can't discuss the substance of the case.'

Less than twenty minutes later, Greg Patterson arrived in Jenny's office carrying an overnight case and with the pallid, sunken features of a man who hadn't slept properly in days. Jenny had learned to read the stages of bereavement in a relative's face as clearly as a doctor diagnosing the progression of jaundice. He had passed through shock and anger – the stage at which his wife had become temporarily arrested – and tipped over the brink into acceptance and despair. He seemed bewildered by the emotions that were assailing him and fidgeted nervously with his cufflinks as he spoke. Gone was the veneer of corporate sophistication that had carried him through the early days of his loss.

'I'm sorry to take up your time, Mrs Cooper,' he said. 'Your officer kindly explained the situation to me, but I can assure you I don't wish to trespass in any way on your inquiry.'

He was so fragile, Jenny thought he might break.

'How can I help you?' she asked gently.

'I just wanted to let you know that I shan't be attending the remainder of your inquest into Mr Brogan's death . . . I'm content to wait for the outcome of the main inquest – whenever that may be.'

'I see.' She hesitated. It would have been enough just to leave it at that, but curiosity and an overwhelming surge of sympathy for the man persuaded her to push further. 'Not that it's any of my business, Mr Patterson, but may I ask why?'

'You've met with my wife on several occasions . . .' He faltered for a moment, struggling with what Jenny interpreted as a combination of bitterness and embarrassment. 'And you will know that she has formed a number of theories—'

'Yes,' Jenny said neutrally.

'Without wishing to be disrespectful –' he forced the words past a barrier of guilt – 'she's a highly strung woman at the best of times. What happened to Amy is beyond any ability she has to cope rationally, or at all.'

'I understand.'

'You don't, Mrs Cooper, because all you see is what she shows you. Behind closed doors—'

'Really, I don't need to know that.'

'Well, perhaps you ought to know that in my view – for what it's worth – she has become delusional. Perhaps dangerously so . . . She has even accused me of having some sort of foreknowledge of this accident.' He stiffened his face against threatening tears. 'As if I would endanger my own daughter . . .'

Jenny let him continue, sensing this was the first time he had opened up to anyone since losing Amy.

'The fact is she couldn't function alone. She's being propped up and encouraged by these lawyers, who are more than happy to take our money and listen to her wild ideas . . . I don't want any more part of it. My wife and I are no longer speaking . . . I have told the lawyers, they don't represent me.' He groped for words to express his confusion of feelings. 'They have no right to behave this way. Both my wife and I have lives to lead once this is behind us . . . reputations—'

'If it's any comfort at all, most couples who face what you're going through are pushed to breaking point. Give her time. A lot can change in a short while.'

Mr Patterson shook his head. 'It isn't just the inquiry . . . Amy was the last thread holding us together. I'm sorry, I shouldn't have troubled you with this.'

'It's quite all right—'

He rose from his seat and picked up his case. 'I just wanted you to know that it wasn't because I don't care. I do . . . I can't tell you how much.' He turned to the door and let himself out.

*

Greg Patterson's visit brought her sharply back to reality. A man who had just lost his young daughter was seeing more clearly than she was. Jenny felt her righteous anger fade, to be replaced by a vague feeling of shame at her hubris and credulity. Mrs Patterson's increasingly delusional state of mind had become painfully obvious at their last meeting, yet even so Jenny found herself entertaining the possibility that mysterious helicopters had shot Flight 189 from the sky. Had she learned nothing about the dispassionate evaluation of evidence from all her years in the service of the law?

The mist seemed to lift, leaving her standing in the hard, painful light. She understood now what Dr Allen had been hinting at when he said she gave too much of herself to the dead. It was seductively easy to wallow in the misery of others. Succumbing to the temptation of shady conspiracies was nothing more than a failure fully to embrace life. The dead were dead. They haunted her thoughts only because she was weak enough to let them.

She reached for her files and began to order proceedings for Monday. She would call all relevant witnesses but make no judgements until the evidence had been heard and tested in cross-examination. She would call a witness from Forenox to lead with the evidence on Brogan's lifejacket, and Lawrence Cole to testify to the presence of the helicopters. She would instruct Alison to contact all local air traffic control towers to establish whether the craft were real or a figment of Cole's whisky-fuelled imagination. As for whatever contraband might have been stowed in Brogan's yacht, Jenny could do no better than to submit a formal application to Sir James Kendall to release details of any evidence that navy divers might have recovered from the estuary floor. The chances of him doing so were slim, but protocol, at least, would have been satisfied.

It felt good to be back in control. An hour later, her plans complete, Jenny printed out a set of instructions for Alison and carried them through to reception.

She was on the phone. Jenny waited patiently at the side of her desk.

'I'll be over right away. Have next of kin been informed? . . . I see. Do let me know.' Alison looked up with a solemn expression. 'A woman's body has been found in a lay-by just along from where the photographer crashed his car. Dark hair, early forties, attractive, wedding ring, photographs of two young children in her pocket. Looks like a suicide.' Her eyes dipped guiltily to the box of effects which still lay untouched at the side of her desk.

'I'll go,' Jenny said. She handed Alison the instructions, grabbed her coat and hurried out of the door before they could exchange another word.

Jenny rounded the steep corner she remembered as the accident scene she had visited two weeks previously and passed the oak tree, which still bore the fresh scars of the collision on its trunk. A hundred yards further on the road was coned off to a single lane. Inside the cordon was the usual collection of police vehicles that attend a fatality and an unmarked black undertaker's van. She pulled in at the far end and took a moment to steel herself.

She turned, startled, at the sound of knocking on the passenger window. A face she dimly recognized was looking in at her. In the seconds it took to open the window and introduce herself, she placed it as belonging to a police officer she had last seen during her days practising law in the family courts: Detective Sergeant Karen Fuller.

'Good to see you again, Mrs Cooper,' Fuller said, as Jenny climbed shakily out of the car. 'It must be five years.' Having spent two decades specializing in domestic violence and sex crime, DS Fuller seemed to be treating a straightforward suicide as something of a welcome relief from the usual routine.

'Six,' Jenny said, as they shook hands. She remembered the case vividly: Fuller had arrested a woman for soliciting and broke into her home just in time to save the life of her two-year-old daughter, who, besides suffering from advanced malnutrition, had been decorated with cigarette burns by her mother's boyfriend.

'Miss it?' Fuller asked.

'Now you come to mention it, no,' Jenny answered truthfully.

'Can't say it gets any easier,' Fuller said. 'This is a bit of an odd one, though – that's why we called you, just in case you thought it didn't add up.'

Jenny glanced down the inside of the line of vehicles but didn't see any sign of a body.

'She's in the field on the other side of the gate,' the DS said. 'Not long dead – only a couple of hours, the medic estimates. That puts time of death at around nine o'clock this morning. No vehicle here, no identification on her – just this in her pocket.' Fuller dipped into her parka and brought out a small, tagged plastic evidence bag. She held it out for Jenny to see two small, passport-sized photographs of smiling girls, one of about three, the other a little older. 'We think they must be her kids. She's wearing a wedding ring.'

'I heard. How did she do it?'

'The usual – sleeping pills. No note.'

'Any sign of violence?'

'No. Why don't you have a look for yourself?'

Fuller led the way into the lay-by and through a partially open five-barred gate into a large field of dormant pasture. The body lay some twenty yards to their right next to the hedgerow under a sheet of black plastic. Two white-suited scene of crime officers had finished their work and were walking towards them, hefting their bulky rucksacks of kit.

'All ready to move her now, boss,' one of them announced to Fuller.

'Give us a moment,' she answered.

As they neared the spot where the woman lay, the detective seemed to sense Jenny's trepidation. 'I thought you'd be used to this by now.'

Momentarily mute, Jenny shook her head.

Fuller leaned down and pulled back the plastic sheet to expose the fully clothed body of a woman lying on her side, the fingers of her right hand still curled around the small brown plastic jar that had contained the pills. A foot to her right lay an empty bottle of water of the sort you might buy in any convenience store.

Jenny stepped around to the side so she could see the dead woman's face. She was pretty, with pale skin and black, shoulder-length hair. She wore a stylish rust-coloured scarf inside a dark wool coat. Her shoes were flat but smart. Elegant; just as she had been in the photographer's pictures. There was no doubt in Jenny's mind that it was her.

She stepped back and swallowed hard.

Karen Fuller looked at her puzzled.

'Is it her, Mrs Cooper?'

Both women turned at the sound of Alison's voice. Buried in her anorak, she was marching across the grass from the gate.

She gave Jenny no time to protest or question what she was doing here. 'It is her, isn't it?'

Fuller looked to Jenny for an explanation.

'My officer—'

'I know who she is. What's going on?'

Jenny started to stumble through the story of the fatal car crash and the pictures on the dead man's camera.

'It is—' Alison said. She turned on Jenny. 'I was going to see her yesterday, except you had to change your plans again, didn't you?'

'Alison, please—'

'I was on my way out of the door when you called.'

'This really isn't appropriate.'

'I had it all planned. I was going to tell her that her secret was safe and that no one need ever know. I even had the number of a grief counsellor with me.'

'It might have made no difference at all,' Jenny protested.

'You know your problem, Mrs Cooper? You're so caught up with your own dramas you've forgotten what your job is. Your predecessor, Harry Marshall, never forgot, not for a moment. Honour the dead and protect the living, those were his rules. You should try learning from them.'

'You know who this woman is?' Fuller asked, incredulously.

'Her name's Angela Wesley. She lives in Victoria Avenue, Clifton, and she worked part-time as a special needs teacher. Her husband runs his own insurance brokerage.'

'Have you got a phone number for him?'

'I'd rather tell him in person,' Alison said.

'I'll come with you.' Fuller looked accusingly at Jenny. 'I'd be grateful if you'd write me a statement setting out everything you know about this case, Mrs Cooper.'

Propelled by an impulse she felt the need to neither question nor resist, Jenny drove the few miles across country to the spot overlooking the estuary to which she had retreated the morning Brogan and Amy Patterson had washed up on the shore.

Leaving her Land Rover at the side of the road, she wandered over the dunes to the head of the beach, seeking comfort in the stark clarity of the open water. A keen east wind bit into her face and cut through to her skin.

Alison had spoken out of guilt, but she was right; she had failed the dead woman. They both had. No written law had been violated, but with hindsight it was obvious that she had been the photographer's lover, and even more obvious that Jenny's duty had been to make sure that she knew that someone who wouldn't judge her understood her predicament.

Braced against the cold spits of rain whipping into her face, she found herself alone again with the dead, and no matter how hard she tried to box them up and file them away, they refused to be contained. Brogan strode listlessly back and forth across the foreshore; Amy Patterson huddled and shivered in a hollow between the dunes; Nuala Casey wandered in search of a waymarker in a landscape as alien to her as the moon's.

Jenny lifted her eyes to glimpse a passenger jet passing between the clouds: a tiny arrow streaking across the sky. She thought of its occupants, protected by a skin only inches thick, breathing air held at pressure by a handful of valves and seals, the entire machine kept aloft by flimsy boxes of electronics and their prayers. And then she pictured the scene inside Flight 189 as the aircraft pitched upwards, hurling bodies from their seats. She heard their screams as it plunged downwards in a vertical dive. There would have been no opportunity for silent dignity throughout its six-minute journey to earth; it would have been chaos, as close to hell as it was possible to imagine.

She turned back to her car knowing what she had to do: her job. Without fear or compromise, she would seek out the truth. If there was an answer to why Flight 189 was lost, she felt sure the key to it lay with Nuala Casey. She needed access to the belongings that she had with her on the plane. If she could have counted on the law being fairly administered, she would simply have issued a request to Sir James Kendall in the expectation that he would oblige her, but there was more chance of 189 miraculously appearing from the clouds and coming safely in to land. Not for the first time in her career, she would have to enforce the law alone.

Driving back through the Gloucestershire countryside towards the M5 motorway, Jenny spoke Dr Kerr's number out to the hands-free. He picked up the call against the sound the voices and the high-pitched whine of surgical saws.

'Dr Kerr? It's Mrs Cooper. Are you still at the D-Mort?'

'Until tomorrow. You're not going to tell me you've postponed your inquest again – my diary's in chaos.'

'I've no plans at the moment,' she answered, reasoning that a half-truth was better than an outright lie. 'You're still doing the autopsies?'

'Mostly re-examining. This one's for a life insurance company – don't ask.'

'Actually, I've got a request of my own.'

'I thought you had lost jurisdiction.'

'Different passenger. It turns out I'm friendly with someone who had an ex-girlfriend on board. A thirty-year-old woman by the name of Nuala Casey.'

'Have you got the identifying number?'

'No. But your report says she had early-stage lymphoma.'

'Yes, I remember.'

'You said her medical records showed no diagnosis. The thing is she was a pilot herself, for Ransome Airways. I'm reading between the lines here, but I suspect that if she thought she was ill, she would have gone to a private doctor first – kept it off the record so as not to jeopardize her pilot's licence.'

'The chances are she would have still been asymptomatic, the odd swollen gland maybe.'

'Is there any chance you can get access to her possessions in the evidence store? Apparently she had a phone she kept all her appointments on.'

'Sorry, Jenny – we don't have any access to personal effects. Once they're bagged it's all handed to the police. There's still technically a criminal investigation going on.'

'And it's all stored at the D-Mort?'

'As far as I know.'

'Oh well, never mind,' Jenny said, pretending to be satisfied with his answer. 'But if it's all the same, I wouldn't mind calling by to have a word about the lymphoma.'

'There's not a lot to tell.'

'We'll see. In about an hour?'

'No problem.'

Jenny recognized the soldier at the barrier from her first visit and flashed him a friendly smile as he checked her name off his list of expected visitors. Waved through without a hitch, she parked in the officials' car park and collected her visitor's tag at the reception desk. She checked her watch: she had fifteen minutes before Dr Kerr was expecting her.

She headed off along the walkway, but instead of turning right to the mortuary continued straight on towards the stack of modular offices that she had first passed with Simon Moreton. There were noticeably fewer people on the site than during her previous visits, but the fact only served to make her feel more conspicuous.

Pretending to be caught up in a phone call, she dawdled a little distance from the evidence and effects store, and noticed that the rectangular building was made up of nine cabins: three high and three wide. The entrance, clearly signed, was through a door in the centre of the bottom middle cabin. The windows on the lower tier were all firmly closed; several upstairs were open a touch. To the left of the building a set of steps led up to a door which would doubtless open only from the inside.

Drifting a little nearer, she glanced through a ground-floor window and saw a single male figure sitting at a desk working at his computer. All along the walls there were metal racks containing deep wire-mesh trays. Each tray was labelled with text which was too small to read from this distance and contained sealed plastic evidence bags, many of them holding entire suitcases. With no idea how to get what she wanted, Jenny decided she had no option but to wing it.

She climbed the three steps to the main door, knocked twice, then stepped inside to see a young broad-shouldered detective rising from behind his desk. He had the startled look of a man who wasn't expecting visitors.

'Sorry to disturb you,' Jenny said, flashing him a smile. 'Jenny Cooper, Severn Vale District Coroner. I presume you're in charge of evidence and effects.'

'That's my boss, DI Prentice,' the young man said warmly, seemingly grateful for a break in the tedium of his day. 'He's at a meeting this afternoon. Paul Knight – detective constable. I administer the database.'

'Pleased to meet you.' She shook his hand and noticed that the air smelt stale and musty. She had heard that all the evidence recovered from the two halves of the sunken hull had been dried out in specially designed trailers, but the process had evidently been far from perfect. At each end of the cabin a large electric heater stood alongside a dehumidifier.

He motioned her to a chair. 'What can I do for you?'

Taking a seat, Jenny glanced left and right and saw that the individual cabins were connected by open doorways with no doors in the frames. In the far right-hand corner of the cabin in which they were sitting was a compact open stair-case leading to the upper level. The rear wall was lined with industrial racks with trays three deep. Each section was numbered alphabetically, and each tray bore the name of an individual passenger. Those immediately behind Knight read *Donoghue, Richard (M), Downing, Elaine (F), Eason, Anthony (M)*. From this, she concluded that Nuala Casey's tray would be off to her left near the entrance to the next cabin, possibly the other side of the doorway.

What *did* she want from him? She had to think quickly.

'You may know that I'm conducting the inquest into the death of Gerry Brogan – the man whose yacht was struck by the aircraft.'

'The IRA guy.'

'He had a dubious history, certainly,' Jenny responded patiently. 'Anyway, you might also know that I initially had jurisdiction over the case of Amy Patterson, the ten-year-old child whose body was washed up in my district.'

'Yes, I know,' Knight said. He turned to his computer and scrolled through a list of names.

'I'm aware that no effects can be released yet, but I wonder if you could answer a couple of questions for the parents – it is rather a special case. The child was travelling alone.'

Knight gave a cautious nod. He found what he was looking for and clicked on what Jenny assumed was Amy Patterson's name.

'What do they want to know?'

'Her father received a brief phone call from her during the plane's final descent. They would like to know if her phone was recovered, if it works, and if you intend to examine any data on it. I think they would like to find out if she was trying to call her mother, or . . . you understand.'

'I'd help you if I could, but all phones are being examined by a team of data retrieval experts. It's a private firm up in Manchester that we're using. Everything recovered will be released to relatives in due course. Actually, they were told that – it should be on the website.'

Jenny felt herself begin to blush. She was a bad liar at the best of times. 'They're very upset, probably a little confused.'

'Was there anything else?'

'Yes—' What was she going to say? She hadn't a clue. She would just have to move from a white lie to an outright one. 'Mrs Patterson thinks her daughter might have been wearing a silver necklace – it was a family heirloom. It would mean a lot to her if it's been found. I saw the body, I should have been able to tell her, but I really couldn't remember.' Jenny offered a silent prayer for forgiveness, then reminded herself that she was the one acting in the interests of justice.

Knight scanned what Jenny presumed was a list of possessions logged next to Amy Patterson's name. He shook his head. 'Sorry, I don't see any mention of a necklace. We haven't recorded every single item in everyone's luggage, though, just the individual items found on the body. Aside from her clothing, it says she had a wristwatch, a phone and purse, that's all.'

'Oh, that is disappointing.' She couldn't let it end here. She needed to get to Nuala's tray. 'I don't suppose you could just double-check for me?'

'I don't think we'll have made a mistake.'

'Please?' Jenny implored. 'Just so I can reassure her that I did everything I could.'

'I can't break the seals on any evidence bags, Mrs Cooper.'

'Of course not—' She held his gaze until his frown dissolved.

'All right, I'll have a quick look for you.' He got up from behind the desk. 'I'll have to ask you to stay here, though.'

'Fine,' Jenny said. 'Thank you.'

As Knight moved off across the linoleum floor towards the staircase, Jenny slipped off her shoes. Her heart beat hard against her ribs as he neared the top of the second flight and disappeared into the cabin above. Hearing his heavy footsteps passing directly overhead, she tiptoed away from her chair along the row of trays towards the letter C. She heard him stop and pull open a tray. Jenny reached the furthest rack in the cabin – it began with *Clark, Samuel (M)*. Damn! She slipped through the doorway into the next cabin, alive to every tiny movement on the floor above, and spotted *Casey, Nuala (F)* on the bottom tray of the nearest rack. Glancing through the mesh she could see a bag containing a small black suitcase on top of which was another holding items of clothing. Close to the front were two other much smaller bags, one containing what appeared to be a wash bag, and in another beneath it, a wallet. The tray was too heavy to pull out without making a noise, but there was gap of about five inches between the top edge and the bottom of the one above. She reached a shaky hand through and touched the bag containing the wash bag. She heard Knight cough and shove a tray back into a rack.

Jenny quickly pulled out the wash bag and stuffed it into her right-hand coat pocket. Knight was moving back towards the stairs as she reached in again and closed her fingers around the wallet. She thrust it into the left-hand pocket and dashed silently back through the doorway and across the central cabin, overtaking Knight's footsteps and arriving at her chair a moment before his foot hit the first tread on the way down. She smoothed her pocket flaps, slipped on her shoes and took a deep breath, all at once.

Knight reached the turn in the stairs. 'No sign of a necklace, I'm afraid.'

'Never mind. I'm so sorry to have troubled you,' Jenny

said. She got up from her chair, her heart still racing. 'I expect it's in the case. I'll explain to them. You've no idea when the phone data might be available?'

'It'll take a few weeks to process them all,' Knight said. 'We'll keep them posted.'

'You're doing a great job.' Jenny heard herself say. 'I'm sure all the families are very grateful.'

The five paces to the door felt like five hundred. She stepped outside into a sheet of drizzle knowing that she had just done something from which there would be no way back.

NINETEEN

JENNY HAD INTENDED TO KEEP her meeting with Dr Kerr in the staff canteen brief, fearing that any moment DC Knight would discover what she had taken and come after her, but she was out of luck and was forced to listen to the story of his day. Together with an American pathologist flown in especially for the task, he had spent most of it conducting a second post-mortem on the body of a wealthy New York investment banker. The dead man had two separate life insurance policies, each worth many millions, one of which excluded liability in the event of death being caused by 'physical trauma suffered in a civil aviation accident'. Lawyers had advised that if the man could be proved to have died from a heart attack before the plane struck the water, the family had a good legal case against the insurance company, who were refusing to honour their policy. When no evidence of a coronary could be found, the other pathologist had suggested that they look again.

Dr Kerr lowered his voice and leaned across the table. 'Do you know what he said to me?'

'I've no idea.'

' "If we look hard enough we might even find 100,000 dollars each." Can you believe that?' His astonishment was quaint.

'I hope you did,' Jenny said. 'Offers like that don't get made in a mortuary every day.'

He looked genuinely shocked.

'I'm *joking*,' Jenny said, but he didn't seem persuaded.

'You wanted to talk about Nuala Casey,' Dr Kerr said, changing the subject.

'Yes. You detected signs of lymphoma which you said were probably asymptomatic.'

'That's right. It was in the very early stages.'

'She was a pilot. She had frequent medicals. You can't fly if you're in anything less than excellent health. If anyone would have been alive to symptoms, it would have been her.'

'It's possible she was feeling a little below par. I think I've read that some patients can suffer symptoms similar to depression before anything manifests physically.'

'And if you're a person unfamiliar with psychological symptoms, that could be quite disturbing.'

'I have no insight into her mental condition, Jenny.'

'No, of course not.'

It was intriguing, nonetheless. She had learned enough through her own experience to know that suffering from unwanted thoughts could lead one to behave in unusual ways. If Nuala was ever going to take a risk she might not otherwise have done, the period at the end of her life was it. Separated from Michael and having denied herself the possibility of motherhood, she would already have been in a deeply negative state of mind.

'You said you know a friend of hers—' Dr Kerr ventured.

'More of an acquaintance,' Jenny said offhandedly, instinctively wanting to keep Michael's identity a secret.

'Is that all?'

'There is just one other thing. I don't suppose you could take another look at Amy Patterson for me.'

'For you? It's not your case, Mrs Cooper.'

'But she was with Brogan until the end.' It was Jenny's turn to speak in a whisper. 'This is strictly confidential—'

Dr Kerr gave a guarded nod.

'You found flash burns on Brogan's face. I've got forensic evidence that there was some sort of explosion after he entered the water – there's chemical residue on his lifejacket. I can't get hold of her lifejacket or clothing to run similar tests – don't ask me to explain – but if you could have a look at the areas of her body that might have been out of the water, I'd be grateful.'

'What sort of residue?'

'I think you might be better off not knowing,' Jenny said, 'but if you find anything worth swabbing –' she dipped into her jacket pocket and pushed one of Forenox's business cards across the table – 'you can book it in under my account. The guy handling it's called Ravi Achari. And tell him if he leaks any more results, I'll put a bomb under him.'

Jenny left the D-Mort and headed back towards Bristol in the gathering dusk. She was desperate to examine the contents of the two evidence bags, but had decided to act on a plan which, although it would do nothing to protect her, would ensure the continuity of any valuable evidence the bags contained.

She arrived at her Jamaica Street offices shortly before five, hoping that Alison would have taken the opportunity to leave early. She hadn't. Jenny felt the leaden atmosphere even before she stepped through the door.

Alison appeared in the doorway of the corridor leading to the kitchenette pointedly drying up one of the several cups Jenny had allowed to accumulate on her desk. 'DS Fuller would like you to give her a statement by tomorrow morning.'

'Fine. Though I'm not sure how it helps anyone.'

'The dead woman's husband might not agree.' Alison turned back into the kitchenette and thumped the cup on the drainer. There was more clanking of crockery – her way of making Jenny feel as guilty as an ungrateful child.

'You spoke to him?'

'Of course.'

She was determined not to make this easy.

'How was he?'

'Pretty much as you'd expect.' Alison reappeared and marched across the room to her desk, where she proceeded to shuffle her papers into orderly piles.

'Did he have any idea?' Jenny asked.

'He had been worried that she might have been seeing someone, but he'd never dared ask. I get the impression he worshipped her . . . That was probably the problem. No woman likes a doormat.'

'He didn't know about her lover?'

'Not a clue. He'd noticed she'd been a little subdued lately, that's all.' Her desk tidied, she turned to face Jenny. 'I left him the photographs.'

'Do you think that was a good idea?'

'Yes, I do, as a matter of fact. I think one thing this sorry episode has taught me is that everyone's better off hearing the truth, no matter how painful it is.'

Jenny looked at her, trying to fathom the subtext. When Alison was being particularly cryptic she was usually talking about herself.

'You mean you and your husband—'

'No, Mrs Cooper,' she snapped back. 'I was thinking more about Mrs Patterson and her ridiculous notions. Everyone knows she's working you like a puppet – it's all over CID. And they also know how much trouble you're in with the Ministry. You'll struggle to find anyone who rates your chances of surviving. They're taking bets on how long you'll last – the smart money's on less than a week.'

'I'm surprised it's that long,' Jenny said, and headed for her room.

'Don't you think someone should go and talk to the photographer's wife?' Alison called after her. 'The poor woman deserves to know what was going on.'

Jenny stopped at the door and took a deep breath. 'I'll call by on my way home.'

'Best not,' Alison said. 'You seem a bit preoccupied. I don't think you'd be much comfort.' She grabbed her coat from the peg and went.

Listening to Alison's heavy footsteps along the hallway, it felt like a parting of the ways. They had weathered many quarrels, but there was a darkness to Alison's current mood that Jenny had never witnessed before. Her natural instinct was to chase after her to try to patch things up, but with two bags of stolen evidence in her pockets it seemed a futile, even a dishonest gesture. It was as if Alison had somehow intuited that Jenny had finally put herself beyond the pale and was furious with her.

With her office door securely locked and the blinds drawn shut, Jenny placed the two bags on her desk and took out her cellphone. Switching it to video mode, she sandwiched it between two piles of books, making sure she had a clear picture of the bags and the area in which she was about to work.

She spoke out loud, stating the time and date, and describing her actions as she performed them. It was vital for the continuity of evidence that the film showed the unsealing of the bags and their precise contents. Without such a record, any evidence the bags contained could never be proved in a manner that would satisfy a court.

'These are two evidence bags that I have today removed

from the evidence and effects store at the disaster mortuary for the purposes of my inquiry,' Jenny began in a dry forensic tone. 'They were removed from the tray containing the effects of the female passenger Nuala Casey. One contains a brown leather wallet, the other what appears to be a black fabric wash bag bearing the Ransome Airways logo. I will examine the wash bag first.'

She took a pair of scissors from her desk-tidy and snipped through the plastic cable tie which sealed the neck of the bag shut. She pulled the wash bag out. It had the same musty smell that had pervaded the evidence and effects store. The fabric was stained with salt residue from the brackish water of the estuary.

'I am now unzipping the bag, which is damp to the touch. There are a number of items inside.' She proceeded to remove them one by one. 'A toothbrush, travel toothpaste, skin fresheners, a sanitary towel and a small tablet of soap bearing the name of the Cavendish Hotel, Fleetcombe, Berkshire.' She checked the inside for any pockets or gaps in the lining. There were none. Continuing to describe her actions, she repeated the process in reverse order before sealing the evidence bag securely with Scotch tape.

She turned to the second bag and resumed her dictation. 'This is a plain brown fold-over wallet, also still slightly damp.' She opened it. 'In the pockets on the right there are two credit cards – one Mastercard, one Visa – and what I assume to be a bank debit card. On the left we have a driver's licence, Heathrow airside ID, a gym membership card and a loyalty card for a coffee shop.' She turned the wallet on its side. 'I'm looking into a pocket running the length of the wallet, which contains a number of pieces of paper, all water-damaged.' She brought them out, separated them from one another and spread them across the desk. There were more than twenty. 'I can see these are mostly receipts from shop tills and ATMs.' She went through them one by one. They dated back to mid-December, and contained nothing more remarkable than records of visits to high street stores and sandwich shops; on 24 December, however, she found something bigger. 'This is a receipt from Linden Electronics for an Oregon GPS device costing £499.' She assumed it related to the gadget Nuala had stowed in her flight case.

There were several receipts from Christmas Eve and Christmas Day itself from Heathrow and Dubai airports, then none until 29 December. On that day Nuala had evidently filled up her car at a petrol station close to her flat and travelled out to the Cavendish Hotel, where at shortly before ten a.m. she paid for a half-day session in the spa. There followed a few more run-of-the-mill receipts from the first week of January, and Jenny found herself beginning to lose heart: she had taken one of the greatest risks of her career for no benefit whatever. She pulled apart three pieces of paper that had been folded together. The first was for a taxi fare. It was dated 9 January, the day of the plane crash. The second was for a return journey on the Heathrow Express bought at six a.m., and the third was a ticket issued by the Paddington Station left-luggage office five minutes later.

Jenny felt a rush of excitement. She tried not to let it sound in her voice as she concluded her commentary. 'I am placing all the receipts back in the wallet except the left-luggage ticket, which I will now take to the office at Paddington Station.' She held it up close to the camera so that every detail could be recorded. 'I will inform Nuala Casey's next of kin immediately her items of luggage have been retrieved.'

Her task complete, she turned the camera around to face the small safe which sat on the floor in the corner of the room. She filmed herself stowing the bags inside it and added for the record that she was the only person who knew the combination.

Jenny remained on edge throughout the entire two-hour drive along the motorway, her white-knuckle grip on the steering wheel sending shooting pains along her arms and into her shoulders and chest. Her eyes were smarting with the strain of staring out into the wet, moonless night, but she had no intention of stopping until she arrived at her destination.

She tried Michael's number repeatedly, but he wasn't answering. Fearing that he might be screening her out, she left a message insisting he call her. He didn't. Eventually, a tired-sounding woman picked up the phone at Sky Driver's office, but after consulting her computer she claimed that Michael had clocked off earlier that afternoon after a return flight to Newmarket. Jenny guessed that meant he was working 'off the log' again. It wasn't the night to be flying a light aircraft, she thought, let alone dog-tired and suffering far more grief than he dared to admit.

It was eight p.m. when she wove through the crowds of bleary-eyed commuters staring hopefully up at the departure screens and made her way to the left-luggage office at the head of platform twelve. Repeated terrorist attacks in recent decades had resulted in a blanket ban on left-luggage lockers, meaning that each bag had to be checked in over the counter and passed through a scanner. The rules printed on the back of the ticket were clear: the checked bag would only be handed back in exchange for the original ticket.

There wasn't much business being done at this time of the evening, and the Polish girl manning the office was glancing sleepily at a magazine. She took the ticket and went in search of Nuala's luggage without a word. Jenny glanced up at the security cameras on the ceiling which covered every angle and realized that evidence of her collection would be sitting on the company's servers for months, if not years, to come.

'What kind of bag is it?' the girl asked, walking alongside a row of suitcases.

Jenny had a moment of panic. 'I'm not sure. It belongs to my friend—'

The girl looked at her uncertainly, but seemed to relent. Besides, there was no clause requiring the collector and depositor to be the same person; whoever presented the ticket was entitled to exchange it for the luggage. The girl wandered further along the row, briefly disappeared behind some racks, then reappeared with a slender black laptop case, which she placed on the counter.

The girl checked the ticket taped to it against Jenny's. 'That's it.'

'Thank you,' Jenny said. 'That's definitely her case.'

She was climbing the steps out of the station to Eastbourne Terrace when her phone rang. It was Michael. About time.

'Jenny?'

'Michael, where are you?'

'In some dive of a hotel on the M4. I'm flying from Newbury to France and back tomorrow. What's so urgent?'

'I've got Nuala's laptop, not the company one, her personal laptop.'

'Where . . . How?' He sounded as nervous as she was.

'By making myself a criminal. I hope it's worth it.'

'Jenny, *where* did you get it?'

'Paddington. She checked it into left luggage before getting on the flight to the States. Do you want to look at it with me?'

'*Jesus*—'

'Michael?'

280

'I thought it must have gone down with her.'

'It didn't. Which particular dive on the M4 do I aim for?'

'No expense spared, eh?'

'The company gets a discount – you can see why.' Michael closed the door to his room in the Reading service station and drew over the night lock. As motel rooms went it was adequate, but Jenny felt there was something faintly tragic about a former fighter pilot living no better than a truck driver. He looked worn out and smelt of beer. Dressed in faded jeans and an old Levi's T-shirt, he could have been a roadie for an ageing rock band.

'Should you be drinking the evening before you fly?' Jenny said.

'Could you sleep in here without a drink?'

It was a fair point. She pushed aside his dirty cup and set the bag on the desk by the TV. Michael let her take the chair and sat on the end of the bed. They exchanged a glance, Jenny wanting to say something reassuring but not knowing what.

'Just open it,' Michael said.

She unzipped the bag and pulled out a slender laptop – the kind of upmarket model she had never been able to stretch to. She checked inside the bag. There was nothing else. Putting it to one side, she flipped open the screen and switched it on. As she had expected, it asked for a user password.

She looked to Michael.

Michael shrugged. 'Tyax?'

She keyed in the now familiar word and the desktop dutifully appeared, revealing a small set of half a dozen icons. Nuala kept her computer as spotless as her flat.

'Where to first?' Jenny asked.

'Look – top left. She backed up her phone.'

He was right – there it was. Nuala had actually bothered

to install the program most people toss away the moment they take their new phone out of the box. Jenny clicked open the application and found a number of folders. One held a diary, one a list of contacts, and a third contained photographs. A line of text at the bottom of the window recorded the date of the last back-up as 4 January. Michael insisted on looking at the photographs first. There were shots of skylines taken in shiny new Middle Eastern cities and a handful of Sandy Belling and her baby.

'You seem disappointed,' Jenny said.

Michael shrugged. 'I don't know what I was expecting. She always used to take lots of pictures.'

That was when she was happy, Jenny might have said, but made no comment. She turned to the diary file. It opened to reveal a month per screen. Starting from the previous June the entries revealed that Nuala had done little except work flat out, flying three or four round trips to European destinations each week until October, when her schedule altered to two runs to either Dubai or Abu Dhabi. The few non-work events entered were usually *Meet Sandy*, *Pilates* or *Gym*. There was nothing out of the ordinary until 6 November. An entry for that date read: *Meet AF H/R T1 17.30.*

'Heathrow Terminal One?' Jenny deduced.

Michael nodded.

'Any idea who AF is?'

'No. Try her contacts.'

Jenny opened the contacts file in a separate window and scrolled through the list of names until she reached F. There was no one listed with an initial A.

'Keep going through the diary,' Michael said.

There was nothing more in November beyond the usual routine. December, however, revealed something different. Interspersed between flights to the Middle East were five meetings with *MD* on the 2nd, 7th, 12th, 19th and 28th.

More interesting still were the locations: *Heston E/B*; *H'smith Starbucks*; *Langley Plough*; *Windsor Costa*. The final entry read: *Mick D, Datchet Royal Oak*.

'Five meetings with Mick D in one month,' Jenny said. 'Do you know him?'

'No.'

'Service stations, coffee shops, pubs. All within thirty minutes of Heathrow. Not what you'd call romantic locations.'

'Look in her contacts again.' Michael's tone was curt and Jenny shot him a look.

'Sorry—'

'Thank you.' She worked through the list to D. There were three entries, none of them relating to anyone called Mick. He wasn't listed under M either. A faint bell rang in the back of Jenny's mind. 'Hold on – didn't Nuala write the initials MD on one of the documents in her files? They're at my house—'

'I remember,' Michael said. 'It was on the FAA directive ordering Airbus operators to upgrade to heated pitot tubes.'

'So we're looking for a pilot?'

'Not necessarily. Try going online and running a search.'

Jenny connected to the motel's wireless network and entered her credit card details. Hooked up expensively to the internet she searched *Mick D Airbus*. In less than two seconds the search engine threw up a list of apparently obscure and irrelevant results.

'There – number four,' Michael said.

Jenny looked at the entry. It was listed under *Tech Log* and in the text beneath it were the words, *Engineer Mick Dalton describes his path to becoming* . . . She clicked and a page appeared from a trade magazine. Scrolling down, she came to a brief column profiling Mick Dalton, Senior Engineer, Ransome Airways. The photograph was of a balding middle-aged man wearing black-rimmed glasses.

Michael nodded slowly. 'Remember him?'

'No—'

'The guy who left Nuala's flight case in the car park – that's him. Check her emails – she used that more than she did the phone.'

Jenny closed the internet browser and clicked on the email tab. An inbox opened and began to fill with newly arriving messages. They were mostly junk – discount and investment offers, but the one midway down the list caught her eye. It flashed with an insistent red exclamation mark and the subject field read: *URGENT*. It was dated 10 January, the day after the crash.

'Are you going to open it?' Michael said impatiently.

Jenny paused, frightened of what she might find, then forced herself to double-click the message. A new window opened and a lot of indecipherable computer code spread across the screen.

'Stop it!' Michael called out.

He leaped up and grabbed the mouse from her hand but it was already too late. The computer screen turned solid blue and the cursor vanished. Michael hit the enter key. There was no response.

He slammed the edge of the desk with his fists. 'Shit!' He looked at Jenny. 'You know what that was, don't you?'

'I've got a pretty good idea.'

Michael switched off the power, removed the battery, then tried to reboot, but the laptop remained frozen on the same blank screen. He quickly switched it off again, reasoning that the damage done by the Trojan Horse contained in the email could be limited and some of the data on the computer's hard drive retained, but Jenny didn't hold out much hope. Whoever planted the virus had known exactly what they were doing, and they had acted quickly.

'We didn't even get to look at her documents,' Jenny said.

Michael sat back on the bed with a look of disbelief. 'Who the hell sent that?'

'Whoever shut down Airbuzz?'

'If the left-luggage ticket was in her wallet, why not just go and collect her computer?'

'You're presuming whoever it was had access to the physical evidence. Maybe they didn't?'

They sat in silence for a moment, both contemplating what might have been.

'I feel stupid,' Jenny said. 'Anyone knows you don't open messages like that.'

Michael sat, shoulders hunched, pale and exhausted. All the energy seemed to have drained from his body.

It was up to Jenny to make the running. 'I need to speak to Mick Dalton. Where do I get his number?'

'David Cambourne?'

'No. I don't want them talking.' She got out her phone and handed it to Michael. 'You know how airports work – there must be someone you can call at Heathrow.'

Jenny waited on tenterhooks while he first dialled a main switchboard for the British Airports Authority, then slowly worked his way through three other offices before finally being patched through to the chief engineer on duty for Ransome Airways. Michael placed a hand over the receiver. 'Who shall I say I am?'

'Tell him you're with the coroner's office.'

Moments later he was writing down Dalton's number on the motel menu card and Jenny was simultaneously entering the digits into her phone. She had pressed dial even before Michael had rung off.

She waited nearly half a minute for the phone to be answered. A male voice said a cautious hello.

'Mick Dalton?' Jenny enquired.

'Who is this?'

'Jenny Cooper, Severn Vale District Coroner. I need to meet with you, Mr Dalton – this evening if possible.'

Dalton was silent for a moment. 'It's past ten o'clock—'

'Would you prefer me to call on you at work?'

'No—' He hesitated. 'I thought I'd already dealt with the coroner's office.'

'It was you who left Miss Casey's flight bag in the Heathrow car park, wasn't it? Mr Cambourne must have mentioned my name.'

Silence.

He was frightened. She would have to leave him no choice. 'I'm quite certain you've been contacted by Sir James Kendall's office since then, and that you have been asked not to speak to anyone else, but they can't stop you from talking to another coroner, nor are they entitled to. I'm dealing with the death of a man killed on the water. I've also seen Nuala Casey's diary and a number of her papers. You met with her five times last December and I've seen your initials on sensitive documents in her possession.'

Now she had terrified him.

'Mr Dalton? . . . Mr Dalton, are you there?'

'I can't . . . I can't afford to lose my . . . I . . .' He ran out of words. Jenny sensed that she had brought the sky crashing down on his head.

'Do you think the truth about something this huge can be concealed for ever? Six hundred people died, Mr Dalton. You can't afford not to talk to me.'

TWENTY

DALTON PICKED THE RENDEZVOUS: a lay-by off a country lane named Drift Road, a short distance from the motorway and halfway between the motel and Heathrow. Tired as he was, Michael insisted on coming with her, saying that it wasn't safe for a woman to drive out to such a remote spot alone. Jenny didn't know whether to feel grateful or patronized, but as she turned off the M4 onto a winding lane virtually empty of traffic, she was glad not to be by herself.

They pulled into the lay-by shortly before eleven p.m. and waited in silence for Dalton to arrive. Over the course of ten minutes several vehicles passed by but none pulled over.

'Do you think he's too scared?' Jenny said.

'Given that he's already driven past three times, I'd say he was a little nervous.'

'How do you know it was him?'

'I memorized the number plate.' A headlight beam clipped over the top of the hedge ahead of them. 'What's the betting this is him again? Fourth time lucky.'

The headlights' rate of progress appeared to slow. A left-hand indicator blinked and Jenny made out the outline of an estate car pulling in to face them head-on.

She reached for the door handle.

'Stay here,' Michael said. 'Let him come to you.'

They waited, letting Dalton sweat. In less than a minute he had switched off his headlights and stepped outside.

Jenny wound down her window. 'Jump in the back, Mr Dalton – it's cold out there.'

'Who's with you?'

'Michael Sherman. He's a pilot, a friend of Nuala's.'

Dalton stalled, confused by the information. It was what Jenny had feared.

'Is this an official conversation?' he asked.

She had to make a snap decision and decided to follow her instinct. 'This one's strictly unofficial. Off the record. Never happened.'

Still standing next to his car, Dalton peered warily through the windscreen of Jenny's Land Rover, showing no sign of coming closer. Before she could stop him, Michael opened the passenger door and climbed out.

'I'm sure we've met, Mr Dalton – one of those company parties. Nuala took me to a couple. I met Dan and Diane Murray, too. We were over talking to her the other day – poor woman's left with teenage kids.'

Jenny saw Dalton nod. Michael stepped forward, extending a hand and Dalton reluctantly shook it.

'Don't worry about a thing. I'm sure Mrs Cooper won't keep you long.'

He shepherded him towards the Land Rover.

Dalton climbed into the back seat but refused to close the door, leaving it open a crack and sending a cold breeze onto Jenny's neck. Insisting on inspecting her ID, he examined it closely by the light of a miniature torch attached to his key chain. His every tic and movement confirmed Jenny's impression of his cautious, fastidious nature.

'I've no reason to think you're not who you say you are, Mrs Cooper,' he said finally, handing her wallet back between the front seats, 'but before you tell me what you'd like to know, perhaps you could explain exactly *why* I should talk to you?'

'Nuala Casey was interested in aircraft defects, and if I understand correctly, overall responsibility for the safety and maintenance of Ransome's Heathrow fleet lies with you.'

'Everyone in aviation is interested in safety.' He paused, then qualified his statement: 'Nearly everybody. But you'll forgive me – you still haven't answered my question.'

Jenny decided on a subtler course than the one she'd originally had in mind. 'You were a friend or colleague of many of the people who died on Flight 189. I'm assuming you don't want it to happen again.'

'No,' he replied sombrely.

Jenny waited a moment, letting the tension between them dissolve. Her gut told her that he was a decent man who would talk just as soon as he felt he could trust her.

'The fact is I'm interested in finding out what brought that plane down and letting it be known,' Jenny said. 'And although it saddens me to say it, I don't believe that the other agencies investigating this incident necessarily share that ambition.'

There was silence in the back seat.

'I'm going to ask you some questions. I have no recording equipment, this isn't a formal interview, I'm just anxious to cast a little more light, that's all.' She glanced in the rear-view mirror and made out the outline of his face. He was staring intently through the window at the road. 'Nuala had written your initials, MD, on a copy of a US Federal Aviation Authority directive issued after Air France 447 went down in the Pacific. Can you explain why that was?'

'Perhaps she wanted to ask me about it. She was very interested in aircraft safety issues.'

'You didn't give it to her.'

'No. I did not.'

Jenny didn't believe him, but left it alone.

'I've heard about a couple of incidents involving Ransome aircraft last year. One was a flight to Zagreb that overshot its destination. I understand that it was in danger of running out of fuel.'

'That's no secret. It was reported to the AAIB. It was a navigational error. I'm afraid no one's got to the bottom of that yet. For what's it worth, I believe the first officer made an error when he programmed in the route which he subsequently sought to disguise.'

'Was that first officer David Cambourne?'

'I believe so. Look, that was one of our oldest Boeings.' A note of impatience entered his voice. 'Most of our fleet is brand new, but that aircraft is over twenty-five years old. There's insufficient memory in the on-board computer to program in the whole route. The first officer has to program the second half of a journey as they're flying. It's most likely to have been a human error.'

Jenny glanced at Michael. He seemed happy enough with Dalton's answer.

'There was an incident on a 380 last summer. Dan Murray was in his first month captaining the aircraft. His wife described it as a glitch with the thrust levers as he was coming in to land. I think I remember this correctly – autothrust should automatically have disengaged, but it didn't. They were lucky not to have shot off the end of the runway.'

'I remember,' Dalton said. 'It happened here at Heathrow. The equipment was tested a total of fifty times and the fault never repeated itself, nor was there anything in the flight data commensurate with such a fault. It was clearly a case of human error. The most likely cause of overrun is landing too far along the runway. Captain Murray was relatively new to piloting the 380 at the time.'

Jenny was dubious. 'Forgive me for saying so, but that

sounds like the party line, Mr Dalton. You don't really think that Captain Murray would have invented a fictitious fault to cover up his own error.'

'Pilots invariably don't know they are committing an error, and after the event – quite naturally – their memories remain false. Flight data is a far more reliable source of information than a pilot's recollection.'

'Spoken like a true engineer,' Michael said.

'I can assure you, an aircraft built and maintained by intuition rather than logic would not be a safe one.'

Jenny touched Michael's arm, urging him to leave this to her.

'We've seen an addendum to his contract of employment that Dan Murray was asked to sign shortly after that incident. It obliged him not to report any such incident to the authorities directly, but to go through the airline.'

'I'm afraid I can't comment on that,' Dalton said.

'Can't or won't?'

'We all have contracts of employment. Many contain things we find objectionable. Can we move on, please?'

'All right, Mr Dalton, perhaps you can help with this: there are references to an AF in Nuala's diary. She met this person at Heathrow early last November. Do you know who that might have been?'

'It might have been Alan Farraday. He was another 380 pilot.'

'For Ransome?'

'Yes.' Dalton shifted uneasily in his seat. 'I'm not sure I'm comfortable with this any longer.'

'Please, I'm sure this is a matter I can clarify elsewhere, but it would be very helpful if you could save me the effort.'

Dalton gave a frustrated sigh. 'I doubt that very much – there's no official record, but if you can guarantee I won't be quoted as the source—'

Jenny and Michael exchanged a glance.

'You have my word.'

Dalton hesitated before answering. 'Farraday was a very experienced pilot. There was an incident last October. He was flying a 380 between Los Angeles and Sydney when he suffered multiple computer failure. He ended up flying on direct law – effectively manually, insofar as that's possible on an Airbus – for twenty minutes, and with no communications. He and the first officer obeyed all the prescribed protocols and the incident passed off safely. They successfully rebooted the primary flight computer, which continued to function perfectly.'

'You say there's no official record.'

'Not that I'm aware of, but there was a small article in the Australian press. I'm only repeating what you might have found on the internet.'

'How can that be? Surely a major incident like that has to be reported by law.'

'I heard about it anecdotally, Mrs Cooper, several weeks after the event. It was never reported to me in the usual manner, and no one from the AAIB has questioned me about it. After I had heard, I carried out tests on the aircraft's avionics independently and detected no faults.'

'How common is this sort of thing? Could that incident have been due to human error?'

'In my opinion, human error is possible but unlikely. As for the rate of occurrence, I can only say that such incidents are rare but not unknown. In the early years of my career my time was spent almost entirely with mechanical faults traceable to worn or defective components. Now I'm concerned chiefly with electrical faults and computer anomalies.'

'I've heard that phrase a lot recently,' Jenny said.

'They happen,' Dalton answered. 'Thirty years isn't long

enough to have perfected such a complex technology. We're still learning to walk, and sometimes we fall over.'

'What you're saying is that Ransome hushed this thing up,' Michael said.

'One might draw that inference,' Dalton answered, 'though I'm not saying that I have.'

'What do you think caused the failure?' Jenny asked.

'A software error, I expect. Even the best-written programs are bound to contain a few. Or possibly an electronic fault. The good news is that, unlike earlier Airbus models, the 380 has modular avionics. It means the on-board computers aren't closed and entire units, but made up of integrated modules which can be periodically updated or replaced. In theory, at least, it's a system that makes it easier to correct faults once they become apparent.'

'But not if they're not reported.'

'I'm sure the people who ought to know do,' Dalton said. 'This is a *business* after all.'

As he spoke, his gaze turned to follow a car that was driving past. It was moving more slowly than the handful of vehicles that had gone by during their conversation, and it seemed to agitate him.

'Will we be much longer?'

'If you don't mind, I need to ask you about your meetings with Nuala in December.'

'What about them?' he said impatiently.

'What did you discuss?'

He didn't answer. Jenny checked the mirror and saw him craning his neck to watch the progress of the car's headlights along the road behind them.

'Mr Dalton?'

'They were private conversations.'

'I appreciate that, but there was clearly something in particular she was asking you about.'

'Yes—'

'What was it?'

'I think that vehicle's turning around.'

Jenny checked her mirrors. 'I don't see anything. Please, this is very important. We know Nuala ran an anonymous forum for pilots online to discuss their concerns. We also know that it was shut down almost immediately after 189 was lost.'

'Very prudent. Journalists would only have used it to whip up hysteria.' He had turned right round in his seat and was looking apprehensively out of the back window.

Jenny told herself to keep patient. She was making progress, albeit slowly.

'You don't strike me as a frivolous man, yet you met with her five times in various locations. You also assisted Mr Cambourne in getting Nuala's flight case to us. You can understand that I might conclude that, firstly, you were discussing something important and, secondly, there was something you wanted me to know.'

'The GPS—' Michael interrupted. 'You wanted us to see the GPS in her flight case. Did the navigation go down on Farraday's flight, too?'

'I did hear that both navigation displays were behaving erratically.'

'So she had her own GPS when she flew – is that what was going on?'

'She did take that precaution, though whether the GPS signal would penetrate the hull of a modern aircraft, I couldn't say.'

'Did you speak to Farraday?'

'Not personally.'

'Did Nuala?'

'They had been in communication. What form that took precisely, I don't know.'

Jenny was starting to lose patience. 'Can we just cut to the chase – was Nuala trying to get you to get to the bottom of what happened on Farraday's flight?'

'Yes.'

'And did you?'

'No.'

Michael cut in. 'Had she discovered other incidents?'

Jenny turned her head at the sound of a car drawing up alongside them in the road. It was a dark saloon; its headlights were off and the occupants invisible.

'I told you—' Dalton said, panicked.

'Sit tight,' Michael said calmly.

Dalton started to push open his door.

'Stay there, I said.'

Dalton froze, silent save for his anxious, laboured breathing. They waited, but the car didn't move. It stood fewer than ten feet away from them, its engine idling.

'Who is that?' Jenny said.

'I don't know, but I've seen the car before,' Dalton said. 'Someone's been watching my house—'

'Ignore it,' Michael said. 'Keep talking.'

Jenny said, 'Perhaps I should be talking to Farraday.'

'You don't know?' Dalton replied.

'Know what?'

'Farraday died in a motorcycle accident in November. His first officer was Dan Murray's co-pilot, Ed Stevens.'

Jenny felt her heart thud so hard she thought it might burst. 'You're sure it was an accident?'

'How could I be sure?' Dalton said.

Michael opened the glove box. Jenny saw him close his fist around the locking wheel nut she kept in there, but before she could work out why he might want to change a wheel, he threw open his door and jumped out.

'Michael!'

He ran at the idling car and hurled the nut straight through the windscreen. She heard glass smashing, a man shout from inside and the squeal of tyres as the car took off, the headlights lighting up as it cleared the lay-by.

Michael ran back to the passenger door. 'Get after it. He'll freeze to death before he gets half a mile.'

Without thinking, Jenny turned the key in the ignition, but as Michael leaped in, Dalton jumped out.

'Leave him,' Michael barked.

Jenny pulled out into the road and slammed her foot to the floor, but the car's headlights were already far in the distance and her hands were shaking so hard she could barely grip the wheel.

Jenny was too shattered to make the two-hour journey home and there were no rooms vacant at the motel. Michael insisted she have the bed in his while he took a blanket and pillow and lay on the floor.

During the drive back from their encounter with Dalton he had phoned Sandy Belling and caught her during an overnight turnaround in Cairo. She confirmed that Alan Farraday had died commuting home from work. According to the police account he had lost control of his bike and launched over the central reservation of the M4 motorway en route to Heathrow. He had been divorced six months previously and lived alone. The rumour among his colleagues was that he had been drinking.

'Are you still awake?' Jenny said.

'Uh-huh,' Michael said groggily.

'Do you believe that about Farraday?'

'They happen.'

'What do?'

'Accidents. No one who's interested in living rides a motorbike in November anyway.'

'I still think it's too much of a coincidence.'

'It was an accident, that's all.' Michael said. 'Airlines want to protect their business, but they don't kill people. The moment you start believing that stuff, you're officially insane.'

'What's making you so angry?'

'I don't believe in conspiracies.'

'But we've just been followed—'

'By a private detective. The airline's jumpy and they've got wind that Dalton's a loose cannon.'

'Is that what you think Nuala was?'

'She was a nice girl, but she would have believed in fairies at the end of the garden if enough people told her they'd seen them.'

'I don't understand . . . Dalton clearly thought something was being covered up, too. And do you remember when we spoke to Sandy Belling last week – she mentioned the military-sounding man who called her asking whether Nuala had her computer with her? She said he frightened her.'

Michael fell silent. A while later, he said, 'I want to let Nuala go.'

'Wouldn't she have wanted you to find out the truth?'

'She went looking for trouble and she found it.'

Jenny heard him roll over and let out a deep despairing sigh. She listened to his jerky breathing interrupted by moans and troubled, half-formed words. Worried for him, she reached down from the bed and stroked his head until slowly he became calm, and she too felt the heaviness of sleep descend.

When she woke, he was gone.

TWENTY-ONE

THE FROST LAY THICK AND HARD for the entire weekend. It was the kind of cold that prised its icy fingers under every door and clawed at Jenny's skin when she left the warmth of her cottage to fetch firewood from the little tumbledown mill at the end of the garden. Not a bird or a rabbit stirred. The deer that came early each morning to drink from the stream stayed hidden in the shelter of the woods. At any moment she expected a call informing her that her inquest would not be allowed to continue, but her overseers remained as ominously silent as the crows perched on the birch tree opposite her study window.

Michael's phone remained switched off and he refused to answer her messages. When she allowed herself to think of him, it was with anxious concern. Their encounter with Dalton had caused his mood to darken even further. It was as if being confronted with the proof that Nuala had indeed got hold of dangerous information made him see it as confirmation that the world was after all as bleak a place as he had feared. She wanted to tell him it was all right, that there was nothing he could have done, that Nuala would have wanted him to keep safe, but at the same time she could hear him say that none of that was true, that Nuala had deliberately steered a perilous course, hoping against hope that he would do what she longed for and step in to rescue her.

Aside from a brief conversation with her hung-over and monosyllabic son, the only other voice she heard all weekend belonged to the matron at her father's nursing home, who interrupted her work with a call to say that he was stable but beginning to weaken. She didn't state explicitly that he was past the point of no return and that his only daughter's place was at his side, but that was the subtext she delivered in her quietly disapproving tone. Jenny assured her that she would be over in the next day or two, just as soon as work calmed down.

It was nearly midnight when she turned out her desk lamp and packed her briefcase with all that she needed for court. She had no idea what tomorrow would bring, but as she climbed the narrow wooden stairs to bed, the vixen screeching across a frozen field sounded out a portent.

The door to the hall in Sharpness was unlocked when Jenny arrived shortly before eight-thirty. Alison was already setting out the furniture and cranking up the radiators.

'You're early, Mrs Cooper,' she said in the brisk, judgemental tone Jenny had heard so many times in recent weeks.

'Would you like a hand?'

'I can manage, thank you.' She hoisted another chair from the top of a stack and thumped it on the floor.

'Thank you for organizing the witness statements,' Jenny said in an attempt to mollify her.

'There's no need to thank me for doing my job.'

'I didn't give you much time.'

'I've had to get used to that.' Another chair crashed onto the boards. 'Though I must say I've had rather more than usual to cope with, what with you devoting so much attention to this case. There have been eight more deaths reported over the weekend.'

'You've been to the office this morning?'

'It doesn't run itself.' She scraped the chairs into a line, her every movement a minor act of revenge for some perceived crime Jenny had committed. 'Lucky for you I did – there was an email from Dr Kerr. I left his report on your desk. I told him to be here promptly.'

'Thank you.' She gathered her strength. 'Alison, is this about the photographer's wife?

'Someone had to talk to her.'

'How was she?' Jenny asked, refusing to be cowed.

'Beside herself,' Alison said. 'She had spent the last two weeks thinking he'd been speeding because she'd had a row with him on the phone. They'd planned to go out that Saturday evening, but at the last minute he took off on a job. She had no idea he'd gone to meet another woman.'

'Do we know for sure that's what he was doing?'

'He'd rented a hotel room in Stroud. She obviously went over to meet him there.' Alison sighed impatiently. 'You don't get it, do you? While we've been sitting on our hands the poor widow has been blaming herself for her husband's death.'

'It couldn't be helped.'

'Of course it could have been helped. We could have been doing our jobs properly instead of the bidding of some crackpot American.'

'Is that what you think this is?'

Alison stopped what she was doing and turned to face her. 'I'm not going to lie to you, Mrs Cooper, I've had Simon Moreton on the phone to me this weekend wanting to know every last detail of how you've been running this case and every other one you care to mention. He didn't come out and say it, but he didn't have to – he thinks you're unbalanced.'

So that's what Moreton had been doing all weekend – gathering ammunition. 'What did you tell him?'

'The truth, what did you expect?'

'Do you think I'm unbalanced?'

'I certainly didn't tell him that,' Alison said, dodging the question. 'And for what it's worth I think you could be a very good coroner, but you seem to have a self-destructive streak—'

'Why didn't you call me and tell me this was happening?'

Alison shook her head. 'I can't cope with this any more, Mrs Cooper. It happens time and again. You go overboard, the Ministry gets furious and I get stuck in the middle.' Her voice filled with emotion as the bottled-up resentment of weeks and months came spilling out. 'All I want is to do my job and sort my life out, and I'm not prepared to sacrifice what's left of it for the sake of your crusades. I'm fifty-seven years old, I've got no husband, I live alone in a poky flat and you act as if we're both prepared to risk it all – and for what?'

'I'm sorry if you feel—'

'I don't *feel*, Mrs Cooper. It's what you *do*. You don't know when to stop. You say you care about all these people, but you don't care enough about those closest to you, let alone yourself.' Her eyes flooded with tears. 'I'm sorry. Excuse me.' She hurried out of the hall.

Jenny had never felt more grateful for the magic contained in a small white pill than when she stepped out to face a packed and hostile courtroom. Not even Alison's was a friendly face. The lawyers – Hartley for Ransome Airways, Bannerman for Sir James Kendall, Crowthorne for the North Somerset Police and Rachel Hemmings representing the Pattersons – were bristling with resentment at the repeated delays and obfuscation over evidence. Mrs Patterson couldn't have looked more mistrustful and disappointed if Jenny had announced that she was in the pay of a hostile foreign power. And evidently the handsome fees she was generating for Galbraith's firm were no longer enough to keep a smile on her solicitor's face. His expression said that he had been through several days of torment and couldn't wait for his ordeal to be over.

The rows behind the lawyers were full to bursting. Among the closely packed journalists, news reporters and assorted observers who could have been from airlines, intelligence agencies or one of the many government departments touched by a major transport disaster, Jenny picked out the unsmiling face of Simon Moreton. And squeezed in at the end of the back row, almost forgotten, was the slight, timid figure of Brogan's girlfriend, Maria Canavan.

As she took her seat she reminded herself why she was putting herself through this ordeal. She pictured Amy Patterson's slender body lying on the beach. She recalled every detail of her delicate, trusting features and thought of her freezing to death in the icy water. That was enough. She couldn't understand why it wasn't enough for everybody.

Jenny turned to the jury, thanked them for their patience and assured them that she intended their duty to be over shortly. They would hear from five witnesses: a member of the public who had discovered a lifejacket believed to be Brogan's; a forensic scientist who led the team which had examined it; a local man who had spotted strange aircraft over the estuary minutes after the crash; another who claimed to have heard them; and the brigadier in command of the nearby Beachley army base.

Giles Hartley QC rose unprompted from his seat. 'This is all extremely interesting, ma'am, and certainly news to me, as I'm sure it is to my learned friends. It is customary, indeed expected, however, that the coroner provide copies of witness statements in advance of a hearing.'

'I appreciate that, Mr Hartley, but how can I put this

delicately?' Jenny glanced at Moreton. 'The evidence raises certain security implications that were judged too sensitive to risk being leaked to the world at large.'

'I see,' Hartley said, and unable to resist probing at an open wound, continued: 'I hope you're not suggesting, ma'am, that you have bent to any improper pressure? You do appreciate that a higher court would look very dimly on such an admission. Indeed, if such were the case, these proceedings could be brought to an immediate halt.'

'Nice try, Mr Hartley,' Jenny said. 'I can assure you, I haven't bent to any pressure, nor do I intend to.' She aimed her next remark at the journalists in the hall. 'Any and all information I have received in relation to Mr Brogan's death will be heard. It has never been my practice, nor will it ever be, to suppress evidence.' She glanced again at Simon Moreton. 'I can think of no greater crime against justice.'

His face remained a tablet of stone.

'And while we're on the subject of incomplete evidence, Mr Hartley, I still expect to hear from Mr Ransome. Tomorrow morning?'

'I shall take instructions, ma'am.'

'No, Mr Hartley. You will convey my instructions to him. He will give evidence first thing tomorrow morning.'

Hartley nodded with an expression of faux sincerity. 'Very good, ma'am.'

'May we have the first witness, please?'

Alison walked the length of the hall and knocked on the door of the small side room she had allocated for witnesses. Moments later she returned with a witness Jenny had not seen before: Thomas Evans.

A solid, no-nonsense man in his mid-fifties, Evans was known to nearly everyone in the town of Chepstow as the owner of a local firm of building contractors. Though by no means a wealthy man, he owned a modest thirty-foot ocean-going yacht which, when it wasn't moored in Bristol marina, he kept in the mouth of the River Wye beneath the walls of Chepstow Castle.

On the morning of the crash he had intended to go down to the boat to try to fix the seals on a faulty pump, but had become caught up with the unfolding news of the disaster on television. It was mid-afternoon by the time he rowed his dingy out to the middle of the river, and it had been dark for nearly an hour by the time he finished his job. He was up on deck making sure the boat was securely tied to the buoys before he left for the night, when he saw something glowing in the water off the port side. He fetched a boathook and fished it out. He saw immediately that it was a lifejacket, and a good one, too.

'Please show the witness exhibit TE1.'

Alison brought the evidence bag out from a holdall stowed under her desk and handed it to Evans. It contained the lifejacket enclosed in the sealed polythene bag in which it had been securely couriered back from Forenox.

'Is that the item you retrieved from the water?' Jenny asked.

'It is,' Evans said.

'Was it floating on the surface when you first saw it?'

'No. That was the odd thing. It was sort of suspended a few inches below. When I fetched it out I saw that it had a hole in it – a puncture.'

'What did you do with it?'

'To be honest I thought someone must have dumped it, thinking it was damaged beyond repair. But I thought I might be able to patch it up. I stowed it below, intending to have a look at it next time I was on the boat.'

'Who did you think might have dumped a lifejacket?'

'There were tens of rescue boats out on the water that day. Could have been anyone.'

'I see. And did you check to see if it had any identifying marks?'

'I saw that it came from Dublin, that's all. Like I said, I thought it had been abandoned.'

'Was there anything else about it that you noticed?'

'Not that night, but later on – I saw that one of the straps had been cut. I guessed whoever discarded it must have done it to try to make it safe. You couldn't wear it like that – there's nothing to secure it.'

Evans went on to explain how he had received an email circulated to local yacht club members from the police asking whether anyone had seen helicopters flying over the estuary shortly after the plane went down. It also mentioned that information was being sought about an Irish yacht that was hit by the plane. It was then that he made the connection with the lifejacket he had found the previous weekend and contacted Chepstow police station.

'How far from the site of the plane crash was your yacht moored, Mr Evans?'

'Over the water? About six miles or so.'

'And what was the tide doing at the time you picked up the lifejacket?'

'It was going out – just about low water, in fact.'

'So the jacket was coming downstream along the River Wye towards the Severn estuary?'

'It was.'

Jenny referred back to the notes she had made during the evidence given by Dick Corton from the Marine Accident Investigation Branch during the previous week's session. 'High tide on the 9th was at approximately ten-thirty a.m., or one hour after the plane went down. That being so, if the lifejacket went into the water at approximately nine-thirty and was carried by the tide, it shouldn't have been inland, it should have been miles to the west.'

'You'd think so,' Evans said, 'but if it had made it as far as the Wye it could have got snagged up on a buoy line or a rope or something. There was plenty for it to catch on.'

No expert on tides or geography, Jenny sketched a diagram of the estuary in her legal pad. The mouth of the Wye was right beneath the Welsh end of the Severn Bridge. The distance from there to where Evans's yacht was anchored was approximately a mile. From the mouth of the Wye to the crash site was closer to five.

'You're familiar with the tides in the estuary, Mr Evans?'

'I've been sailing it since I was a boy. There was no bridge to Bristol then – it was boat or swim.'

He raised a chuckle from the jury and an arch smile from Giles Hartley.

'Can you tell me, in your opinion, how this lifejacket could have travelled five miles up the estuary, turned left and been carried at least another mile up the Wye in one hour?'

Evans shook his head. 'Couldn't happen.'

Hartley shot to his feet. 'With respect, ma'am, Mr Evans is an amateur sailor, not a maritime expert. His opinion on tidal flow is hardly reliable scientific evidence.'

'Point taken, Mr Hartley. If you consider it necessary I'll allow you to call such an expert – would that satisfy you?'

Wrong-footed, Hartley replied that he reserved the right to do precisely that, and let Jenny continue.

'Assuming the lifejacket could have gone in the water at a point closer to where you found it, how close would it have to have been to get as far as Chepstow in under an hour?'

'The thing is,' Evans said, 'for anything to come up the Wye from the estuary it's got to go in the water tight up close to that side. There's no way it came all the way over from the other side where the plane went down.'

Jenny looked over at Mrs Patterson. Suddenly animated, she was conferring with Galbraith and Rachel Hemmings.

Wait until you hear what's coming next, Jenny thought to herself.

'Thank you, Mr Evans. You've been most helpful.' She looked at the lawyers. 'Any questions for this witness?'

'If I may?' Rufus Bannerman said, polishing his glasses with a handkerchief as he stood to cross-examine. 'Mr Evans – you said it yourself, there were tens, if not hundreds of boats out searching for survivors on the estuary that day. You were aware of them no doubt.'

'Yes, I was. I was listening to them on the radio, in fact.'

'The ship-to-shore radio on your yacht?'

'Yes.'

'Did you see any search boats come as far as where your boat was moored?'

'They definitely came up as far as Beachley.'

'Which in effect is the mouth of the River Wye?'

'It is.'

'Thank you, Mr Evans, that's all.'

So much for her amateur oceanography. Bannerman hadn't only holed her theory beneath the waterline, he had sunk it without trace. She released Evans from the witness chair and asked Alison to fetch Lawrence Cole.

Her fears about his credibility as a witness were more than realized when she saw him approaching from the back of the hall dressed in a suit which had evidently spent thirty-five years in the wardrobe save for the occasional – and ever more uncomfortable – wedding or funeral. He looked exactly what he was – a petty criminal who'd done a bad job of scrubbing up for his day in court.

When Alison handed him the oath card, he reddened with embarrassment. 'Sorry, ma'am,' he muttered, 'not too good with letters, like.'

Hartley sat back in his chair with a smile, enjoying the prospect of an illiterate witness to taunt.

'Repeat after me,' Alison began, 'I swear by Almighty God that I shall tell the truth, the whole truth and nothing but the truth.'

Cole mumbled his way through a rough approximation of what he had just heard. It would have to do.

Jenny led him gently through the preliminaries, aware that the only times he would have seen the inside of a courtroom would have been when he was facing a criminal charge. He gave his name as Lawrence Arthur Cole, he was sixty-three years old and a casual labourer by profession.

'Mr Cole, can you please tell the court what you saw on the morning of 9 January.'

He scratched his head and looked vaguely puzzled. Hartley raised his eyebrows.

'The morning the plane went down,' Jenny prompted.

'Oh,' Cole said, 'yes, well, let's see now –' he cleared his throat noisily – 'I'd been fishing down on the river. Not much luck that morning, far as I remember. The tide was too high, the water was all stirred up. Your fish won't see the bait when it's all dirty, like.'

Jenny waited patiently for him to get to the point.

'I was just giving it up for a bad job when I heard the plane coming over. Making a sound like one of those World War Two bombers, it was.' He gave a low growl for the benefit of the jury. 'I looked up and there it was – appearing out of the fog. Huge great thing. I'd never seen one like that before, not there anyhow.'

'Can you describe what it looked like? Was it intact? Could you see any flames?'

'I didn't see nothing wrong with it,' Cole said. 'It looked normal, but like it was coming in to land.'

'Did you see it touch the water?'

He shook his head. 'Too foggy. It disappeared off to the west. I heard it come down though. It wasn't a bang, more like a rumble of thunder – a boom, that's what it was.'

Jenny became aware that the room had fallen eerily silent. She realized it was the first time that anyone had heard live testimony of Flight 189's last moments. The lawyers were all taking careful notes; Mrs Patterson was wiping tears from her cheeks.

'I knew what had happened – it was plain as day. I packed up my kit and hurried back up the lane – I wanted to hear what they were going to say about it on the wireless. Anyway, it was no more than ten minutes later, I was just about to turn down the track to my place when I heard this chop-chop-chop coming from the same direction the plane had come. I turned round and saw these two black helicopters skimming over the water, like. No more than a few feet up they were. And the one in front had this orange searchlight.'

'Was there anything else that struck you about them?' Jenny asked.

'Little wings, they had – on the underneath, like.' He produced a folded scrap of paper from his jacket pocket. 'I drew a picture.' He held up a sketch similar to one he had made for Jenny in his caravan, only substantially larger and more detailed. He had an unrealized talent.

Jenny gestured Alison to hand it to the jury first, making the impatient lawyers wait their turn.

'Where did the helicopters go, Mr Cole?'

'Same way as the plane.'

'And then?'

'It was only a couple of minutes later – I was going through the gate to my place when I thought I heard a bang. It wasn't as loud as the first one, and it was different – like when you hear a shotgun echo off the side of a valley.'

'Just the one bang?'

'That's all I heard.'

'Did you see or hear the helicopters again?'

'No, I was inside listening to the news. I couldn't believe it—' He shook his head. 'Wild horses wouldn't drag me onto one of those things.'

Jenny gave Rachel Hemmings the privilege of being first to cross-examine. Stoically ignoring the constant flow of whispered instructions issuing from Mrs Patterson behind her, she treated Cole with the kid gloves she must have used so effectively in the family courts.

'Mr Cole, would you say you're an observant man?'

'I suppose so.'

'You spend a lot of time by the estuary?'

'I do.'

'Have you ever seen anything like those helicopters before?'

'I can't say I have.'

'And you're sure about the timings – less than ten minutes after the plane went down.'

'Certain of it. It's not half a mile from the beach to my place. I was in a hurry, too.'

'Have you ever seen a search and rescue operation mounted on the water?'

'Once or twice. I've seen the rescue helicopter go over quite often, mind. This wasn't one of them – they're bigger like, and they don't have the wings.'

'That is unusual, I agree.'

Galbraith thrust a note in front of her. It was clear that this was an instruction from Mrs Patterson that she wasn't being given the option to ignore.

'What you describe as the "wings" on these two helicopters – did they appear to have anything attached to them?'

Cole looked blank.

'What you have described is, I'm given to understand, a military-style helicopter that might have guns or missiles.'

He shook his head. 'I'd be lying if I said there were. I didn't get a clear enough look at them, to be honest.'

'But the bang you heard a few minutes later – you described it as an explosion?'

'Like a big firework going off, that's what it sounded like.'

'I understand. Now one final thing – you said that you saw no obvious damage on the aircraft or smoke trailing from it as it passed over.'

'That's right.'

'Would I be correct in assuming you only saw one side of the aircraft – its right-hand side?'

'Yes – that'd be it.'

'And there was dense fog over the water, from which smoke may have been indistinguishable?'

Cole thought for a moment. 'I hadn't thought of that, to be honest with you.'

'Thank you, Mr Cole. You've been most helpful.'

'Does anyone else have questions for this witness?' Jenny asked.

Bannerman nodded towards Hartley, who was looking at something on a laptop screen which had been shown to him by his instructing solicitor. Jenny caught a glimpse of a page from an online newspaper. Hartley rose to address the witness, wearing a faintly amused smile.

'Would you say that you are a trustworthy man, Mr Cole?'

'If I can trust you, I am,' Cole answered defensively.

'What an interesting answer,' Hartley said. 'Well, I'm sure we can trust you to be honest under oath, so would you please tell me this – given the fact that you pleaded guilty to a charge of stealing diesel fuel last October, can I ask if you have been convicted of any other offences in the past?'

Cole turned warily to Jenny.

'He's entitled to test your credibility, Mr Cole,' she said. 'I'm afraid you'll have to answer.'

He turned back to Hartley, who was waiting expectantly. 'It's no secret. I've been in court a few times over the years.'

'What sort of offences have you committed? Perhaps we could begin with the most serious.'

Cole scowled. 'Burglary.'

'Domestic or commercial?'

Jenny cut in. 'How many years ago, Mr Cole?'

'I was no more than a kid.'

'Any offences of violence?'

'No.'

'Theft?'

Cole gave a reluctant nod.

'How many convictions?' Hartley asked.

Cole shrugged. 'Ten or so.'

'And you nevertheless consider yourself trustworthy.'

'I know what I saw.'

'You didn't see any smoke or flames, did you?'

'I never said I did.'

'Quite. And neither did you see anything to connect the bang you claim to have heard with any of the aircraft you claim to have seen.'

'It came from that direction.'

'I'll treat that as a "yes", shall I?'

Cole shrugged. He was getting impatient with Hartley's tone.

Hartley continued. 'These helicopters with "wings", how many were there?'

'Two.'

'Had you been drinking, Mr Cole?'

'I beg your pardon?'

'Had you been drinking down by the river? It's not unusual for an angler to have a nip or two, is it?'

'A drop to keep warm, that's all.'

'You don't think it might have been a drop too many?'

Cole's face hardened. 'I wouldn't come all this way to tell lies, would I?'

'Of course not. All I'm suggesting is that your recollection may not be altogether sound. One's perception of the passage of time, as we know, is apt to become a little distorted under the influence of alcohol, and senses somewhat dulled. Perhaps you saw a rescue helicopter twenty minutes later and heard a search flare being fired?'

'You can twist it whatever way you like, I know what I saw.'

'The question is, whether what you perceived corresponded with reality.' Hartley smiled at the jury. 'I wonder, Mr Cole. I wonder.' With a little theatrical shake of the head, he sat down. He didn't need to labour the point any further.

Susan Roberts, the farmer's wife whom Jenny had briefly spoken to nearly a week ago, had probably never been in a courtroom before. An anxious witness, her eyes darted from one lawyer to the next, then back to Jenny as she struggled to control her nerves while going through the preliminary formalities. She had given Alison only a brief, one-page statement and Jenny had it on the desk in front of her. If she repeated what she had told her officer, it would be enough to bolster Cole's shaky testimony, but no more.

'You were in your kitchen overlooking the estuary with your husband and child when the plane went down?'

'I was.'

'How far from the crash site is your house?'

'A mile or so.'

'The D-Mort is set up on one of your fields, is that right?'

She nodded, preferring to speak as little as possible.

'Tell me what you saw, Mrs Roberts?'

'Nothing. I was feeding the baby.'

'Then what did you hear?'

She paused and tugged at her cuff. 'A bit of a bang, that's all.'

'Can you be any more specific?'

She shook her head. 'Could have been a bird scarer, I suppose. That's what it sounded like.'

Jenny looked at the statement in front of her. It wasn't what she had told Alison less than forty-eight hours before.

'Did you hear anything else after that?'

'No. My husband thought he heard something. He went down to the field and saw the rescue helicopters and that. It was too foggy to see the plane.'

Jenny studied her face. She could tell the woman was lying, but why?

'You made a sworn statement to my officer the day before yesterday. In it, you say you were in the kitchen when you heard a loud explosion coming from the direction of the river. Your husband went outside to investigate. Later he told you that he had been hearing helicopters from the moment he set foot outside your front door, and that shortly afterwards they moved away. Isn't that what you said?'

Mrs Roberts gave another fearful glance in the direction of the lawyers, each of whom had been handed a copy of her statement by Alison. Mrs Patterson was craning over Rachel Hemmings's shoulder to read it.

'It's the way she asked the questions – those weren't my words, exactly.'

Jenny looked at Alison and saw her bristle with indignation.

'Are those your words or aren't they?'

'No.'

Alison's face had turned a bright shade of crimson. Jenny had never before heard her accused of not recording a witness's words accurately.

'You signed the statement, Mrs Roberts.' She held it up for her to see. 'There's your signature.'

'There was a bang, an explosion, whatever you like to call it. My husband went outside to see what it was. That was the beginning and end of it.'

'Has someone told you to downplay your evidence, Mrs Roberts?'

Her eyes fixed on the floor, Susan Roberts shook her head. If she were an advocate, Jenny would have been permitted to harry and cajole her, but as a coroner she had to avoid the appearance of bias at all costs.

'Mrs Roberts, what did your husband tell you about hearing helicopters?'

'He said he heard some. They were buzzing round all day.'

Giles Hartley and Rufus Bannerman exchanged a glance of mock consolation.

Jenny tried one more time. 'Have you discussed the contents of your written statement with anyone other than your husband since you put your signature to it?'

There was a pause that stretched for several long seconds.

'No,' Mrs Roberts said finally.

It was the one of the baldest lies Jenny had ever heard from an otherwise honest witness, but there was nothing she could do. From the corner of her eye Jenny saw Simon Moreton's mouth curl into a smile.

TWENTY-TWO

THE HELICOPTERS FADED FURTHER into the mist with the arrival of Brigadier William Russen in the witness chair. A trim, compact man with an impatient military manner, he had provided only the briefest statement affirming that he was aware of no helicopters in the vicinity of the Severn Bridge until the arrival of the first rescue helicopters nearly forty minutes after Flight 189 went down. There was only one helicopter at his camp on that morning, a Puma, and it was out of action undergoing routine maintenance. He insisted that there were not, nor had there ever been, any Apaches at the camp or any other aircraft that resembled one.

His evidence was precisely what she had expected it be. Hartley and Bannerman both looked delighted by what they were hearing, if not somewhat baffled as to why Jenny would have called a witness who was so obviously going to contradict the already tenuous evidence of Lawrence Cole. But there was more than a hint of method in her madness, and it would take a little while longer for it to play out.

'Brigadier,' Jenny continued, 'if two such helicopters had indeed flown past your camp, would you necessarily have noticed them? You're not an airport, you don't have radar, and I don't suppose you have people visually scanning the estuary at all times of the day.'

'I accept it's possible that aircraft might pass by with

which we have no radio contact. Not every civilian helicopter pilot flying at low altitudes does us the courtesy of announcing himself.'

'So it is possible that two helicopters passed by without you noticing them?'

'Possible, but unlikely, especially the kind of machines you've mentioned. As far as I'm aware, all those operated by the British forces are currently abroad.'

'And just so that I'm clear about this – if you were to see two suspicious aircraft over the estuary, what action would you take?'

'We would seek to make radio contact, and if that failed or proved unsatisfactory, I would refer the matter up the chain of command.'

'There is a prescribed procedure for dealing with potentially hostile aircraft, I take it?'

'Yes,' the brigadier said smartly, 'but of course I'm not at liberty to disclose precisely what that is in a public arena.'

'If the aircraft was deemed a sufficient threat, I presume an RAF jet would shoot it down.'

'That has never happened in the UK, but yes, it is theoretically possible.'

'Thank you, Brigadier.' Jenny turned to the lawyers. She could see that Rachel Hemmings was being loaded with questions from Mrs Patterson, who had been furiously writing notes throughout the witness's evidence. 'I'm going to ask the brigadier to remain in court until the final two witnesses have been heard. He may have something to say about their testimony. I suggest you may want to save your cross-examination until that time.'

Hartley, Bannerman and a brooding Crowthorne were more than happy to cooperate, and after a brief skirmish with her client, Rachel Hemmings too agreed to hold fire.

'Very well. Please take a seat, Brigadier.'

Jenny spotted him glance briefly at Moreton, whose fore-head was creased in a frown. Moreton then gave a hint of a nod and the brigadier did as Jenny had bidden, following Alison's direction to a vacant seat.

'We'll hear from Dr Ravi Achari, please.'

The forensic scientist was younger than Jenny had pictured him – only twenty-six – and with his delicate features could have passed for eighteen. Quietly spoken and slightly built, he didn't look a match for Giles Hartley, but Jenny didn't need him to impress, she just wanted the facts about what he had found. He told the court that he held a doctorate in analytical chemistry and had worked as a chemical analyst at Forenox for nearly two years. He didn't have experience on his side, but he certainly gave the impression of being at the cutting edge of his field.

Jenny directed Alison to hand him Brogan's lifejacket and watched the lawyers' reaction as Achari methodically described the processes of spectrometry and chromatography which had yielded his results. As she suspected, the three men on the advocates' bench appeared unsurprised at the revelation that minute traces of plastic bonded explosive had been discovered embedded in the fabric of Brogan's lifejacket, but the evidence caused a sensation in the Patter-son camp. Jenny, the jury and all the people sitting around her heard Amy's mother excitedly whispering about terror-ists and the sophisticated weaponry she supposed they possessed.

But her reaction turned to one of puzzlement as Achari described the recent severing of the lifejacket's webbing and the tiny traces of metal swarf found both on the strap and at the site of the puncture. She didn't have a ready narrative for this twist and, nor yet, did Jenny.

'Tell me, Dr Achari, in your opinion, was the explosion

that caused this residue one that took place above or below the water?'

'Above, I'm fairly sure. My recent conversation with Dr Kerr substantiates that – I understand Mr Brogan had flash burns on exposed areas of his skin.'

'I see. And are you able to say how far from the explosion Mr Brogan might have been?'

'Of course it all depends on the size of the blast,' Achari said, 'but these particles were not deeply embedded in the fabric, and as far as I can ascertain, the flash burns were not intense. All I can offer is an educated opinion that the subject was at least fifty yards away from the blast, possibly much further – perhaps as far as two hundred yards.'

Hartley and Bannerman glanced at one another. Jenny intuited that this was a fact they hadn't fully grasped from whatever information Moreton had managed to extract from Achari's superiors at Forenox.

'Let's put that in context, shall we?' Jenny said. 'According to a witness we heard from last week, Mr Corton, a marine accidents investigator, Mr Brogan's yacht would have gone down literally seconds after being struck by the descending aircraft. That being the case, if the explosion emanated from his boat, it's hard to see how he could have got more than fifty yards away from it in only a few seconds.'

'I agree,' Achari said.

Hartley couldn't contain himself. 'Ma'am, no one could say how quickly Mr Brogan's yacht went down apart from Mr Brogan. It's a complete unknown.'

'I accept it's uncertain, Mr Hartley, but I have a note of Mr Corton's testimony in front of me.' She read aloud. ' "Given the extent of the damage to the yacht, I would say it went down almost immediately." Do tell me if you have a different recollection.'

Hartley looked to the attractive young junior counsel sitting obediently at his side. She flipped through her verbatim notes, then shook her head.

'Those may be his words, but I remain unsatisfied as to their meaning. I would caution against too literal an interpretation, ma'am.'

'I thank you for your advice,' Jenny replied, straining to remain courteous. She turned her attention back to Dr Achari.

'I understand that Dr Kerr asked you to carry out another set of tests over the course of the weekend that has just passed.'

'That's correct.'

Jenny glanced over at Moreton and the lawyers and saw that the revelation had caused the ripple of alarm she had expected. This was information they didn't have and their faces showed traces of panic. Moreton was already reaching for his phone.

'What did he ask you to examine?'

'He sent a hair and a tissue sample. I understand that both were taken from the rear of the skull of a child who was a passenger in the aircraft – Amy Patterson.'

Hartley shot to his feet. 'Ma'am, not only have we not been put on notice of this evidence, it appears to relate to a person who is not the subject of this inquest.'

Jenny couldn't resist a dose of sarcasm. 'I'm surprised this evidence is news to you, Mr Hartley. I understand you were fully briefed on Dr Achari's findings relating to Mr Brogan's lifejacket.'

'I have no idea what you are talking about, ma'am,' Hartley replied, daring her to raise the stakes and accuse him of dishonesty – a charge that would send him immediately scurrying to the High Court to accuse her of bias.

'Sit down please, Mr Hartley. I wish to hear the evidence. You were saying, Dr Achari?'

Achari opened the folder he had brought with him to the witness box and produced a number of photographs of small sealed Petri dishes containing labelled samples. Alison passed them around the jury.

'I examined both samples microscopically, using the same techniques I had applied to the lifejacket samples. In each I detected minute traces of uncombusted plastic bonded explosive. This, too, lacked the chemical marker required by the Montreal Treaty, making its origin impossible to trace. In addition, the hair sample showed definite signs of heat exposure: there was evidence of singeing, particularly at the tips. This is consistent with the girl having been briefly subjected to a high temperature such as that caused by an explosion.'

Moreton was now making his way along the row towards the aisle, a phone pressed to his ear. The legal teams behind Hartley, Bannerman and Crowthorne were in frantic consultation, but for once Mrs Patterson was still and silent. She looked at Achari with wide staring eyes; the shock of hearing something truly revelatory knocking her completely off her axis.

Jenny said, 'Is there any particular significance relating to the part of the skull from which the samples were taken?'

'Dr Kerr carried out microscopic examination of both the front and back of the skull and found evidence of heat exposure only at the back.'

'Amy Patterson was facing away from the explosion?'

'She was.'

'Are you able to say at what distance she was from it?'

'She was closer to the blast than Mr Brogan. You'll see from the photographs that, viewed under the microscope, her tissue sample showed at least a 20 per cent greater concentration of PBX particles than the sample taken from his lifejacket.'

It took a moment for the full implications of Achari's finding to register.

'Tell me if you think this assumption is correct,' Jenny said. 'If Mr Brogan's yacht sank approximately three hundred yards upstream from where the wreckage of the plane was recovered, and the tide was coming in, then Amy Patterson, who was wearing a lifejacket, would have been swept towards the yacht. She was closer to the explosion than Brogan, which in my understanding suggests that the explosion was more likely to have come from the direction of the aircraft than from the yacht.'

'I would draw the same conclusion.'

'And would you also conclude that Brogan must have been swimming against the tide *towards* Amy Patterson?'

'I am certain that he was much closer to the blast than three hundred yards.'

They were rare moments in court proceedings when even the most determined and resilient advocates felt their cases explode and scatter in fragments around them. The looks of utter dismay that spread across the faces of Hartley, Bannerman and Crowthorne testified that this was just such an occasion.

'One final question, Dr Achari,' Jenny said. 'In your opinion, was Mr Brogan's lifejacket cut before or after the explosion?'

'Afterwards. Definitely. The explosive residue was present on nearly the entire left face of the jacket. If punctured, a much greater portion would have been submerged.'

Jenny looked up at the sound of someone entering at the back of the hall. It was Moreton, and he was moving purposefully towards Hartley and his team. She knew full well what was coming next and that she had only a few seconds left in which to play her final card. Turning to Bannerman, though intending her remarks chiefly to be heard by the watching reporters, she said: 'The evidence we have just heard is as relevant to Sir James Kendall's inquiry into the deaths of the aircraft's passengers as it is to mine, suggesting as it does that there was a chain of events leading to Mr Brogan's death, one of which included an explosion on or near the downed aircraft. I am therefore making formal request that Dr Achari and his colleagues be allowed to test the aircraft for explosive residue. I expect access to be granted immediately.'

Hartley was already on his feet. 'Ma'am, counsel cannot be expected to cross-examine on such –' he groped for an appropriate word – '*incendiary* evidence without time properly to consult.'

Jenny aimed her answer at Moreton, who was now right in the middle of the crisis talks that were centred around Hartley's back-up team.

'Well, I have to say, Mr Hartley, I don't intend to delay a verdict a moment more than I have to. If it'll make it any easier, I have no objection to your clients having their own experts examine the aircraft alongside Dr Achari.'

'Take it,' she heard Moreton hiss.

Rachel Hemmings interjected: 'My clients would also like a representative present.'

'I see no problem. Mr Bannerman – does your client wish to do the same?'

'I'm sure he does, ma'am.'

'Mr Crowthorne?'

He nodded.

'Then when can we inspect? I'm happy to wait for your solicitor to make the necessary phone calls.'

Moreton leaned over the shoulder of Bannerman's

instructing solicitor as he put a call through to Sir James Kendall in his office at the D-Mort. Jenny pretended to be absorbed in the copies of Achari's lab photos which had been handed to her, but her mind was racing ahead to what might happen next. Journalists were already hurriedly leaving the room to file their copy. The rolling news would soon be filled with accounts of phantom helicopters and explosions. Events were running out of Moreton's control. There was a chance, albeit vanishingly slender, that in spite of all their efforts, the truth might just force itself to the surface.

Bannerman finished consulting with those behind him and turned back to Jenny. 'Sir James Kendall is happy for you to inspect the wreckage at your earliest convenience.'

Jenny could hardly believe her ears. 'Thank you, Mr Bannerman,' she said, failing to conceal her surprise. 'Dr Achari and others will be there at nine o'clock tomorrow morning.'

It was the presence of so many reporters that must have tipped the balance, Jenny concluded, as she headed for the sanctuary of the office while the proceedings adjourned in a babble of excited chatter. Until only a few years before, the first instinct of an authority with something to hide was to keep it from ever reaching the light; now that strategy was more and more unlikely to work. The emphasis was on managing the story and pumping out information and misinformation until no one could untangle truth from fiction, safe in the knowledge that twenty-four-hour news programmes didn't have the time or patience even to try.

Closing the door behind her, Jenny saw that her hands were shaking. She had spent the entire morning in a drug-induced calm that was fast disintegrating. She had made more progress than she had dreamed possible, but she was just one woman alone. It wouldn't take much ingenuity on the part of the Ministry to put her out of action.

Stop it, stop it, she told herself. *You're letting yourself get paranoid again. Keep calm. Just do the right thing. It'll be fine.* Soothing words were all very well but they were doing little to dampen her physical symptoms of anxiety. Breaking Dr Allen's rules, she delved into her handbag and rooted around until she found the single pill that she kept for dire emergencies. Her relief as the temazepam worked its almost instant magic was like that of arriving safely on the ground after a turbulent flight. The adrenalin drained from her blood and after only a few short moments she was herself again.

A sharp knock at the door sent another unwelcome jolt through her fragile nerves. Alison entered without waiting to be asked. She had lost none of the attitude with which she had greeted her earlier that morning.

'Mr Galbraith is insistent on having a meeting with you,' she announced.

'What about?'

'Apparently he has something he would like you to see.'

'He knows I shouldn't be seeing one set of lawyers in the absence of the others.'

'I'm sure he does, Mrs Cooper. I'm just telling you.'

Jenny glanced out of the window and saw the car Bannerman had arrived in pulling away. Hartley's and Crowthorne's had left even earlier. Only a handful of news crews remained loitering outside the hall.

'He can have a couple of minutes – just him. And I'd like you to remain present.'

'Perhaps you could make do with the tape recorder? I ought to get back to the office.' She turned to the door. 'I'll fetch it for you.'

She returned a short while later with an excited-looking Nick Galbraith.

'Thank you, Mrs Cooper – I really do appreciate this, and I think you will too.' He opened the lid of a laptop and set it on the desk.

Alison placed the aged Dictaphone she used to record court proceeds next to the computer and switched it on. 'I'll see you back at the office, Mrs Cooper,' she said tartly, and exited the room, leaving the two of them alone.

'I won't discuss the proceedings, Mr Galbraith—'

'I'm not asking for that, Mrs Cooper. I merely wish to make you aware of some evidence that might be of use to you. It's news footage that was aired on Taiwan Television during the last hour. A journalist we both know, Mr Wen Chen, emailed me the link just minutes ago. I've forwarded it to you.'

He tapped on a link in an email which brought up a video of a news segment. The newsreader was speaking in Taiwanese. The screen behind her contained three images: an A380 in flight; a good-looking Chinese man in a black polo-neck, and a woman Jenny recognized as the fashion model Lily Tate.

'The man's Jimmy Han,' Galbraith said.

Unfairly handsome as well as rich, Jenny thought, but as dead as everyone else on board.

The image on screen changed to time-coded closed-circuit television footage of what appeared to be the lounge of an expensive modern hotel.

'It's the Ransome VIP lounge at Heathrow,' Galbraith explained. 'There's Han.' He pointed to a figure sitting on a leather sofa in the lower left portion of the screen. Lily Tate wandered into shot – Jenny heard the newsreader speak her name – then settled in a chair at a right angle to Han, who appeared to look up and engage her in conversation.

'I think the story is about whether Han and Lily Tate had

something going on,' Galbraith said, 'you know the sort of thing.' The footage was now on a continual loop, replaying a moment during which Lily Tate appeared to reach out with her toe and touch Han's leg. 'But look up here—' He pointed to the top right-hand corner of the screen, where two male figures could be seen entering through a door and making their way in Han's direction. One was a middle-aged man, the other younger, around thirty, and they appeared to be deep in discussion. 'The one on the left is Alan Towers, MD of Winchester Systems. I told you his business – high-tech weapons systems. The one on the right is young Dr Ian Duffy, a man at the cutting edge of light-based computing technology. Only Towers had been transferred onto this flight from Saturday's, but don't forget – they're both travelling on to Washington.'

'They certainly appear friendly.'

'Now watch what happens—'

Galbraith moved the slider along the bottom of the screen a touch. Han and Lily Tate were still in conversation when Han looked round as if in response to someone speaking his name. He said something to the model, which Jenny inferred were probably words to the effect of 'Be right back', and got up from his seat. He crossed to his left and Alan Towers stepped into frame, hand outstretched. They shook hands warmly, then Towers turned to his right as if to introduce Duffy. The footage ended with an abrupt freeze-frame which then zoomed into a close-up of Lily Tate's face: she was frowning at the two new arrivals, seemingly annoyed at their interruption.

'That's all there is,' Galbraith says, 'but it couldn't be any clearer. You've got a weapons manufacturer, a computer giant and a research scientist whose published aim was to design the hardware for the next big thing – computers incapable of being hacked.' He flipped to a page on the internet: a precis of a scientific paper entitled *Light-Chip Technology and the Future of Quantum Computing*.

'I'm sure it's fascinating,' Jenny said, though doubting it very much.

'Computers that use lasers instead of electrical current run on a fraction of the power and with billions of times the capacity of conventional ones. If you want a satellite-controlled weapons system to keep an eye on the entire surface of the globe and one which is also incapable of being penetrated by the opposition, that's the technology you're going to need.'

'Is there anything else that links them together?'

'Not that I can find. Their PAs both claim not to have heard the other's names being mentioned.'

'Do you know where were they going in Washington?' Jenny said.

'Another blank,' Galbraith replied. ' "Business meetings" was all I could get out of them. Had even less luck with Han's people. He's often over there apparently, retains some lobbyists and waves the flag for Chinese democracy. The Communists loathe him.'

Jenny tried to incorporate this information into one of the several possible scenarios she had mapped out to explain the explosion on the water and failed. Only one thing had become clear: if these men had all been going to the same meeting in Washington, then Nuala had to have been going there too.

'One last thing before I get out of your hair,' Galbraith said. 'It's purely anecdotal—' He stopped himself mid-sentence, then nodded towards the Dictaphone as if inviting Jenny to turn it off.

'I think that'll do for now,' Jenny said. 'Thank you for bringing this to my attention, Mr Galbraith.' She waited for a moment, then reached down and pressed the red button, ending the recording.

'It's just this,' Galbraith said hurriedly. 'Mrs Patterson says she and her now estranged husband have been pretty good at the no-pillow-talk rule – it's written into his contract of employment. But as far as she's concerned, the rules of the game have changed since their daughter's death. She managed to hack into his online email account and picked up the gist of some of the contracts his company, Cobalt, are working on. It used to make high-end software systems for companies requiring tight security – banks, drugs companies, that sort of thing. But it seems the gamekeeper's turned poacher – it looks like they've moved on to providing the tools for clients to break into other people's systems. Corporations, unelected governments – as long as they pay, they don't seem to care. Anyway, as you might expect, she couldn't wait to hit him with it. And she did, in a round-robin email to him and all his colleagues last Thursday afternoon.'

Thursday. Greg Patterson had come to see her on Friday morning. No wonder he had been so distressed.

'Not the wisest move, perhaps,' Jenny said. 'What happened?'

'She got the inevitable lawyer's letter, and Greg Patterson's done a disappearing trick. He's not at work, not at home, he's not answering calls and as far as we know he's not turned up at a hospital – alive or dead.'

Jenny remembered the overnight bag he had carried with him – he had clearly left London in a hurry, not stopping to pack more than he needed to disappear quickly.

Galbraith said, 'Another thing she found out from his email – it was Cobalt's CEO, Dale Cannon, who pulled him off the flight.'

'For any particular reason?'

' "Business in London". But she doesn't think Cannon knew that Amy was due to travel with her father. Apparently Cobalt executives never discuss family matters among themselves. It's considered unprofessional.'

TWENTY-THREE

JENNY STAYED ON AFTER GALBRAITH had left and watched the video clip several times through on her own laptop. With each viewing, her sense that something connected the three men with Nuala Casey and with the fate of the aircraft they were about to board grew stronger. And in the light of what Galbraith had told her it didn't seem absurd to question whether Greg Patterson and his company were somehow involved. But as powerful as the circumstantial evidence was becoming, she still struggled with the notion that so many innocent lives could have been sacrificed to effect a handful of assassinations; aside from the shocking brutality of such an act, who would go to so much effort in a cover-up?

Equally puzzling was the reaction of Moreton and his anonymous government colleagues to the morning's evidence. The appearance of the mysterious helicopters so soon after the crash seemed to indicate an element of foreknowledge, but the official reaction wasn't consistent with that. If the authorities had received a warning that a civilian airliner was being targeted, coroners wouldn't have been allowed anywhere near the incident for months. It would have been strictly a police and security services investigation conducted under a cloak of secrecy. It was as if she was uncovering information faster than them – whoever they were.

On top of everything else, Achari's findings left no doubt that there had been an explosion on the water and that Brogan's death was far from accidental. Technically, the presence of explosives residue was sufficient evidence of a crime having been committed for the police to step in and request that she postpone her inquiries while they conducted a criminal investigation, but no such request had been made. She didn't believe for a moment that she was still being allowed to run free because that was the right thing to do; she could only surmise that her inquest was still in motion because just now Moreton and his colleagues were in disarray. Flight 189 was supposed to have been struck by lightning. It was the story that had been officially announced to the world. And she, the only potential fly in the ointment, was supposed to return an uncontroversial verdict of accidental death in the case of the one victim killed on the ground.

Her mind exploding with frightening possibilities, Jenny hurriedly packed away her computer and decided that she couldn't afford to wait for Achari to examine the aircraft's wreckage. If she really was ahead in this race, she would have to fight to stay there.

'Cigarette, Mrs Cooper?' Detective Inspector Owen Williams leaned across his desk in Chepstow police station and offered her his open packet.

'Are you sure we're allowed?'

'You'll see the Welsh flag flying from the roof of this station, not the bloody swastika.'

Jenny smiled as she took one and shared the flame from Williams's match. She hadn't smoked in months and had forgotten how much she enjoyed it. It was the aroma of the few carefree years between leaving home and getting married far too soon; it made her feel young and interesting, and stupidly invincible.

'I can tell this is going to be good,' Williams said.

'How's that?'

'You've got that look about you, Mrs Cooper – a woman on a mission.'

'I don't suppose you've caught up with what happened at my inquest this morning?'

'I did hear something on the car radio – explosives, wasn't it?'

'You don't sound surprised.'

'I'm a policeman, Mrs Cooper. Nothing surprises me, especially when it comes to those bastards.' He nodded in the direction of England. 'It's obvious – one of those helicopters let a rocket off.'

'That's one possibility. But why?'

'Your man Brogan had form a mile long. You can't tell me no one knew he was there.'

'Who are you thinking of?'

Williams blew a thin stream of smoke up towards the single light bulb that lit his gloomy cubbyhole of an office. 'I shouldn't be telling you this, but every few weeks we get these intelligence alerts sent through from HQ in Cardiff. It looks like a quiet stretch of water out there, but there are vessels bringing in drugs, people traffickers, criminals trying to escape the country. If there's been a tip-off we're all told to keep an eye out.'

'And was there a tip-off about Brogan?' Jenny ventured cautiously.

'Not specifically, but let's just say there's an ongoing problem with Irish villains thinking they can sneak their wares in across the water.'

'What sort of wares?'

'Marijuana mostly. They're growing more of it than they are potatoes – all indoors, of course. It's what's keeping the Real IRA in business.'

'That's still no reason to fire a rocket at Brogan.'

'Maybe they'd run out of bullets?'

Jenny shook her head. 'I'm not sure, but look, I could do with a favour. There are some witnesses I want to get to my inquest in the morning. I need help tracking one or two of them down, and once they're found they might need a little persuading.'

'But you're over the border, Mrs Cooper. Now, if you'd done the sensible thing and held court in Chepstow—'

'It's covered. The border runs down the middle of the estuary. When Lawrence Cole saw those helicopters they were definitely in Wales. Brogan's lifejacket was cut off him and dumped your side of the line – that's got to be something you're entitled to investigate all the way up the chain.'

Williams dabbed his ash dubiously into a saucer.

'I'm not asking you to launch a criminal investigation, not yet. I just want you to serve a witness summons and give them a lift in the back of your car if they're tempted not to comply.'

'Who are we talking about?'

'Greg Patterson – the father of the little girl who was washed up at Aust; Mick Dalton – the chief ground engineer at Ransome Airways; and the personal assistant of a man named Dr Ian Duffy, who was a passenger aboard 189.'

'You're going to tell me it'll mean sending my men into Indian country.'

'Kensington, Berkshire and Cambridge.'

Williams smiled. 'I don't know why, but there's something about driving a vehicle saying Gwent Police through the middle of London that makes me feel like Owen Glendower on his way to thrash Henry IV.'

'You'll do it?'

'With pleasure. But you did know that Glendower is the only Welshman ever to have been Prince of Wales. Six hundred years of Englishmen—'

'I can't say that I did.'

'You should learn the history of your adopted land, Mrs Cooper. I don't run these errands just for fun, you know.'

Jenny was too preoccupied with framing questions for Patterson and Dalton that would fall within the technical limits of her inquiry to notice the black government car idling close to the front entrance to her office, or the midnight-blue saloon tucked in close behind it. She dashed into reception hoping to bypass another prickly conversation with Alison, but was met by the sight of Simon Moreton standing inside the open door to her room sipping a cup of coffee from one of the china cups Alison reserved for those she deemed VIPs.

Alison was at her desk, sorting officiously through a pile of mail. 'If you'd switch your phone on, Mrs Cooper, I could keep you informed,' she said, without looking up.

'Ah, Jenny,' Moreton said. 'I was frightened you'd disappeared.'

'No such luck.'

Stepping forward to join him, she closed the door and glanced over her desk, checking that he hadn't helped himself to her paperwork.

'I wouldn't dream of it,' he said, settling in a chair. 'Alison kindly made coffee for both of us. Would you like some?'

He was being unnervingly polite. It made her suspicious.

'Yes, please.'

Jenny sat behind her desk, unsure what to make of him. She could deal with him angry or flirtatious, but he was managing to be neither. 'I know you didn't come here to kiss and make up.'

'I'll be honest – you pulled off something of an unexpected spectacular this morning. I know you've a lively imagination, Jenny, but really – haven't you even explored the possibility that Brogan let off a distress flare, or that a rescue helicopter might have dropped one?'

'I don't know why I'm discussing the evidence with you, but distress flares are made of phosphorus, not explosive.'

'I'm reliably informed they have an ignition agent that can be mistaken for explosive, but there we are – that's a matter for the experts to quibble over. Now what interests me is something outside the formal limits of your inquiry, but which I suspect you might be able to help with.'

'And what's that?'

'You've been taking an interest in one of the other pass-engers on board – a young lady by the name of Nuala Casey?'

Jenny tried not to let the cup she was holding rattle in its saucer. 'Have I? Who told you that?'

'I couldn't tell you the original source exactly – you know how labyrinthine these things are. But in the interests of getting everything out in the open, it might be helpful if you were to tell me why she, in particular, caught your attention.'

Mick Dalton – that's who it would have been. He had been frightened into talking to whoever had been following him. Jenny could imagine Ransome Airways having hauled him over the coals, extracting all he knew, then deciding to cut their losses and do a deal with the authorities in the hope of staying in business.

'She was a pilot.'

'I'm aware of that.'

Of course he was.

'A friend of hers approached me, that's all.'

'A friend?'

'An ex-boyfriend. Also a pilot. He wanted to know what she was doing on the plane.'

'Why did he come to you?'

'You'd have to ask him.'

'And you discovered what exactly?'

Jenny set her cup down on the desk, her trembling fingers threatening to betray her.

'Simon, only last Thursday you and I were at a press conference at which the world was told that Flight 189 was hit by lightning. Accident. Act of God. No human agency. Are you telling me you no longer believe that?'

'Hmm.' The question seemed to unsettle him. 'I must confess to having my doubts.'

'And Sir James Kendall?'

'He remains open-minded. Contrary to what you might be tempted to believe, Jenny, no one wants anything less than the truth.'

'You could have fooled me.'

'There may be valid reasons for not hurling it directly at the public without weighing the consequences first, of course.'

'Well, that's where you and I will always differ, isn't it?'

He gave a resigned smile. 'I can't pretend that I still entertain any hope of ironing that particular flaw out of you.'

'At last.' She sat back in her chair with the feeling that she had scored a minor victory.

'I suppose I would have felt guilty if I had ever succeeded in making you compromise your principles. I get the impression you could live with almost anything but that.'

'What do you want from me, Simon?'

He sat back in his chair and gazed thoughtfully up at the ceiling, as if the question was a philosophical one requiring deep contemplation. 'I suppose I'm trying to appeal to the part of your nature that might be tempted by a pragmatic solution to all of this. The evidence you're uncovering is fascinating, and I'm sure in the fullness of time and with all the resources at Sir James Kendall's disposal, it will be slotted into the complete narrative we all want so desperately to emerge.'

'You want me to abandon my inquest and turn all my evidence over to someone else.'

'Strictly on a basis of trust. You have my word – no sleeping dog will be left undisturbed, no fact hidden.'

'Why? What exactly are you afraid of?'

'The *implications*, Jenny. We need to know what they are.'

She shook her head. The gulf between them remained an unbridgeable void. 'Why will you people never accept that you're the servants and not the masters?'

'My way is safest, Jenny. Please, for once – be kind to yourself and take my advice.'

She resisted. 'You know my answer, Simon.'

'Yes,' he said, as if he had expected nothing else. He stood up from the chair, their conversation at an end. 'I admire you, Jenny; I mean that sincerely.' He smiled at her fondly and left the office.

There was something in his manner which had been strangely pathetic. It left Jenny with a curious feeling of guilt, as if she were partly responsible for the furious dressing-down she imagined would be waiting for him following his failure to curb her waywardness.

Forcing her thoughts to more pressing matters, she unloaded the contents of her briefcase onto her desk and grabbed a legal pad. Hartley and Bannerman would both be conferring with teams of lawyers, trawling every statute and precedent for a means to derail her. She wouldn't just have to be good, she would have to be the best she had ever been.

Moreton had been gone less than a minute when Jenny heard the doorbell ring.

'Tell whoever it is I'm busy,' she called through the closed door to Alison.

It was too late. The visitor had already been buzzed into the hall.

Jenny shot up from her seat and looked around the door. 'I've no time for visitors. Make an appointment for tomorrow.'

'It's Detective Sergeant Fuller.'

'I don't care. I'm not available.' She slammed the door shut and returned to her desk.

'I'm sorry – Mrs Cooper's too busy to see anyone at the moment.'

'Thank you,' Jenny said out loud to herself.

Karen Fuller wasn't taking no for an answer. Without knocking, she marched in with a detective constable at her shoulder.

'I did tell them,' Alison called out.

'You're under arrest, Mrs Cooper.'

While Fuller recited the caution, all Jenny could think of was what she would like to do to Moreton, the devious bastard.

Jenny decided that complete cooperation was the best policy. She opened the office safe and handed over the evidence bags without being asked. She also handed Fuller her phone containing the video record she had taken of her opening them. The items hadn't been stolen, she stated calmly, she had merely seized evidence relevant to her inquest from a competing jurisdiction. The issue was a technical one between her and Sir James Kendall, not a matter for the police. Fuller was having none of it, and told Jenny she was being taken to New Bridewell police station.

*

Her nerves calmed by a beta blocker, Jenny declined the offer of legal representation and faced Detective Sergeant Fuller and her taciturn colleague, Detective Constable Ewan Ashton, alone. It was a moment she had hoped wouldn't come, but for which she had been mentally preparing since her visit to the evidence and effects store at the D-Mort. While far from bulletproof, she at least had a defence which sounded plausible. During the brief journey across town to the police station Jenny had tried to prompt Fuller into revealing who had told her about the evidence bags, but she remained tight-lipped. Jenny guessed that if it wasn't one of the officers at the D-Mort who had reported her, the trail would lead back somehow to Mick Dalton. Michael had been sure that whoever had followed him to their rendezvous had been working for the airline – a private detective or internal security – but Jenny secretly suspected the police. Either way, it made little difference; Fuller had arrived knowing exactly what she had done.

In a drab, oppressive room, Jenny confronted her interrogators across a table stained with the rings of a thousand cups of the weak, sugary coffee that was the only refreshment on offer. Fuller laboured through the formalities with the sinister fastidiousness Jenny supposed she had developed to intimidate the child-molesters, wife-beaters and other inadequates she spent the bulk of her working life pursuing.

Giving the impression she had all the time in the world, Fuller finally opened her small black notebook and read aloud the notes she had made in Jenny's office immediately after her arrest. They recorded precisely Jenny's account of removing the two bags from the evidence and effects store at the D-Mort and taking them back to her office, the procedure she went through in filming their unsealing, and her subsequent trip to the left-luggage office at Paddington. She had a mastery of detail, Jenny could give her that.

'Do you accept that what I have just read to you is a fair and accurate record of what you told me earlier today?' she asked.

'It's entirely accurate,' Jenny said.

'And you admit that you removed the items from the evidence and effects store without permission?'

'I didn't require permission,' Jenny said. 'I am a coroner lawfully conducting an inquest. The bags contained evidence relevant to my inquiry.'

'Did you abide by the procedures laid down in the Coroners and Justice Act? Schedule 5 requires you to have the permission of a senior coroner before entering and searching any premises for the purposes of obtaining evidence.'

'I didn't. And the reason I didn't was that it had already been made perfectly apparent that no such permission would have been granted.'

'So you admit you were acting outside the law?'

'On the contrary: I was seeking to ensure that evidence the law requires to be examined was obtained for my inquiry. The Ministry of Justice and Sir James Kendall, on the other hand, are the ones failing properly to apply the law. We could argue about it until we're blue in the face, but the proper place for that argument is the High Court, not a police station.'

Fuller persisted, 'But you accept that the property was not yours to take.'

'I accept no such thing. And what's more, you should know that the law of theft requires an intention permanently to deprive the owner of his or her property. I had no such intention. I took temporary possession for the purposes of my inquest, nothing more.'

Jenny's assertions were part strict legal fact, part bluster and argument, but it was enough to make Fuller unsure of her ground. She wasn't the brightest detective Jenny had ever met, but she was smart enough to want to avoid becoming embroiled in a claim of unlawful arrest. Less than fifteen minutes into the interview she suspended her questioning and left Jenny alone in an empty room for nearly the best part of three hours while she consulted with Crown Prosecution Service lawyers.

It was the middle of the evening when Fuller and Ashton returned. They appeared calm and relaxed, as if they'd both enjoyed a good dinner in the police canteen. Jenny had had only some lukewarm coffee and a stale biscuit. The effects of the beta blocker had worn off and she was fast becoming anxious and jittery. Fuller sensed it as soon as she stepped through the door.

'Sorry to have kept you, Mrs Cooper. Why lawyers can't give a straight answer when you need one is beyond me.' She eased her solidly built body into the chair opposite, carrying the smell of the canteen on her clothes.

'Because there isn't one?' Jenny countered.

'We got there in the end,' Fuller said. 'The good news from your point of view is that the CPS are dubious about a burglary charge. They're not too confident about attempting to pervert the course of justice, either. Even better news, they're not sure that what you did at the left-luggage office amounted to fraud.'

Jenny nodded, trying hard to disguise her elation.

Fuller switched on the tape recorder. 'Interview resumed at twenty-one-oh-eight. Persons present: Detective Sergeant Karen Fuller, Detective Constable Ewan Ashton and suspect Mrs Jenny Cooper. Before we continue, Mrs Cooper, do you require a solicitor to be present?'

'No.'

'Very well. This won't take long.' She referred to a set of notes she had brought back with her. 'Thank you for your patience. The purpose of this resumed interview is simply to clarify a couple of points we discussed earlier. In the video you took of yourself opening the evidence bags, you describe removing a left-luggage ticket from the wallet. Is that correct?'

'Yes.'

'And you took that ticket to the left-luggage office at Paddington Station?'

'I did.'

'What then happened to the ticket?'

'I imagine it was thrown away.'

'You didn't retain it?'

'No. I exchanged it for Miss Casey's left luggage: a laptop computer.'

'Thank you,' Fuller said. She exchanged a glance with the detective constable, who had remained silent throughout. 'Anything you wish to add?'

'No. That covers it,' he replied.

Fuller turned to Jenny. 'Our lawyers have advised us that the lawful owner of that ticket is Miss Casey's next of kin. You have permanently deprived him of it, and are therefore guilty of theft.'

'You are joking?'

'It wasn't yours to dispose of, Mrs Cooper. You know the law.'

'You're charging me with the theft of a scrap of paper?'

'Yes. Interview terminated at twenty-one-thirteen.' Fuller switched off the tape recorder. 'But you know lawyers – they're bound to have changed their minds by the morning. I'm in no particular hurry. We'll talk again tomorrow.'

For the second time during her tenure as coroner, Jenny suffered the humiliation of being booked into a police cell. So much for innocent until proven guilty. They took away her few possessions and stripped her of her jewellery. She

was fingerprinted, photographed, DNA-swabbed and subjected to a humiliating search before being locked in a
graffiti-stained cell whose thick walls did nothing to muffle
the screams and yells of the drunks, junkies and street-
walkers who were to be her neighbours for the night.

She sat hugging her knees on the hard cot shelf feeling
shocked and numb, but as much as she tried, she couldn't
imagine having done anything differently.

TWENTY-FOUR

'MRS COOPER?'

Jenny opened her eyes and blinked against the harsh fluorescent light. Alison was standing in the doorway of the cell alongside the custody sergeant.

'I've come to bail you out.'

Slowly coming to consciousness, Jenny swung her feet over the edge of the shelf and onto the hard floor. Everything ached. Her neck was cricked and she had lost all sensation in one arm.

'What time is it?' she croaked.

'Six. You've got to be back here for another interview at ten. I thought you'd appreciate a wash and change of clothes.'

Jenny hoisted herself to her feet. 'What about the inquest?'

'You don't have to worry about that. I've told everyone it's postponed. Come on, let's get you out of here.'

Alison led her along the narrow corridor, through the reception area and out of the security door into the biting pre-dawn air. Neither spoke as they made their way the short distance along the street to where Alison had parked, but in the confined space of the car the tension between them mounted until neither could bear the silence any longer.

'You might as well spit it out,' Jenny said.

Alison stared at the road ahead.

'You've had enough, I don't blame you.' Jenny sighed. 'But thanks for rescuing me. I appreciate it.'

Alison gave her a concerned glance. 'Do you think you're quite all right, Mrs Cooper? You have been under a lot of strain—'

'Don't believe everything Simon Moreton tells you.'

'This is very serious. I don't think you should be flippant. If I were you I'd be getting a good lawyer. Why don't I make some calls for you?'

'Before you leave, you mean?' Jenny instantly regretted her acid remark. 'I'm sorry. I don't blame you, honestly. I know I haven't exactly been easy to work with.'

Alison turned off a deserted Whiteladies Road and into Jamaica Street. 'I wasn't intending to mention my future, but now you've brought it up I might as well tell you that I will be handing in my resignation. I'll work out my four weeks' notice, of course.' She pulled over into a space behind Jenny's Land Rover.

'What will you do?' Jenny said, feeling more than a little betrayed now that the inevitable moment had finally arrived.

'There's plenty of time to work that out.'

'You'll miss it.'

'We'll see. I really should drive you home – you're not in any fit state.'

'I'm fine.' Jenny reached for the door handle.

'You forgot this.' Alison handed her the bail sheet, which she had left on the parcel shelf. 'For God's sake make sure you're back at the station before ten. It was hard enough getting you out this time – I don't think Fuller likes you.'

'I don't exactly have a crush on her either.' Jenny tucked the sheet into her pocket and climbed out of the car. Before closing the door, she said, 'I don't suppose there have been any messages from Michael Sherman?'

Alison shook her head.

'No. Of course not.'

The police had at least shown the decency to break down the kitchen door, which couldn't be seen from the lane, but that was as far as their generosity had extended.

Every shelf and cupboard had been ransacked. Her study had been turned upside down. The floor was ankle-deep in paper, the drawers of her filing cabinet in an upturned heap on top of them. Both Nuala's laptops were gone, as well as the box of USB sticks on which Jenny backed up all her own files. Upstairs they had tossed her clothes into a single heap on the bed. Some kind soul had found the few items of silk underwear she possessed and spread them out on top. She would have felt less violated by a gang of drug-crazed burglars.

The chaos was too overwhelming to begin to deal with. She extracted some clothes from the tangled pile and carried them through to the bathroom. Her most urgent need was to wash the smell of the cells out of her hair. By the time she had showered, dressed and tried to hide the lines that had aged her ten years overnight, it was nearly eight o'clock. It would take forty-five minutes to drive back to the police station, which left her a little over an hour to decide her next move. Shutting her eyes to the mess, she made her way back downstairs.

From amongst the pans and utensils littering the kitchen floor, she picked out the stove-top espresso pot she had owned since before she was married. She made the strongest coffee she could and steeled herself to return to her study to check her messages. There were none, or at least none the police hadn't already listened to and deleted. Out of curiosity she checked the number of the last caller and saw that her ex-husband had tried to phone late the previous night. He must have heard about her arrest on the local grapevine. Great.

She fetched out her mobile and retrieved DI Williams's number. He answered from his car.

'Mrs Cooper? I thought you were in Bristol nick.'

'I got bail, well, four hours' worth. I suppose you gave up on those witnesses?'

'You know me better than that. Like you said – I've got grounds for a criminal investigation.'

'You're serious?'

'Deadly, Mrs Cooper. I've got a team of boys heading for Dalton's place, another on their way to Cambridge and I'm currently driving past Harrods thinking I wouldn't live in this hell-hole if you paid me – eight o'clock in the morning and it's bloody pandemonium.'

'Does anyone else know what you're doing?'

'Only my super, but he's as sound as a bell. Pembrokeshire man – loathes the bloody English.'

'Well, keep it that way. Call me when you've got news.'

'Will do. You look after yourself.'

Jenny rang off and dialled Michael's number. Frankly, he didn't deserve her attention, but she felt he ought to know that she had got herself arrested and more than likely lost her job trying to find out what had happened to his ex-girlfriend. She expected to get the usual automated message with which he seemed to screen all his calls, but there was no answer service of any kind, just a voice saying the number she had dialled was unavailable. She dialled directories, requested the number for Sky Drivers and ended up with another machine; this one informing her that office hours were between nine a.m. and six p.m. She felt a surge of anger. How dare he ignore her after all that had happened?

She looked at the time: it was ten past eight. If she drove quickly she might just make it.

Jenny pulled into the car park next to the Sky Drivers office at Bristol airport at shortly after nine. Making her way to the block that housed the offices of the small airlines and freight companies, she scanned the rows of parked cars looking for the old blue Saab she remembered seeing Michael driving, but there was no sign.

Sky Drivers inhabited a small set of rooms on the third floor. Jenny arrived outside on the landing, pushed through the door to the compact reception area and found it empty.

'Hello?'

A girl with a belly ring showing above the waistband of her trousers drifted vaguely through from a back room carrying a mug of herbal tea. She clearly wasn't expecting visitors.

'Can I help you?'

'Jenny Cooper – Severn Vale District Coroner. I'm looking for Michael Sherman.'

'Mike?'

'Yes. I need to speak to him. He's not answering his phone.'

'Right.' The girl sat in the swivel chair behind the desk and blinked through puffy eyes at her computer screen. 'I've got a feeling he booked himself out.' She brought up a spreadsheet and located Michael's name. 'Yeah – four days. Actually, he's not back until next Monday.'

'Do you have any idea where he is?'

The girl looked up at her with a hint of suspicion. 'Are you something to do with the inquiry into the plane crash?'

'Yes, I'm a coroner,' Jenny said, and, responding to some gut instinct, asked, 'has he mentioned it?'

'Kind of . . .' She appeared a little confused.

'You said he booked himself out. Is this something he did recently?'

She glanced back at the screen. 'Yesterday . . .'

'You seem unsure.'

'No, it's just that I thought it might be something to do with you – or with the inquiry, I mean . . . what with his girlfriend being on board and everything.'

'*Girlfriend?*'

'Nuala . . . Nuala Casey.'

'I know who she is. I thought their relationship had been over for some time.'

'Yeah, so did I, I guess.'

'What do you mean?' Jenny said. 'Were they together or weren't they?'

'Oh . . . I'm not really sure I should be talking about it.'

'I'm asking you – formally – was Michael Sherman in a relationship with Nuala Casey immediately before she died?'

The girl hesitated, realizing she had crossed some sort of line and no longer had the option to retreat. 'I don't know about *immediately*, but she came by a few weeks ago to meet him.'

'When?'

'Just after Christmas, I think . . .' She clicked over to a screen containing a diary. 'It would have been around the 28th. He and I were the only ones sad enough to be working.'

'What did she want?'

'She came to meet him, that's all. She sat over there and waited for him to come back from a flight.'

'How did she seem?'

'Quiet . . . She didn't talk much. I think she was doing something on a computer.'

'What about when Michael arrived – did they seem close?'

'Friendly. I'm not sure they kissed or anything . . .' She pulled a face as she tried to remember, as if something wasn't quite sitting comfortably in her recollection. 'You know, I'm not sure he was expecting to see her. That's right, I think he was a bit surprised. It was almost as if she'd come to break some news to him or something.'

'Did you hear their conversation?'

She shook her head. 'No. They left pretty quickly.'

December 28th. Jenny thought back to the entries in the diary on Nuala's laptop. She had cancelled a flight on that day. And on the 29th she had been at the spa at the Cavendish Hotel in Berkshire. Had Michael been lying to her about his relationship with Nuala? Why would he do that? Did he know more than he had told her?

Jenny said, 'Do you know what Michael was doing on 29 December?'

The girl gave her a guarded look. 'Is he in some sort of trouble?'

'No . . . Please, just tell me where he was.'

She consulted her screen. 'He was flying. He took a family party over to Guernsey at ten in the morning and flew back that afternoon.'

'You're sure about that?'

'I arranged it myself. They're some of our best clients – the Colthards, you know, the National Hunt trainers. They always ask for Michael. I think they like the fact he was in the RAF.'

'And Nuala didn't come here again?'

'No . . . But she hadn't been here for, well, nearly a year, I suppose.'

'Did he ever talk about her?'

'He doesn't really talk about anyone.'

It sounded as if Nuala had come to seek him out, but why? And why hadn't Michael told her? He was hiding something, he had to be. Jenny glanced at the clock behind the desk. It was nine-fifteen. If she didn't leave soon she'd be in even more trouble.

'Look, I really need to speak to him. Is there any way of getting hold of him? Is there anyone who might know where he is?'

'You've tried his home?'

'He's not answering. Is he always like this?'

'Mostly . . .'

Jenny detected uncertainty in her voice. There was something on her mind that she wasn't articulating; a connection that she was beginning to make.

'Do you think Michael knows something about the crash?' the girl asked. It was more than an idle question. There was a history of suspicion in the way she delivered it.

Jenny didn't have time to tease it out of her gently, she needed answers now.

'What's your name?' Jenny asked.

'Jemma. Jemma Reynolds.'

'And your position here?'

'Bookings and secretarial.'

'So you see everyone who comes through here and take all the calls.'

She nodded. 'Nearly all.'

'Tell me, has anyone apart from me come to see Michael or been trying to contact him since the plane went down in the Severn?'

'He is in trouble, isn't he?' She shook her head. 'I knew it.'

'There has been someone, hasn't there?'

Jemma looked guiltily up at her. 'My boss told me not to talk to . . . Michael's our best pilot—'

Jenny gave her a look that told her that no excuse was going to be good enough. It worked.

'There was a man who came in twice a day or two after the accident looking for him. He said he was with the investigation ... I think his name was Sanders – that's it, Wing Commander Sanders.'

Sanders. She'd heard the name before – it was the man Sandy Belling had mentioned. He had been calling her asking about Nuala. But what would an RAF officer be doing as part of the investigation? Could he have been with the AAIB?

'Did he leave any details?'

'A number. I've got it here somewhere.' She searched through the files on her computer desktop.

'Can you describe him?'

'Fifties. Fit-looking. An officer type. He didn't say it, but I got the impression he might have known Michael from the RAF.'

'Did Michael say who he was?'

'No. I gave him his number, that's all. Here it is.' She reached for a message pad and jotted down a number.

'Thanks. If Michael calls, tell him I'm looking for him. And tell him to switch his phone on.'

Jenny walked quickly out of the office and dialled Sanders's number as she clattered down the stairs. Damn. His phone was switched off too. Why did men have such a problem with communication? At least she had a lead. She dialled her office number and found Alison at her desk.

'You are on your way, Mrs Cooper? You know it's nearly half-past nine.'

'I'm nearly there. There's something I need you to do for me.'

She shouldered through the doors and out into the car park as a passenger jet was taking off from the main runway. Deafened by the noise, she ducked back inside.

'You sound like you're at the airport,' Alison said.

Ignoring the comment, Jenny said, 'Don't worry, I'm just

leaving. There's someone I need you to track down – Wing Commander Sanders. He's something to do with the main inquiry. I need to speak to him urgently.'

'What about?'

'It doesn't matter. Just find out who he is, what he does and where I can get hold of him.' She dictated his number, eager to end the call before Alison could object.

'Mrs Cooper—'

'Yes?'

'I had a call from the photographer's widow this morning – she'd seen the press reports of the inquest . . .' Alison hesitated, as if not quite believing what she was saying. 'The helicopters . . . Before Christmas her husband had taken pictures of some odd-looking helicopters flying over Herefordshire. They had no markings. Apparently he posted them on the internet to see if anyone could identify them. Other people contacted him to say they'd seen them too. In the week before the accident he'd had anonymous phone calls, all from the same person, telling him to take the photos down. She hadn't made any connection between the calls and what happened to him until she read about the evidence—'

Jenny felt her heart pressing hard against her ribs. She remembered the second set of tyre marks on the road caused by a vehicle following the photographer's. 'Did she take any of these calls?'

'No, but he described the caller's voice to her – he said he sounded military, like a senior officer.'

'Where are the pictures now?'

'That's another thing – the day he died, his office was burgled. He kept all his pictures on two hard drives locked in a cupboard. They were both taken.'

'I see,' Jenny said. 'On second thoughts don't call Mr

Sanders yet. I think this is one development I might discuss with the police.'

Hurrying back towards her car, Jenny tried to fit what she had just learned with what she already knew about the events leading up to the crash. Sanders, it was clear, was part of a concerted attempt to suppress the truth of what had happened to 189. But just who he was and who he worked for wasn't something she yet had enough information to work out. All that she could be certain of was that he had proved himself an extremely dangerous and determined individual. She suspected him of being the man who had disrupted her roadside meeting with Dalton and, given his possibly fatal harassment of an innocent photographer, it didn't seem incredible to think that his shadow might even stretch over Captain Farraday's death.

As for Michael, her instincts told her that he hadn't been lying about his relationship with Nuala having ended, but he certainly hadn't told her the whole truth. Given the meetings she had been having with Dalton, it was hard not to conclude that Nuala had come to Michael on the 28th with information that she was unable to cope with alone. She had turned to the one person she thought she could trust. Had her trust been misplaced? Had Michael decided not to mention their meeting on the 28th because he felt he had failed her in some way? On the 29th he had continued with his work and Nuala had gone to the Cavendish Hotel. Her actions struck Jenny as odd. Given the post-mortem findings it was possible that she hadn't been feeling well, but would her response have been to travel thirty miles from London to visit a spa? Somehow, it didn't seem in character.

Jenny reached her car and, with her head still buzzing, made one final phone call.

She counted a full ten rings before Sandy Belling answered.

'Hello?' Sandy sounded fraught. Her baby was crying noisily.

'Sandy, it's Jenny Cooper – the coroner.'

'Can I call you back?'

'Just one thing – the Cavendish Hotel in Fleetcombe, do you know it?'

'Yeah.' The crying ratcheted up to a full-blown scream. 'Look, I have to go —'

'Nuala went to the spa there on 29 December. Does that seem like something she would have done?'

'I don't know . . . it's normally just management that go there.'

'The Ransome management?'

'I think Guy Ransome owns shares in the place. He holds all his board meetings there. Sorry —'

She hung up.

It was nine-thirty. If the traffic was heavy she would be late for her appointment with Fuller. As she drove towards the exit barrier, Jenny dialled directories, and asked to be connected to the Cavendish Hotel. Pretending to be an accounts clerk at Ransome Airways, she asked the receptionist to confirm which meeting rooms Ransome had booked out for 29 December. The receptionist put her through to a young man in the back office who consulted his records and came up with a blank.

'Sorry, there were no meeting rooms booked that day.'

Jenny continued to fish. 'You're sure? I'm certain we had some of our personnel there that day.'

'All the meeting rooms were clear,' the young man said. 'The only item charged to Ransome Airways on that date was Mr Ransome's suite.'

356

'Oh,' Jenny said, playing dumb. 'Which days was that for?'

'The 27th to 1 January. You won't receive an invoice until the end of this month.'

'Oh, of course. Sorry to have troubled you.'

The clerk said an impatient goodbye and rang off.

She had her answer. Nuala had gone to see Ransome. It made perfect sense. A month of ever more frightening meetings with Dalton, then a trip to consult Michael, who would have given her the only sensible advice: if what she had learned was truly serious, she had a duty to take it up with the boss. And being the cheapskate he was, Ransome had made her pay for her own spa session while she waited for an audience.

She needed to make a call that would demand her full attention. She pulled into a lay-by and dialled the number.

The receptionist was as obstructive as Jenny had anticipated: Mr Ransome was in a meeting and couldn't be disturbed; no, she didn't know when he would be finished.

Jenny took a deep breath and tried not to yell. 'Listen to me – this isn't optional. I'm a coroner investigating deaths caused by one of his aircraft. I don't care if he's with the Pope and the President of the United States, you're going to call through to him and tell him that Mrs Cooper wants to talk about the meeting he had with Captain Nuala Casey on 29 December last year. And if he still won't speak to me, you can tell him it won't just be one plane, it'll be his whole airline that'll come crashing to the ground. Have you got that?'

'Hold, please.'

Jenny held, gritting her teeth against the inane muzak that was intended to soothe impatient callers. She had twenty minutes to make it to New Bridewell and the traffic heading into Bristol was slow and heavy. She would be lucky to arrive before ten-thirty. Fuller could add failing to answer bail to the list of charges she would have cajoled a more amenable CPS lawyer into drawing up.

A minute ticked by. She was nearing the end of her tether when the receptionist's voice abruptly returned. 'Putting you through now.'

'Guy Ransome speaking.' He was as prickly as his staff.

'Jenny Cooper, Severn Vale District Coroner. I'm investigating the death—'

'I know what you're investigating. What can I do for you?'

'You met with Captain Nuala Casey on 29 December. She and your chief engineer, Mick Dalton, met several times during December to discuss recurring and unexplained faults on your aircraft.'

He remained silent. It was time to scare him. 'I have spoken with Mr Dalton and I have seen Miss Casey's personal computer. I know all about the illegal conditions you inserted into your pilots' contracts of employment following Captain Dan Murray's overrun on landing a 380 at Heathrow last summer, and I'm also aware of Captain Farraday's incident over the Pacific. If that's not enough to ground your entire fleet instantly, I don't know what is.'

'I don't understand,' Ransome said, striking a conciliatory tone. 'Is this some sort of threat, Mrs Cooper?'

'My job is to determine the truth, Mr Ransome. You declined to appear at my inquest, but I think it's only right that you now make a statement recording everything you know.'

He paused before responding.

'What's this about a bomb on the water?'

'I'm sure your lawyers have told you – explosives residue was found on the bodies of both Mr Brogan and Amy Patterson. There was an explosion close to your plane that appears to have been connected with two Apache helicopters which arrived on the scene very soon after it went down. They were gone some time before the search and rescue Sea Kings arrived.'

'My lawyers also told me you had been arrested for stealing evidence.'

'Seizing, not stealing – there's a difference. And you're right to point out that what I've discovered hasn't exactly been welcomed. But the way I see it, you're better off owning up to a fault and fixing it than being responsible for another six hundred or more deaths.'

'I'm not responsible.'

'You knew your aircraft had a problem, Mr Ransome.'

'No. I did not.' He was emphatic. 'Where are you, Mrs Cooper?'

'A short distance from Bristol airport – why?'

'If I sent a helicopter for you, would you agree to come and meet me?'

'Now?'

'Now would be perfect.'

TWENTY-FIVE

IT WAS TEN THIRTY-FIVE when the Bell JetRanger painted in full Ransome livery swung in a tight arc over the landing pad at Bristol Flight Centre in the south-east corner of the airport, and settled on the ground. Jenny had ignored the repeated calls from Alison, keeping her phone switched on only in the frustrated hope that Michael might still break his silence. Detective Sergeant Karen Fuller hadn't wasted a moment. She had phoned at two minutes past ten to inform Jenny that she was officially in breach of bail and was liable to be arrested on sight. Jenny thanked her for the heads-up, but told her not to waste her day waiting: she wouldn't be in a position to talk to her until at least the close of business.

The pilot jumped down from the cockpit and waved her over. He was evidently in a big hurry. Bracing herself against the downdraught from the idling rotors, she made her way towards the waiting machine.

'Mrs Cooper?' the pilot shouted over the noise of the engine.

'Yes.'

'Brendan Murphy. Welcome aboard.'

He opened the passenger door and helped her inside.

Jenny guessed that Brendan was a pilot whom Guy Ransome trusted for his experience. Silver-haired, but still an imposing physical presence, he exuded confidence and authority.

In moments they were airborne and leaving the airport behind. Skimming over the treetops and into a clear sky, Jenny felt like a fugitive making a jailbreak. Then it dawned on her: a fugitive was precisely what she was, and right now Karen Fuller would be emailing her photograph to every police station and patrol car in the country.

They tracked the M4 motorway eastwards, and in a little under thirty minutes were shearing off to the south and homing in on a grand Georgian estate surrounded by parkland. An ornamental lake shimmered silver in the winter sun. She had become used to the shuddering motion of the helicopter as it snatched at rather than glided through the air, but the sudden downwards swoop towards their destination had her forcing herself back into her seat.

Brendon threw her a friendly smile. 'Just imagine you're a bird.'

Guy Ransome's personal assistant was waiting on the lawn at the rear of the hotel where the helicopter landed. She led Jenny along the gravel path towards a balustraded terrace than ran the entire length of the building, explaining that Mr Ransome was currently concluding a meeting and would be with her shortly.

The Cavendish was a hotel of the kind that would have impressed her ex-husband: loaded with chandeliers and ostentatious antiques. Jenny had never felt comfortable in such places, suspecting that in opulent surroundings men too often perceived women as part of the decoration.

She was shown into a large suite on the first floor and left alone to wait for Ransome. The view from the large windows took in the full sweep of the surrounding parkland. Sitting in the centre of a large table was a complex scale model of an Airbus A380 with the top half of the hull removed. Curious, Jenny took a closer look and saw that the seats in the cabin could be arranged in different configurations. Someone had left notes scribbled on a pad which appeared to show profit margins according to passenger numbers. Five hundred, six hundred, even eight hundred passengers were envisaged per flight. Amidst the tangle of figures the writer had circled the figure 800 and written: '*Insurance? Safety?*' It was reassuring to know there were limits.

She had been waiting less than five minutes when Guy Ransome entered. For all his impressive height and immaculate tailoring, he showed every sign of having endured a very testing two weeks.

'Mrs Cooper.' He shook her hand and gestured her to sit on one of the suite's two sofas. 'Have you been offered coffee?'

'I'm fine,' Jenny said, anxious to get down to business, though suddenly unsure of her angle of attack.

Seizing on her uncertainty, Ransome took the initiative. 'We both clearly have information the other would like to possess. The only problem remains what we each do with it.'

'I'm not in the business of keeping secrets, Mr Ransome.'

'You're not in business at all – that's what concerns me. But on the other hand, if my lawyers inform me correctly, you're not in much of a position to be believed even if you were to go public with anything I might choose to share with you.'

Jenny paused to consider her next move. Ransome was prepared to trade, but wanted to control the flow of information to protect his airline. If she were to pursue a strictly ethical line she would have to refuse all attempts to gag her, but if she had learned one thing during the previous fortnight, it was that it doesn't always pay to play by the rules. Getting justice wasn't that different from getting ahead in business: in this fallen world, sometimes you have to play dirty.

'I'll be honest with you, Mr Ransome,' Jenny said, preparing to be anything but. 'What concerns me most is that whatever brought your plane down doesn't happen again. Everyone wants that, I know. Until yesterday I would have said I was prepared to do whatever it takes, but faced with the prospect of losing my career I'm not sure I feel quite so bullish.' She met his gaze, trying to signal that she was vulnerable. 'In a way, you're the passport out of my predicament. You see, if I know what happened to your aircraft I'm in a position to negotiate to keep my job. And if you have all the information I have, you're in a position to save your business.'

Ransome stared at her for a long moment. She could tell he was trying to read her like he would a rival proposing a deal.

'You want me to help you keep your job—'

'And I help you to make your aircraft safe.'

'You don't make money killing your customers, Mrs Cooper.'

'Then I think we understand each other. Who goes first?'

'I will,' Ransome said. He had decided to trust her. 'You say you know about Dan Murray's overrun and the problem with the autothrust failing to disengage?'

'Mick Dalton told me it could have been pilot error, but I don't think he believes that.'

'Anomalies happen. You can trace a faulty servo or a leaking valve easily enough, but a one-off computer glitch is a different order of challenge altogether. If every plane that had one was grounded, there'd be virtually no carriers left in the air.'

'What about Captain Farraday's experience? Losing all flight computers and the ability to control the aircraft for twenty minutes is more than just a glitch.'

'Maybe it is, maybe it isn't. A similar thing happened on a BMI A321 from Khartoum to Beirut in the summer of 2010 – all computers went down for several minutes before somehow resetting themselves. I admit it's terrifying, but I don't build aircraft, I just operate them.'

'Farraday had been talking to Nuala Casey.'

'Farraday was talking to anyone who'd listen. That was why we altered the pilots' contracts – not to keep secrets, but to stop rumours. Having the internet buzzing with wild stories won't make a single plane any safer. I'm very sorry about his accident, but I can assure you that's all it was.'

There was nothing overly polished or pre-rehearsed about Ransome's explanations and Jenny felt that he seemed relieved to be sharing his problems with someone outside his inner circle. She watched him reach up to his tie knot and loosen his top button. Look sympathetic, she told herself, play the understanding woman.

'Nuala Casey thought Farraday's incident was more than just an anomaly,' Jenny said. 'That's why she came to see you here after Christmas, isn't it?'

'Partly . . .' He hesitated, then changed the subject. 'What do you have to say about the theory that my plane was shot down by a missile?'

'I don't believe that. There's no evidence of a mid-air explosion.'

'I heard about the Patterson girl's phone call – is that what you're basing your conclusion on?'

'The passenger post-mortems are the most persuasive evidence. There's no sign of injuries caused by an explosion in the air.'

Ransome considered her answer for a moment, turning

over the possibilities in his mind. He switched the subject back again. 'What do you know about Nuala?'

'I know she sent a one-word text to her ex-boyfriend while the plane was heading for the ground. It was a password connected with an online forum she ran—'

'I know about Airbuzz,' Ransome interjected. 'But before you jump to conclusions, Mrs Cooper, it wasn't me who had it taken down. Look, there's another layer to all this . . .' He leaned forward towards her, as if taking her into his confidence. 'Tell me about the helicopters. Did one of them fire a missile?'

'That's what the evidence suggests. And I'm beginning to think that Sir James Kendall's inquiry must have known that very soon after the crash. It also looks as if whoever was in the helicopters cut Brogan's lifejacket from him too.'

'Who do you think was in them?'

'I honestly have no idea.'

Ransome sat back, looking like his bleakest fears had been confirmed. 'We got hold of a leaked report from one of the salvage crew that said the avionics bay was partly blown away – it's directly beneath the cockpit. I'm told the photograph of the "lightning strike" was taken from the other side – from an angle at which you can't see the damage.'

'Where all the flight computers are housed?'

Ransome nodded. 'I took it up with the security services. They weren't happy that I knew, but they didn't deny that it had been hit. But if they had any idea who did it, they weren't letting on.'

'Who do you think it was?' Jenny asked.

'I can make an educated guess, but I'm still struggling with the reason why.' He turned his head abruptly towards the window as if fighting to control a surge of anger. He was bitter about something; something outside his control.

Jenny said, 'You tell me your theory and we'll see if it fits with what I know about some of the passengers who were on board.'

'You mean Jimmy Han?'

'Among others.' She had his interest. 'Why don't we start from the beginning?'

The airline's problems had begun in May of the previous year, Ransome said, starting with an unannounced visit from an American named Doug Kennedy. He claimed to be working for the US Federal Aviation Authority, but would later admit that he was attached to the Central Intelligence Agency. Ransome had since come to believe it was the other way around: Kennedy was a senior CIA agent who formed part of a team responsible for international aviation security. 'He had an Englishman with him by the name of Sanders – ex-military, I'd guess; he seemed to be acting as Kennedy's man on the ground.'

Sanders again. Now Jenny was beginning to understand his involvement more clearly. She kept her knowledge to herself and allowed Ransome to continue.

'We receive security bulletins all the time,' he explained, 'but never personal visits. Kennedy told me that more than one intelligence source in the Far East had tipped off US agents to expect attacks on Western interests doing business with Taiwan, including airlines like ours that fly there. He said I was to report anything suspicious directly to him, and under no circumstances was I to speak to the British security services. If for some reason he wasn't contactable, I was to speak to Sanders. He didn't trouble himself with explanations – he simply told me that if I didn't cooperate fully my US landing slots would vanish overnight and with it my business.'

'What was his problem with the British?'

'He was rather colourful on the subject – said our government was "halfway up Beijing's ass", and that ministers would still be sipping tea with the ambassador when Chinese tanks were rolling up Whitehall. He was a real armchair cowboy, even had the boots to go with it.'

'What kind of attacks was he anticipating?' Jenny asked.

'He didn't say.'

'Did you talk to him again?'

'He called me once or twice over the following months, but as far as I was concerned there wasn't anything much to report. We had some technical problems, as you know, but nothing I equated with the kind of threat he had warned me of. I confess, I'd more or less forgotten about him when Captain Casey contacted my assistant asking for a meeting. I already knew about her forum and, I'll be honest with you, I had recently taken legal advice about the best way to deal with her before she harmed my airline. Naturally, I was curious about what she had to say that was so urgent, so I invited her over.

'We met here in this room. She told me that she had been speaking to my chief engineer, Mick Dalton, about what she considered was an unacceptably high incidence of faults in our flight computers and that they resembled those that had been cropping up on aircraft operated by a number of other airlines. It turned out they all had one thing in common: landing slots in Taiwan. That was interesting enough, but then she informed me that she had been contacted by Doug Kennedy, who had traced her through her internet postings. Apparently he was very exercised about a threat to computerized aircraft control systems and wanted her to attend an emergency summit he was organizing in Washington. He had expressly instructed her not to tell me – I think he assumed that for selfish reasons I would have tried to silence her – but I told her she should go; no one could have been more concerned about the safety of my aircraft than me. We agreed she would report back in confidence, and ten days later she headed out on Flight 189.'

The fog was finally starting to lift. 'And was this summit specifically concerned with aircraft computers?' Jenny asked.

'As far as she knew. But she thought that what had really grabbed Kennedy's attention was a new message thread on Airbuzz about the dangers presented by integrated modular avionics.'

'You've lost me—'

'Older aircraft had sealed flight computers. They were closed systems. If a fault developed, you would replace the whole unit. On the most modern aircraft such as the A380 the computers are modular – one module for engines and fuel, one for the aileron actuators, one for cabin pressure and so on. If there's a problem with one part of the system you unplug a module and slot in a new one. It's cheaper, allows for more frequent updating, and in theory it's an easier system to maintain. The only snag is that you're introducing vital components into a single aircraft from multiple suppliers, some of whom are using commercial off-the-shelf software. In other words, any one of a number of companies can produce a module to run a vital system—'

The penny dropped. Jenny finished his sentence for him. 'And if faulty or malicious software were somehow introduced into it—'

'That's the worry,' Ransome said. 'But big modern planes mean cheaper seats. And if I'm not the cheapest, I'm not in the sky.'

They looked at each other, the enormity of the story leaving them at a loss for words.

After a moment, Ransome said, 'You mentioned other passengers on 189.'

'Yes. Jimmy Han you know about, but there were several

others with onward flights to Washington. It seems some of their tickets had been rearranged to ensure they were all travelling together —'

She was interrupted by the phone ringing on the coffee table between them. Ransome answered it and listened to a message from his assistant. He looked across at Jenny. 'There's a Detective Inspector Williams wanting to speak to you.'

Williams? How had he traced her here?

She took over the receiver. 'Hello?'

'Mrs Cooper – you're with Mr Ransome.'

'How did you know where I was?'

'It just came over the police radio – I expect you'll have company in a minute. Listen, I'm at Heathrow Terminal Four. Your Mr Dalton's just hopped on a plane to New York – Flight 199. I almost caught up with him, but it took off five minutes ago. And you'll never guess who was raising hell at the departure gate – a Mrs Michelle Patterson. She was trying to get her husband off the flight and telling anyone who cared to listen that his company were responsible for what happened to 189. She told me he was attempting to flee jurisdiction before he was arrested. Can you tell me what the hell's going on?'

Jenny's mind was racing ahead. She called over to Ransome. 'New York Flight 199 that's just left Heathrow – get me a passenger list now!' Picking up with Williams, she said, 'I need some more time. Can you put a message out that you've apprehended me.'

'Lie, you mean?'

'Call it misinformation.'

'Call it shafting those English bastards and I'll do it with pleasure, Mrs Cooper.'

'Thanks. I owe you.'

Jenny replaced the receiver and joined Ransome, who was

issuing instructions down another line. Moments later his assistant was running through the door with an open laptop.

'The passenger manifest—'

The assistant set the machine down on the meeting table and opened the newly arrived email.

Taking control of the computer, Jenny scrolled through the list of names listed in alphabetical order, their corresponding seat numbers in a column on the right.

'Who are you looking for?' Ransome asked.

Jenny didn't hear him. Having spotted Dalton's name she skipped straight down to the 'Ps'. There was *Patterson, Greg (Mr) 18C*, then scrolling down she picked out *Sanders, Thomas (Wing Cmdr) 55C*, and right below him, *Sherman, Michael (Mr) 57A*. What was Michael doing on the flight with Sanders and Patterson? Could they have been summoned to Washington, too?

'What's going on?' Ransome demanded.

'When was the last time you spoke to Kennedy?'

'Shortly after 189 went down. Why?'

'Just tell me what was said.'

'I called him. Naturally, I wanted to know if he had any insight into what had happened. He was adamant that what happened to 189 was nothing to do with any of the threats he'd mentioned last year. He was insistent we keep flying at all costs.'

'Or what?'

Ransome didn't answer.

'He must have said something,' Jenny insisted.

'He repeated his earlier threat ... He said we'd lose our US landing slots.'

'I try hard not to leap to unfounded conclusions,' Jenny said, 'but I have a feeling that the problem with your planes might be bigger than anyone dare contemplate. It seems the computers operating them have developed minds of their own, but of course computers don't have minds, do they? They just do what someone has told them to do. And what if that someone isn't the pilot?'

'It wouldn't happen again. It couldn't—'

'Surely that depends on whether the person trying to make their point feels they've made it. You could trust Kennedy and carry on regardless, but if I were you I'd get this aircraft back on the ground as quickly as possible.'

TWENTY-SIX

FLYING CONDITIONS OVER ENGLAND were as favourable as could be expected in late January. Skies over Heathrow were bright and departures were running on time. Captain Patrick Finlay and First Officer David Cambourne had conducted their pre-flight preparations in a subdued atmosphere and Flight 199 had secured a take-off slot for eleven fifty-four a.m., six minutes ahead of schedule. Taxiing away from the stand at Heathrow, Finlay gave silent thanks. He had been the pilot originally scheduled to fly 189, but had been put out of action by a bout of full-blown flu that had laid him low for nearly a fortnight. Dan Murray and many of the cabin crew had been good friends. It would take a long time to accept they were gone.

David Cambourne was a reassuring presence alongside Finlay in the first officer's seat: quiet, dependable and thorough. Despite having been close to First Officer Ed Stevens and having been on friendly terms with many of 189's cabin crew, he was dealing with his grief like a true professional. The briefest glance in a meeting room in the canteen had sealed their tacit agreement that the crash wouldn't be mentioned. They had an aeroplane with 576 passengers on board to get safely to New York; nothing was more important than that.

As Finlay lined up at the head of the runway for the first

time in nearly three weeks, he was surprised not to feel in the least nervous. Like Dan Murray, he had cut his teeth flying older Boeings and hadn't flown an Airbus until his early forties. Since the crash he had heard other pilots voicing their suspicions of fly-by-wire technology in the media, but he remained resolutely in favour. As a young first officer he had had his one and only brush with disaster when his captain – a man nearing retirement – had decided to try to fly over a tropical storm en route to Barbados in an ageing DC9. The Airbus simply didn't allow a pilot to stray so far from the boundaries of safety. Better to trust to the cold logic of computers, he reasoned, than to the whims of stubborn pilots who thought they knew best.

'Beautiful day,' Finlay said, as he awaited the final word from the tower.

'Enjoy it while it lasts,' Cambourne replied, glancing at the weather display on his navigation screen. 'Dense high-level cloud over mid-Wales and a hundred-mile-an-hour headwind all the way from Anglesey to Iceland.'

Finlay ran a swift mental check on his fuel contingency. Ransome's insistence on loading light always made him a little insecure, especially on a transatlantic crossing, but he was confident that he had taken on more than enough to cope with a little wind.

He watched the American Airlines 747 that had been queuing ahead of them slowly lift from the ground and take to the air.

Word came through from the tower. 'Skyhawk 1-9-9 cleared for take-off runway two seven left, wind two three zero at ten.'

First Officer Cambourne replied: 'Cleared for take-off runway two seven left, Skyhawk 1-9-9.'

Captain Finlay released the brakes and moved the four thrust levers forward. The flight management computers did the rest, pushing the engines up to the pre-set take-off thrust level of 88 per cent of maximum power. As the aircraft weighing over one million pounds slowly picked up speed, it struck Finlay that the thrust lever he was gripping tightly was for no one's benefit other than his own. It was merely an electrical selector switch whose function could as easily have been performed by a tiny joystick a few centimetres high. One day soon pilots would lose the emotional attachment to controls that mimicked the manual levers of the analogue age; flying a plane would be more akin to a video game and, some even predicted, more safely done remotely from the ground.

Moments later the only sound in the cockpit was the gentle hum of the engines as Flight 199 began its slow, sweeping pre-programmed turn to the west. Finlay ran his eye over the array of screens that seemed to envelop him and felt there was something deep in the human psyche that was profoundly excited by a machine so far removed from the baseness of nature. As they passed through 5,000 feet, leaving the ugly sprawl of London far behind, he realized what that was: the world below was stuck in the inexorable cycle of life and death; this wonderful craft was a glimpse of immortality.

Michael looked down from his window seat at the green Berkshire countryside flitting beneath wisps of cloud. He had expected to feel uneasy aboard the 380, but it appeared so solid and enormous, and the seats were so comfortable, that he was already beginning to sense the gentle pull of sleep. God knows, he could do with some. Sitting at the bar in the departure lounge, he had declined Dalton's offer of a pill, preferring a large Bloody Mary, and then another. Sanders had drunk tonic water. He was still on duty and wouldn't relax until he had safely delivered both men to Kennedy.

Michael had a lot of questions for the American when they met, and if he didn't get answers he fancied he might punch the bastard's lights out.

It had been a hell of a two weeks, a hell of a twenty years. There had been numerous pilots he'd known whom he hadn't expected to see grow old, but Nuala was never one of them. He had had a colleague in the RAF who had become so tightly wound during their first tour in Afghanistan that he would have laid money on him putting a bullet through his head if he managed not to be shot down; more than a decade later he was still very much alive and well. It was Nuala, the sensible, capable one, who had fallen from the sky; Nuala, the kind and beautiful girl he had loved, but was so scared he'd hurt that he'd walked away.

He had lost count of the times he had replayed the events of their final meeting in his mind. He had walked into the office at the end of the day to find her sitting with a computer on her lap. She had looked as startled as he was, and was wiping tears from her cheeks the moment they stepped the other side of the door. She hadn't meant to cry – he understood that – but couldn't help herself. She was still in love, and he was still fighting it. She had wanted him to touch her, a hand on her arm, a kiss on her forehead – anything – but he had denied her it all. He recalled the relief he had felt when she told him it wasn't a personal visit, but that she needed advice – the kind only he could give.

She had insisted they talk somewhere where they couldn't be overhead. Michael took her to pub a few miles from the airport. It had felt incongruous sitting in a 400-year-old snug bar listening to her talk excitedly about state-of-the-art avionics, but at least she was no longer crying. She had always been happiest talking about planes: her eyes would light up like a little girl's. Male pilots were addicted to the freedom from responsibility flying brings, but for Nuala it was much more than that; she seemed fused with her passengers and crew in a way no male pilot ever was or wanted to be. He suspected that flying solo would have brought no joy to her at all.

She had talked non-stop for nearly two hours. He was treated to a detailed history of the evolution of fly-by-wire philosophy and technology which had culminated in the A380. She adored the aircraft and revered its architects and builders as heroes, which was why the faults she had come to believe had crept into its computers had troubled her so deeply. But there were some incidents which seemed beyond all normal explanation. Dan Murray's near disaster with the disobedient thrust lever had been one of them, and Alan Farraday's instrument blank-out another. What troubled her most of all was that there was no pattern to these errors, and by all accounts Ransome's engineers were as baffled as she was.

It was Farraday who had forced the issue. Nuala had told Michael how Farraday had grown more anxious about the error he had experienced over the Pacific repeating itself. Unhappy with Mick Dalton's failure to trace the cause of the fault, he had recruited Nuala to help persuade the chief engineer to copy the entire contents of the aircraft's flight computers onto a separate hard drive, which he intended to have analysed by independent experts. Dalton had carried out the download, compressed the files and transferred them to Nuala. She was all set to transfer them to Farraday when he came off his motorbike.

She had met Dalton several times during December to discuss Farraday's case and that of several other Ransome pilots who had experienced anomalies, hoping to trace them back to the same root but without success. Growing increasingly anxious for answers, she had cast the net wider on Airbuzz and been alarmed to discover a rash of reports of similar incidents from pilots working for several different airlines. The problem was so widespread that she started to canvass opinion on the forum as to whether a pilots' committee should be formed to present their concerns to aviation authorities across the world.

A plan was beginning to take shape when she was visited at home on a Sunday afternoon by an American who had introduced himself as Doug Kennedy, and who claimed to be from the Federal Aviation Authority. She had immediately suspected that he was no mere airline official. She described him as having the hardness of an experienced military man beneath a cloak of civility. He knew all about Airbuzz and claimed that the FAA had also known that she'd been behind it for more than two years.

But far from threatening her, Kennedy had attempted to be friendly. The FAA was as concerned about the incidents as she was, he assured her, which was why they were planning on holding a series of high-level meetings to discuss each one. He wanted her to come to Washington for a week to share what she knew with a committee of industry experts. There would be engineers, avionics specialists, security and counter-terrorism officials present. They had the full backing of the US government and wouldn't stop until they had solved the problem. Nuala hadn't known whether to feel relieved that such powerful people were taking an interest, or frightened that she had been outed as a potential trouble-maker. Anticipating her concern, Kennedy assured her that her connection with Airbuzz would remain secret, but she was requested not to discuss their meeting or her invitation to Washington with anyone, especially her employers. She had agreed, and even signed a document to that effect, which Kennedy handed her before leaving.

That was shortly before Christmas. Over the next few days she had grown more and more uncertain about the mysterious American. She could find no mention of him on the internet and he had left only the sketchiest details of the arrangements: she was to be waiting in the lobby of the Embassy Suites Hotel, Washington, at nine a.m. on 10 January. She was to bring any relevant information she had along with her and to use her best endeavours to gain more in the interim.

Finally, on 28 December her concern had got the better of her and she travelled to Bristol to seek Michael's advice. It became clear to him that she had become involved in something huge, but that she was only a tiny cog. The Americans would want her information, her silence and her insight into the mood of fellow pilots. His only concern was that she might find herself arrested in the States for some offence she had unwittingly committed, but she assured him that that had been another of Kennedy's guarantees: her liberty was secure. She had committed no crime in spreading information via her forum, though he questioned the ethics of further alarming an already jumpy public.

Nuala's greatest worry had been that if she obeyed Kennedy's orders and Ransome Airways got wind of what was happening, she wouldn't only lose her job but she would never work for a commercial airline again. Michael had no hesitation in advising her to tell Ransome everything: acting deceitfully was the one thing guaranteed to destroy her career.

Whether Nuala would have set off for Washington if he had told her not to, he could never know. What he could find out was whether her presence on the aircraft along with the others bound for Kennedy's secret meeting was just an unfortunate coincidence or the very reason it went down. He would come away from Washington with an answer; he would make sure of it. He would stick a gun on Kennedy if he had to. Hell, it wasn't as if he had anything left to lose.

The view from the window was hazy now they had climbed past 10,000 feet. He glimpsed the ground through fleeting gaps in the cloud; all that he had left behind seeming increasingly irrelevant as the plane powered towards the other side of the world. His only regret was that he hadn't told Jenny Cooper a little more. She had crept up on him somehow, moving from stranger to friend within days. She had stirred up all manner of unexpected feelings in him – guilt, fascination, anger, desire – and if Nuala's ghost hadn't been hovering so close, he was sure he would have taken things further.

Jenny, Jenny. She cared so deeply. He should at least have told her about his last meeting with Nuala, but just as he was learning to trust her he had become frightened for her. Once he had heard about the Apaches and the explosion on the water the danger was more than theoretical. Kennedy and whichever branch of the mighty US state he represented clearly had serious weaponry at their disposal, and on British soil. Where the helicopters had sprung from remained an intriguing mystery to him. The mothballed former US airbase RAF Fairford in Gloucestershire was a possibility, but the old SAS HQ at Hereford was closer and a natural place for the US to establish a black operations capability, no questions asked. At full speed a couple of Apaches could have reached the crash site within fifteen minutes. If they were scrambled at the first sign of the aircraft being in trouble they could have made the Severn only ten minutes after 189 hit the water.

It had been unclear to Michael at first what had happened out on the estuary, but he'd since begun to form an idea. It seemed to him that Kennedy wanted all the information about whatever was going on in the aircrafts' avionics for himself, or at least for his government. Knowledge was power. Witnesses, physical evidence, anything that might have handed the answers to others would have to have been neutralized. The man Brogan remained an enigma, but Michael's best guess was that, having found him alive, the Apache crew were ordered either to kill him or bring him in. Maybe there had been a struggle and he had fought them off. They would have been in a hurry to clear the area before they were seen – search and rescue helicopters would have been only minutes away – which would explain why they might have made do with puncturing his lifejacket and cutting him adrift in the expectation that he would drown. But from the facts Michael had picked up from Jenny he was sure that the Irishman had swum to the little girl in the water and attempted to save her. Perhaps that was the deal he cut with his would-be assassins – spare my life to let me help the girl. Michael doubted anyone would ever know the full facts for certain.

What he did know was that Nuala had intended to take a copy of the data from Farraday's flight computer to Washington on a portable hard drive. When Jenny got hold of Nuala's laptop he had been certain it would contain a copy, too, but Kennedy's people were good: their Trojan horse had worked far better than they could ever have hoped. The hard drive was wiped and the data lost. Until that moment he had been planning to tell Jenny everything; in his fantasy, the two of them would have copied the files and spread them far and wide across cyberspace. Screw Kennedy. Robbing him of his precious information was going to be sweet revenge. But fantasies seldom came true, and his was no exception.

Lying on the motel floor while Jenny slept he had tried again to start the laptop but to no avail. Tyax, Tyax, Tyax . . . the word went round and round his mind until he had wanted to bang his head against the wall. Then it had come to him, like a shaft of sunlight through a heavy sky: all those months ago she had sent him photographs of their trip to

Canada. There had been too many to email so she had posted them on her account at datadrop.com for him to download. She knew he would never get around to setting up his own account so she had instructed him to use hers – Tyax was her password.

He left the motel room before Jenny woke and flew his clients through rough weather across the Channel to Guernsey, having hardly slept. He rushed to an internet cafe in St Peter Port and logged on to datadrop. He keyed in Nuala's email address, entered 'Tyax' in the password box and there it was: hidden amongst her hundreds of backed-up files was 'A380 FC'. The compressed data fitted onto three small memory cards that were currently zipped in his jacket pocket: the contents of two of the aircraft's six flight computers on each.

His elation had been short-lived. Tommy Sanders was waiting for him on the ground at Newbury. He remembered him from his first tour in Iraq, a sly bugger who was known for eating more dinners in the US Air Force mess than his own. Always greasing up to the Americans and offering his men to do their dirty work. There were no tears shed when he hit thirty years' service and was put out to grass.

'Michael, old friend,' he had said, striding across the grass with an outstretched hand. 'How the devil did you get mixed up in this lot?'

Good question.

He had been charming, naturally, but there was no arguing with him. He was working directly for Kennedy and it had been his man following Dalton to their meeting at the lay-by the night before. The Americans were demanding to know everything there was to know about the downing of Flight 189 and failure to cooperate 'wouldn't be tolerated'. Michael hadn't troubled to ask what form their intolerance might take. He had seen the CIA at work over many years in the Middle East and needed no lessons in what they were capable of.

The retired wing commander seemed delighted to be working for the big boys at last and not an embarrassingly ill-equipped limb of a colonial army. Michael could see the back of his head two rows in front of him. He was already wearing his headphones and watching the start of a Clint Eastwood movie: *Dirty Harry*. That was Tommy Sanders all over: peace through superior firepower.

'One to go,' both pilots called out in unison.

The altimeter ticked swiftly upwards through 30,000 to 31,000 feet, the height at which they would level off over mid-Wales before moving slowly on upwards to 41,000 once they were out over the Irish Sea. They had cleared the Severn estuary and were heading towards the NUMPO waypoint in South Wales. Clear skies had turned to high-altitude cloud that was becoming thicker by the second. The hum of the engines adjusted to a lower, almost inaudible register. Airspeed was a steady 465 knots.

The aircraft jolted slightly as they encountered the first belt of serious headwind. Captain Finlay adjusted the attitude a touch and kept a close eye on the artificial horizon. Even though the aircraft's computers were busy transmitting instructions to the flying surfaces to carry out minute adjustments, he retained the illusion of being in complete control. The nose dipped through a pocket of turbulence and a ripple travelled through the aircraft's hull as they bounced through it.

'Seat belts?' First Officer Cambourne asked.

'Seat belts,' Finlay answered, his eyes fixed on the screens in front of him.

Cambourne reached up to the overhead switch and activated the seat-belt warning lights. In the cabin, the chief steward would be telling passengers to return to their seats and remain belted in.

'We'll have plenty of this as far as Iceland,' Cambourne said, consulting the weather display on his navigation screen. He checked the positions of other transatlantic aircraft up ahead following the same route. 'Doesn't seem to be causing anyone any problems.'

Finlay nodded. Some minor turbulence was fine, in fact he found it reassuring to be buffeted a little by the weather.

While Cambourne checked in with Shanwick to get the all-clear to proceed across the Atlantic, something caught Finlay's attention on his multi-function display. On one of three screens that sat on the console between his seat and Cambourne's, was a message reporting a problem with flight computer one. He pointed it out to his first officer. 'Take a look at that, would you?'

Cambourne quickly ended his conversation with Shanwick and turned his attention to his screen, which was showing the same message indicating that action was required to re-boot a malfunctioning flight computer. It wasn't one he recognized from his most recent simulator training.

He turned to the onboard information terminal. 'I'm going to look this one up.'

'No problem,' Finlay answered.

Cambourne pulled out the keyboard and tried to focus on the screen as he bounced in his seat.

Cambourne called up a list of error messages and tracked his finger down the screen looking for *FC1 FAULT 00/81 Re-boot*. 'It's not here.'

'Say again?' Finlay said, glancing over.

'It's not listed in the manual.' Cambourne turned back to his multi-function display and saw another error message appear: *ELEC AC BUS 1 FAULT*. He flicked to the electrical system topographic on the system display screen. It showed no fault. Another message: *DC ESS BUS FAULT*. There was no corresponding sign of a fault on the system display. 'Two electrical faults that aren't showing up on the system display.'

'Work through them,' Finlay answered calmly. 'There'll be something.'

Cambourne turned back to the onboard information terminal with the aim of reminding himself of the correct protocol when two displays failed to correspond, but as he navigated back to the main menu the screen froze on the list of errors. He hit the enter key a second time. The screen flickered, switched momentarily back to the main menu, then dissolved to black, a single white cursor blinking in the upper left corner. 'What the hell's wrong with this now?' He hit several more keys, but the screen remained stubbornly blank. 'I've lost the OIT,' Cambourne said.

'So have I,' came Finlay's deadpan reply.

Cambourne spun around in his seat and saw that Finlay's screen had also gone blank. Both men were having the same thought at once: that shouldn't have happened; the terminals were operated by separate computers. The whole point was that if one set of screens went down, the other didn't.

'Skyhawk 1-9-9, this is Bristol.'

'Skyhawk 1-9-9, go ahead, Bristol,' Finlay answered.

'Skyhawk 1-9-9, you are requested to turn around and land the aircraft as soon as possible. Suggest Filton.'

'Skyhawk 1-9-9, who is making this request?'

There was a crackle of static as the controller briefly conferred with someone Finlay assumed was his superior.

'Skyhawk 1-9-9, the instruction comes from Ransome Airways. My information is that you have failed to transmit any ACARS messages sent during the last five minutes—'

Cambourne was watching another unfamiliar message

appear on his multi-function display when it too flickered and turned to black. He glanced across at Finlay's and saw the same thing happen to his. Finlay glanced down at the console as the system display dissolved into a series of jagged white lines . . .

TWENTY-SEVEN

IF IT HADN'T BEEN for the turbulence Michael might have drifted into sleep. Instead he lay back in a semi-doze, watching the cloud vapour whip over the leading edge of the portside wing. He thought of Nuala, and for the first time fully appreciated the job she had done. Flying a handful of jockeys and rich playboys to and fro was one thing – they were risk takers by profession – but assuming responsibility for hundreds of civilian passengers who had placed their complete faith in you was something else. It was a load she had willingly carried every day, but he hadn't even been able to bring himself to take responsibility for her. In an attempt to distract himself from his guilty feelings, he glanced out along the wing and noticed that something was different: the light at its tip had stopped blinking. Odd. He craned round to see if he was simply at the wrong angle when the aileron moved swiftly downwards and the aircraft turned violently to the left.

Passengers screamed. They were falling.

Jenny had passed an anxious and frustrating ten minutes in Guy Ransome's suite while he barked orders into two telephones at once and finally succeeded in getting his message through to the National Air Traffic Control Service. He tried to be patched through to the aircraft's cockpit but failed. Communicating with an airliner in flight was an exclusive business, it seemed; not even the airline's owner could cut through the bureaucracy.

Having had the message back from Bristol, he slammed down the phone and turned to Jenny. 'Bristol has made contact with them. They're turning round and landing at Filton. It's the only big airport close enough to land a 380 that can be safely cleared in time.'

'Is the plane all right?'

Ransome forced back his shoulders and glanced off out of the window. 'They have a computer fault.'

'What sort of fault?'

The phone rang. Ransome snatched up the receiver. 'Yes . . . I see. Where are they now? . . . Instruct Brendan to be ready to go in two minutes, and tell them she'll be down directly.' He ended the call and turned to Jenny. 'The police are here. Do you want to go with them or come with me to Filton?'

'How do I do that?'

He nodded towards the next room. 'Fire escape.'

'All right. Let's go.'

She grabbed her bag and followed him. He paused to pull over the bolt on the main door, then stepped through to a passageway which led to the bedroom. French windows opened to a small balcony at the side of the building which connected to a narrow fire escape. Ransome went through and started down the steps. Behind them, Jenny heard a knock on the main door of the suite, and an insistent voice on the other side calling for it to be opened. She hurried after Ransome as the knocking turned to violent pounding.

She could hear the sound of the helicopter engines slowly winding up as she clattered down the final two flights and followed Ransome along the path which led to the corner of the building. The helicopter was fifty yards away on the open stretch of lawn behind the terrace.

'Stop there!' The voice belonged to one of two detectives who had made it onto the fire escape.

Jenny broke into a run.

'What was that?' Finlay yelled, as he fought to stabilize the aircraft after its sudden unprompted lurch to the left.

'No idea,' Cambourne answered, straining to keep his cool. Stick to the rules, he told himself. But he didn't know of any that covered this situation.

'What's wrong with these bloody screens? How do we re-boot them?'

'I'm trying.' Cambourne searched across the bank of switches above his head, hoping for inspiration. He was working from the assumption that several flight computers couldn't malfunction at once without there being an electrical fault. Perhaps one of the four generators was malfunctioning. But without a system display to indicate which of the aircraft's circuits was faulty, he was shooting in the dark.

Finlay steeled himself and took a deep breath. He was aware that his mind was cluttered with extraneous thoughts. The computers were the first officer's responsibility. His task was to get the plane on the ground using whatever tools he possessed. He checked the two screens in front of him: the primary flight and navigation displays were still in working order. On the radar he could see the half-dozen planes in the corridor behind him peeling off to the east. The airspace had been cleared. He had an unobstructed hundred-mile run back over the Brecon Beacons and the Severn estuary into Filton, on the north-west outskirts of Bristol. It could have been worse: many airports didn't have runways long enough to allow a 380 to land.

Finlay radioed the tower at Bristol. 'Skyhawk 1-9-9, Bristol, we're having some more electrical problems. We're working on finding out which systems are faulty. We may need some assistance on the ground . . . Bristol?'

There was a click, then a constant static hiss over Finlay's headphones. He glanced over at Cambourne. His face had turned a deathly white.

'This isn't making any sense,' the first officer said.

'Sir, please return to your seat.' The stewardess pursued Michael along the aisle as he made his way forward towards the entrance to the cockpit.

'I need to speak to the captain.'

'You have to return to your seat.'

The chief steward appeared, blocking his path. 'Sir, back to your seat at once, please.'

Michael spoke in a low whisper so as not to be overheard by passengers sitting nearby: 'Did you know Captain Nuala Casey?'

Confused, the steward nodded.

'So did I. I'm a fellow pilot, and I think I might know more than whoever is flying this plane about what happened on 189.'

'What's going on?'

The voice behind Michael belonged to Tommy Sanders. His usual swagger had been replaced by a look of alarm.

'Tell these people to take me to the cockpit while they still can,' Michael said.

Sanders's face froze in fear.

'Jesus Christ.' Michael shoved past the steward and ran the length of the cabin to the cockpit door.

Captain Finlay and First Officer Cambourne had swapped seats. Finlay didn't like to fly in this position, but there it was, he had no choice. The priority was to get as low as possible and quickly; he needed to be able to see the ground.

The interphone buzzer sounded.

Cambourne responded: 'Yes?'

'Michael Sherman, formerly of the RAF. I was a friend of Captain Nuala Casey—' Cambourne heard what appeared to be sounds of a scuffle breaking out in the background.

'Ignore him,' Finlay barked.

'Are you in trouble?' Michael insisted. 'I may be able to help.'

'Tell him to get back to his seat,' Finlay snapped.

'I think I know something about what happened on 189. Their stall must have been caused by loss of airspeed indication. I've got Nuala's GPS with me—'

Cambourne hesitated.

Finlay relented. 'All right. Let him in.'

Cambourne glanced left and saw that the two screens in front of the first officer's seat now occupied by Finlay were starting to break up, too.

'I said let him in – we've got no instruments.'

In the moments it took for Michael to pass through the two safety-locked doors that separated cabin and cockpit, Finlay took decisive action. He switched off all four of the aircraft's main generators and activated the auxiliary power unit. The lights in the cockpit flickered and died.

'Shit.' The APU wasn't functioning either. He activated the ram air turbine and waited on tenterhooks for the first sign that the propeller-driven generator had successfully dropped out from beneath the undercarriage and started to supply power to the aircraft's vital systems.

Michael stepped out from the pitch-black void between the two doors as the cockpit lights blinked dully back into life.

'Loss of power?'

'We're on the RAT,' Finlay said.

Michael scanned the ten dead screens in the cockpit. 'You've lost everything?'

'I think I'm somewhere between direct law and mechanical back-up.'

'Meaning?'

Finlay moved the joystick subtly right and pressed the right rudder pedal. 'I've got joystick controls, left and right rudder, manual trim and thrust, but no instruments of any kind.'

For a moment, the three men fell silent. 'Where's that GPS?' Cambourne said desperately.

Michael pulled the small hand-held unit out from his jacket pocket and switched it on. It took frustrating seconds to boot up.

'You may not get a signal in here,' Finlay said, 'the shielding—'

He was right. Standing behind the cockpit seats there wasn't even a single bar of reception.

'Give it to me,' Cambourne said, snatching it from him. He pressed it up hard against the cockpit window and two bars appeared. 'It's working – just.'

A map appeared plotting their position above the town of Pontypridd in South Wales. They were heading on a south-easterly course.

'Here, let me.' Michael leaned forward and adjusted the display to include crude speed and height readings as well as an electronic compass. 'Don't forget this is ground speed, not true airspeed.'

'I'll take anything I can get,' Finlay said. 'Has someone got a phone? We'd better call Bristol before they shoot us out of the sky.'

Greg Patterson's shirt clung damply to his skin. Like him, his fellow business-class travellers were sitting stiffly in their comfortable seats flinching at every bump and sudden move-ment. The effortlessly smooth craft on which they had begun their flight now felt erratic and brittle. There was a strange, high-pitched whine beneath the sound of the engines. The cabin temperature had dropped and the air felt thinner. There had been no announcement from the cockpit, but no one in his section had yet called over a stewardess to demand an explanation. They didn't want one. The plunge, the flickering lights, the failure of the seat-back screens all pointed to there being a serious problem, and the frequent fliers – which was most of them – would have noticed that the plane had turned around and was now heading downwards.

But only Patterson knew just how serious a problem it was likely to be. To die now would be the least he deserved for having let Amy travel alone. Since losing his only daughter he hadn't found the courage to confront his boss, the founder and CEO of Cobalt Inc., Dale Cannon, or even to tell his wife what he knew. He was astonished and sickened by his own cowardice. His father had served as a front-line infantryman during three tours of duty in Vietnam and he had inherited none of his mettle.

But in nearly ten years working for Cobalt, Patterson had now come to realize that he had learned to separate the interests of business from its ethical consequences to a degree that would shock any reasonable human being. Dale Cannon, not the brightest man who had ever lived, though certainly one of the most cunning and amoral, had pulled off the trick of harnessing the intellectual curiosity of a number of highly intelligent men and women by exploiting their greed. His theory – that if you offered a high enough reward, a scientist would do just about anything if it could be passed off as advancing the sum total of human knowledge – had worked with a degree of success that reflected very bleakly on human nature. Cobalt's software had generated billions of dollars in revenue. It had started with broadly laudable aims: to protect vulnerable and sensitive systems from outside attack, but Cannon had been unable to resist the lucrative offers from less salubrious customers. Cobalt had accepted contracts from the Saudi and Iranian governments to ensure that polluting Western influences didn't make it to their citizens over the internet, and from security services as opposed in their philosophies as Israel's Mossad and Pakistan's ISI. In the purely commercial realm, it had worked on submarine control systems and advanced avionics, helping develop modular systems that could be updated and replaced at will.

Dale Cannon's increasingly reckless choice of customers had been a long-standing and growing source of tension among a number of his senior executives. Matters had come to a head two years before when three of Cobalt's top programmers were poached by a Chinese corporation to work on highly secretive government projects. All senior personnel, including Patterson, knew that this meant the Chinese would now have the means to penetrate and disrupt any number of systems, including the latest avionics in both military fighters and commercial airliners. But Cannon refused to discuss these dangers and, worse still, rebuffed all approaches by American government officials, convinced that they were determined to put him out of business.

Patterson had been secretly counting the days until the escalating Cold War in cyberspace claimed its first human victims. It had come later than he expected, but the warning signs had been present for several years. Localized disruptions in electricity and gas supplies throughout Europe had gone largely unreported, but he had noticed them; there had been blips in air traffic control systems too. These were given mundane explanations by local media, but surely no one could have ignored the twenty-minute diversion of a quarter of internet traffic through Chinese servers that had occurred in April 2010. Yet it seemed they had, at least until six weeks ago, when Doug Kennedy and two associates – one of whom was retired Wing Commander Tommy Sanders – turned up in Cobalt's London offices threatening to drive them out of the free world unless they gave up the secrets of their technology. Dale had acted cool, initially playing along, then pulling Patterson out of their first Washington meeting merely to prove that he wasn't going to be the government's poodle.

Immediately it was known that Patterson wasn't travelling, several colleagues contacted him urging him to go to Washington in any event. Not only the company's but their own futures were potentially on the line, they argued. One even feared that they might face federal indictments. Patterson had been sorely tempted, but in the end his cowardly streak had again got the better of him. And to his everlasting shame, when Cannon telephoned to offer his condolences after the crash, he had felt pathetically grateful.

He railed against his predicament. It should have been Dale Cannon sitting in this seat now. It was all Cannon's fault. When Sanders had approached him several days after the accident and subjected him to a lengthy interrogation, he had been left in no doubt that the CIA were convinced that viruses, which had probably started their lives as lines of code written in the sealed rooms of Cobalt's Lombard Street offices, had found their way into the avionics of commercial airliners. They had undoubtedly passed through several sets of hands since and many stages of malignant evolution, but it was Cannon's money that had nurtured them to life, his manipulation that had persuaded young minds to leave their consciences at the door.

Recruited to the near-impossible task of putting the genie back in the bottle, Patterson had worked hard over the ensuing days to gather as much data as he could to take to Kennedy in Washington, but had amassed far less than he might have done if his wife hadn't behaved so recklessly. He had been on the verge of persuading a colleague to hand over passwords to one of Cobalt's most secure servers when, in a grimly ironic twist, Michelle had released the contents of his private emails to the world, forcing him to take flight immediately to save what he had already collected.

How extensively the viruses were distributed and how precisely they were controlled remained unknown. If Sanders was to be believed, it appeared – anecdotally, at least – that many aircraft and airlines were already affected, meaning that no commercial flight could be considered completely safe. When Patterson had queried the wisdom of taking a 380 across the Atlantic to attend their Washington meeting, Sanders had replied that the first rule of warfare was that lightning never struck twice. Like a fool he had accepted the logic, not stopping to think that the analogy was entirely false: lightning was a random event; Cobalt's programs were precision weapons.

The plane banked to the right and steepened its angle of descent. The strange whine grew louder, piercing his eardrum like a dentist's drill. Patterson clamped his eyes tight shut and prayed that death would come quickly.

Sitting in the rear seat of the helicopter, Jenny struggled to hear the conversation Ransome was having on his phone over the noise of the engine. It seemed there had been some communication with the aircraft. She was desperate for news. It was selfish of her – there were probably many children, mothers and fathers and young people with their whole lives ahead of them on board – but all she could think of was Michael.

'What's happening?' she asked as he rang off.

He didn't answer.

'What's going on with the plane?'

'Their only communication has been by cellphone and they're navigating using a hand-held GPS.' He seemed more angry than distressed. '200 million pounds' worth of aircraft . . .'

Jenny felt the knot in her stomach tighten. 'Where are they?'

'Approaching the Severn estuary between Newport and Cardiff. They've dumped their fuel and are heading in to land at Filton.'

They broke through the blanket of low cloud at 6,000 feet and the landscape opened out beneath them. The estuary spanned the horizon from right to left, sparkling orange and yellow in the slanting sun.

'300 miles per hour,' Cambourne called out, no longer bothering to attempt the translation to knots. '9,500, 9,000 . . .'

'Yes?' Finlay barked.

'We've lost reception – "searching for satellites".'

Attempting to assist, Michael leaned forward from his seat behind Cambourne's, but there was nothing to be done. Even pressed right up to the windshield the message remained stubbornly on the screen. 'It's probably the battery – it uses more juice on a weak signal.'

'Where the hell does that leave us?' Finlay said.

'Grateful we're in daylight,' Michael said. 'I know this bit of country, I'll navigate. Turn five degrees left.'

'Where are the RAF when you need them?' Cambourne said. 'Someone to guide us down wouldn't go amiss.'

'Trying to find a working plane, I expect,' Michael replied. 'The nearest Tornado's probably in East Anglia. Expect them to arrive just about the time we're touching down.'

Finlay had flown simulators on direct law, but no matter what the instructors said, it was a million miles from reality.

Without the flight computers making their constant automatic adjustments, the aircraft had all the finesse of an oil-tanker in a force nine gale.

'Keep her going down, nice and steady, ten miles to landing.' Michael tried to sound reassuring, but his heart was beating so hard he could hardly force out the words. He had no idea how Finlay was remaining so calm; the man was made of steel.

The nose tipped down further as Finlay manually adjusted the trim and throttled back. The engines were now turning at little more than idling speed as they began their gliding descent towards an airport which remained invisible to him. As they crossed onto the southern side of the estuary the city of Bristol spread out ahead of them, but Finlay had no idea where to locate the runway.

'I see it,' Michael said. 'Five degrees right. Six miles to go—'

Finlay was flying blind, relying solely on Michael's visual cues. Without him, ditching on water would have been the only viable option, but with this little control he was sure they wouldn't have stood a chance.

'You can see the M5 motorway going from left to right,' Michael said. He pointed dead ahead. 'There's Filton.'

Finlay's eyes finally picked out the thin strip of concrete he was aiming for. He eased to the right, then back a touch to the left. He estimated they were at 1,500 feet with four miles to go. All he had to do was hold a steady course and bring her gently in.

'Gear down.'

Cambourne operated the lever that would bring the 380's landing gear down by force of gravity alone. There was no display to tell them it was engaged. It would have to be an act of faith.

The three men in the cockpit exchanged apprehensive

glances. They could all see the runway dead ahead, there was nothing more to be said. The only one who could get them on the ground was Finlay. He gave a thumbs-up and adjusted the trim for the final approach. For the first time in twenty years he was flying in the raw. He pretended he was back in the little two-seater Cessna in which he had first taken to the air.

The helicopter reached the eastern fringes of Bristol in time for Jenny and Ransome to see the 380 gliding like a distant eagle towards the far side of the city, the sun glinting off its starboard wing. Even five miles away it looked huge and graceful. There was no smoke trailing, no outward sign of distress as it continued its slow descent. Jenny closed her eyes and said a silent prayer.

With two miles to touch-down Finlay realized he had brought the 380 in a little low for comfort, but better to strike at a shallow angle than come in too steeply. They couldn't have been at more than 500 feet. Cambourne shot him an anxious glance. Finlay eased the throttle lever forward; the engines flared but the nose skewed ten degrees to the right.

He wrestled the controls, pumping the pedal rudder with left foot. 'What's wrong with the right engines?'

'Must be the fuel pumps,' Cambourne said.

Finlay had the nose lined up again, but they were falling quickly. Leaning on the rudder, he touched the throttle, but this time the sheer to the right was matched with a sudden flick-up of the nose as they met a pocket of warmer air. Suddenly the runway was at ten o'clock and coming up fast.

Finlay fought the rudder and started to bring the nose round once more, but it refused to come fully square. They were heading for the ground at an angle that would see them career across the grass and into the hangars. He had run out of options. He pushed the joystick hard left. The plane tilted. Back right. The starboard wing started down, but not in time. The tip of the port-side wing clipped the airport's perimeter fence. Dragged suddenly to the left, the plane thumped hard onto the ground with the sound of splintering metal. Finlay jammed on the brakes, but the aircraft was already leaning over onto its left side. The forward landing gear gave way under the strain, sending the nose plunging towards the tarmac. Michael threw his hands over his face as shattered glass and a hail of sparks flew through the cockpit window. He heard Finlay cry out in pain. Then all was peace.

The plane was tilted sideways, supported by the remains of its port-side wing. The smoking wreckage of two engines was scattered over the runway for several hundred yards behind it. The tip of the nose cone had been ripped away and the cockpit was staved in. Smoke was still curling upwards from the foam-smothered fuselage. Jenny absorbed every detail as the helicopter circled, then came in to land on the grass.

Ignoring the protests of the fire crew, she jumped out and followed Ransome as he strode towards the wreckage. Two escape slides had been activated and traumatized passengers were sliding down, some with bloody wounds on their foreheads where they had struck the seats in front.

A pair of fire-fighters were in the forward doorway at the top of a ladder. Others were clambering over the broken wing to reach the door at the mid-section. There were hands at the cabin windows, and at one the battered features of an unconscious man. She scanned the faces of the walking wounded looking for Michael, but didn't see him; neither was there any sign of Dalton or Patterson. The only person who caught her eye was a straight-backed figure of about sixty who was shouting instructions to a bemused policeman. Ransome had noticed him, too, and was hurrying towards him calling his name: 'Sanders. Sanders, you bastard!' The man turned with a startled expression as the airline boss threw a punch directly into his face which sent him sprawling to the ground. The bewildered policeman ran over and after a brief tussle Ransome found himself laid out on the ground; a knee was forced into his back and his wrists tethered in plastic restraints.

He called out to her to intervene. 'Tell them who he is, tell them,' Ransome yelled, but her attention had been caught by a bloodied figure who had been helped to the forward door and was now standing at the top of the ladder. As if prompted by some sixth sense, he turned his head. It was him. It was Michael.

TWENTY-EIGHT

WHEN THE CELL DOOR OPENED, Moreton was smiling. 'To the best of my knowledge, Jenny, you have the proud distinction of being the only British coroner ever to have been arrested twice in two days. I suppose congratulations are in order.'

Too weary to pick a fight, she held back from making the caustic remark that his sarcasm deserved and levered her aching body off the concrete shelf in the all-too-familiar cell beneath New Bridewell police station.

'You would have thought the police had better things to do,' she said.

'The rule of law has to be upheld, even in extremis,' Moreton answered, 'though you'll be glad to know that no charges will be laid against you.'

'Who do I have to thank for that?'

Moreton smiled. 'Consider it a gesture of goodwill.'

She had been arrested by a sharp-eyed constable even before she had had a chance to meet Michael off the plane, and had spent a long eight hours locked up without communication or explanation. The fact that Detective Sergeant Fuller hadn't come down to gloat suggested that her fate remained the subject of debate, but Jenny was taking nothing for granted. Stepping out of the cell and into the corridor, she realized she felt the giddy rush of liberation – she had begun to convince herself that this time she really would be cast into the outer darkness. Perhaps Moreton wasn't so unprincipled after all.

She followed him along the corridor past locked cell doors with the names of the noisy, unhappy occupants scribbled on wipe-clean boards screwed to the dull green walls. He seemed in a hurry to escape, as if frightened that he might become contaminated by his unsavoury surroundings.

As they stepped into the welcome fresh air, Moreton said, 'I trust the experience has discouraged you from straying again.'

This time Jenny couldn't hold her tongue. 'Would you have preferred an aircraft with six hundred people aboard to have gone down in the Irish Sea?'

'Fair point, Jenny, I won't deny it, but let's not squabble – we've a meeting to attend. I hope you don't mind coming as you are.'

'What meeting? Where?'

'Not far – but do try to be sensible. This really is for the best.'

During the short journey to the city council building on College Green, Moreton updated her on the details of the crash landing. Thankfully there had been only three fatalities, but unfortunately one of them had been Captain Patrick Finlay, who had been struck on the head by debris from the nose cone flying through the broken cockpit window. Miraculously, First Officer Cambourne had escaped with minor wounds, as had most of the cabin crew. Over half the surviving passengers had suffered broken limbs and minor head injuries, but none was in a life-threatening condition. Of the two who had died, one had suffered a coronary and the other a fatal blow to the head caused by failing to wear a seat belt. The quick action of the fire crews had prevented an engine fire, which had ignited on landing, becoming an inferno that would have engulfed the entire plane. The full picture was still being formed, but in the words of the emotional rescue worker whose impromptu interview was being continually played on the rolling news, the angels that had failed to arrive for Flight 189 had certainly turned up for work today.

The Aircraft Disaster Management Committee had up-rooted itself from London and set up a temporary HQ in a large second-floor meeting room at Bristol City Hall, only a five-minute walk from Jenny's office and a stone's throw from the Marriott. In her makeshift office on the opposite side of College Green, Mrs Patterson would doubtless be convening a committee of her own, unaware that her husband was currently sitting less than a hundred yards away with many of the answers she craved. But Greg Patterson was in no mood to show Jenny even a hint of gratitude, and barely lifted his eyes to acknowledge her presence as Moreton introduced her to the other seven men and one woman arranged around the large table. To Patterson's right sat Guy Ransome, who greeted her with a wan smile; to his left, Wing Commander Tommy Sanders – the man whom Jenny had seen next to the plane at Filton issuing orders. The woman, who reminded Jenny of a particularly fierce judge she had once known, was Eleanor Hammond from the Secret Intelligence Service. The five remaining men were Assistant Chief Constable Raymond Butler of the Avon and Somerset Police, Amrit Singh, a senior civil servant who sat on the government's Joint Intelligence Committee, Air Chief Marshal Colin Talbot, Senior Investigating Officer Edward Marsham from the Air Accident Investigation Branch, and Sir James Kendall.

Singh, a genial, round-faced man in his mid-fifties, acted as chairman.

'Pleased to meet you, Mrs Cooper. Please accept my apologies for the manner of your delay.'

'Apology accepted,' Jenny said in a tone dry enough to draw an anxious glance from Moreton. 'Before we begin, can I ask what's happened to Michael Sherman and Mick Dalton? I believe they were travelling with the two gentlemen sitting opposite me.' She nodded towards Patterson and Sanders.

'They're being debriefed, Mrs Cooper,' Eleanor Hammond interjected, 'as these gentlemen will be in due course, and you also – if you would be so kind as to cooperate. Mr Patterson and Mr Sanders have been asked to assist us this evening as their connection to events is of a slightly different order from the others.'

'Thank you,' Singh said, eager to maintain a brisk pace. He addressed himself to Jenny. 'Mr Ransome has been good enough to explain to us the circumstances of your meeting with him earlier today.' And without a trace of irony he added: 'We are most grateful for your contribution to the return of Flight 199. It's quite possible that without your intervention the tragic event of a fortnight ago would have been repeated.'

Jenny wanted to shout out in protest that those now nodding in congratulation had done everything in their collective power to silence her, but somehow the words seemed to stop in her throat.

Acknowledging her unspoken thoughts, the urbane Singh deftly piled on more praise. 'Mrs Cooper, a robust system of justice requires determined and independent judges and coroners, and your embodiment of these qualities is to be applauded. Your suspicions have indeed been wholly vindicated.'

Jenny waited for the 'but'.

Singh didn't let her down. 'That said, we do have something to offer in mitigation. Until we spoke to these three gentlemen this afternoon –' he waved a hand in the direction of Ransome, Patterson and Sanders – 'we genuinely had no idea that maliciously corrupted avionics were the most likely cause of 189's problems.'

Jenny glanced at Sir James Kendall. He was keeping his eyes fixed firmly on his notebook.

'There was no doubt that something had struck the aircraft, but we remained at a loss to explain precisely what.'

'You didn't know about the Apaches?'

Singh's eyes flicked uneasily to Air Chief Marshal Talbot, who seemed to place the ball back in the civil servant's court. A wise man, Jenny thought.

'Or about Mr Sanders's role in trying to suppress evidence of their existence? People have died. I suggest that your debriefing includes questions about the death of an innocent photographer named Jon Whitestone, and whether Mr Sanders had a hand in Captain Farraday's fatal accident.'

Sanders remained impassive. Singh considered his response with extreme care, exchanging glances with Eleanor Hammond to be sure of her approval before continuing. 'Your comments have been noted. You have my word that all relevant matters will be dealt with. But you must appreciate, Mrs Cooper, that nothing of what we have discussed in this room must be repeated once you have left it.'

It was more than a polite request, Jenny sensed. Her answer and the faithfulness with which her actions reflected it would determine her entire professional future. She had no doubt that to step outside the rules of this inner circle would place her permanently beyond the pale. The question was: did she want to be taken to the Establishment's heart, or was this the moment for a new departure?

'Mrs Cooper—?'

'The families of the dead deserve to know what happened – and I include Whitestone's and Farraday's among them.'

'They do indeed, but they can't know everything, I'm afraid, not even Mrs Patterson. They will be given certain information, of course, but by Sir James, not by you.'

Air Chief Marshal Talbot interjected: 'We can't ground the world's airliners, Mrs Cooper, and nor do we have to. With the help of Mr Patterson and, we hope, his company, this threat will be dealt with.'

Jenny shot Patterson a look.

'I will be happy to fill you in on the details once I have your assurance,' Singh said. 'You must understand that some things are simply too delicate and important to be subjected to all the rumour and conflation that would occur in the public arena.'

'What about my inquest?' Jenny asked.

Singh passed the question to Assistant Chief Constable Butler. 'We're hoping you can bring it to a sensible conclusion, Mrs Cooper. My force has been as mystified by the circumstances of Brogan's death as I know you have been. We've been making inquiries and we're fairly certain that he had been engaged as an informer for Customs and Excise in a joint operation with the Irish Garda's Drug Squad. We believe the Garda tempted him back from the Caribbean with the offer of immunity in exchange for helping them to penetrate the criminal activities of the Real IRA. He had a mixed cargo of cannabis and cocaine on board, which he was en route to delivering to his accomplices further up the Severn. There is some suggestion that he was concerned that his cover might have been blown – the Garda has never quite managed to purge itself of officers sympathetic to Republican terrorists – hence the gun, one suspects.'

'And I'll be receiving a statement to this effect?'

'You will,' Butler replied.

'But it wasn't the plane that caused his death, it was what happened in the water.'

'I can only repeat my earlier request, Mrs Cooper,' Singh said. 'It goes without saying that all of us only want what's in the public interest.'

She had made up her mind to get up from the table and leave the room when Patterson broke his silence. He spoke in a feeble, faltering voice. 'Mrs Cooper, I thank you for all that you tried to do for my family. Your task would have been so much easier if I had had the courage to tell you what I knew . . . I understand you were responsible for turning the plane around so quickly this morning. I probably owe my life to you . . . You have my word that I will be dedicating my efforts to making sure a disaster of this sort is never allowed to happen again.'

She could see in his eyes that he meant it. He was no longer the buttoned-up corporate man she had first met in the mortuary a fortnight ago. He had the look of a penitent now.

'Mrs Cooper?' Singh asked again.

'All right. Agreed.'

'Thank you.'

Looks of relief spread across the committee members' faces. Moreton let out an audible sigh. At last he had delivered.

Singh spoke for no more than ten minutes, succinctly placing all the facts as he knew them in chronological order. Much of it Jenny already knew or had surmised: she had deduced that malware had been remotely inserted into the A380's flight computers, possibly before the components were even installed in the aircraft, and she had also known that Ransome Airways' booking system had been manipulated by the same unseen hands into grouping Han, Patterson, Towers, Duffy and Nuala Casey on the same flight. What she hadn't fully grasped was the sheer enormity of the electronic war in which the downing of 189 was the first bloody skirmish, or the precise intention behind Kennedy's Washington summit.

The battle had been escalating for at least ten years, Singh explained. China saw the advent of global electronic communications as the number one threat to its internal stability, and to defend against this had erected what had become known as the Great Firewall, through which only approved internet traffic could flow. The US had then set about finding means of bypassing it in the hope of igniting the sparks of a mass democracy movement in the Communist superpower. In retaliation, the Chinese government sponsored efforts to use the internet as a means of threatening vital infrastructures in Western countries: power, water, telecommunications, electronic banking, stock markets and aviation. Controlling and disrupting such systems remotely was every bit as effective as other means of warfare, and China possessed vastly superior manpower with which to wage it. As the balance of power slowly tilted towards the East, it became increasingly apparent that this was a Cold War the West was in danger of losing.

Doug Kennedy was put in charge of a team fighting the war on the aviation front. A series of suspicious mishaps in air traffic control systems, coupled with an unexplained spate of errors in previously dependable fly-by-wire aircraft, pointed to outside interference. His task was to isolate the problem and gather together the personnel to fix it. The summit set for 10 January was the result of many months of careful persuasion. Aided by Sanders in the UK, Kennedy had sweet-talked, cajoled and ultimately threatened his way into persuading some big players to come to Washington. Captain Nuala Casey was on the guest list because of her unique overview of the latest reported malfunctions on commercial aircraft. Cobalt, represented by Greg Patterson, was targeted for its singular expertise in both preventing and orchestrating viral attacks on complex computer systems. Alan Towers and his associate Dr Ian Duffy were well ahead of the competition in developing hardware with the potential to be immune from outside interference. Kennedy wanted them prised out of the purely commercial sphere and under the watchful supervision of the US government. Jimmy Han was already a loyal friend of the US and needed little persuasion to offer his manufacturing muscle as one of the world's largest manufacturers of computer hardware. Already exiled from his homeland, he was in the front line of the struggle for Chinese democracy, a cause he felt would ultimately triumph only when information flowed freely amongst his billion and more compatriots.

'As you can appreciate, Mrs Cooper,' Singh said, drawing towards a conclusion, 'between them, those four men and one woman represented a body of knowledge whose value could safely be considered priceless – easily worth the loss of a few hundred innocent lives.'

'Will there be retaliation?' Jenny asked, realizing how naive she sounded as soon as the words left her mouth.

'It all gets weighed in the balance,' Talbot answered. 'I am sure that at some point there will be consequences.'

Silence fell across the table. Glances were exchanged, indicating that the committee's business was drawing to a close.

'We appreciate your cooperation, Mrs Cooper,' Singh said. 'It won't go unacknowledged.'

Simon Moreton took his cue to see her out. 'Thank you, Jenny. Can I offer you a lift home?'

Jenny turned back to Singh. 'You haven't told me what happened on the water.'

'We're still trying to establish the precise facts,' Talbot cut in. 'It seems likely that American personnel were acting directly on Kennedy's orders. We can presume they attempted to destroy the avionics of the downed aircraft rather than let them fall into our hands, and it probably also follows that they made every effort to ensure that there were no surviving witnesses to their actions. In the latter respect, at least, they were successful.'

'The Americans don't trust us?' Jenny needled. 'I thought we cooperated fully over terrorism.'

More uncomfortable glances were exchanged. Jenny suddenly felt foolish but didn't understand why.

'We're considered leaky,' Sir James Kendall said, speaking for the first time. 'It's our press and, I'm afraid, people like you they fear, Mrs Cooper. Somehow we've lost the knack of keeping a secret.'

Ignoring his note of disapproval, Jenny persisted. 'Someone tried to kill Brogan, or at least ensure he didn't survive. That can't be allowed to go unpunished.'

No one answered her.

'And what will the public be told? No one is going to believe it was a lightning strike after what happened today. You can't continue to issue misinformation for ever.'

Singh took up the baton again. 'Please try to be content with what you have already achieved, Mrs Cooper. Not even you can improve the situation any further. The contaminated avionics will be analysed; a solution will be found.'

Jenny wasn't content, far from it, but she could truthfully say there was nothing more she could have done.

Several inches of snow had fallen overnight, covering the valley in a white shroud that had frozen hard in a searing east wind. The snow ploughs had left the tiny lane from Melin Bach untouched, forcing Jenny to creep slowly down the hill cutting the first tracks of the day. The smothered landscape looked as subdued as she felt. The radio bulletins carried the latest speculation that Flight 199 had been forced to land because of a faulty electrical component supplied to the aircraft's manufacturers. Familiar-sounding officials re-assured the listening public that very occasionally faulty components slipped through the net, but that this would never be allowed to happen again. Jenny almost found herself believing them.

Likewise, she almost trusted Simon Moreton's assurances that diplomats were now working day and night to ensure that no more airliners were plucked from the sky, but it was little salve for her conscience. When, in a few days' time her inquest resumed, it would end in an open verdict, leaving Brogan's girlfriend, Maria Canavan, with unanswered questions and a lingering suspicion that the man she had loved had been an unredeemed criminal. Mrs Patterson, too, would never be allowed to know that in the interests of keeping their shady mission secret, the operatives in the Apache helicopters had left her daughter to the mercies of the freezing river. Picking her way through the winding miles of snow-covered forested gorge, she felt like a traveller on a journey that might never end.

The uneasy sensation stayed with her even as she broke out of the wilderness and crossed the bridge into the tamed English countryside. Following the motorway into Bristol, she scolded her imagination and reminded herself that she had banished irrational feelings to the past, but there it was: a real and undeniable sensation, as tangible as any in the corporeal world; a presence that sat neither next to nor behind her, but seemed to occupy every aspect of her space, and which was urging her to something. Who could it be? Was it Brogan or Amy Patterson? Don't be so stupid, she told herself. You're over all that now. You've been into the darkest places; you've shared everything with Dr Allen there ever was to share; there are no ghosts left to haunt you.

But as she crunched across the pavement in Jamaica Street the sensation seemed to grow stronger still. Approaching the entrance to her building, she started in alarm as a burly, red-faced man threw open the front door and marched angrily out. It was Alison's husband.

'Terry?'

He glared at her and stormed past, wrenching open his car door.

Jenny hurried inside and along the hallway. She called out Alison's name.

'Mrs Cooper?'

She was sitting calmly at her desk, dressed in a neat navy suit, her hair elegantly set. The room was serene and orderly. Fresh flowers stood in a vase on the waiting-area table.

'I just saw Terry . . . I thought for a moment—'

'That he'd strangled me?' She let out an ironic laugh. 'I could have strangled *him*. He would have deserved it, too – the tramps he's been consorting with in Spain.'

Jenny took a moment to reorientate herself, but something remained definitely wrong.

'What's going on, Alison? I thought you were—'

'Leaving?'

'You did say—'

'I'd prefer not to, if you don't mind, Mrs Cooper.'

They looked at each other, Alison's expression pleading that she would rather they left it at that and carried on as usual.

But Jenny was not content to let more unfinished business linger.

'What happened?'

Alison composed herself, determined not to spoil her elaborate make-up with tears. 'I decided to take a lesson from the dead photographer and his lover. They were so desperate not to hurt the people who loved them . . .' Her voice wavered. 'You can't live without hurting someone, Mrs Cooper. That's just how life is. And if you're the one who always lets themselves be hurt, you end up hardly living at all . . . I gave Terry thirty years and he repaid me by walking out when it suited him. Now it's my turn. He came here begging me to take him back but I told him no, I've started seeing Paul and he's making me very happy.' She gave a bittersweet smile.

'So happy I can even cope with staying here with you.'

'Good,' Jenny said, raising a smile at Alison's joke. 'I wasn't sure how I'd manage.'

'Let's face it, you wouldn't, would you?' Back to her old self, Alison pushed a pile of death reports topped with a bundle of mail across the desk. 'I'm afraid we've let things get behind.'

'What's new?'

Jenny picked up the papers and carried them through to her office with a heavy heart. Her immediate future held little to look forward to: chained to a desk, ever more estranged from her son, and any prospect of seeing Michael again seemingly having vanished like the mist. And standing at her shoulder the presence that still refused to leave. Sitting at her desk in the quiet of her office, she understood how it must feel for a blind man to know that someone is silently watching.

The rude interruption of the telephone came as a welcome relief.

'Jenny Cooper.'

'It's Mrs Stewart,' the frosty voice announced. 'I really don't think your father's going to last the day.'

TWENTY-NINE

She stepped into the spotless room and forced herself to confront the emaciated figure lying semi-conscious beneath blankets tucked tightly under the mattress. He looked as if he had already been laid out; his breathing was slow and shallow, his lips slowly turning blue. His body was a shell, but the spirit that still clung to it remained as strong and present as an ogre. She felt his fear of death as strong invisible hands around her throat. He wasn't resigned to this, and nor was she.

'Dad?' Jenny whispered.

No response.

She extended a wary hand and touched his clammy forehead.

Not a flicker. He was unconscious; slowly descending the final steps. It was safe.

Unsure what to do, she drew up a chair and glanced around the family photographs the nurses had loosely tacked to the walls. She featured in many of them: a fussily dressed baby in her mother's arms, a smiling seven-year-old, posturing teenager, proud graduate. She realized they were all her father's pictures brought from home by his second wife before she, too, had abandoned him to his lonely fate. They were sufficiently thumbed at the corners to suggest that he must have studied them from time to time, and even as a mad thing confined to the shrinking cell of his collapsing mind he had never torn them from the walls.

Did it mean that he still loved her?

Did she still love him?

Since her memory had returned, an unkind part of her had secretly longed for his life to end. She had convinced herself that when he was gone she would be clear and free. But now the moment had come, it felt anything but a liberation. What would she do without the man who had patrolled the passageways of her unconscious mind for more than thirty years? Where would she find herself?

Adrift.

Alone.

Despite the warmth of the room she felt strangely cold. She fought the urge to weep and plead with him not to leave. 'I don't want to be by myself. You *can't* leave me.' The words flooded unprompted into her mind. She was a small and frightened child suddenly overwhelmed by the urge to show him all the affection that she had withheld for most of a lifetime. She moved closer and stroked his face.

'I'm sorry, Dad . . .' she whispered. 'I do love you.'

She circled his cheek with her fingers but his skin grew colder.

'Dad . . .'

The tiny movements of his chest had stopped. The gentle rasping on each breath had faded to silence.

'No—'

Somewhere in the corridor outside a door slammed. Nurses chattered; life went on. Jenny looked up at a photograph of her father on the beach at Weston on a hot summer's day. Slim and tanned, he was beaming as he held her five-year-old self in his powerful arms. She reached up and took it down. Tucking it into her pocket, she went to tell Mrs Stewart that he had gone.

The snow had frozen hard and more was starting to fall. Jenny inched the Land Rover up the lane to Melin Bach through the raven-black darkness, wishing for once that she lived somewhere with neighbours and street lights. Halfway up on the steepest part of the hill she passed a car that had been abandoned in the gateway to a field, the driver having surrendered to the elements. It was no night to be travelling; it was a night to be safely indoors hoping for warmer days to come.

It had come as no surprise to her that it had taken the coldest day of the year to break her father's iron grip on life. He had held on to it with the same fierce determination with which his ancestors had clung to the decks of their storm-lashed trawlers in the Irish Sea. Some people slipped from this world without protest, glad to be free of its troubles; others fought to the last moment, resisting the inexorable tides of death until the waters closed over their heads. He had held on until she had arrived at his side. It was still too early, and her feelings too raw for her to say exactly what had passed between them in his final moments, but she already sensed that the malevolent presence that had haunted her for so long had gone. She dared to think that at journey's end they might finally have forgiven one another.

She rounded the final bend and parked the Land Rover on the cart track at the side of the cottage. Retrieving the torch she kept in the glove box, she braced herself to face the freezing night. Picking her way back onto the lane towards the front gate, the security light fixed to the outside wall of the house lit up. She heard footsteps crunching on the snow.

'Hello?' she called out nervously.

'Jenny – it's me.'

Approaching the gate she saw a frozen figure outside the open-fronted porch. It was Michael.

'Sorry. I didn't mean to frighten you.'

'That's all right—'

Her momentary panic subsiding, she went through the gate, struggling to adjust her thoughts. She hadn't been ready for this. Making her way up the path, she could see that he was shivering uncontrollably. He was wearing only a thin sweater over his shirt.

'You're frozen—'

'I couldn't get my car up your hill.'

'You haven't even got a coat.'

'I came straight from the hotel where they were debriefing me.'

She reached her keys from her bag with cold, clumsy fingers and unlocked the door. 'They kept you all this time?'

'Thorough isn't the word.'

She stepped inside and switched on the light. He followed her in. She turned to look at him: his face was bruised and stitched in several places. His eyes were dark and hollow.

'You look terrible.'

'I'm fine. I called your office. I heard your father—'

'He's gone.'

'I'm sorry.' He looked stricken. 'I shouldn't have come . . .' He stepped back towards the door.

'No.' She caught his arm. 'Please.'

He slowly turned to face her. 'This feels wrong, Jenny . . . I shouldn't . . . Another time.'

'What?'

He dipped his head.

'What is it, Michael? Tell me.'

'I owe you an apology – for the time I frightened you in the Cessna. I don't know what possessed me.'

'You told me. I even remember her name.'

He looked up.

'Believe me,' Jenny said, 'I know what it's like to be haunted. But what I've learned is that if you turn to look them in the eye ghosts vanish.'

'You know, you scare me a little, Jenny.'

'The feeling's mutual.' She shrugged off her coat and hung it on the peg. 'Come through into the kitchen, it's freezing out here.'

'There's something I want to say first – you might want to throw me out after you've heard it.'

She looked at him, feeling all of the things that she had felt since she first saw him at the D-Mort. He was delicate, damaged, and promised to be more work than she could handle, but he was too darkly beautiful to turn away.

'Try me,' Jenny said.

'I . . . I don't know how to say it.'

'Then maybe you shouldn't say anything.'

Jenny let his cold fingers slip between hers.

'Thank you,' Michael said. 'I won't.'

He kissed her gently on the lips. Jenny smiled and led him into the warmth.

AUTHOR'S NOTE

I confess to having always been a nervous flyer. Three childhood experiences helped nurture this wholly rational fear. The first was a trip in a light aircraft owned by a friend of my mother's – an aerobatics enthusiast – whom I vividly recall carrying out some distinctly amateurish-looking repairs under the hood to enable the old crate to get off the ground: they involved a length of wire, some pliers and a lot of cursing. While we survived that particular flight – despite the alarming coughing noises from the engine – a few years later the pilot crashed during a foolhardy manoeuvre and was rendered semi-paralysed. Even then, he continued to fly with modified controls. On another occasion, I was on a flight with my parents and brother from London to Malaga, southern Spain, when gentle music started playing over the cabin speakers and the adults around me began whispering agitatedly about engine failure. This was duly confirmed by the anxious-sounding Spanish pilot, who carried out an emergency landing at Madrid airport. Thankfully he brought us safely down, but the incident confirmed my mounting suspicion that planes weren't as invincible as I had been led to believe. Finally, aged fourteen, I was on a return flight from Milan with a school party when the plane ran into a violent storm over the Alps. It was one of those in which the cabin crew turn ghostly pale and those who aren't tightly strapped in are hurled out of their seats. A boy sitting across the aisle struck his head on the overhead locker, causing a wound that required many stitches. For nearly thirty minutes we all thought we were doomed. Thankfully, I have never had to endure a repeat performance.

However, despite what my fevered imagination tells me, planes do not very often fall out of the sky, and when they do it is most often due to human error or shoddy maintenance. It is a testament to the immense skill and expertise of aircraft manufacturers that problems in construction or design are very rarely the reason for aircraft failure. For the avoidance of doubt, I must stress that the fly-by-wire technology pioneered by Airbus has undoubtedly made aviation safer, not least by significantly reducing the possibility for human error. I must also emphasize that there has never to my knowledge been a case of a commercial airliner's avionics having been maliciously corrupted. Academics and military strategists are increasingly discussing such possibilities (see for example Frank D. Kramer et al, *Cyberpower and National Security*, NDU Press, 2009), but the threat remains a strictly theoretical one. And, heaven forbid, should terrorists of the future develop such capability, there is nothing to my knowledge about the Airbus A380 which would make it any more vulnerable to attack than a Boeing or any other make of aircraft. I chose the A380 as an inanimate 'character' in this book simply because at the time of writing it is the ultimate in commercial aviation, and as such the most potent and visible symbol of our ongoing conquest of the skies.

Next time you fly – or perhaps you are in a plane right now? – do remember that a short drive through town remains statistically far more dangerous than your flight by a factor of many thousands to one. The most perilous parts of your journey are the ones to and from the airport. I am reliably informed that you are precisely eighty-seven times more likely to choke on the ice cube in your gin and tonic than to perish in a crash. So sit back and enjoy the movie – the numbers say it'll never happen to you.

ACKNOWLEDGEMENTS

I would like to thank David Swan, who between being a busy pilot and father to a young family, found time to advise me on the intricacies of modern passenger aircraft and to read drafts of my manuscript while criss-crossing the globe (though only once safely on the ground). It's always a challenge for a rigorous professional to accept the writer's need to serve the interests of story-telling alongside factual accuracy, but he did so with grace and patience. I am deeply grateful.

If you enjoyed THE FLIGHT you'll love

The Chosen Dead

**the next thrilling novel in the
Coroner Jenny Cooper series**

*'I've already told you, Mrs Cooper. I don't believe in
conspiracies.'*

'But you'll let me know what you find.'

*He nodded, and then, with all the effort of contradicting
beliefs to which he had held fast for years, said, 'Do you
think I'm in any danger?'*

'I don't know how to answer that question,' Jenny said.

When Bristol Coroner Jenny Cooper investigates the fatal
plunge of a man from a motorway bridge, she little suspects
that it has any connection with the sudden death of a friend's
thirteen-year-old daughter from a deadly strain of meningitis.
But as Jenny pieces together the dead man's last days, she's
drawn into a mystery whose dark ripples stretch across conti-
nents and back through decades.

In an investigation which will take her into the sinister
realms of unbridled human ambition and corrupt scientific
endeavour, Jenny is soon forced to risk the love and lives of
those closest to her, as a deadly race to uncover the truth
begins . . .

Out now

An extract follows here . . .

THREE

Present day

JENNY COOPER WAS FREE. Eight years after she had frozen mid-sentence in front of a bemused courtroom and felt the walls close in, she had emerged from the long dark tunnel of recovery and completed her last ever appointment with Dr Allen, the psychiatrist who had become such a troubling fixture in her life. He had seemed almost disappointed that she hadn't suffered a panic attack for more than a year and was coping well with her job as the Severn Vale District Coroner. In the absence of symptoms to analyse, he had been reduced to sermonizing and platitudes: 'Remember that life is precious, Mrs Cooper. It exists by chance but thrives by will. Always keep hold of your purpose.' She had promised that she would and had stepped out into the bright morning to feel the warmth of the sun on her face as if for the first time.

No more pretending. No more deceit. No more shame. She was well again. It was official.

Jenny drove her Land Rover out of the car park and turned towards Bristol, saying goodbye to the Chepstow Hospital for the final time. In future she would drive past on her journeys to and from the office not with a sense of dread, but with only a fading memory of the years in which she had struggled to put her shattered life together. She felt like the sole survivor of a bomb blast; a woman who had emerged whole from the wreckage but couldn't quite understand how or why. Don't question, Jenny, she told herself, you're done with all of that. Just live.

Just live. What did that mean?

Driving over the mile-wide expanse of the Severn Bridge, the sharp, fresh air of the estuary blowing in through her open window, she allowed herself to believe that it meant no more than being an ordinary, forty-something single woman, with mundane worries of the kind millions of women like her coped with every day. She was anxious about her future with Michael, the man who only sometimes referred to himself as her 'boyfriend'. She fretted about the lines appearing in her still-attractive features and about the few pounds she was struggling to shed from around her middle. And she was missing Ross, her son, who was at university in London and who she feared would have grown even more distant when she went to collect him tomorrow. Ordinary worries. Nothing that couldn't be overcome; nothing that need defeat her. After nearly a decade of being a 'case' she had rejoined the common flow. She felt an unaccustomed sensation: was it happiness? No, it was something even more precious than that: it was contentment.

Her brief moment of peace was rudely interrupted by the phone. The display on the dashboard behind the wheel said *Unknown Caller.*

'Hello.'

'Mrs Cooper?'

'Speaking.'

'Detective Inspector Stephen Watling, Gloucestershire. We met last summer – the kids in the canoe.'

She felt herself crashing back to earth.

'I remember.' Images of swollen, drowned teenage bodies

invaded her mind. She pushed them away. 'What can I do for you?'

'Body on the M5. Male. Thirties. Looks like he jumped from the bridge into the traffic – he was lying just along from it.'

'Are there any witnesses?'

'No. He was found at the roadside this morning by a verge-cleaning crew.' It seemed an enraged choice, made by a man intent on inflicting his suffering on innocent strangers who would experience the trauma of running over his body in the road.

'Right.' So far it sounded like an unremarkable suicide. She waited for the rest.

'We think we know who he is. A two-year-old boy was found early this morning about a mile away in Bristol Memorial Woodlands. He's the man's son. His car was still parked there.'

'What's happened to the child?'

'He's alive. Hypothermia but no injuries. He's been taken to the Vale Hospital. Mother's on the way.'

Now she understood. DI Watling was trying to pass the awkward conversation with the child's mother over to her. Satisfied the dead man had killed himself, it had become the coroner's problem.

'Won't you be talking to her anyway?' Jenny said.

'I'll send a family liaison along – Annie Malik, she's good. I'm tied up on a drugs inquiry.'

What could be more important than that? Jenny wanted to answer, but held her tongue. She had made enough enemies in the police.

'What's the mother's name?'

'Karen Jordan. We think the guy was called Adam. Adam Jordan.'

'All right. Tell your officer I'll be ready to speak to Mrs Jordan in an hour, but I'd like to see the body first.'

It was a task most coroners would have left to their officers. The days of being obliged to view the body *in situ* were long past. The coroner had increasingly become an office-bound official who kept contact with the bereaved to a minimum, but Jenny had never been able to operate that way. Having spent the first fifteen years of her legal career in the family courts dealing with the fallout from domestic violence and abuse, there wasn't one human emotion that she hadn't learned to cope with. Death was far easier to manage than a bitter struggle over a damaged child, her role so much more clearly defined than that of an advocate fighting an ugly case: gather the evidence and determine the cause of death. She was to the legal profession what the pathologist was to medicine: the last word.

Some things she never got used to. The heavy perfume of the mortuary – pine-scented detergent and decomposing flesh – was chief among them. A warm day in July was guaranteed to be close to intolerable. A virulent outbreak of hospital infection had been killing elderly patients at three times the normal rate for the past month. Superbugs loved the summer, and their victims were lined up on gurneys in the long straight corridor, two deep. Jenny instinctively covered her mouth as she hurried past and pushed through the swing doors into the autopsy room.

Dr Andy Kerr glanced up briefly from his work, then carried on, his muscular arms bare beneath the elbow save for a pair of blue latex gloves. He was dissecting the body of an emaciated young man with a shaved head, separating the lungs and removing them from the narrow ribcage. Two others, each wrapped in a shroud of white plastic, were waiting their turn for the knife.

'No locum today?' Jenny said, nodding towards the empty second table.

'Called in sick.'

'Coping?'

'No,' he said, in the unflappable Northern Irish way of his she had come to find so reassuring. 'Maybe when they can smell us in the staff canteen they'll hire in some more fridges.'

'I just wanted to check on a suspected suicide – Jordan. I doubt you've had a chance to look at him.'

'Only a glance.' He placed the lungs on the steel counter alongside the liver and heart, and rinsed his bloody gloves under the tap. 'It's that one there.'

She waited for him to dry his gloves on a paper towel and come over. He tugged his mask down beneath his chin and smiled. At thirty-five he still looked unnaturally youthful for a senior pathologist, his eyes bright and keen. His work was clearly suiting him.

'You told me you weren't squeamish any more,' Dr Kerr said. 'Have a go.'

Jenny shook her head. 'Please?'

He lifted the plastic by the corner and pulled it back to reveal a face that had been staved-in by an overwhelming impact. Jenny felt an involuntary shudder travel the length of her spine. There were no visible features remaining above the lower set of teeth. The torso was spectacularly bruised and most of the ribs were broken. The right arm lay straight, but the left was dislocated at the shoulder and broken in several places, fractured ends of bones jutting through the skin. Dr Kerr drew the sheet all the way back and revealed another massive set of injuries around the waist. The pelvis was shattered and both legs showed every sign of having been driven over by a large, heavy vehicle. Jenny's eyes went to his hands: they were almost untouched. The fingers were delicate and slender like a pianist's. There was one ring: a plain wedding band.

'Jumped from a motorway bridge,' Jenny said.

'Looks like it,' Dr Kerr said. 'I'd say he'd been run over several times. Look at the crushing injuries across the lower legs – that was done by big wide tyres.'

'No one stopped.'

'They never do.'

Over the initial shock, Jenny leaned forward for a closer look. She ran her eyes over the forearms, looking for the tell-tale signs of an addict, but there were none.

She noticed the skin was deeply suntanned above the waist and below the knees, and the man had been slim and muscular. No tattoos or other jewellery; no powerful smell of alcohol that usually accompanied male suicides.

'Anything in the clothing?' Jenny asked.

Dr Kerr shook his head and reached beneath the trolley for the list of effects that was kept alongside the bag containing the bloodstained clothes. He handed it to Jenny. It revealed that Jordan had been wearing jeans, a T-shirt, cotton sweater and canvas shoes. The police had retained his wallet. There was no record of a phone, money or keys – the usual items that men carried in their pockets – nor was there any evidence of prescription drugs.

Jenny said, 'We'd better have a full suite of tests on bloods and stomach contents. I've never known a suicide be entirely clean.' She turned away, Dr Kerr's cue to draw the plastic over the body.

'Is something troubling you?' he asked, reading her frown.

'No,' Jenny lied. 'I'm sure I'll learn a lot more from his wife. When can you have him ready?'

'Give me a couple of hours. We'll clean him up best we can.'

'Maybe a mask?'

Dr Kerr nodded. 'Don't worry.'

Jenny left the mortuary and crossed the car park to the main hospital building. She was dreading the encounter with the widow, not for all the usual reasons, but for the unusual ones she knew were coming. Fit, good-looking, well-dressed young men seldom jumped from motorway bridges; less still did they leave their two-year-old children to spend a night alone outdoors. It felt like the worst and most unsettling kind of death: a suicide that had come from nowhere.

Jenny heard the woman's anguished cries even before she had pushed through the door. They emanated from behind a curtain drawn around a bed in the children's ward, and were disturbing everyone within earshot. Staff exchanged glances, parents at other bedsides attempted to distract their fragile sons and daughters from the sound. Jenny was momentarily paralysed, overcome by the widow's all-consuming grief. She stopped and gathered strength, reminding herself she had to appear strong even if she didn't feel it.

A nurse appeared carrying an IV bag. Jenny intercepted her, fishing her identity wallet from her pocket. 'Jenny Cooper. Severn Vale District Coroner. I'm looking for Mrs Jordan.'

'I'm not sure now's a good moment.' She nodded towards the curtained-off bed.

'Is the child all right?' Jenny asked.

'Mild hypothermia. It's not life-threatening.'

'The police said he wasn't found until this morning.'

'He was admitted just under three hours ago.'

The woman's cries grew louder. The nurse responded to the anxious faces up and down the ward. 'Excuse me.'

'This isn't helping him, is it?' Jenny heard her say patiently. 'Maybe it's best you come with me. Just for a while.'

Mrs Jordan was younger than Jenny had imagined, perhaps not yet thirty, with long, crow-black hair and wide blue eyes that her anguish did little to dull. There was no question of talking to her in her current state, but curiosity caused Jenny to wait a moment longer while another nurse drew back the curtain to reveal a cot bed containing a tiny child. He was barely more than a toddler and was hooked-up to a heart monitor and several drips. He had his mother's eyes and they were wide open, staring unfocused into space.

Jenny felt the silent buzz of her phone. She fished it out of her pocket and saw her officer's name, Alison, on the screen. She headed out into the corridor to take the call.

'Mrs Cooper. Did DI Watling get hold of you?'

'Yes. I'm at the hospital now. I tried to call you.'

'Sorry. I was out of the office for a while.' She paused. 'How's the little boy?'

'Fine. Physically, at least.'

'Oh . . . Good.'

Jenny registered a flatness in Alison's voice and sensed that something was troubling her. 'What is it?'

'Nothing. Would you like me to visit the scene of death? We ought to have some pictures.'

'Won't the police have done that?'

'They've already emailed them. They're not very clear. What about where the boy was found?'

'Anything you think would be helpful.'

'Righto. I'll see you back at the office.'

'Alison?'

She had already rung off. Jenny held the phone in her hand for a moment, unsure whether to call back to tease from her whatever it was she had failed to say, but was interrupted by the nurse, who had appeared from a doorway to her right.

'Now might be a good moment, Mrs Cooper.'

Jenny looked at her, taking a moment to reorient her thoughts.

'I've told her you're waiting,' she said with a trace of impatience. 'She's calmed down a little.' The nurse started back towards the ward.

Jenny approached the door. Pausing outside it, she glanced through the observation pane into an unoccupied side room. Beyond the empty bed, Karen Jordan was standing at the window looking out over rooftops to a line of distant hills. She wore jeans and a plain T-shirt that hugged her slender frame, and dabbed at her eyes with a wad of paper towel. Even with a door between them, Jenny felt her bewilderment like a radiating force. She knocked lightly and stepped inside.

'Mrs Jordan?'

The young woman turned, a sob catching in her throat.

Jenny moved cautiously towards her. 'Jenny Cooper. I'm the coroner.'

Karen Jordan stared at her with eyes frozen in an expression of shock.

'Would you mind if I asked a couple of questions about your husband?'

She shook her head, her lips clamped tightly together.

'His name was Adam Jordan?'

She nodded.

'His age?'

'Thirty-two.' The words came out in a hoarse whisper.

'Occupation?'

'He worked for a charity. It's called AFAD – Africa Aid and Development . . . He came back from South Sudan at the end of May.'

'Is there anything about your husband's state of mind that I ought to know?'

She shook her head violently, her hair sweeping across her face and clinging to her cheeks. 'No.'

'I was told he had parked at the Bristol Memorial Woodlands – that's a cemetery, isn't it?'

'A natural burial ground. Adam's father died last autumn. He'd gone there with Sam, that's all. I was working.'

'Sam's your son?'

She nodded.

'Was your husband close to his father?'

'I suppose—' Her voice cracked.

Thinking it better to get the painful conversation over quickly, Jenny persisted. 'Can you think of any reason why your husband may have taken his life, Mrs Jordan?'

'He didn't!'

'I see. And how do you know that?'

'He was my husband.' She stared at her with wild, enraged eyes. 'Don't you tell me I don't know my own husband!'

Jenny wanted to tell her the agony would pass, that as despairing as she felt now, it would not get any worse, but she was unreachable. There was no question of putting her through the ordeal of an identification. She turned to the door and quietly left her to cry herself out.

extracts reading groups
competitions books new
discounts extracts extracts discounts
competitions extracts
books extracts
new
events books
extracts titles reading groups
interviews
new events extracts
discounts
new books events
events new
discounts extracts discounts
www.panmacmillan.com
extracts events reading groups
competitions books extracts new